LIGHT ON THE BOOK TRADE

PETER ISAAC 1921 – 2002

LIGHT ON THE BOOK TRADE

ESSAYS
IN HONOUR OF PETER ISAAC

Edited by
Barry McKay John Hinks
and Maureen Bell

OAK KNOLL PRESS
AND
THE BRITISH LIBRARY

PRINT NETWORKS

This series, edited by Barry McKay, John Hinks and Maureen Bell, publishes papers given at the annual Conference on the History of the British Book Trade.

1. Images & Texts (edited by Peter Isaac & Barry McKay)
2. The Reach of Print (edited by Peter Isaac & Barry McKay)
3. The Human Face of the Book Trade (edited by Peter Isaac & Barry McKay)
4. The Mighty Engine (edited by Peter Isaac & Barry McKay)
5. The Moving Market (edited by Peter Isaac & Barry McKay)
6. Light on the Book Trade

© Oak Knoll Press and the contributors 2004

First published in 2004 by

Oak Knoll Press
310 Delaware Street
New Castle
DE 19720

and

The British Library
96 Euston Road
London NW1 2DB

Library of Congress Cataloging-in-Publication Data

Seminar on the British Book Trade (19th : 2001 : Worcester, England)
Light on the book trade : essays presented at the Nineteenth Seminar on the British Book Trade in honour of Peter Isaac /
edited by Barry McKay, John Hinks, and Maureen Bell.
p. cm. Includes bibliographical references and index.
ISBN (US) 1-58456-085-1
(UK) 0-7123-4797-6

1. Book industries and trade--Great Britain--History--Congresses.
2. Printing--Great Britain--History--Congresses.
3. Books--Great Britain--History--Congresses.
4. Great Britain--Intellectual life--Congresses.
I. Isaac, Peter C.G. II. McKay, Barry, 1948- III. Hinks, John. IV. Bell, Maureen. V. Title.
Z329 .S46 2002
381'.45002'0973--dc21   2002072587

Designed, and composed in MONOTYPE Bulmer by Barry McKay
Printed in England by St Edmundsbury Press, Bury St Edmunds

Contents

List of Contributors		vii
BARRY McKAY	Peter Isaac: a Landmark Removed	ix
MAUREEN BELL	Introduction	xi
JOHN FEATHER	The History of the English Provincial Book Trade: a research agenda	1
LUCY LEWIS	'For no text is an island, divided from the main' Incunable Sammelbande	13
DAVID STOKER	Freeman and Susannah Collins and the Spread of English Provincial Printing	27
MICHAEL POWELL	Taking Stock: The Diary of Edmund Harrold of Manchester	37
BARRY McKAY	Books in Eighteenth-Century Whitehaven	51
DAVID HOUNSLOW	From George III to Queen Victoria: a provincial family and their books	61
DAVID N GRIFFITHS	Print, Privilege and Piracy in the Book of Common Prayer	73
JOHN HINKS	John Gregory and the 'Leicester Journal'	85
JOHN GAVIN	Literary Institutions in the Lake Counties Part IV: Catalogues	95
MARGARET COOPER	Influential and Mysterious: The Career of Septimus Prowett: Bookseller, Publisher and Picture Dealer	107
CAROLINE ARCHER SUE WALKER & LINDA REYNOLDS	Typography in Nineteenth-Century Children's Readers: the Otley Connection	119
WALLACE KIRSOP	Baker's Juvenile Circulating Library in Sydney in the 1840s	131
IAIN BEAVAN	Staying the Course: the Edinburgh Cabinet Library, 1830-1844	141

DIANA DIXON	Paths Through the Wilderness: Recording the History of Provincial Newspapers in England	153
BRENDA J SCRAGG	James Everett and the Sale of Adam Clarke's Library, 1833: a newly discovered manuscript	165
PHILIP HENRY JONES	Thomas Gee Senior	175
R J GOULDEN	False Imprints and the Bridger Specimen Books	189
WARREN McDOUGALL	Charles Elliot's Book Adventure in Philadelphia, and the Trouble with Thomas Dobson	197
Bibliography of Writings by Peter Isaac		213
Index		217

Contributors

Caroline Archer is a freelance author and journalist specialising in typography and graphic communication. She has written for magazines in Europe, America and Asia and is the author of a book on the Kynoch Press. She is currently working on two books that will be published in 2003 and 2004. At the time of writing the paper she was a research assistant in the Department of Typography at The University of Reading.

Maureen Bell, Reader in the English Department of the University of Birmingham, teaches Renaissance literature, early women's writing and the history of the book. Her research interests include women in the early-modern book trade and the provincial trade in the seventeenth century. She is assistant editor of Vol 4 of *The Cambridge History of the Book in Britain* and is currently working on 'A Chronology and Calendar of Documents related to the London Book Trade 1641-1700'.

Iain Beavan, Senior Curator (Projects) in Historic Collections, University of Aberdeen, has written widely on the Scottish book trade, and in particular on the nineteenth-century period. His most recent research has centred on the Edinburgh publishing and bookselling firm of Oliver & Boyd.

Margaret Cooper, bookseller and former Open University tutor, is continuing her study of the Worcestershire book trade, and also working on the library of 12,000 volumes beueathed to a Bristol independent school by the antiquarian C J Ryland.

Diana Dixon lectured at the College of Librarianship Wales and Loughborough University before taking early retirement in 1997. Currently she is researching the access to English provincial newspapers at University College, London. She contributes the 'Annual Review of Work in Newspaper History' to *Media History* and has written a number of articles on the history of the provincial press.

John Feather is Professor of Library & Information Studies at Loughborough University. He is the author of *The Provincial Book Trade in Eighteenth-Century England* (1985) and *A History of British Publishing* (1988).

John Gavin is a Cumbrian by adoption, and has had a varied career through chance rather than choice; literary, scientific and environmental interests provide a linking thread.

R. J. Goulden of the British Library (British Books 1801-1914), has long been investigating the Kentish book trade, 1750-1900, and is the author of *Kent Town Guides 1763-1900* (1995), *Faversham Book Trade 1730-1900* (1996) and *Sittingbourne and Milton Regis Book Trade 1770-1990* (1999). His long-term intention is to compile a directory of the Kent book trade covering the eighteenth and nineteenth centuries.

David Griffiths is a retired Anglican priest living in Lincoln, where he was once Cathedral Librarian. His *Bibliography of the Book of Common Prayer* was published in 2002 by the British Library.

John Hinks is a librarian turned book historian who has completed his doctoral research at Loughborough University on the history of the book trade in Leicester. His interests include radical political publishing and bookselling (c1790-1850) and book-trade networks in the English Midlands.

David Hounslow is a former children's bookseller.

Philip Henry Jones, a lecturer in the Department of Information & Library Studies of the University of Wales Aberystwyth, has made a special study of the nineteenth-century Welsh-language book trade. He edited, with Eiluned Rees, *A Nation and its Books* (1998).

Wallace Kirsop is Honorary Professorial Fellow in French Studies at Monash University and General Editor of *A History of the Book in Australia* (to appear in three volumes from 2001 to 2003).

Lucy Lewis holds a doctoral thesis from London University on the subject of 'British Boethianism 1380-1436', which she completed in 2000. Based at Cambridge University Library, she works as Assistant Editor for the *Annual Bibliography of English Language and Literature*, and is also a tutor in medieval literature for the Madingley Hall centre for Continuing Education. Recently, she edited a collection of essays and extracts called *Spinning Lifelines: Women's Autobiographical Writing*, which she produced with the help of a National Lottery grant. She has also published two articles on Thomas Usk's *Testament of Love*.

Warren McDougall, an Honorary Fellow of the Faculty of Arts of the University of Edinburgh, is editor of the eighteenth-century volume of the *History of the Book in Scotland*. He is currently indexing the archive of Charles Elliot

Barry McKay, an antiquarian bookseller who specializes in bibliography and the art and history of the book, is engaged in research into the book trade in Cumbria and into chapbooks.

Michael Powell is Librarian of Chetham's Library, Manchester. He has published on the local history and bibliography of Manchester and its region, and is currently carrying out research on collectors and owners of books in the Northwest.

Linda Reynolds is a lecturer in the Department of Typography & Graphic Communication at The University of Reading. Her particular interests are design evaluation methods, legibility, and the use of colour. She was previously Senior Research Fellow in the Graphic Information Research Unit at the Royal College of Art, where she worked mainly on projects funded by the British Library.

Brenda J Scragg has published several catalogues of the John Rylands Library exhibitions on nineteenth-century book arts and children's literature. Her book trade research specializes on Manchester.

David Stoker is a senior lecturer in the Department of Information & Library Studies, of the University of Wales, Aberystwyth. He has been intersted in the early Norwich book trade since 1970.

Sue Walker is Head of the Department of Typography & Graphic Communication at The University of Reading. One of her research interests is typographic design for children.

Professor Peter Charles Gerald Isaac
A Landmark Removed

PROFESSOR PETER ISAAC died suddenly on 15 June 2002 as this book was being completed for the press. The papers that it contains, which were presented in his honour, are therefore now published both to fulfil that honour, and in his memory.

He retired after a distinguished academic career, spent largely in the civil engineering department of Newcastle University and as an advisor and consultant on public health matters at both national and international levels. Then, at an age when most men would settle for a quiet and leisurely retirement, he began what can only be held as a second career as one of the foremost scholars of the English provincial book trade. In his thirties Peter began a life-long passion for bibliography, initially as a collector of works printed by Newcastle-born William Bulmer. This resulted in his first publication of a bibliographical nature, appropriately an 'introductory essay' on Bulmer, which appeared in *The Library* in 1958.

This passion intensified after his retirement in 1981 but, with an engineer's insistence on understanding the workings of things he soon passed beyond the stage of merely accumulating titles and needed to understand the technicalities of printing in the hand press days. This led him to establish his own private press, the Allenholme Press. The first publications were two short collections of papers, inevitably, on Bulmer, followed by his first essay into the history of the provincial book trade, an account of the caricatures produced by the Alnwick pharmacist and printer William Davison. Peter's interest in Davison never waned and a small, but significant, contribution to the study of the provincial book trade *William Davison of Alnwick Pharmacist and Printer* appeared from the Clarendon Press in 1968.

Peter's avowed second love (after Bulmer) was the history of the book trade in provincial England. In 1965 a small group of professional and amateur bibliographers met to form a research group, *The History of the Book Trade in the North*. Since then, under his inspiring (and occasionally benignly dictatorial) editorship, this group has produced almost one hundred working and miscellaneous papers, and several substantial books.

In 1980 Peter was one of a group invited to the University of Leeds to meet to discuss various aspects of the history of the provincial book trade, and from this small beginning has grown the British Book Trade Seminar. Another outcome of the Leeds seminar was the decision to commence work on the British Book Trade Index, a biographical database of everyone who could be traced, who had any connection – no matter how tenuous – with the book trade. This monumental undertaking has recently been transferred from its centre in his overcrowded study to Birmingham University.

In 1990, to celebrate the twenty-fifth anniversary of the History of the Book Trade in the North, many of Peter's fellow workers in the field gathered at Durham to present and receive a series of papers which showed just how much had been achieved in a comparatively short time. The proceedings of that gathering, *Six Centuries of the Provincial Book Trade*, appeared under his editorship in the same year. Also in 1990, he returned again to Davison of Alnwick and edited for the Printing Historical Society (another society which he was to chair) a facsimile of Davison's rare *New Specimen of Cast-Metal Ornaments and Wood Types*. This he introduced with a typically taut and magisterial essay.

In 1983/4 Peter was Sandars Reader in Bibliography at Cambridge and an expanded and revised version of his lectures appeared in 1993 as *William Bulmer the Fine Printer in Context 1757-1830*. In this work the accumulated results of a near-lifetime's research came together in a seminal study not only of the productions of a fine and significant printer, but also of the entire milieu in which he lived and worked. It set a demanding standard for any similar study.

In 1996 Robert Cross of St Paul's Bibliographies and Robert Fleck of Oak Knoll Press agreed that the proceedings of the British Book Trade Seminar should be properly published. Thus, the first volume of the 'Print Networks' series, *Images and Texts*, appeared in 1997 under our joint editorship. I believe we can justly claim that the volumes so far published have placed both the British Book Trade Seminar and the Print Networks series at the very forefront of Book History studies. I use capitals for Book History, as Peter did, for the field of study is now a respectable academic discipline, pursued in many universities on both sides of the Atlantic.

In 1994 Peter became President of the Bibliographical Society. Never before has either an engineer or scholar, whose interests were largely in areas previously not held in high regard by the bibliographical establishment, been given this honour. In bibliography, as in engineering, Peter Isaac explored new terrain, and it is a mark of the man that he was awarded a D.Litt. for his scholarly works in bibliography, his lifelong passion. He was not the earliest scholar of the provincial book, but he was unquestionably one of the finest. Without his contribution, energy and organization it is doubtful if the discipline would enjoy quite such an elevated status. His forceful personality conquered dissent, converted sceptics, encouraged enthusiasts, and inspired followers who will, indeed must, continue his work. As Philip Henry Jones, one of the contributors to this collection, remarked upon hearing of Peter's death, 'a landmark has been removed.'

Barry McKay

Introduction

MAUREEN BELL

THIS VOLUME, the sixth in the *Print Networks* series, is published with a particular sense of occasion.[1] Like other volumes in the series it presents the proceedings of the annual British Book Trade Seminar; unlike the other volumes, however, it has a particular purpose in honouring Peter Isaac's contribution to the development of the study of the book trade in Britain and, especially, in the provinces.

Peter Isaac has often drawn attention to 'the human face of the book trade', reminding us in *The Moving Market* that 'books are more than objects; they are written by people, produced by people, distributed by people, bought by people, and possibly read by people'.[2] His commitment to books *and* people is evidenced not only by the British Book Trade Seminars themselves and the associated *Print Networks* series, but also by his founding of *The History of the Book Trade in the North* and its working papers, his editing of *Quadrat*, and his vision and practical determination in establishing the massive collaborative project of the *British Book Trade Index*. His understanding of the history of shared human endeavour which is represented by books as artefacts is consequently a *lived* understanding: made tangible and alive in the collegiality, collaboration and sheer fun that he has fostered, drawing into his orbit fellow researchers of all ages and from all walks of life, encouraging their projects and always alert to the significant contribution to be made by those with practical experience: of the book trade, of libraries and archives, of family businesses.

The editors have expanded the usual format of the volume, inviting additional contributions from colleagues keen to pay tribute to Peter's achievement. John Feather's keynote paper sets the framework of the volume by surveying the landscape of research on the provincial book trade and setting an agenda for future scholarly projects, and the papers which follow exemplify many of the approaches, methodologies and sources that he identifies. The kinds of sources used by the authors collected here are many and various: the book itself as material evidence (with attention to size, format, binding, type, inscriptions, illustrations, annotations); local archival and documentary sources, including local newspapers; sale catalogues and circulating library catalogues; business letters and private diaries; the surviving archives of printers and publishers; and the ephemera of a printer's specimen books. The chronological span of the collective endeavour called 'the history of the book' is, moreover, well-represented here, with papers presenting evidence ranging from the first English printed texts to the most recent editions and transformations of the *Book of Common Prayer*.

Lucy Lewis takes us to London of the fifteenth and early sixteenth centuries to point to the sammelband format as possible evidence of the marketing strategies of the earliest printers. Her account of pairs of printed texts by Caxton and de Worde which survive bound up together shows the relationship, from the earliest English printing, between the expectations and needs of buyers and readers and the decisions about physical form made by printers and booksellers. Texts which printers conceived of as relating to similar subjects and interests, so that they were printed in the same formats, were collected and bound together by booksellers or by readers to create physical pairings in much the same way that scribes and owners brought together manuscript compilations. The importance of format as a key to success in publishing did not diminish over time as evidenced, for example, by the way in which publishers' series proliferated in the nineteenth century. Iain Beavan's account of Oliver and Boyd's 'Edinburgh Cabinet Library', launched in the 1830s, shows how a small octavo non-fiction series was planned both to be uniform with an edition of a fiction series – the Waverley Novels – and to be suitable for binding up with competing 'useful knowledge' series. The significance of format is also evident in Margaret Cooper's dicussion of Septimus Prowett's sumptuous large-format illustrated books, for which he commissioned work by the leading artists of his day. Typography, as well as format, can be an important feature of marketing strategy, and the pioneering work of the Yorkshire Joint Stock Publishing & Stationery Company of Otley in suiting the typeface and type size of its children's readers to the needs of the young is uncovered by Caroline Archer, Sue Walker and Linda Reynolds. In his survey of that most successful of long-term sellers, the *Book of Common Prayer*, David Griffiths clarifies the confusing variety of decisions about format, typography, rubrication and content made over four and a half centuries by printers and publishers responding to changing religious, social, legal and economic circumstances.

A focus on place is of course fundamental to the study of the provincial trade and, as John Feather notes, 'Without a chronological framework, there can be no history.'[3] Several of our contributors are distinguished for their long-term research into the book trades of particular towns, cities and regions and into the careers of individual traders, the development of local businesses and family firms over several generations. Amongst the papers collected here the reader will find new perspectives on the book trades of numerous towns and cities (Denbigh, Edinburgh, Leicester, Manchester, Norwich, Otley, Philadelphia, Sydney, Whitehaven, Worcester) and regions (Cumbria, Kent). Working to provide a chronological history for the book trade in Whitehaven, Barry McKay mines a range of sources (letters, newspapers, imprints and local archives) to reconstruct the beginnings of the town's book trade. The career of John Gregory, proprietor of Leicester's first newspaper, is documented by

INTRODUCTION

John Hinks with careful attention to the specific social and political context of the eighteenth-century town and the wider region served by Gregory's newspaper. Philip Henry Jones reconstructs the career of Thomas Gee senior, printer-publisher of Denbigh in the early nineteenth century and until now overshadowed by the importance of his son of the same name; a career in which local politics and in particular the politics of Welsh culture were a significant factor.

One of the crucial tasks for future research is the reassessment of the relationship between London and the provinces. London's dominance as the major centre of production and the role of the provinces as mainly concerned with distribution are, broadly speaking, accepted as accurate generalisations, but the establishment in provincial towns of printing presses, and in particular of local newspapers from the early eighteenth century, complicates this neat division of production and distribution. As John Feather notes, it is in mapping the *regional networks*, often based on newspaper ownership and distribution, that there is still much to be done. David Stoker addresses the complex connections between London and the regions in terms of book trade personnel, revealing the way in which the London business of the printer Freeman Collins and his wife Susannah, with its succession of apprentices, served to develop the provincial trade in Exeter, Reading, York and especially in Norwich, providing the latter city with printers and sustaining a Norwich printing business for a decade in the early years of the eighteenth century. Margaret Cooper's detective work in pursuit of Septimus Prowett exposes a London-based publisher's brief flirtation with a business in Worcester early in his career. Iain Beavan's work on Oliver & Boyd, focusing on the relationships between publisher and authors, also points up trade connections between Oliver & Boyd in Edinburgh and other branches of the trade: paper was supplied from Hertfordshire, wood engravings were printed in London, and the London wholesalers Simpkin, Marshall were agents for distribution. Particularly tantalising in relation to the question of regional networks and the geographical interdependence of the trade is the new evidence adduced here by Richard Goulden, whose investigation of printers' specimen books, in themselves rare survivals, points to a symbiotic relationship between a Tonbridge printer and the stationers and booksellers of the immediately surrounding area.

Geographical interdependence within the book trade stretches beyond the British Isles, and as Wallace Kirsop remarks below, 'the pattern adopted for setting up bookselling businesses in nineteenth-century Australia was not unlike that being studied by Warren McDougall for the United States fifty years earlier.'[4] The British colonies offered established British businesses expanding markets and proved attractive to young men with experience of the trade and ambition to succeed. McDougall's account of the relationship between the Edinburgh bookseller Charles

Elliot and Thomas Dobson, his young clerk sent to Philadelphia to sell Elliot's books, tellingly illustrates the human as well as financial costs of transatlantic trading. The subject of Kirsop's investigation, William Baker, seems not to have had the secure backing enjoyed by Dobson, but like Dobson he exploited his opportunities. Originally a lithographer and engraver in Dublin, Baker moved to Australia where, in a spirit of enterprise and opportunism, he developed his career as both publisher and proprietor of shops and circulating libraries.

A notable development of book history in the past decade has been the increased concentration on readers and reading practices, which are notoriously difficult to reconstruct. The study of the buying, borrowing, owning and reading of books (and as Peter Isaac reminds us, books 'bought by people' are only '*possibly* read by people') relies on two lines of approach: one, the systematic collection and analysis of evidence (from subscription lists, private and institutional library catalogues and records of circulating and other public libraries) and the other the individual examples of particular collections and particular readers (often from the evidence of their own libraries, surviving books and personal letters and diaries). Both approaches are represented in this volume. John Gavin, taking the computer-aided and systematic approach, reports on his project to record information about a range of early libraries in the Lake Counties and proposes a system for analysing library catalogues by using contemporary subject classification. Wallace Kirsop investigates Baker's 'Juvenile Circulating Library' in 1840s Sydney within the context of the career of a 'go-a-head' publisher exploring every opening in the market for books in Australia. The startling appearance of forty-nine copies of Byron's *Don Juan* in a juvenile library provides a useful (and intriguing) warning that trusting to library catalogues as unproblematic evidence can seduce us into creating 'borrowers of the mind'.

Individuals and their books are also central to the papers offered by Brenda Scragg, David Hounslow and Michael Powell. Brenda Scragg's account of the manuscript notes made by the Methodist minister James Everett in his copy of the sale catalogue of Adam Clarke's books (1833) takes us into the worlds of two Manchester Methodists whose interests in writing, collecting, reading and (in the case of Everett) bookselling prove mutually illuminating. In exploring the books owned by Lydia Haskoll (1756-1826) David Hounslow vividly demonstrates the long life and cross-generational influence of books in a book-loving family. The persistent appeal of children's books is a salutary reminder that while individual titles go out of print and out of fashion, a single copy remains alive as a potent element in the cultural life not only of its contemporary readers but often of successive generations. 'Reading!…how I venerate thee!' proves an apt motto not only for those Haskoll family members who read, annotated and treasured Lydia's books across three centuries,

INTRODUCTION

but also for Edmund Harrold, the Manchester wig-maker whose diary of 1712-16 Michael Powell enthusiastically excavates. Harrold's diary (featuring drink, sex and books) not only reveals the reading practices of a man continually searching for moral improvement (and, engagingly, failing to find it) but, importantly, offers new evidence of an extensive business in books well outside the usual sphere of the book trade. As a barber Harrold supplemented his services by trading in books, exchanging, lending and bartering them with customers, cataloguing collections and conducting auctions. Here, the survival of one man's diary opens up a substantial world of informal book-dealing completely outside the local book trade.

Harrold's diary, like the printers' specimen books discussed by Richard Goulden, demonstrates that much crucial evidence for the ways in which books were produced, traded and read is dependent on chance survivals. The serendipity of the fortuitous find will always be part of the excitement of research into the history of the trade. Conversely, one of the frustrations of research is the difficulty of systematic work when surviving evidence is scattered or difficult to locate. Diana Dixon does a valuable service in addressing the methodological problems of newspaper research. Although, as she demonstrates, many strides have been made in bringing newspapers under firmer bibliographical control, the very nature of the periodical press – its short runs, frequent changes of ownership and of titles – means that systematic study of newspapers in particular towns or regions is still peculiarly difficult. Amongst the many approaches, methodologies, types of evidence and angles of research represented in this volume, Diana Dixon's good-humoured approach to the 'vast wilderness' of her subject stands as testimony both to the frustrations and to the rewards of a field of research in which there is still much to be done.

Like the many books, newspapers, diaries, letters, library lists and sale catalogues discussed within its covers, this volume will have its own future as material evidence of more than the texts it contains. We hope that, in providing its readers with historical information about books and the people who have made and used them, it will also stand as a warm tribute to Peter Isaac who, as friend and colleague, has tirelessly and generously invited us to accompany him in the shared endeavour of shedding light on the book trade.

NOTES

Publication was originally intended to coincide with the meeting of the twentieth annual seminar, held at the University of Exeter in 2002: an apt occasion not only to honour Professor Isaac's achievement in his own substantial research into the history of the trade, but also to celebrate his energy in building and sustaining through two decades a community of researchers, a network of shared interests and a convivial sense of collective endeavour. Peter's unexpected death shortly before that seminar has necessarily changed the context of publication from festschrift to a memorial volume still celebratory in intention.

1. An earlier volume, containing the proceedings of the eighth annual seminar, was published as *Six Centuries of the Provincial Book Trade in Britain*, edited by Peter Isaac and Barry McKay (Winchester: St Paul's Bibliographies, 1990).
2. Peter Isaac and Barry McKay (ed), *The Moving Market: Continuity and Change in the Book Trade* (New Castle, DE: Oak Knoll Press, 2001), x.
3. See below, 2.
4. See below, 135.

The History of the English Provincial Book Trade: a research agenda

JOHN FEATHER

THE STUDY OF THE ENGLISH PROVINCIAL BOOK TRADE has been bedevilled by its very name. In England – unlike France and some other countries – the word provincial carries with it an undertone of inferiority and narrow-mindedness which is implicitly contrasted with the social and intellectual sophistication of metropolitan life. Despite the perception, provincial cultural and economic life in early modern and modern England was, and is, a vigorous entity in its own right, separate from that of London and yet intimately related to it. The relationship is far from being one of dependence. Indeed, for 150 years from the middle of the eighteenth century onwards, the true drivers of the economy were the extracting and manufacturing industries which were, by and large, in the midlands and the north rather than in London and the home counties. For at least a century before that, however, a distinctive social life had been developing in provincial towns, which was to bear its full fruit between 1750 and the outbreak of World War One. This provincial history – the history of England outside its capital city – has attracted much attention in recent decades, and we now know a great deal about it.[1]

The history of the book trade is one part of this history of provincial England. The study of this trade helps us to understand some aspects of that history, but in its turn the trade can only be fully understood if we put it in its broader context. The provincial book trade was never a self-contained entity in two respects. First, it was always part of the economic, social and cultural structures of the towns and cities in which it was practised. Booksellers, printers and others engaged in the trade took part in civic affairs just like their fellow citizens. We find them as churchwardens, councillors, aldermen and mayors, property owners, investors, and occasionally miscreants. They participated in religious, political and social activities. They were connected with families in other trades by blood and by marriage. In other words, the people in the trade were part of a community, and typically part of a community which, even in the late nineteenth century, was small, intimate and introspective by modern standards. Their trades were as integrated into the local economy as they were into local society. They were suppliers to other traders, and were supplied by them. They had shops, warehouses and workshops; they were employers of labour, or were themselves employed by others.

The book trade, however, could never be entirely inwardly focused on its own local community. Until the end of the seventeenth century, booksellers outside

London were necessarily dealing in books which were produced in London or on the continent. Even after printing was legalised in the provinces (or, more accurately, the restrictions on printing were abandoned), the London booksellers continued to dominate the trade. The transformation of the copy-owning booksellers into what we can recognise as publishers, which began in the 1780s and was complete by about 1820, merely reinforced existing patterns. The heart of the provincial book trade has always been in distribution rather than production.

The understanding of the provincial trade was distorted for many years by a general failure to recognise this essential fact. In itself, the failure is understandable. The most visible evidence of the existence of a trade in printed books lies in the books themselves. Books survive in quantities which are unmatched by the numbers of survivors of any other artefact of remotely comparable cultural significance. With rare exceptions, they declare their origins, and thus provide us with the initial means of recovering some basic data about the book trade – who was involved in it, what they did, when they did it, and where they worked. The earliest studies of the provincial trade were largely based on the study of imprints.[2]

From them, and a from a limited range of documentary sources, it seemed to be possible to compile lists of those involved in the trade, which duly took their place in a multitude of local and national directories. This process reached its culmination in the series of dictionaries published by the Bibliographical Society between 1905 and 1932.[3] Many similar directories of traders in particular localities have also been compiled and published, and they continue to appear from time to time.[4]

The compilation of lists of names, places and dates is an essential element in the study of the provincial trade. Without a chronological framework, there can be no history, and without factual foundations historians build on shifting sands. Recovering the raw facts about the past of their localities has been the greatest contribution of local historians to our understanding of the history of England. If it was not until the last decades of the last century that academic historians came to recognise the immense contributions which local antiquaries had made to our knowledge of the English past, the fault lies with the historians as much as it does with the antiquaries. In the present context, glib dismissal of the value of lists, indexes and catalogues betrays a fundamental failure to appreciate the need for foundations upon which a history of the book trade can be built.[5] The British Book Trade Index, conceptualised and largely realised by the honorand of this volume, will be a unique and invaluable resource for future historians of the trade precisely because it provides this infrastructure of fact on a scale never previously attempted.[6]

The continued investigation of archival and bibliographical sources for evidence of the existence and extent of the book trade is of fundamental importance. In the last twenty years, major projects have been undertaken in the north-west of England, in the west midlands, in some parts of the south-east, and in the northern counties. Some of these are individual efforts,[7] some are the work of groups or societies.[8] What they all have in common is that they are driven by the desire to augment our knowledge of the trade. Every investigation reveals more booksellers, more agents for newspapers and more stationers. It is becoming clear that there were few communities in England even before the building of the railways where printed matter was not available. The trade extended far beyond the narrow limits of those towns where there was a printer, although even printing was becoming comparatively common by the middle decades of the nineteenth century.

A good deal of this work has been based on the exploitation of new sources, or of sources which had not previously been fully explored. These have included collections of printed ephemera (often among the most revealing products of the trade for its historian),[9] documentary evidence including a few isolated but precious examples of accounts and other internal documents from booksellers,[10] and, of course, local newspapers.[11] As this work has continued, however, there has also been a greater awareness of the need to put it into the broader context of the history of provincial life and work.

What have we learnt from all of this effort? Do we need to modify our overall picture of the operation of the provincial book trade? At the highest level of generalisation, the answer is that we do not. It remains the case that London was at the centre of the book trade in England, and that it was the most important single centre of the publishing industry. We should not, however, underestimate the importance of provincial publishing, and of the development of regional centres of the trade where both publishing and distribution flourished from the late eighteenth century onwards. Newcastle-upon-Tyne is an interesting example of such a centre. Geographically isolated, but economically dominant in its region, and looking northwards to Scotland almost as much as it looked south to the rest of England, Newcastle's book trade has a long history. That history has been well-documented, although not yet written as a coherent narrative and analytical history, with the partial exception of some aspects of the newspaper trade.[12] During the eighteenth and nineteenth centuries, Newcastle was a significant centre of printing and publishing, first of chapbooks and other popular literature and later of works of more general interest.

Newcastle is an extreme example of a phenomenon which has emerged from a number of studies of the trade over the last twenty years or so: local and regional networks. Their existence has been known for some time, particularly in the early years of the provincial newspaper trade in the first half of the eighteenth century.[13] The vast areas over which some of the early newspapers were circulated laid the foundations for the book distribution network which provided the basis for the well-organised national trade that can be detected by the end of the eighteenth century. In some cases, the association of book distribution with local newspapers continued for many decades; it sometimes became highly competitive. Particularly in the south and west of England where the prosperous and comparatively leisurely pre-industrial lifestyle survived well into the nineteenth century, a regional book distribution network was a highly desirable business.

Two areas which have been studied in recent years can be taken to exemplify the regional networks which were critical to the development of the book trade in the later eighteenth century. A number of booksellers in Worcester were involved in the distribution of newspapers, books and other goods not only in the city but in a substantial surrounding area in and beyond the county.[14] In the south-west of England, there was a sufficient market for some competition to develop between printers and booksellers with regional aspirations. Although this was not quite as open as it might superficially seem, because of cross-ownership of newspaper titles, the mere existence of rival networks, some of which had comparatively long life-spans, confirms that we are dealing with a trade which had worthwhile financial returns.[15] There is much more to learn about these regional networks. Some booksellers whose names are familiar from imprints almost certainly had a key role in regional distribution which might be more fully exposed by deeper work in archives and (especially) local newspapers. But all the evidence we have suggests that the basic patterns of the eighteenth-century trade sketched by Pollard and the present author – a trade dominated by London producers, with extensive and growing regional distribution systems – will not be significantly amended.[16]

Much work, however, remains to be done, even for the eighteenth century. At the most basic level, there are significant areas of England whose book trade history has not been written, even if some of the basic archival work has been completed. These areas include parts of the north-west, large parts of Yorkshire, and several midland counties. Even where the spade-work has been done, there are comparatively few genuinely analytical historical studies of the trade. Nottinghamshire and Sussex can be taken to exemplify this category. Moreover, although administrative units such as boroughs and counties were important (perhaps more so in the eighteenth century than subsequently), economic studies of the trade need to take full account of the trade networks which encompassed regions which crossed their boundaries and sometimes overlapped with each other. Local bibliographies and lists of traders provide an invaluable framework, but they are only the starting point not the ultimate goal.

When we turn to the nineteenth century, the gaps are even more conspicuous. We could speculate on a number of reasons for this, some of which are very general and some quite specific. At the most general level, the focus of nineteenth-century urban and local history has tended to be on the industrial cities, while in the eighteenth century there has been a greater concentration on the historic county and market towns.[17] The book trades did, of course, exist in the industrial towns of the north and the midlands, but they were not part of the most vibrant sector of their economies. There was a flourishing cultural life in nineteenth-century Leeds or Manchester (and in many smaller towns as well), of which bookshops and circulating libraries were an integral part, but this was an outgrowth of the industrial economy rather than being an economic driver in its own right. In economic terms, booksellers were just another group of retailers, dealing in a non-essential luxury product. Printing was perhaps more significant, although for reasons which had little to do with literary or even political culture. Printing was needed for stationery, packaging, advertising and all the paraphernalia which accompanies the manufacture and sale of goods. Printers were integrated into the urban economy, but were essentially one of many service providers who enabled industry to function. Neither booksellers nor printers belonged to economically dominant groups in nineteenth-century cities, and as a result they seem to have played a far less conspicuous role in civic social and political life than they had done in many places in the eighteenth century.

When we turn to more specific issues, the would-be historian of the nineteenth-century provincial book trade faces a problem quite different from that which confronts historians of earlier centuries. While the latter must make the best use they can of any material which survives, for the nineteenth century there is almost too much. Trade directories multiplied in numbers, were often revised annually, and are increasingly reliable. Official records, such as those of births, marriages and deaths were better kept, are more likely to have survived, and are comparatively easily accessible. Local newspapers proliferated. By the second half of the nineteenth century, even quite small towns had their own weekly paper, many places had a daily, and in some cities and larger towns there were two or more competing titles. In other words, three of the key sources for book trade history – contemporary directories, documentary records and local newspapers – have reached an almost deterrent scale. The availability of the 1901 census on the World Wide Web, with sophisticated search facilities promised for the near future, makes another massive and complex source readily accessible.[18] A recent analysis of the sources for a history of printing in nineteenth-century Manchester exemplifies both the potential for research and the pitfalls for researchers.[19]

The tradition of research into the provincial book trade may also have militated against the development of nineteenth-century studies. The sheer scale of the sources which would underpin book trade directories has been a deterrent to those who might otherwise have done the work.[20] The reason which was proffered was that by the middle of the nineteenth century, the trade directories, and particularly the *Post Office Directory*, were so comprehensive that compilation of directories of specific trades was no longer necessary.[21] The point is a valid one, but it reflects the antiquarian approach to the provincial book trade, rather than the more analytical approach of the historian. It has, however, left a gap. Even now we have far better bibliographical resources for the nineteenth century,[22] it is still difficult to paint a general picture of the trade. Many key documents, even at national level, remain comparatively unexplored, including the records of the Stationers' Company, and even many of the business records whose existence is now known and recorded.[23]

It is no surprise that the growing body of work on the nineteenth-century book trade is focused on the publishing industry. Indeed, it was not until the second quarter of that century that there was a publishing industry in anything like the modern sense. Thereafter, however, it operated in a way which, in some key respects, is still familiar today. Above all, it was a national (and increasingly international) trade. There was a growth in provincial publishing in the nineteenth century, but as in the previous century much of what was published was of limited local interest. The handful of exceptions merely emphasises the continued dominance of the London trade and the great publishing houses which dominated that trade by about 1870, although some interesting and important work has been done on publishers in provincial cities.[24]

The availability of new aids to research such as the British Book Trade Index (BBTI) and Nineteenth Century Short Title Catalogue (NSTC), as well as smaller but no less significant listings such as those prepared under the NEWSPLAN project, opens the way for a new approach to the study of the nineteenth-century provincial book trade. It has been possible to create these new tools because of the use of computers, and it is the computer which will facilitate their full exploitation by future scholars. It is now possible to handle data on a scale which was previously impracticable. This may change the social mode of the research process. In the past, almost all of the ground-breaking work has been done by individuals, or small volunteer groups. Few of them have held academic posts directly concerned with book trade history, and many have not been academics at all. A new research culture which involves bringing in research assistants and technical support and creates a demand for significant funding may make a fundamental change to this tradition. It will be important to ensure that the genuine enthusiasm of the local historians, and those simply fascinated by the history of print and printing, is not lost.[25]

At the same time, however, we need to reflect on the broader context of the subject. More accurately, there are two contexts which we have to consider. The first of these is national, and concerns the book trade as whole. It is clear that the structure of the trade changed significantly between, say, 1800 and, say, 1850. But how? when? and why? These questions are not entirely without answers. Much work has been done on the emergence of publishing as an activity with a separate identity, and how the publishers came to dominate the trade as their predecessors – the copy-owning booksellers – had done before them.[26] There have also been authoritative studies of some of the key issues which concerned the London publishers from the 1830s to the end of the century. These include copyright (and especially international copyright), the contentious issue of the wholesale and retail prices of books, and the development of new internal structures in the trade which were more effective than the somewhat anachronistic Stationers' Company.[27]

There are still, however, many significant gaps. For those whose interests lie in the provincial trade, the most important of these is that there is still no adequate account of nineteenth-century wholesaling and distribution. We know that in the second half of the eighteenth century, there were well-established systems for the national distribution of London books, for the regional distribution of provincial books and, to lesser extent, the national distribution (or at least London sale) of some books of provincial origin.[28] A hundred years later, the patterns were very different. The wholesale trade was dominated by one firm – Simpkin, Marshall – whose competitors operated on a much smaller scale. Physical distribution, both nationally and locally, had been transformed by the building of the railways. Books and a few associated products were no longer unusual in being centrally produced and regionally distributed rather than being sold in the region where they were made. As part of these changes, the book trade developed new mechanisms for distributing not only books, but also information about books. New working tools for provincial booksellers, notably *The English Catalogue of Books,* began to be evolved.[29] A trade press emerged, not least *The Bookseller* founded in 1858, which survives today as the principal means of distributing information in the trade and as the most important single medium for publishers' advertising to retail booksellers.[30] The chronology of these developments is reasonably clear; the chain of cause and effect – if there was one – is not. Until it is established, there can be no holistic analysis of the provincial book trade in the nineteenth century.

The second context is local. Pride in locality was a hallmark of Victorian Britain. There were great monuments to that pride in public buildings and public spaces, and in philanthropic support (often with official blessing) for such institutions as civic universities and orchestras. Across the midlands and the north, towns and cities vied with each other to have the best town hall, the best parks, the largest population, even the best tramways and the best annual performance of *Messiah*. It was this vibrant urban culture which was the context in which the provincial booksellers operated in the nineteenth century, and of which they were an integral part. At a local level, their most important direct contributions took the forms of newspapers and circulating libraries. The development of the provincial newspapers in the nineteenth century has probably been more thoroughly studied than any other aspect of the trade in this period. Socially, culturally and politically, local newspapers were an important element in the life of Victorian England. In the largest cities, there was a flourishing and competitive market for dailies and weeklies, and for morning and evening papers, often reflecting both national and local political partisanship.[31] They did not, of course, have the market to themselves. The London newspapers were reaching a national market in the middle of the eighteenth century; a hundred years later they were genuinely national, leaving London every evening by train to be read at breakfast tables throughout the land.

Circulating libraries were to be found in many towns by the end of the nineteenth century. As the century wore on, however, the market changed, and came to be dominated by a major national company, Mudie's, which almost took on the status of an institution.[32] Mudie's could only operate as it did because of the improved physical communications which characterised the nineteenth century. The availability of cheap transport for large quantities of heavy goods, like books in bulk, made it economically feasible to establish almost identical libraries in towns and cities across the country. Later competitors, notably W. H. Smith, followed the same pattern.[33] The typical circulating library in an eighteenth-century provincial town was actually founded and run by a bookseller. By the late nineteenth century, it was a branch of a national chain. There were, of course, some surviving small-scale enterprises, but they were under pressure from the national chains, and, from 1850 onwards, from the newly founded municipal public libraries.[34]

Any study of the provincial book trade in the nineteenth century will have to take account of the tensions between local and national provision, and between national suppliers, local suppliers and their customers. It seems that at least some of the documentary sources exist from which it should be possible to answer some significant questions which can less easily be addressed for the eighteenth century. It will be particularly interesting to attempt to assess the economic importance of provincial outlets to the London publishers. Accounts of the origins of the Net Book Agreement normally follow the views of the London publishers of the 1890s that provincial underselling (that is, price competition) was significantly damaging the profitability of the trade as whole, and in particular of the London publishing houses.[35] At the very least, this proposition, accepted for scholars by decades, needs to be re-examined.

As with other issues in the history of the retail book trade, a provincial perspective will be a valuable counterbalance to the London perspective of the publishers.

The provincial book trade was already the subject of historical study when the Net Book Agreement became operational on the first day of the twentieth century. Since Allnutt published his first tentative list of early provincial printers in 1879, hundreds of scholars, and tens of thousands of hours of work, have been devoted to the topic. Of those scholars, the majority have been interested in the trade in a particular town or county, and at a particular time. Some have devoted themselves to the work of one aspect of the trade, such as printing, bookselling or circulating libraries. There have been studies of individual firms, sometimes over several generations. The tools which are now available to us enable us to embark on scholarly projects which were inconceivable a generation ago, and impractical until the 1990s. A Web-delivered version of BBTI is only one example – although one of critical importance – of a resource which will almost immeasurably facilitate the study of the provincial book trade.

The factual infrastructure on which our accounts of the trade are built has become more accessible than ever before. That very accessibility has, however, exposed gaps of both knowledge and understanding. Peter Isaac, true to the great tradition of his first profession, has systematically created a device which enables us to do things. The task now is to make use of it to the full.

NOTES

1. Exemplified by Peter Borsay, *The English Urban Renaissance: culture and society in the provincial town, 1660 – 1770* (Oxford: Clarendon Press, 1989).

2. The first attempt was that by W H Allnutt, 'Printers and Printing in the Provincial Towns of England and Wales' *Transactions and Proceedings of the first annual meeting of the Library Association* (London: 1879), 101–3, 139, Appendix V; and 'Tables of places in England and Wales, with their earliest specimens of typography', 157 – 64. For the early history of these studies, see Paul Morgan, *English Provincial Printing* (Birmingham: Privately Printed, 1958), 1–4.

3. E Gordon Duff, *A Century of the English Book Trade* (London: The Bibliographical Society, 1905); R B McKerrow, *A Dictionary of Printers and Booksellers in England, Scotland and Ireland, and of foreign printers of English books 1557 – 1640* (London: The Bibliographical Society, 1910); Henry R Plomer, *A Dictionary of the Booksellers and Printers who were at Work in England, Scotland and Ireland from 1641 to 1667* (London: The Bibliographical Society, 1907); Henry R Plomer, *A Dictionary of the Printers and Booksellers who were at Work in England, Scotland and Ireland from 1668 to 1725* (London: The Bibliographical Society, 1922); and G H Bushnell, E R McN Dix and Henry R Plomer, *A Dictionary of the Printers and Booksellers who were at Work in England, Scotland and Ireland from 1726 – 1775* (London: The Bibliographical Society, 1932).

4. For those published before 1980, see John Feather, *The English Provincial Book Trade before 1850. A checklist of secondary sources* (Oxford: Oxford Bibliographical Society, Occasional Publication 16, 1981). As the date of publication suggests, an updated version is now needed.

5. I am referring to the comments of F W Ratcliffe. 'The Contribution of Book Trade Studies to Scholarship', in: Peter Isaac [ed] *Six Centuries of the Provincial Book Trade in Britain* (Winchester: St Paul's Bibliographies, 1990), 1–11, which betrayed a woeful misunderstanding of the field.

6. BBTI has been some twenty years in the making, and is now accessible at http://www.bbti.bham.ac.uk . It has attracted support from a number of institutions and organisations over the years, including most recently the Arts and Humanities Research Board, but it would not have started, would not have survived and would not have reached near-completion without Peter Isaac's enthusiasm and sheer hard work.

7. Such as the work of David Knott on Kent in, for example *The Book Trade in Kent. Working paper: Isle of Thanet directory ca. 1776 to 1838*, (Privately Distributed, 1989); Ian Maxted on the west country in, for example, *Books with Devon imprints. A handlist to 1800* (Exeter: J Maxted, Exeter Working Papers in British Book Trade History, 6, 1989); or John Hinks on Leicester in his 'Freedom and Apprenticeship Records as a Source for Book Trade History', *Book Trade History Group Newsletter*, 41, 2001, 11–13.

8. The first of these groups was The History of the Book Trade in the North, founded in 1965, in which the dedicatee of this volume was a key player; among the Group's many products are C J Hunt, *The Book Trade in Northumberland and Durham to 1860. A biographical dictionary* (Newcastle upon Tyne: History of the Book Trade in the North, 1975) and P J Wallis,*The Book Trade in Northumberland and Durham to 1860. A supplement* (Newcastle upon Tyne: History of the Book Trade in the North, 1981). Other groups include those based in Birmingham (P B Freshwater [ed] *Working Papers for an Historical Directory of the West Midlands Book Trade to 1850,* Nos. 1-7 (Birmingham: Birmingham Bibliographical Society, 1975 - 87)), and Liverpool (M R Perkin, *Book Trade in the North West Project. Occasional Publications,* Nos. 1-3 (Liverpool: Liverpool Bibliographical Society, 1981-92)).

9. See, for example, Ian Maxted, 'Single Sheets from a Country Town: the example of Exeter' in Robin Myers and Michael Harris [ed] *Spreading the Word. The distribution networks of print 1550 – 1850* (Winchester: St Paul's Bibliographies, 1990), 109–29.

10. The few pre-nineteenth-century records include those of the Clay family of Daventry, Rugby and Warwick (Jan Fergus and Ruth Portner, 'Provincial Bookselling in Eigheenth-Century England: the case of John Clay re-considered', *Studies in Bibliography*, 40 (1987), 47–63, and papers and financial documents from the Mountforts of Worcester (Margaret Cooper, *The Worcester Book Trade in the Eighteenth Century,* (Worcester: Worcestershire Historical Society, Occasional Publications 8, 1997), 29. A number of provincial printers, publishers, booksellers and stationers are listed in Alexis Weedon and Michael Bott, *British Book Trade Archives 1830 – 1939. A location register* (HOBODS, 6: Oxford and Bristol: History of the Book – On Demand Series, 1996).

11. Used to great effect by many scholars; a recent example is to be found in the work of John Hinks on Leicester to be found elsewhere in this volume, and at greater length in his recently completed Loughborough University PhD thesis.

12. See note 8, above. For newspapers, see Frank Manders, 'History of the Newspaper Press in Northeast England', in: Peter Isaac [ed] *Newspapers in the Northeast. The 'fourth estate' at work in Northumberland & Durham* (Newcastle upon Tyne: History of the Book Trade in the North, PH 78, 1999), 1–4.
13. For the example of *The Northampton Mercury*, see John Feather, *The Provincial Book Trade in Eighteenth-Century England* (Cambridge: Cambridge University Press, 1985), 17–18.
14. See Cooper, *Worcester Book Trade*, together with Martin Holmes, 'Samuel Gamidge: Bookseller in Worcester ($c1755 - 1777$)' in: Peter Isaac and Barry McKay,[ed] *Images & Texts. Their production and distribution in the 18th and 19th centuries* (Winchester: St Paul's' Bibliographies, 1997), 11– 52, for Worcester and the upper Severn valley.
15. This is the conclusion which I draw from the research reported in C Y Ferdinand's 'Local Distribution Networks in 18th-Century England' in: Myers and Harris, *Spreading the Word*, 131–49, dealing with Hampshire and adjacent counties.
16. Graham Pollard, 'The English Market for Printed Books' *Publishing History*, 4 (1978), 7–48; and Feather, *Provincial Book Trade*.
17. Of course I recognise that this generalisation can be challenged in almost every detail, not least because some of the historic towns were being transformed into industrial cities by the end of the eighteenth century. But in outline, the point is sufficiently valid to sustain the present argument.
18. At http://www.census.pro.gov.uk.
19. Brenda Scragg, 'Some Sources for Manchester Printing in the Nineteenth Century' in: Isaac and McKay, *Images & Texts,* 113– 9.
20. As Ratcliffe, 'Contribution of Book Trade Studies', pointed out, almost none of those who have done the groundwork have been full-time academics in this field. The majority have not been academics at all, including booksellers, librarians, and simply interested amateurs. In re-iterating this point, I do not endorse Ratcliffe's implied deprecation of them.
21. The compiler of the most authoritative list of directories commented that 'as directories had become fairly common and fairly uniform by the 1850s, that would seem a convenient period at which to stop'. Jane E Norton, *Guide to the National and Provincial Directories of England and Wales, excluding London, published before 1856* (London: Royal Historical Society, Guides and Handbooks 5, 1950), 15. Hunt, *Book Trade in Northumberland and Durham,* does not explain the choice of 1860 as a terminal date, although he implies that the provincial trade is of less interest after the middle of the nineteenth century (p.xii). The north-east model seems to have been followed by both the west midlands and north-west England groups (see note 8, above).
22. Notably, of course, the *Nineteenth Century Short Title Catalogue* (NSTC).
23. There are exceptions. Michael Turner's long-term work on 19th-century apprentices will no doubt bear fruit in due course. Some scholars have made use of the copyright registers which were kept after 1842. And, in any case, the Stationers' Company was less important than it had been before the late eighteenth century. But the fact remains that there is a unexploited (and largely unexplored) corpus of material. See Robin Myers. *The Stationers' Company Archive. An account of the records 1554 – 1984* (Winchester: St Paul's Bibliographies, 1990). A small fraction of the material was used by contributors to Robin Myers [ed] *The*

Stationers' Company. A history of the later years 1800 – 2000 (London: Worshipful Company of Stationers and Newspaper Makers, 2001). For book trade business records, see Weedon and Bott, *British Book Trade Archives*.

24. Exemplified in two recent papers by John R Turner, 'Conditions for Success as a Provincial Publisher in Late Nineteenth-Century England,' Publishing History 41, (1997), 63 – 73; and 'A Sales Ledger of J. W. Arrowsmith Ltd.' *Publishing History* 44 (1998), 77 – 87. These are about publishers based in Newcastle and Bristol respectively.

25. See the comments of John Sutherland in his Foreword to Elizabeth James [ed] *Macmillan: a publishing tradition* (Basingstoke: Palgrave, 2002), xvii.

26. The account in Terry Belanger, 'From Bookseller to Publisher: changes in the London book trade, 1750 – 1850' in: Richard G Landon [ed] *Book Selling and Book Buying. Aspects of the nineteenth-century British and north American book trade* (Chicago, IL: American Library Association, 1978), 7-16, is still essentially valid.

27. I am referring to works such as Simon Nowell-Smith, *International Copyright Law and the Publisher in the Reign of Queen Victoria* (Oxford: Clarendon Press, 1968); James J Barnes, *Free Trade in Books. A study of the London book trade since 1800* (Oxford: Clarendon Press, 1964); John Sutherland, 'The Institutionalisation of the British Book Trade to the 1890s' in: Robin Myers and Michael Harris [ed] *The Development of the English Book Trade, 1700 – 1899* (Oxford: Oxford Polytechnic Press, 1981), 95 – 105; and Myers, *The Stationers' Company*.

28. John Feather, 'The Country Trade in Books' in: Myers and Harris, *Spreading the Word*, 165–83, is a summary account of the practices. See also P J Wallis, 'Cross-Regional Connexions' in: Isaac, *Six Centuries* 87-100.

29. This was its final and most familiar title, in use from 1860 onwards. But its predecessor series under various titles had existed since the late 1830s. See the brief listing in Joanne Shattock, [ed] *The Cambridge Bibliography of English Literature*, (3 ed., Cambridge: Cambridge University Press, 1999), vol. 4, col. 85.

30. Again, the publication has a longer history, going back to *The Monthly Literary Advertiser*, founded in 1805; see *CBEL*, col. 85.

31. The pioneering and classic study is Alan J Lee, *The Origins of the Popular Press in England 1855 – 1914* (London: Croom Helm, 1976).

32. Guinevere L Griest, *Mudie's Circulating Library and the Victorian Novel* (Newton Abbot: David & Charles, 1970), 15 – 34.

33. Charles Wilson, *First With the News. The history of W. H. Smith 1792 – 1972* (London: Jonathan Cape, 1985), 355 – 73.

34. The position of independent bookshops at the end of the twentieth century provides an interesting analogy. For the early development of public libraries see Alistair Black, *A New History of the English Public Library. Social and intellectual contexts, 1850 –1914* (London: Leicester University Press, 1990).

35. The classic account is, of course, that by Barnes, *Free Trade in Books*, 143–46, whose views have been broadly accepted by most subsequent writers on the subject.

'For No Text Is An Island, Divided From the Main': Incunable Sammelbande

LUCY LEWIS

WHERE DOES a book begin and where does it end? To a fifteenth-century reader of Caxton's 1480 edition of the *Description of Britain*, the question might seem a somewhat artificial one. Not only does this text have no title-page (a feature which did not become common in printed books till the sixteenth century)[1] but it announces its association with another, longer text (the *Chronicles of England*) in a preamble which is not formally demarcated or labelled as 'introduction' or 'preface':

> Hit is so that in many and diuerse places the comyn cronicles of englond ben had and also now late enprinted at westmynstre And for as moche as the descripcion of this londe whiche of olde tyme was named albyon and after Britayne is not descriued ne comynly had ne the noblenesse and worthynesse of the same is not knowne Therfore I entende to sette in this booke the descripcion of this said Ile of Britayne with the commoditees of the same

The text, then, is not presented in isolation, but in relation to another text. This association is reflected in the physical fact of the collocation of the *Description* and the *Chronicles* in several surviving volumes. In fact, another textual relationship, not stated here but apparent to any student of fifteenth-century letters, lies behind the edition, for the *Description of Britain* is an extract from the *Polychronicon*, a global history which Caxton was to print in full in 1482. Caxton's focus on British history and geography in these early productions reflects his consciousness of himself as England's first printer, and patriotism is a theme running through the metatextual statements (introductions, epilogues and the like) that he made in many of his editions.[2] However, he began his career as a printer in Bruges, and cannot therefore be seen solely as an insular printer.[3] This paper is not concerned with geographical islands, however, but with conceptual and textual ones, specifically with the unit of the fifteenth-century book, its boundaries and its internal organisation.

It is a commonplace of cultural history that the advent of the printing press coincided with, and even contributed to, a revolution in habits of thought and techniques of learning.[4] The age of printing has been seen as a new dawn, inaugurating greater internationalism in learning, new standards of textual accuracy and integrity and a new democracy of letters. In many ways, of course, this is true: texts and information were much more easily and speedily disseminated than ever before, and the mass production of editions at relatively affordable prices made it possible for readers to have private, personal access to texts which would have been much more difficult (and costly) to acquire in manuscript form. However, the 'revolution' in patterns of reading was not total or sudden and the forms in which early printed texts were presented and marketed reflects this. It may seem anachronistic to speak of 'marketing practices' when discussing the book trade of the late fifteenth century, but the evidence of incunable sammelbande makes such a phrase appropriate, as this paper sets out to show.[5] The grouping together, usually in pairs but sometimes larger units, of incunabula in predictable or at least habitual configurations at a point shortly after publication is an intriguing feature of early printing history in England. The incunable sammelband bears some affinities with the medieval manuscript compilation in which different but often related titles existed side by side. These affinities are not coincidental, but reflect the continuity in reader tastes, habits and expectations that bridged the transition from the age of manuscript to that of print.

A volume viewed recently at the Pepys Library, Magdalene College, Cambridge, illustrates some of the rewards and difficulties experienced when studying sammelbande. The volume (shelf-mark is 2051) contains three editions: two incunabula and one early sixteenth-century imprint.[6] The binding is not original, but appears to date from the period when the Pepys collection was being assembled in the late seventeenth and early eighteenth centuries. However, manuscript annotations throughout the volume show that the editions were associated – that they were at least in common ownership if not actually bound together – from a very early date. It is for this reason, and not because they now share a binding, that they are treated as sammelbande here. The editions, in order of appearance in the volume, are: *The Chastysing of Goddes Childern*, printed by Wynkyn de Worde c1494 (STC 5065), *The Treatise of Love*, printed by Wynkyn de Worde c1493 (STC 24234) and the pseudo-Bonaventuran *Imitation of the Blessed Life of Christ*, printed by Richard Pynson in 1506 (STC 3623).[7] A very early hand (from the late fifteenth or early sixteenth century) has made copious marginal annotations, bearing directly on the printed text, in the first two editions, but not in the third. An ownership signature in what appears to be the same hand does, however, appear in the later edition. On the final leaf of the pseudo-Bonaventura, above and below the printer's mark, we find the following words: 'Robard Spencer lederseller of London aremit of the chappell of saynt katheryn at charyng crosse'. Annotations in a later, seventeenth-century, hand also appear in all three editions and were probably made by the last owner before the copies were acquired by Pepys.[8]

If Robard Spencer was the first owner of these three copies, as seems likely, it would be interesting to know whether he acquired them all at the same time or separately, and whether the decision to combine them was his. Incunable editions were sold unbound but it was not unusual to commission a binding for books at the time of purchase. In the absence of an original binding this is likely to remain a mystery. The slightly different treatment of the third edition in the volume, which is free of annotation in the earlier hand, suggests that it may have been acquired at a later stage than the other two, at a point when perhaps the owner's reading habits had changed in line with a general trend towards 'clean copy' and a more passive form of reading.[9] The printed, marginal commentary provided by the printer in the pseudo-Bonaventuran edition perhaps obviated the need for reader annotation of this kind. It is also noteworthy that the pseudo-Bonaventuran edition has worm-holes whereas the other two do not. This is probably due to the poorer quality paper used in the later edition but may suggest that it was not contained in the same binding at the earliest stage of its history, although it seems to have shared the same owner.

Attempts to reconfigure such collections of texts in their original forms, although rewarding, are beset by a number of difficulties. First is the loss of original bindings, which would supply valuable information.[10] This is a widespread problem thanks to the predilection of collectors through the centuries to disbind and rebind editions, often with the laudable motive of preserving the contents but sometimes with a less disinterested view to their saleability. Another problem is that the conventions of bibliographical description applied to incunabula are often more suited to the modern book than to such early productions. The focus on the individual edition as a discrete entity existing in a state of quasi-Platonic abstraction is in some ways inappropriate to the productions of the earliest printing presses, as bibliographers are beginning to realise. A more fruitful approach is to adopt some of the strategies of codicology, a discipline originally adapted to the study of manuscripts, and to pay closer attention to copy-specific features of the texts, such as for example ownership marks and manuscript rubrication.[11] This will add an understanding of publishing, dissemination and reception to the already fairly well adumbrated picture we have of printing processes *tout court*. In the case of the Pepys volume, relevant information had been recorded by cataloguers but in different places so that a composite picture of this early configuration of texts was not readily available. The first two editions were described in J C T Oates's appendix on incunabula in the 'Printed Books' volume of Catalogue of the Pepys Library, compiled by N A Smith. The fact that they were found with another early edition, and possibly shared an early owner with it, was not recorded in that appendix. The pseudo-Bonaventura is described in a different part of the volume, with no cross-referencing, because it is not an incunable, and so a somewhat artificial bibliographical distinction between books printed before and after 1500 potentially obscured a not insignificant aspect of the texts' early readership history.

At this point, further clarification of the term 'sammelbande' and its application may help to focus the observations made in this paper. The term is used to refer to copies of editions which were associated from the earliest point in their history. A good guide to such combinations may still be found in Seymour De Ricci's *A Census of Caxtons* which notes both combinations that are still to be found and offers speculation on ones which may have existed but have since been disrupted.[12] Although the locations of the volumes he describes are not always up-to-date, there has been no change for many, indeed for the majority, of volumes. A more recent guide is to be found in Paul Needham's *The Printer and the Pardoner*, Appendix B.[13] However, Needham applies the term 'sammelbande' somewhat broadly to include any incunable texts that were bound together at an early stage. This paper will concentrate on a narrower category: those editions which seem to have been paired or associated on a regular basis. This regularity distinguishes them from 'tract volumes', or miscellaneous collections of printed material assembled together through the vagaries of individual readers' tastes. In the case of *The Chastysing of Goddes Childern* and *The Treatise of Love*, texts which appear together a number of times, a more systematic selection procedure seems to have been at work than reader choice, although reader demand may of course have prompted or suggested the pairing in the first place.[14] What remains hard to establish is whether these combinations were deliberately planned by the printers when they embarked on a project or whether the phenomenon had nothing to do with the printers but was rather an innovation of the booksellers, who were in a good position to assess reader demand. It is important to note at this stage that texts which occur in sammelbande combinations may also occur individually or in combination with other, quite different, texts, suggesting that there was some flexibility in the 'marketing' of these editions.

Returning to Wynkyn de Worde's editions of *The Chastysing of Goddes Childern* and *The Treatise of Love*, it is worth noting that the subject matter of the editions makes the pairing logical and natural. Both drew their titles and were partly drawn from the *Ancrene Riwle*, a manual for female religious. Another volume containing the two editions together, held at Sidney Sussex College, Cambridge, bears early ownership signatures by two female members of Syon Abbey: Edyth Morpeth and Katheryn Palmer who, as female religious, would have found the texts of especial utility. The former died in 1536 and the latter, who was Abbess of Syon, died in 1576. The volume later came into the possession of Dorothy Abington, who signs her name on the opening page. Dorothy was the sister of Thomas Habington (1560-1647), who was arrested over the Babington Plot (his brother Edward was executed for his involvement) and endured an enforced retirement in Worcestershire, where he pursued antiquarian research. Close study of this volume revealed some interesting similarities with the Pepys volume. In both, leaves B2 and B5 of *The Treatise of Love* are missing. In the Sidney Sussex copy, remnants of the missing pages remain as stubs, whereas in the Pepys volume nothing remains. Although this may of course be coincidence, another unusual feature suggests that it may be a clue to an irregularity in the printing procedure: the text ends unusually early, some three lines short, in the last column of B4a. It could be that B2 and B5 (conjugate leaves) were printed separately and that miscalculation meant that the intervening text failed to fill the space. However, further investigation has shown that these are the only two editions to lack these two leaves: the remaining copies in England are all perfect, as is the copy in the Pierpont Morgan Library. A fragment exists in the Bridwell Library of the Southern Methodist University, consisting of leaves D3 and D4. Another possible explanation for the missing two leaves in the Pepys and Sidney Sussex copies is censorship: perhaps the material printed on these leaves caused offence to some readers? In point of fact, the text is pretty orthodox here, unless an emphasis on the importance of good deeds in achieving salvation was deemed to undermine the doctrine of divine grace as omnipotent. The text reads: 'Fayr lord seyth he ye haue no no [sic] nede of my good dedys but for all that good wyll not saue a man yf he helpe not therto hym self as seynte Austyn seyth. Qui fecit te sine te non iustificabit te sine te.' Although there had been some controversy, earlier in the middle ages, over the Pelagian heresy, which was thought to challenge divine omnipotence by asserting the necessity of earning reward through merit, it is hard to see anything especially objectionable in this passage.

One of the rewards of studying sammelbande is the discovery of connections between different volumes. For example, the Syon Abbey provenance of the Sidney Sussex volume adds to the evidence of de Worde's links with the Bridgittine order. In 1499 Wynkyn de Worde printed *Jerome* by a Syon brother, Symon Wynter, and in 1500 *A Ryght Profytable Treatyse* by another brother, Thomas Betson. Much later, in 1519, he was to print *The Orchard of Syon*. Sue Powell has argued that Syon spirituality and the reading tastes of the order's members influenced the form of two sammelbande editions originally printed by Caxton and later reprinted by Wynkyn de Worde. These are John Mirk's *Festial*, and the *Quattuor Sermones*, with which it is almost invariably bound.[15] Bearing in mind Sue Powell's argument about these two editions, and connecting this with the evidence of the Sidney Sussex volume containing *The Chastysing of Goddes Childern* and *The Treatise of Love*, it might be worth considering whether the sammelband format itself was one favoured by members of this religious house. Possibly they were accustomed to reading devotional and preaching texts in manuscript compilations which allowed cross-comparison and integrational reading, and this habit determined the way in which they selected and organised the printed material that they acquired.

John Mirk's *Festial*, or *Liber Festivalis*, was a well-known sermon collection dating from the fourteenth century. Caxton first printed the work in 1483, but reprinted it in a somewhat different form in 1491.[16] The second edition included three new sermons to celebrate the 'nova festa' – the Visitation, the Transfiguration and the Blessed Name of Jesus – and a short text called the *Hamus Caritatis*. Powell notes that the Visitation was accorded particular devotion at Syon, that the Holy Name was revered in the writings of Richard Rolle and Hilton (both favourite Syon authors) and that the sermon on the Transfiguration contains a direct reference to Syon Abbey. The feast of the Holy Name acquired a certain prestige through the patronage of Lady Margaret Beaufort, who was officially recognised promoter of the feast in England by the Pope in 1494.[17] Powell suggests that Lady Margaret Beaufort, who had for some time been a patron of Caxton's, may have acted as an intermediary between Caxton and Syon Abbey. The *Hamus Caritatis* closes with an injunction that the reader should seek the aid of St Bridget. The *Quattuor Sermones*, according to Powell, displays similar Syon connections. It is a composite text combining material from two different sources and is not found in any manuscript or printed book prior to Caxton's first edition of 1483.[18] The title by which it is now known is taken from the running heads in a later Wynkyn de Worde reprint and is not connected with it in the earliest editions. The version of *The Lay Folks' Catechism* used as one of the sources for the *Quattuor Sermones* divides the preaching material into two blocks, each of which incorporates an excerpt from the *Revelationes* of St Bridget of Sweden. A manuscript containing this version of the *Catechism* is now owned by Trinity College Cambridge and in it may be found other texts suitable for female religious, including *The Chastising of God's Children*. Caxton may have reckoned on the appeal of such material for members of Syon, or have been advised to that effect by a client.

The fact that Caxton (followed by Wynkyn de Worde) printed the *Quattuor Sermones* and the *Festial* with separate signature sequences suggests that the binding of the two editions together may not have been envisaged by the printers from the outset. In fact, although the two texts are almost always found together, the first edition of the *Quattuor Sermones* was printed slightly before the *Festial*. C A Webb published an essay in 1970 which demonstrated that there were two separate editions of the *Quattuor Sermones* accompanying the single, 1483 edition of the *Festial*, not the single edition which had been known as Duff number 299.[19] What seems to have happened is that, after the *Festial* was published, and Caxton (and/or the booksellers) perceived that it sold well in combination with the *Quattuor Sermones*, a decision was made to print more copies of the latter so that the successful pairing – which had not perhaps been envisaged from the outset – could continue. Thereafter, editions of the two works were printed virtually simultaneously by Caxton, his successor Wynkyn de Worde, by Richard Pynson and by Julian Notary.[20] The two texts were not printed with the same signature sequence until the edition by Wolfgang Hopyl, a German living in Paris, in 1495. Contrary to what might be expected, the *Quattuor Sermones* did not ride on the back of its longer, and more well-known, companion text: it was not 'parasitic' in the sense of gaining a readership only through its association with the *Festial*. Significantly, it had been printed before the edition of John Mirk's sermon collection. Moreover, it had a ready-made, niche audience (Syon Abbey) whereas the appeal of the *Festial* (at least in its initial 1483 form) was general and less well-defined, if broad. Far from being parasitic, the Bridgittine *Quattuor Sermones*, with its references to the *Revelationes*, seems to have affected the reworking of the *Festial* edition in 1491, the year in which Caxton introduced the three new, Syonite, sermons. It is not surprising that Caxton should target his publications at a particular institution, like Syon Abbey, for its members had distinct and easily-identifiable reading tastes and priorities, and this would have made it a valuable client for early printers like Caxton. At a time when the financial risks of producing an edition which failed to find a market were real, it was wise to cater for a readership that could be more or less relied upon.

Although the *Quattuor Sermones* was not parasitic upon the *Festial*, there can be little doubt that its association with the longer, more well-established, text would have helped it find a wider audience than it might otherwise have achieved. In that sense, the relationship between the two was intriguingly symbiotic. A slightly different, but equally interesting, textual relationship is that between the *Chronicles of England* and the *Description of Britain*, which are frequently found together in the same volume. In other words, they form another sammelband pairing. The *Chronicles of England* was first published by Caxton on 10 June 1480, according to the colophon. [21] For the most part, it is a version of the English *Brut*, a translation of the Anglo-Norman *Brut d'Engleterre*, which was in turn based on Geoffrey of Monmouth's *Historia Regnum Britanniae*. In his edition, Caxton added a continuation to cover the period 1419-1460, of which he may himself have been the author. The *Description of Britain* was first published later in the same year: 18 August 1480 according to the colophon.[22] In the preface to this, shorter, edition, Caxton makes explicit reference to the earlier publication, as quoted in the introduction to this paper. In this opening paragraph, Caxton is clearly attempting to give a context for the work he is now presenting to the reading public. This was wise, as the text was a new and untried one: it was his own reworking of a section from the *Polychronicon* of Ranulph Higden, translated by John Trevisa from Latin into Middle English at the end of the fourteenth century. A full edition of the *Polychronicon* was to follow in 1482. The explicit link made with the *Chronicles of England* in the preface suggests that Caxton may have planned the marketing of the two together. It would have been good business strategy to launch a less familiar work on the back of a more standard and well-known one, almost in the way that, in the 1950s, a B-movie accompanied a main feature, to draw a somewhat facetious modern parallel.

Wynkyn de Worde followed in Caxton's footsteps by publishing paired editions of the two works which, however, retained separate signature sequences and publication dates. His 1497 edition of the *Chronicles of England* is consistently found together with his 1498 *Description of Britain*.[23] The latter edition has a fine full-page woodblock on its first page. Besides being of interest as an early form of 'title-page' at a time when printed books rarely had such a thing (colophons containing publication information, sometimes with the addition of a printer's mark on the final leaf, were still conventional) the striking appearance of the opening page in this edition suggests that Wynkyn de Worde did not necessarily envisage it being merely appended to the earlier edition. The full-page woodcut would have made a good first page for a book standing alone. The fact that, in practice, it accompanies the *Chronicles* may have as much to do with booksellers and readers as with the original publisher. By this time, the *Chronicles* had been published by other printers (William de Machlinia, the St Albans printer and Leeu of Antwerp) without the *Description*, and Caxton himself had printed a second edition without an accompanying *Description* in 1482.[24] This history of dissociation might have influenced Wynkyn de Worde to market the two as separate (but potentially complementary) texts. Although Caxton's 'list' of titles seems to have been developed strategically, so that one book generated interest in another, the conjoining of editions may well have been the idea of booksellers. Thus a conceptual pairing of texts by the publisher would be translated rather literally by the bookseller as a physical pairing.

So far, this paper has concentrated on textual configurations which seem to have been invented for marketing purposes: frequent pairings of editions which were apparently planned by the publishers. Before concluding, some consideration will be given to the other kinds of configurations: those produced by booksellers and readers. There is evidence to suggest that editions sometimes remained unsold in the booksellers' shops for a reasonably long period after printing and that some sammelband configurations can be seen as a way of shifting stock. For example, Needham has observed that editions of the *Book of Good Manners* (1487) and the *Royal Book* (1485-6) were often bound with the later *Doctrinal of Sapience* (1489) or *Dictes or Sayengis of the Philosophres* (1489). The first three of these texts are found together in the volume now known as the Rosenwald Sammelband, which retains a very early binding (dating from *c*1530).[25] The combination of texts is in many ways natural and appropriate – they all have an ethical theme – however, it is a little surprising that the *Royal Book* and *Doctrinal of Sapience* should be found together, since

The descrypcyon of Englonde.

Here foloweth a lytell treatyse the whiche treateth of the descrypcyon of this londe whiche of olde tyme was named Albyon And after Bryptayne And now is called Englonde and speketh of the noblenesse and worthynesse of the same.

1498 edition of the *Description of Britain* printed by Wynkyn de Worde. Reproduced by permission of the Syndics of Cambridge University Library. Shelfmark: Inc. 3-J-1-2 [3548]

they share some passages and cover much of the same ground. The *Doctrinal* was intended for simple priests and was aimed at a slightly less sophisticated readership than the *Royal Book,* but both are derived from the French *Somme le Roi*. It seems unlikely that Caxton, who was himself the compiler of the *Doctrinal*, would have intended or expected readers to make a joint purchase of two books with such similar content. The pairing of these two editions, which were published some four years apart, therefore seems more probably the idea of booksellers, or possibly of readers.

One early reader who seems to have had a taste for collecting books is Richard Johnson, whose signature appears in a number of editions. One of his volumes contained five incunabula, four of them Caxtons, now all held at Cambridge University Library.[26] The library received the volume as a donation from the collection of Bishop John Moore, a noted bibliophile. The titles are: *Godfrey of Bulloigne, Virgils Eneid, Of Chyvalry from Vegetius, The Chastysing of Goddes Childern* and Chaucer's *Book of Fame*. Each of the editions individually bears his signature, the purchase price and the date of purchase (1510). The printing dates of these editions are fairly widely spread – the earliest being *Godfrey of Bulloigne* (1481) and the latest being *The Chastysing of Goddes Childern*, a Wynkyn de Worde publication, and the decision to combine them together clearly had nothing to do with Caxton. There does seem to be a rationale to the combination, though: the theme of honour and reputation runs through the different texts, linking them. *Godfrey of Bulloigne* is a crusading romance, and its martial theme connects it obviously with the *Aeneid* and with the Vegetius translation (Caxton's English prose version from Christine de Pisan's French version, the *Fayttes of Armes*). Chaucer's *Book of Fame* (more commonly known to modern scholars as *The Hous of Fame*) continues the theme of reputation and glory, although in a more literary than martial vein, and the *Chastysing* deals with honour in the strictly moral sense of virtue. The combination created in this volume by Richard Johnson suggests that his tastes were those of an early Christian humanist, interested both in the public themes of classical literature and in more spiritual concerns. Other books owned by him were an edition of *Aesop's Fables* in Caxton's translation printed by Richard Pynson in 1500 and John Blacman's memoir of Henry VI printed by Robert Copland in 1523.[27] The ownership of the *Fables* adds to the picture of a reader interested in classical culture, and ownership of the memoir is consistent with his apparent interest in public themes.

Examining patterns of readership, traceable through ownership signatures, bindings and other evidence, can help to reconstruct the literary culture in which publishers worked. The relationship between publishers and readers was reciprocal: publishers introduced new texts to readers at the same time as they accepted suggestions from them. A glimpse of this circular process may be obtained from the preface to Caxton's *Aeneid*, a translation made by himself from a French redaction. The preface describes how his translations have been criticised in the past for using obscure language and how he is aiming in this text at a more accessible style, yet one which retains an elegance and dignity suitable to the story it tells and which will be pleasing to a gentleman:

> And for as moche as this present booke is not for a rude vplondyssh man to laboure therin ne rede it but onely for a clerke & a noble gentylman that feleth and vnderstondeth in faytes of armes inlove & in noble chyualrye / Therfor in a meane bytwene bothe I haue reduced & translated this sayd booke...

Caxton clearly gave much thought, as any sensible businessman must do, to his market. Discriminating between different types of reader would have been as important as identifying which texts were likely to be generally popular and successful, and this must have played a part in the decision to publish certain books simultaneously, so that they could be bought and bound together.

Whilst sammelbande provide tangible evidence of strategic thinking by printers in the incunable period, it should not be assumed that such an approach, which we might call 'marketing', confined itself to such specific projects. Caxton seems to have developed a list of titles that fell into certain categories – the martial, the devotional, the historical – so that readers could add to their collections over time, making connections between books that may have been published at reasonably long intervals and not necessarily purchased at once. It is, for example, interesting to note that Caxton's 1478 edition of Chaucer's *Boece* (a translation of Boethius' *Consolation of Philosophy*) was twice bound with his edition of Cato's *Disticha* (1484).[28] These two ethical, philosophical texts are also separately found with an English-French language treatise, the *Vocabularius* (1480), suggesting that the Boethius translation and the *Disticha* were deemed (by readers and by Caxton) to serve a philological interest as well as a philosophical one.[29] This is borne out by the epilogue to the *Boece*, which draws attention specifically to linguistic issues, praising Chaucer as a translator. Commenting on the difficulty of the Latin, Caxton notes:

> Therfore the worshipful fader & first founder & enbelissher of ornate eloquence in our englissh, I mene Maister Geffrey Chaucer hath translated this sayd werke out of latyn in to oure vsual and moder tong + folowyng the latyn as neygh as is possible to be vnderstande + wherein in myne oppynyon he hath deseruid a perpetuell lawde and thanke of al this noble royame of Englond

Intriguing as they are, the combinations of the *Boece* with the *Disticha* and of both with the *Vocabularius* are not frequent enough, at least in the copies which survive, nor were they published sufficiently close together, to be regarded as linked editions in any formal, programmatic sense. It is simply worth noting that certain generic and thematic patterns recur over Caxton's output and that these had appeal for particular groups of readers with specific needs and interests, whether scholarly, recreational or spiritual. Catering for these particular needs and interests was part of Caxton's conscious endeavour as a printer.

In conclusion, the treatment of English incunable editions by early readers, publishers and (probably) booksellers, shows that the unit of the book was not limited to the individual title: various combinations of texts, some more and some less conventional, were created. This paper has not attempted to give a comprehensive survey of sammelbande, and other interesting examples could have been explored, such as the pairing of John Alcock's *Mons Perfectionis* (STC 278 and 279) with the *Spousage of a Virgin to Christ* (286 and 287), or two grammatical texts by John of Garland, his *Synonyma* (STC 11609 and 11610) and *Equivoca* (STC 11601 and 11602). It is interesting that the issuing of 'paired' editions was something printers sometimes copied from each other, suggesting that the combinations were quickly perceived as standard. For example, the *Synonyma* and *Equivoca* were originally printed by Richard Pynson in 1496, to be copied later by Wynkyn de Worde in 1499/1500. Not enough is currently known about the role of booksellers in the process, and this could be a fruitful field for further enquiry. Although this paper has limited itself to English incunabula, it might be worth attempting a comparative study with continental incunabula to see if such 'marketing practices' as have been observed in England existed elsewhere. The future discussion of editions which were bound together might benefit from a slightly more precise terminology to discriminate between editions which were routinely bound together (like the *Festial* with the *Quattuor Sermones*, or *The Chastysing of Goddes Childern* with *The Treatise of Love*) and those which were combined less predictably, probably at the whim of the reader.[30] Of course, it would be difficult to know where to draw the line in many cases: quantifying such phenomena can never be an exact science when the survival rate of early books is relatively low, and the evidence we have is incomplete. It could be that combinations which now exist in only two or three volumes were once more common. However, some attempt should perhaps be made to make the distinction.

NOTES

1. See Margaret M Smith, *The Title-Page; its Early Development 1460-1510* (London: British Library; New Castle, DE: Oak Knoll Press, 2000).

2. See N F Blake [ed] *Caxton's Own Prose* (London: Deutsch, 1973).

3. Caxton's career, see Lotte Hellinga, *Caxton in Focus: the Beginning of Printing in England* (London: British Library, 1982).

4. See particularly E L Eisenstein, *The Printing Press as an Agent of Change: Communications and Cultural Transformations in Early-Modern Europe*, 2 vols (Cambridge: CUP, 1979).

5. The term 'sammelbande', referring to editions bound together in the same volume, was apparently first used by the bibliographer Seymour De Ricci.

6. See Robert C Latham [ed] *Catalogue of the Pepys Library at Magdalene College, Cambridge*, 7 vols (Cambridge: D S Brewer, 1978), I *Printed Books*, compiled by N A Smith. The two incunabula are described in the appendix on incunabula by J C T Oates, 195-8 (*Chastysing*, 196 and *Treatise*, 198). The pseudo-Bonaventura is described on 20.

7. Alfred G Pollard and G.W Redgrave [ed] *Short Title Catalogue of Books Printed in England, Scotland and Ireland, and of English Books Printed Abroad, 1475-1640*, 3 vols (London: Bibliographical Society, 1976-1991), hereafter STC.

8. Here I rely on the opinion of the current Pepys Librarian, Dr Luckett, who viewed the volume with me.

9. The trend towards 'clean copy', or the decline of readerly annotation, is noted by Paul Saenger and Michael Heinlen in 'Incunable Description and its Implication for the Analysis of Fifteenth-Century Reading Habits', in Sandra Hindman [ed] *Printing the Written Word: the Social History of Books, circa 1450-1520* (Ithaca; London: Cornell UP, 1991), 225-58 (particularly 254).

10. For valuable information on early bindings, see E Gordon Duff, *The Printers, Stationers and Bookbinders of Westminster and London from 1476 to 1535* (Cambridge: CUP, 1906).

11. See the introduction by Lotte Hellinga to the volume she co-edited with Helmar Härtel, *Book and Text in the Fifteenth Century: Proceedings of a Conference Held in the Herzog August Bibliothek Wolfenbüttel, March 1-3, 1978* (Hamburg: Hauswedell, 1981), 11-16. See also the introduction by Sandra Hindman, *Printing the Written Word*.

12. Seymour De Ricci, *A Census of Caxtons* (Oxford: OUP for the Bibliographical Society, 1909).

13. Paul Needham, *The Printer and the Pardoner* (Washington: Meriden-Steinhour, 1986), 69-80.

14. The frequency of their binding together can be seen by consulting De Ricci's *Census*, which lists surviving copies and the contents of the volumes they are found in. *The Chastysing of Goddes Childern* is no. 104 and *The Treatise of Love* is no. 105. These are included along with Caxton editions although printed by Wynkyn de Worde because they use Caxton types and his sign.

15. Sue Powell, 'Syon, Caxton and the *Festial*', *Birgittiana*, 2 (1996), 187-207.

16. The first edition is De Ricci no. 79, STC 17957(I); the second edition is De Ricci no. 80, STC 17959(I). On the textual history of these early editions, see Sue Powell, 'What Caxton Did to the *Festial*: from Manuscript to Printed Edition', *Journal of the Early Book Society for the Study of Manuscripts and Printing History*, 1 (1997), 48-77.

17. See Michael K Jones and M G Underwood, *The King's Mother, Lady Margaret Beaufort, Countess of Richmond and Derby* (Cambridge: CUP, 1992), 83.

18. De Ricci no. 85: 2,3,4,5; STC 17597(II).

19. C A Webb, 'Caxton's *Quattuor Sermones*: a Newly Discovered Edition', in D E Rhodes [ed] *Essays in Honour of Victor Scholderer*, (Mainz: Karl Pressler, 1970), 407-25. The second edition is De Ricci no. 85: 1,6,7,8,9; STC 17957(II). The two editions had been described as one by E Gordon Duff, *Fifteenth-century English Books*, Illustrated Monographs Issued by the Bibliographical Society, 18 (Oxford: OUP, 1917).

20. Pynson printed an edition of the *Festial* in 1493 (STC 17960(I)) which was issued with his edition of the *Quattuor Sermones* (STC 17960(II)) and he reprinted the pair shortly after (STC 17961 (I and II)) and again in 1499 (STC 17966.5(I and II)). Wynkyn de Worde printed an edition of the *Festial* in 1493 (STC 17962(I)) which was probably issued with his *Quattuor Sermones* of 1494 (STC17962(II)). Reprints were issued by him in 1496 and 1499 (STC 17965 (I and II) and 17967 (I and II)). Julian Notary printed the *Festial* in 1499/1500 (STC 17968(I)) and this was probably issued with his edition of the *Sermones* (STC 17968(II)).

21. De Ricci, *Census* no. 29, STC 9991.

22. De Ricci, *Census* no. 35, STC 13440a.

23. The *Chronicles of England* is STC 9996 and the *Description of Britain* is STC 13440b.

24. De Ricci, *Census* no. 30, STC 9992.

25. See Needham, *Printer and the Pardoner* Appendix B, no. 8.

26. See Needham, *Printer and the Pardoner* Appendix B, no. 37.

27. See A I Doyle, 'Books Belonging to R. Johnson', *Notes and Queries*, 197 (1952), 293-4.

28. See Needham, *Printer and the Pardoner,* Appendix B, no. 11 (Exeter College, Oxford) and no. 16 (Bodleian Library, Arch.G.d.13).

29. The *Consolation* was bound with the *Vocabularius* in a volume at Ripon Cathedral, see Needham, *Printer and the Pardoner,* Appendix B, no. 7 (the *Vocabularius* is now in the Cambridge University Library) and the *Disticha* was bound with the *Vocabularius* in a volume belonging to J G Cochrane, Needham no. 14, which was sold to the second Earl Spencer in 1813.

30. A S G Edwards noted the distinction when he wrote: 'An analysis of such "sammelbande" would be of some value not just to students of the history of bookbinding; it would also help to make discriminations between the contemporary trade distribution of books and the vagaries of individual taste.' See Lotte Hellinga and John Goldfinch [ed] 'ISTC, the Literary Historian and the Editor', *Bibliography and the Study of Fifteenth-Century Civilisation*, British Library Occasional Papers, 5 (London: British Library, 1987), 228-37 (particularly 230).

Freeman and Susannah Collins and the Spread of English Provincial Printing

DAVID STOKER

STUDIES OF ENGLISH provincial printing in the eighteenth century have naturally focused upon the towns or cities where the trade was practised, since most of the evidence for the existence of such presses will be local. This approach has resulted in a series of detailed but discrete studies, which are gradually amassing evidence and providing more information about a neglected subject. Yet the topographical approach may obscure links between contemporary businesses in different towns, and the all-important relationship between the provincial book trade and that in London. For example, when describing the first four English provincial presses to be established after the lapse of the Licensing Act in 1695, John Feather comments: 'these pioneer printers have much in common. None was returning to his birthplace... All of them saw a gap in the market... Above all, they all published or assisted others to publish, newspapers'.[1] Thus, there is also a need for analytical studies, which can make such links and paint the wider picture, although the evidence on which they are based, and examples quoted, will be local in nature.

Despite the increased interest in the subject over the last thirty years or so, there remain many unanswered questions relating to the spread of provincial printing in England between 1695 and about 1725. Were the earliest provincial printers known to one another? Was there any other connecting factor between them? What was the attitude of established London printers towards the newcomers who were beginning to move into the provinces? The object of this paper is to explore some of these issues, by combining evidence from different places, and particularly by focusing on the activities of one London printing business, and its relationships with provincial printers. In doing so, the author will, of necessity, have to cover some individuals and events he has written about before, although from an entirely different perspective.[2]

Whereas by the end of the seventeenth century it was possible for a successful provincial bookseller to have learned his or her trade locally, English printing was restricted to London and the universities (apart from a few minor exceptions). With the lapse of the Licensing Act in 1695 there was no workforce in the country able or equipped to take up the new trade. Almost inevitably the first printers in any town before about 1725 will have gained their experience elsewhere – particularly in London. For example, of the thirteen individuals known to have worked as printers in Norwich before 1725, only one, William Chase, did not originate in London. Many of the men (and occasionally women) who took printing to the provinces will have known one another as apprentices, or journeymen working in the capital, or else might be otherwise related.

The fact that most of the early provincial printers served apprenticeships in London does not suggest that all mobility was one way – from London to the provinces. There was also mobility between provincial towns, and occasionally from the provinces back to London. During the early eighteenth century setting up a press in a new town was a very risky business, and might require finance from some established trader as a partner. Several provincial printers moved from town to town until the circumstances were sufficiently favourable for them to establish themselves. Robert Raikes worked as either a journeyman or master printer in London, Norwich, St Ives, and Northampton between the years 1717 and 1721 before ultimately settling in Gloucester from 1722 onwards, and achieving a degree of prosperity.[3] Raikes was ultimately successful as a provincial printer, but others were not so fortunate. Some even left the country. William Parks printed for short periods in Ludlow, Hereford and Reading before he disappears from sight in 1723, presumably to return to the anonymity of London and life as a journeyman printer. However he emigrated to Maryland in 1726, where he began a distinguished career as a colonial printer; and died at sea in 1750 on his way back to England.[4]

A surprising number of similar relationships can be found by examining the subsequent careers of those who worked at one London printing office. Eleven individuals whose names appear as printer on the imprints of provincial books and newspapers, together with at least one other who is known to have run a printing office and newspaper in Norwich, worked in a single London printing office – that of Freeman and later Susannah Collins, either as apprentices, journeymen or as members of the family. Members of this group, (which includes three women), went on to work in nine different English towns and cities, and on at least ten provincial newspapers. One member established one of the great printing dynasties of the eighteenth century, and another the first literary magazine. Whether consciously or not, Freeman Collins and his family played a significant role in the spread of printing from London to the English provinces during the first quarter of the eighteenth century.

Freeman Collins was an example of a provincial boy who went to London and made his fortune. He was born about 1657, the son of Thomas Collins an Exeter clergyman,[5] and was bound apprentice to the London printer Thomas Newcombe on 3 March 1669. He became a freeman of the Stationers' Company 6 May 1676 and two years later he married Susannah, the daughter of the printer James Cotterell. From imprint evidence, Collins appears to have been in partnership with Cotterell at

Black and White Court, Old Bailey from 1680 until the latter's retirement or death about 1685. Thereafter he continued at the same address on his own account. His business prospered, and he ultimately had seventeen apprentices,[6] and by the end of the century was operating five presses.

According to John Dunton, Collins was

> a composition made up of justice and industry, that other printers may imitate, but cannot exceed. He is a moderate Church man. A sincere friend, and so expeditious in dispatch of business, that he printed more sheets for me in ten dayes than others did in twenty.[7]

Much of his printing was for the Stationers' Company, including several editions of the *Psalms in Metre,* and his name is not always identified on the imprints of the works he printed. However he was responsible for the printing of several prestigious works, including the 1695 edition of Camden's *Britannia*.[8] He was also the financier of publications, although on a modest scale, registering nine titles at Stationers' Hall between 1683 and 1694.[9]

Freeman took an active part in London politics rising to the position of Deputy Alderman (which resulted in his nickname 'Deputy Collins'). He was active in the Stationers' Company serving as Renter Warden in 1691, Under Warden in 1707/8 and Upper Warden in 1710 and 1712. Thus, he may be described as a pillar of the London book trade. However, if he was successful in his business dealings, he was singularly unsuccessful in his domestic life. Freeman and his wife are said to have lived in 'perpetual discord, and their house could be no comfortable habitation'.[10] Later evidence indicates that these quarrelsome tendencies were also inherited by his children. He died in January 1713, leaving an estate valued at over £1500 to his 'dear and loving wife', and five surviving children (two sons and three daughters).[11]

During the 1680s and 1690s Collins appears to have maintained contact with his home county, and he produced several works with Devon connections, or else the names of Devon booksellers in their imprints. *A True and Impartial Relation of the Informations Against Three Witches*, 1682, and *An Essay on Hypocrasie and Pharisaism*, 1683, were both printed by Collins either for, or else to be sold by, Charles Yeo of Exeter. Likewise John Newte's sermon *The Lawfulness and Use of Organs in the Christian Church*, 1696, was sold by Humphrey Burton of Tiverton, and William Chilcot's *Sermon Preached in the Cathedral Church of St. Peter in Exon. April 4, 1697,* was printed for Philip Bishop, in Exeter.

One of the apprentices who probably worked on the two latter publications was a young man named Samuel Farlow from Twining in Gloucestershire, who had been bound apprentice to Collins for eight years from 6 May 1689, completing his apprenticeship in May 1697. He is undoubtedly the same man as Samuel Farley who went into partnership with the printer and bookseller Samuel Darker, to establish the first printing office in Exeter in 1698.[12] Darker died in 1700, but Samuel Farley continued in business, establishing a local newspaper *Sam. Farley's Exeter Post-man* about 1704. This was replaced by *Sam. Farley's Exeter Mercury* before 1714. His ambitions also led him to open a printing business in Bristol, and publish *Sam. Farley's Bristol Post-man,* from 1713. In 1715 he closed his Exeter business and opened another in Salisbury printing the short-lived *Farley's Salisbury Post-man*. However either Samuel or his son with the same name returned to Exeter to establish *Farley's Exeter Journal* in May 1723. He died in 1730 having established printing dynasties in Exeter, Bristol, Bath and briefly at Pontypool, involving his three sons and their wives and later six grandchildren.[13]

Collins's next apprentice after Farley was Francis Burges, the son of a London cleric, who was bound 7 November 1692 (aged sixteen) and obtained his freedom 4 December 1699. Burges must have watched Farley's progress with interest and looked out for an opportunity in another city – and the obvious choice was Norwich. The story of Burges and his wife has been told in detail elsewhere,[14] and will therefore only be covered in outline. In April 1701 he visited Norwich and discussed his plans for establishing a press in the city with local dignitaries, including Humphrey Prideaux the Archdeacon of Suffolk. The plan came to fruition; Francis moved to premises near the Red Well in Norwich during the summer, establishing the *Norwich Post* in the November of that year. The first item he printed was a pamphlet justifying his new trade, dated 27 September, 1701, which mentions the existence of presses at Exeter, Chester, Bristol and York.[15] Over the next five years he enjoyed a fair degree of success but he died in November 1706, and the business was continued by his widow Elizabeth until her own death two years later. The business then passed into the hands of Freeman Collins, her husband's former master. There is strong circumstantial evidence to suggest that Elizabeth Burges was the married daughter of Freeman and Susannah Collins.[16]

After Francis Burges, Collins's next apprentice to work in the provinces was William Ayres, the son of a Clerkenwell brewer, who was christened 18 November 1683, bound apprentice 2 October 1699 and became a freeman 6 October 1707.[17] This is almost certainly the same printer who worked in Filber Row, Reading from 1727 until 1734. He printed four small works between these dates,[18] and was also the printer of the *Reading Mercury,* founded in 1723 by David Kinnier and William Parks.[19] However by 1735 the *Mercury* was being printed by William Carnan. Ayres had apparently moved on and it is likely that he is the same William Ayres who was a printer in Winchester between 1739 and 1744, whose name is found on two receipted bills in the Winchester city records.[20]

On 1 July 1706 Benjamin Lyon was bound apprentice to Collins, but no details of his family background were recorded.[21] He became a freeman 5 July 1714, after the death of his master, and may have continued working for Susannah Collins as a journeyman. At Michaelmas (25 September) 1717 he took over the Norwich printing business originally operated by Francis and Elizabeth Burges, and which had been operated by the Collins family since 1708. The business included the successor to the *Norwich Post*, which was by then called the *Norwich Courant*. However whereas Burges had a local monopoly between 1701 and 1706, by 1717 there were two other newspapers operating in the city in opposition. Lyon was required to appear before the Quarter Sessions to answer a charge of having printed a libel, and his name appears as printer on the imprint of *The History of the City of Norwich* in 1718. There is specific reference to his newspaper in May of that year, but nothing is known of him in the city thereafter. He appears to have been driven out of business during the bitter trade war, in which Robert Raikes was recruited to come to Norwich and establish a fourth newspaper.[22] Benjamin Lyon next re-appears eleven years later as the earliest known printer in Bath. His name is found on the imprints of two publications for 1729 and 1730 respectively, from an office near the Northgate.[23] It has been suggested that Lyon may have joined in partnership with Thomas Boddeley, who later established the *Bath Journal*, in 1735, although the evidence is not conclusive.[24] He may been driven out of business by the arrival in the city of Felix Farley (grandson of Samuel Farley).

Collins's business affairs were made more complicated by the death of Elizabeth Burges in November 1708, as he seems to have inherited her business (implying that he had a family or business relationship with her). Immediately following her decease the *Norwich Post* and a number of sermons were printed by 'the Administrator of E. Burges', who was perhaps the workman (or workmen) referred to in an open letter to Elizabeth Burges written by Samuel Hasbart, a distiller and rival newspaper proprietor in 1707, offering to buy her out.[25] In so far that public denials in newspapers sometimes indicate a course of action previously considered, an advertisement in the *Norwich Post* for 19 February 1709 may indicate that his initial wish was to discontinue and sell the business. But Elizabeth had venomously turned down Hasbart's offer to buy her business before her death, and it was no longer on the table.[26]

Collins therefore continued to keep the Norwich business going, and the window tax payment on the printing office for Easter 1709/10 was in his name, which also begins to be found on the imprints of a number of Norwich works until 1713. Yet it is most unlikely that the successful printer with all his civic responsibilities, and in his mid-fifties, ever came to work in Norwich. He seems rather to have operated the business at a distance, by sending experienced and trusted apprentices to manage the press. The first of these was his own son Freeman Collins, who was christened 5 January 1690, bound apprentice 7 July 1707 and became a freeman by patrimony 3 August 1713, after his father's death. The correspondence of the two names has undoubtedly added to the confusion concerning the management of the Norwich press. The career of the younger Freeman Collins in Norwich between 1709 and the end of 1710 has likewise been described in detail elsewhere,[27] and by the spring of 1711 he had apparently tired of Norwich, and was working as a journeyman at Cambridge University Press.[28] Thereafter he appears to have returned to the business in London and following the death of his mother worked on his own account. His son Freeman III became a freeman printer in 1740.[29]

It is not clear who operated the Norwich press after the departure of Freeman II early in 1711, but Benjamin Lyon would have been a possible candidate, or else the next of the apprentices, John Roberts, who was bound 12 April 1708. There is no evidence to say whether either of these men was sent to Norwich in 1711, although the next in line after Roberts undoubtedly was. This was the son of a Rugby cobbler named Edward Cave, born in 1691, who was bound apprentice to Collins 6 February 1710. The life of Cave, written by Dr Samuel Johnson, is quite specific about his period in Norwich, and is a useful source for dating events:

> ... having in only two years attained so much the confidence of his master, that he was sent without any super-intendant to conduct a printing house in Norwich and publish a weekly paper. In this undertaking he met with some opposition, which produced a public controversy, and procured young Cave reputation as a writer. His master died before his apprenticeship expired.[30]

Thus the twenty-one year old Cave was in Norwich during 1712 and the early part of 1713 so he was probably responsible for printing the five surviving works with Freeman Collins's Norwich imprint published during this period,[31] and also possibly two of the three items with the imprint of Susannah Collins in 1713.[32] Cave was likewise responsible for printing the *Norwich Post*, which until 1712 still carried the imprint of 'the Administrator of E. Burges', but which appears to have changed its name soon after Susannah took over responsibility.[33] Unfortunately only one issue of the *Post* has survived for this period, and no copies of the *Courant*, and so it is not possible to elucidate the nature of the public controversy.

Edward Cave left Norwich soon after the death of Freeman Collins, as 'he was not able to bear the perverseness of his mistress'.[34] He returned to London, got married, and served the remainder of his apprenticeship living at Bow. Once he completed his time he worked as a journeyman printer for Alderman John Barber in London. Later through the influence of his wife he obtained a position in the post office and used the experience gained at Norwich to operate as an early news agent supplying newsletters to country newspapers. He also procured country newspapers and sold their news to a London journalist for a guinea a week.[35] Then from January 1731 he edited and printed the first issue of the *Gentleman's Magazine*, which brought him lasting fame and fortune.

Thereafter the Norwich press seems to have been operated by Susannah's other children, who seem to have been equally argumentative as their parents. Their son John's name is found on the imprint of Robert Pate, *A Complete Syntax of the Latin Tongue*, 1713, on the window tax records for 1714/15, and also on some issues of the *Norwich Courant* now lost. Having served his time in Norwich, he returned to London, but as Thomas Gent later recorded he came to no good.

> She [Susannah Collins] had a wicked son, called Master John, who, contracting debts by extravagant living, was thrown into the Counter: she, good gentlewoman, forgetting how he once sued her for some legacy, almost to an excommunication, had pity for him, who had not the least regard for her. She gave me money to release him, which, with some difficulty, I did, from that close prison; and took the loathsome wretch from his filthy bed on the ground, in a coach with me home. It was a great Providence that, in the unpleasant action, I became not smitten with the jail distemper that he was then afflicted with; considering that, a little afterwards, it fell to his aged mother's lot.[36]

The last member of the family to print in Norwich was 'H Collins' who printed two works in 1715, and a third in 1716.[37] Reference to Freeman Collins's will shows that this can only refer to Hannah Collins, one of his three surviving daughters.[38] However, although the children's names are given on the imprints, Susannah appears to have remained in control of the business. Throughout this period the newspaper is described by competitors as 'Mrs Collins' news', and the advertisement for the sale of the business in 1717 refers to it as 'Mrs Collins' printing office'.[39]

Following the sale of her Norwich printing office Susannah Collins continued in business in London, binding three more apprentices. Her last link with the provincial book trade was when Thomas Gent came to work for her as a journeyman, several weeks before his own move to York in 1724 where he married a printer's widow and took over a press, establishing the *York Journal*. Gent portrays Susannah Collins in old age far more sympathetically than Edward Cave had done a decade earlier, but admits it was only because he 'found the art of gaining her temper'.[40] He gives a sad account of the end of her business, following her death on 2 June 1724.

> The executors continued me in their service, at twenty shillings per week, in bringing the materials from their confused condition, and helping to weigh the letters, in order to make a division of the substance amongst them, and cease their jarring disagreements.[41]

The situation of Freeman Collins and his family, with respect to their operation of a second printing house and their other provincial connections, was hardly typical. It does however raise some broader questions. Why, for example, would a Warden of the Stationers' Company, which had petitioned, and was continuing to petition against the liberalisation of the book trade and for the re-instatement of the Printing (Licensing) Act, have become so involved with the spread of provincial printing, which was one result of the lapse of that act? The answer may have been a combination of pragmatism – encouraging his apprentices to take advantage of an opportunity in the provinces rather than struggling to establish themselves in London - and pure chance - when he found himself the unexpected owner of such a business. Collins's printing interests in London were much more important and profitable than the Norwich printing office and its newspaper. Also the restrictions on provincial printing were only a relatively unimportant aspect of the Licensing Act. The London trade was more concerned with controlling their profitable copyrights, and were not too worried about a succession of poor printers moving to the provinces. As John Feather comments 'the trade asked for a Licensing Act; what it really wanted was a Copyright Act, and this it obtained in 1710.'[42]

NOTES

1. John Feather *The Provincial Book Trade in Eighteenth-Century England* (Cambridge: Cambridge University Press, 1985), 16.

2. David Stoker, 'Printing at the Red Well: an early Norwich press through the eyes of contemporaries' in Peter Isaac and Barry McKay [ed] *The Mighty Engine: the printing press at work*, (Winchester: St. Paul's Bibliographies; New Castle, DE.: Oak Knoll Press, 2000), 29-38, and 'The establishment of printing in Norwich: causes and effects 1660-1760', *Transactions of the Cambridge Bibliographical Society*, 7 (1977), 94-111, see 104-5. To keep the duplicated material to a minimum, the reader is refered to these sources for further details. I should also like to acknowledge the assistance of Stephanie Brownbridge (Bath Local Studies Library), Ian Maxted (Devon Local Studies Library) and David Knott (University of Reading) for their assistance in compiling this paper.

3. The opportunity for him to operate the press in Norwich arose because the printer Henry Crossgrove had broken away from his erstwhile financier, Samuel Hasbart, a Norwich distiller. Hasbart was now looking for a replacement printer to run a new newspaper in opposition to his former partner, and had offered a partnership to the Irish printer Thomas Gent (then working in London). However Gent needed to go to Dublin and so recommended Raikes for the position (Thomas Gent, *The Life of Mr Thomas Gent, printer of York*, (New York: Garland, 1974)), 77-8.

4. *Printing and Society in Early America*, William L Joyce [ed] (Worcester: American Antiquarian Society, c1983), 140-3.

5. Michael Treadwell, 'London Printers and Printing Houses in 1705', *Publishing History*, 7 (1980), 18-19.

6. All references to the dates of apprenticeship and freedom are taken from D F McKenzie, *Stationers' Company Apprentices 1641-1700*, and his *Stationers' Company Apprentices 1701-1800* (Oxford Bibliographical Society, 1974, 1978). Only those apprentices known to

have worked in the provinces are considered in this paper, but other Collins apprentices set up in business in London, notably Laurence Veze or Vezey (bound 1687 and in business c1720?) and John and Thomas Dormer who were in business between 1722 and 1739 (H R Plomer, G H Bushnell, and E R Dix, *A Dictionary of the Printers and Booksellers who were at Work in England, Scotland and Ireland from 1726-1775,* ([London]: Bibliographical Society, 1932)).

7. John Dunton, *Life and Errors* (London, 1705), 324-5.

8. Gwyn Walters and Frank Emery 'Edward Lhuyd, Edmund Gibson and the printing of Camden's *Britannia*, 1695', *The Library,* 5 Ser., 32 (1977), 109-37 (128).

9. G E Briscoe Eyre, H R Plomer and C R Rivington, *A Transcript of the Registers of the Worshipful Company of Stationers from 1640-1708,* 3 vols. (1913-1914).

10. Samuel Johnson's account of Edward Cave was originally published as an obituary in the *Gentleman's Magazine*, (February 1754) and republished in John Nichols, *Literary Anecdotes of the Eighteenth Century,* 9 vols. (1812-15), v. 3.

11. Public Record Office, PROB 11/531/5.

12. Apart from the frequent variant forms of surnames found in the Stationers' Registers (cautioned by McKenzie in his introduction), the place names Farley and Farlow appear to have been used interchangeably in Gloucestershire and Herefordshire in the seventeenth century and come from the same Old English phrase 'fern-clad hill', see Eilert Ekwall, *The Concise Oxford Dictionary of English Place-names,* 4 ed. (Oxford University Press, 1960).

13. For a full account of Farley's career and his successors see Ian Maxted, *The Devon Book Trades: a biographical dictionary,* 1991. Available at
http://www.devon.gov.uk/library/locstudy/bookhist/devexef.html
and his *A History of the Book in Devon. 41. The Provincial Press and the Origins of the Local Newspaper,* http://www.devon.gov.uk/library/locstudy/bookhist/west41.html

14. For a more detailed account of the careers of Francis and Elizabeth Burges see David Stoker, 'Printing at the Red Well', 98-101.

15. *Some Observations on the Use and Original of the Noble Art and Mystery of Printing,* (Norwich: F Burges, 1701). No copies have survived but extracts from the preliminaries are given by John Chambers in *A General History of the County of Norfolk,* 2 vols. (Norwich: Stacy, 1829) 2, 1286-7.

16. Apart from the evidence of the transfer of the business, the Collinses had a daughter with the same Christian name, who was baptised 21 October 1683 at St Sepulchre's, London, but was no longer alive when Freeman made his will.

17. Although the Stationers' Registers give the spelling Eyres, the Christening record at Saint James, Clerkenwell uses the spelling Ayres, with the same father named.

18. Catherine M Legg, *A Bibliography of the Books Printed at Reading during the Eighteenth Century,* (University of London, Diploma in Librarianship Dissertation, May 1961).

19. R M Wiles, *Freshest Advices: early provincial newspapers in England,* (Columbus: Ohio State University, 1965); G A Cranfield, *The Development of the Provincial Newspaper 1700-1760* (Oxford: Clarendon Press, 1962), 49, suggests that he took on John Newbery as his apprentice, but gives no source. Newbery later worked for Carnan.

20. Alfred Cecil Piper, 'The Book Trade in Winchester, 1549-1789', *The Library,* 3 Ser, 7 (1916), 191-7 and 'The Early Printers and Booksellers of Winchester, *The Library,* 4 Ser, 1 (1920), 103-110. In the second article Piper mentions hearsay evidence of a James Ayres working as a printer in Winchester c1720, but was unable to verify this.

21. There are two possible candidates named Benjamin Lyon on the *International Genealogical Index*. The first was the son of Will and Susanna Lyon of Dallinghoo, Suffolk (christened

10 June 1689). The second was the son of Luke and Jane Lyon of Cookham, Berkshire (christened 4 September 1693).

22. Trevor Fawcett, 'Early Norwich Newspapers', *Notes and Queries,* NS19 (1972), 363-5.

23. Jennifer Tyler, 'A Dictionary of Printers, Bookseller and Publishers at Work at Bath During the Years 1664-1830', MSc Thesis, 1972.

24. *Bath Weekly Chronicle Notes and Queries,* 6 July 1943.

25. Reprinted in Stoker, 'The Establishment of Printing in Norwich', 100-1, which also provides further discussion on the background to the offer and its refusal.

26. Hasbart's response to Elizabeth Burges was published in the *Norwich Gazette,* 10 January 1708. See also Wiles, *Freshest Advices.*

27. Stoker, 'Printing at the Red Well', 102-4.

28. D F McKenzie, *Cambridge University Press 1696-1712,* 2 vols (Cambridge: Cambridge University Press, 1965), I, 84, II, 336.

29. Freeman II's name does however recur on one more occasion in Norwich when he paid the window tax on the printing office for the years 1716/7, but there is no other evidence of his printing at this time. It is possible he may have briefly returned to the city (Norfolk Record Office 23a). 82.

30. Nichols, *Literary Anecdotes,* v 5, 3.

31. Herbert Addee, *A Sermon Preached at the Cathedral-church of Norwich on September the 7th, 1712* (Norwich: printed by Free. Collins near the Red Well, for Frances Oliver, near the Market Place, 1712); Charles Buchanan, *The Worthy Communicant Examin'd* (Norwich: printed by Fr. Collins, near the Red Well, in the year 1712);William Gibson, *An Essay Being a New Choice Warning to Sinners with Damned Doom* (Norwich: printed by F. C. near the Red Well, 1712); John Knott, *A New Method of Arithmetick* (Norwich: printed by Freeman Collins, near the Red-Well, 1712, and also a 1713 edition).

32. Two folio pamphlet poems, *Æthiops* and *Æthiopides* (both Printed by S. Collins, near the Red-well, for the author, 1713) display a high standard of workmanship, whereas *The Queen's Most Gracious Proclamation of the Peace* ([Norwich] Printed by Susanna Collins, near the Red-Well [1713?]) which must date after 13 July 1713 was poorly printed.

33. Chambers in *A General History of the County of Norfolk,* ii 291.

34. Nichols, *Literary Anecdotes* v 5, 4.

35. Nichols, *Literary Anecdotes* v 5, 5.

36. Gent, *Life of Thomas Gent,* 143-4.

37. T B, *The Holland Merchant's Companion* (Norwich: printed by H. Collins for the author, 1715); *The Impartial Satyrist* (Norwich: printed by H. Collins, near the Red Well, 1715); and John Clarke's *The Happiness of Good Men After Death* (Norwich: printed by H. Collins, and sold by T. Goddard, in the Market Place, 1715/6).

38. Chambers' description of the sorry state of the press under John and Hannah Collins is reproduced in David Stoker, 'Printing at the Red Well', 104-5. There is also the puzzling reference to a 'Samuel Collins' in the window tax records for the property for 1716/17. However in so far that this is the only occurrence of the name, and no one of this name is listed on Freeman Collins' will, I assume that it is a clerical error for Susannah Collins.

39. *Norwich Gazette,* 21 September 1717.

40. Gent, *Life of Thomas Gent,* 143

41. Gent, *Life of Thomas Gent,* 145.

42. John Feather, *Provincial Book Trade in Eighteenth-Century England,* 2.

Taking Stock: The Diary of Edmund Harrold of Manchester

MICHAEL POWELL

IN A CURIOUS, slightly caustic review of the proceedings of the fifteenth annual seminar on the British Book Trade, the reviewer, Brian Alderson, pointed out that the singular contribution of both the seminar and the proceedings is the 'demonstration of the bibliographical records to be gained from an investigation of manuscript sources housed in regional collections'.[1] This paper, like a number of others given at this seminar, is intended to introduce another document from a regional collection, which has yet to be exposed to the full glare of historical scholarship. The document in question, unlike some of the other sources referred to in earlier papers at this seminar, is not entirely unknown to historians. Parts of it were published as long ago as 1867;[2] it features in many standard accounts of the history of Manchester of the late nineteenth and early twentieth centuries; it was the subject of a lengthy, albeit unpublished paper given to a local literary society in Manchester;[3] and more recently it has appeared in an anthology of early modern English diaries.[4] Nor is it unknown to book historians. It was used by Charles Sutton in his account of auctions in Manchester,[5] and was mentioned in a paper given to this seminar on the subject of book auctions a couple of years ago.[6] Having said that, the diary of Edmund Harrold has yet to receive the attention that it deserves from those people whom we must learn to call the SHARPists. What we have is a document of enormous potential to students of the provincial book trade in pre-industrial urban society, a document that offers us extremely valuable evidence of the trade in books, book ownership, reading and the physical contexts of reading.

The document itself consists of a small octavo diary written by Edmund Harrold, a Manchester wig-maker, between 1 June 1712 and 24 June 1716, with some gaps in the later years.[7] It is written in a cramped and not easily legible hand on both sides of some ninety-two leaves measuring 15 x 10 cm. The provenance of the manuscript is revealed in a letter of 1884 from Robert McDowall Smith of Samuel Smith & Sons, Drapers and Silk Mercers of Manchester, to the historian John Eglington Bailey.[8] Smith claimed to have bought the diary many years earlier in his youth from one of the bookstalls in the Market Place near to the steps to the old fish market for the cost of sixpence. Some years later, Smith showed the work to his father-in-law, Benjamin Wheeler, publisher of a series of trade directories for Manchester, who persuaded Smith to show it to the historian John Harland, who in turn published extracts from it in a volume published by the Chetham Society. In 1883 the diary was presented by Smith to Chetham's Library, where it has remained ever since.

The editor of the diary, John Harland, was principal reporter of the *Manchester Guardian*, a man hailed by the historian Donald Read as the father of provincial journalism in the country.[9] In the 1860s Harland pioneered a series of volumes on aspects of the modern and recent history of the north-west of England. These amounted to something of an innovation for the Society, whose officers, editors and even members regarded the modern age with distaste, not to say outright hostility.[10] Harland's work for the Chetham Society – he edited no less than fourteen of its 'Remains' – included the editions of the Manchester Court Leet records of 1552-1586, the Shuttleworth farm and household accounts, 'a vast undertaking which provided an invaluable source for social and economic history',[11] and a two volume collection of short pieces that included eye-witness accounts of the Jacobite rebellions and a biographical essay on Elizabeth Raffald, publisher of Manchester's first trade directory and author of one of the most popular cookery books of the age, *The Experienced English Housekeeper*. It is in this company that his edition of Harrold's diary appeared.

The edition was selective, although one might not guess this from the text, and was highly partial. All of the references to matters of a sexual nature were omitted from the published version. By contrast, virtually all of the references to drink were retained, no doubt in the hope that Harrold's frequent bouts of drunkenness followed by remorse and periods of abstinence would serve as a warning to those members of the gentry that subscribed to the Chetham Society.

The result is that the diary tells us more about the age when it was published than about the age when it was written and reads less as a document of the early eighteenth century than some mid-Victorian temperance tract. From our point of view, it is sad to note that Harland omitted many of the references to books and to book-dealing, clearly regarding this as of less local interest than church attendance, which is recorded almost with enthusiasm. The main fault of the edition, however, lies not with its selectivity but with its inaccuracy. Harrold's is by no means an easy hand, and the diary contains a large number of contractions and abbreviations that make accurate transcription something of a nightmare. His two closest friends, John Brook and John Barlow, for example, are both styled by their initials. According to one recent commentator, the published version is so selectively and inaccurately transcribed as to be virtually worthless.[12] The true value of the diary of Edmund Harrold is thus known only to a handful of scholars who have bothered to work their way through the manuscript.

What then can we say of the work? The diarist, Edmund Harrold, was born in Manchester on 26 April 1679, the son of Thomas Harrold and his wife Hannah. The

Harrolds were settled in Flixton, near Manchester, by the early seventeenth century, and a branch moved to Manchester. Edmund's father Thomas traded as a tobacconist in Manchester up to 1683 when he died, on 13 December, of dropsy, scurvy and asthma. Edmund, though aged only four when his father died, was the eldest of five surviving children.[13] Nothing is known of Harrold's early life. He was possibly educated at Manchester Grammar School but he first troubles the historical record in March 1702 when he married the first of three wives – Alice Bancroft. She bore him a daughter before her death in March 1704. In 1703/04 Edmund was recorded as a barber in Marketstead Lane, a tenant of one Mrs Bevan, for an annual rent of £5.2s.0d, and later lived in a house rented from the Warden of the Collegiate Church, Richard Wroe. When he started his diary in June 1712 he was thirty-three years old; a long-established trader as a barber or barber-surgeon or periwiquier, well into his second marriage to Sarah Boardman of Gorton, father of a second daughter, sister to his daughter Ann from his first marriage (four other children had not survived).

The Manchester of the second decade of the eighteenth century was a large market town of perhaps two-and-a-half-thousand households with a population of a little under ten thousand.[14] According to Celia Fiennes, who visited the town in 1679, Manchester had a pleasant and fair prospect with a large market-place dealing in linen cloth and cotton tickings,[15] and its influence as a centre for retailing spread well into the Cheshire heartland. Politically, the town was backward, as Defoe pointed out in describing it as the greatest mere village in England,[16] and was still governed through the manorial court or Court Leet.[17] By 1700, as elsewhere, local factions were divided along High Church Tory and Low Church Whig lines. The old church, Harrold's chosen place of worship, was joined first by the Presbyterian chapel and then by St Ann's in 1712. The Manchester of this period had few of the social and cultural organisations and institutions that were increasingly common elsewhere. There was, of course, a public library, but the Manchester of Edmund Harrold had no newspaper press and had yet to publish its first book. Bookselling had begun to flourish at the end of the seventeenth century, with no less than seven traders active between 1690 and 1700.[18]

What then lies behind the diary? Towards the beginning of the work, Harrold explained his purpose:

> I've been taken up with a Review of my life, past since 1709, in which I find things amany to trouble me as well as to raise me up. I pray God it may have this effect on me,
> to mend what I have in my power to mend for ye time to come, amen! (4 June 1712)

The idea of using the record of sins as the basis for future reform was a motivating factor behind many of the diaries of this period,[19] and Harrold repeatedly used the record of external events as a way of learning moral lessons. Thus the entry for 2 October 1712 is typical. 'I observe that there is a many ways to spend one's time but ye best & most Comfortable way is in Reading, praying and working; for ye devill's always busie wth ye Idle person, leading him to lust, drunkenness, &c.' As one might expect, the very next day Harrold went out for a drink with some friends and ended up completely drunk. So much for moral lessons. The diary is peppered with pithy aphorisms and the occasional witticism: 'I observe women are sometimes unreasonable in their Censures' (12 November 1712). 'I observe y^t its best to keep good Decorum and to please w[i]f[e]; it makes every Thing pleasant and Easy' (25 June 1712). 'I find y^t ready money is a good Comodity & y^t is very necessary' (11 March 1713). 'When one thinks least of Drinking, one drinks most' (11 August 1712).

If the purpose of the diary was to teach him how to live a good and moral life, then for Harrold the means to achieve this end was to avoid drink. He was a staunch churchman, fasted in Lent, kept many of the holy days, including the martyrdom of Charles I, which he described as being kept strictly in Manchester (29 January 1714), and frequently got up for the six o'clock daily service. The diary gives a very complete record of texts and sermons given at the old church in Manchester; Harrold was able to summarise and criticise sermons and had the ability to convey something of the character and style of the preacher.[20] Alongside all this, indeed often in conflict with it, was what the diarist called his weak side, his fondness for society and his remarkable appetite for the consumption of alcohol. Much of the diary is given over to lengthy accounts of drinking bouts, described by Harrold as 'going on the Ramble'! After a while the word 'Ramble' is all that he entered for the phrase and eventually the word was contracted to 'Ram'. These drunken tours often lasted a week or more: the inns of Manchester were listed (Harrold identifies over thirty), the amounts drunk and the money paid, all recorded in detail before we come to deep contrition, prayers, church attendance, and resolves for the future. In turn these are followed by water and beer, then beer and water, then beer alone, and then inevitably by another ramble.

The physical consequences of heavy drinking bouts were hangovers, gravel kidneys, which were cured with purges and vomiting and fasting, loss of work and loss of income. The emotional or spiritual consequences, however, were seen by the diarist as far more serious.

> This morn I had my old malancholy pain seized on me wth a longing desire for drink. So I went & pd my Rent y^n I s[o]ld J G[rantham] a lock of hair pro Loss 5s 6d; y^n I spent 2^d wth Hall &c; y^n 4d wth Mr Allen Tourney; y^n fought with S. B[oardman] at Janewins about a hat; y^n went into y^e [Hanging] Ditch a Rambl, - Keys, Dragon & Castle, and Lyon till near 12 clk, till I was Ill drunken; cost me 4s from 6 till 12. I made myself a great foole, &c. (7 July 1712)

The next day Harrold, unable to work, mulled over the events of the previous day.

I've mist pub: private prayer 2 times; its a very Great trouble to me y^t I thus exspose my self, hurt my body, offend against God, set bad example, torment my mind & break my Rules, make myself a laughing stock to men, Greive ye Holy Spirit, disorder my family, fret my wife now Quick, wch is al against my own mind when sober, besides loss of my Credit & Reputation in ye world. (8 July 1712)

The lesson that he learnt from all this was to abstain from drinking in the morning in the ale house, a pledge he managed to keep for all of a week!

The idea that an account of the minutiae of daily life would result in moral improvement allowed Harrold scope to record events and indeed reflections on events at length and in detail. Though not in Pepys's class, Harrold still managed to convey something of the time, and gives us a very valuable account of work and leisure in a pre-industrial town. Much of the diary is given over to an account of daily business transactions. His customers were named, and their various requirements recorded, whether these be hair cutting, shaving, or even the unblocking of teats. The different heads of hair and of wigs, natural wigs, bob wigs, boys wigs, long wigs, were described as were particulars of their manufacture, exchange, repair, curling, dyeing, powdering, reversing and even their baking.[21] Visits up and down the regions were conducted for the collection of hair, which fetched about twenty shillings per pound – a poor girl, apparently, would part with her curls for five shillings and sixpence. Dealings, and especially quarrels, with fellow barbers were recorded. This was a highly competitive business and there were at least four other members of the trade in Manchester at this time congregating in their usual haunt, the Fiddler's Inn.[22]

As for public events, Harrold was by no means a generous chronicler and did not describe events in anything like the detail that he accorded his personal life. There are some brief references to local and national events – the consecration of Manchester's second church, St Ann's, in July 1712, the death of Queen Anne and the arrival and coronation of George I, the quartering of the soldiers in the town and the consequent fight against the Jacobite army at Preston, the celebrations of victory and the execution of some of the captives, including a fellow barber. These, however, are few, and the diarist fails to mention a number of important events that took place in this period, notably the riot and destruction of the Presbyterian chapel in Cross Street on 10 June 1715. What is more characteristic of Harrold's diary is an almost obsessional concern with his own life, with his feelings and emotions, his misery and his happiness. Like Pepys, Harrold was fond of the physical side of marriage and his diary records a good deal of casual detail about sexual acts. 'Remarkable for Peter Nedoms being drowned, and Peter Downs being married to Grace Hulme; my wife and I was very merrey there at night. On ye 9th at night I did wife 2 tymes Couch and bed in an hour an[d] ½ time' (10 June 1712). 'I smoked 1 pipe at Aunt's Came Home and ab[ou]t

11 I enjoy wife &c.' The next day… 'both scolded & did wife 2 tymes got[?] we was merry at last' (19 June 1712). 'Came home went to bed, did w[i]f[e] new fash[ion], fell asleep' (25 July 1712). 'Came at [ten], went to bed, did w[i]f[e] old fash[ion], y^n fell asleep' (30 July 1712). 'Spent 4*d*, came home at q[ua]r[ter] past ten, went to bed, did w[i]f[e] old fash[ion]' (6th August 1712). 'Did w[i]f[e] after a Scolding bout: now we are friends' (6 September 1712). 'Did wife and Talk for a long time; we was pleasant' (8th September 1712).

Whilst the records of sexual acts are kept mercifully brief, records of death – the deaths of his children and of his second wife – are described at length and with enormous tenderness and compassion. The entries for 17 and 18 December 1712 read as follows:

> My wife lay a dying from 11 this day till 9 a clock on ye 18 in ye morn; then she dy'd in my arms, on pillows Relations most by She went suddenly, & was sensible till ¼ of an hour before she dyed I have given her workday clothes to mother Boardman & Betty Cook, our servant now relations thinks best to bury her at meetin[g]-place in Plungeon Field, so I will. According to her mind, I'm making me a black suit on her black mantue and peaticoat I bought her on Edwards, and if God gives life and health I will wear y^m for her sake. I besweech God almighty who has taken my dear assistant from me to Assist me with Grace and wisdom to live Religiously and virtuously & to Eye his providence in this dispensation and to weigh and Consider before I act any Thing, and ye Lord direct me to ye Best amen…

Harrold was devastated by the loss of his wife and for the following six months or so drank to an alarming and dangerous excess. The need to avoid celibacy, however, was strong and it took him about three months before he considered marriage. 'I'm now beginning to be uneasie with my self, and to think of women again. I pray God direct me to do wisely & send me a good one or none; if it be his will, I must have one…' (8 March 1713). Harrold attempted to woo a number of potential candidates, before marrying his third wife, Ann Horrocks, on 22 August 1713, after less than three months' courtship and eight months after the death of his second wife.

To the sections devoted to drink and sex can be added a third to complete the trinity and that is books. Most of the diary's opening pages, the entries for June 1712, are given over to Harrold's attempt to sell the works of Isaac Ambrose of Garstang.[23] Disposing of this book, for which he had paid the sum of sixteen shillings, proved difficult and attempts to recover his costs from the bookseller, John Whitworth,[24] were fruitless. Whitworth, according to Harrold, had but two notes – 'either to extol or run down commodities, as it serves his interest'. His philosophy 'was to buy cheap and sell dear', and his offer to Harrold for the Ambrose was seen by the diarist as derisory. In the end Harrold was forced to sell the book at a loss. The lesson was clear. 'I heartily wish y^t by this loss by bks I may take warning for ye future of f buying new ones any more; or few & very Choise Authors And Extraordinary matter' (23 June 1712).

For Edmund Harrold, books were part of his stock in trade, and as saleable commodities they were almost as vital to his economic well-being as wigs. They were located in his shop as well as his home and hardly a week went by in the diary without at least one reference to their purchase and sale. They were routinely swapped for other books or for wigs or for other services.[25] The entry for 15 August 1712 saw him swap a wig for twenty-eight books. On 1st December 1713 he swapped a volume of Sparke for some nineteen pamphlets and books. The following January saw him 'curling J⁰ Dickensons old wig; Bt 13 bks on him for 13^s, to be paid at May 1; & swapt with J W[hitworth] for Hopkins in folio & 2 vols Scot for 11 Bks; got 6d Boot'. What we have is clear and abundant evidence of the exchange or barter of books; indeed so commonplace is this that it opens up an important issue of how a trade in books could co-exist alongside other forms of service trades. In addition, Harrold gives an insight into the way that books could be traded without the immediate exchange of money. On 3 November 1712, for example, Harrold bought eighteen books for five shillings and twopence. This was on credit, the money did not have to be made until the following Christmas. Clearly there was a need to establish good lines of credit. Books were bought on a promise of payment, and were then sold on, hopefully at a profit, enabling the original debt to be settled at ease. When, as with the works of Isaac Ambrose, the book had to be sold at a loss, the consequences were more serious than one might assume. Even more damaging was the loss of books. In January 1715 three books were borrowed, conveyed or stolen out of the shop. 'This night I mised y^m; it has been a great vexation to me – besides loss of 4^s-5^d. Their names - English, Rogue or witty Extravigant. Complt. 2 voll, 4 parts wth Cuts;. Vol. 19 Sermons m[a]rked Geo. Birch gathering' (14-15 January 1715). Their loss is felt almost as personally as the loss of a child.

The sheer amount of detail given over to an account of the trade in books gives the diary peculiar significance.

> Read Bp Tillitsons sermons. There as so for swapping books for S.O[okes]: with J.W[hitworth] and S. Knots [?] & for my self with J[ohn] Dickenson 3 for 2, voll 7^s 3^d aside and for buying Scots 2^d voll of practicall Discourses of J.W. 3^s & An Account of ye Reformation & Societys y^t promotes it for manners cost me 9^d for having [?] Ralph's Acclamations for a Regular life and ye pleasantness of it (25, 26, 27 November 1713)

The same volumes were regularly bought and sold and bought again. At other times they were loaned, a practice that was described almost in terms that would apply to a circulating library. 'Saw J Brk; bor. his Norriss 1st vol & I'm to bor. him Cornelius & lend WB Recreations for it, which I will if [I] can, but its lent' (11

August 1712). Books, however, were routinely hired and borrowed. On 21 July 1712, for example, Harrold went to see the bookseller John Whitworth to hire a book or two but was baulked. An important part of his trade was the supply of books to customers. On 19 October 1712, for example, he bought for Mary Hill a church catechism. 'She says she will have 2 bks on me Esop and Lady's New Year Gift at 12^s.' Mary Hill was an important customer of Harrold, and was someone with whom he could discuss books. Other women, such as Margaret Brown of Ardwick and Madam Birch, also feature in the diary as buyers and sellers.

The references to the buying or selling of books, however numerous, do not allow us to build up a detailed picture of the economics of the business. We cannot say, for instance, how much of his expenditure or indeed his time went on books, nor can we assess how much of his overall income was dependent on a trade in books. In an age when labour specialisation was uncommon, attempts to separate the strands of his income are futile. His trade in books is by no means insignificant; on a few occasions Harrold provided evidence of the quantity of material passing through his hands.

> Jno Dickenson not come wth Hornecks Great Law according to Bargain paid him 7^d In hand & I have Quarles' Boanerges & Barnabas in part. S[ol]d Anatomy in Latin today I bless God for my wife's deliverance I hope she'll do well Im very busie now in ye world, can hardly get time for any thing towards god so Throng in ye world,...Sent Dr Ranour his 2 Books by his scholor y^t he bought on me Pool & London Devines at 12^d both JB[rooks] brought home Norris on humilty... lent him 7 British Pratle. A Emblem in Ralph of Covetousness (24 November 1712).

On 16 August 1712 he acquired through a series of deals some thirty-six books for thirty-six groats. Immediately, Harrold resorted to draw up a catalogue of the books.

Cataloguing of books was an important part of his work. It features whenever he acquired a large number of items and took on increasing importance as Harrold developed an additional career as an auctioneer. From the end of 1713 until the close of the diary, references to auctions and to auctioneering are increasingly prevalent. Initially it appears that Harrold was selling off his own stock, possibly as a result of poor trade. 31 December 1713 saw him 'in sobriety, only I'm ill set for money, very dull Business, also much indisposed in body,... a great Rent and litle Trade, so y^t I'm in a great Straite what to do'. Auctions which, of course, were held at night, after he had completed his normal day's work as a wig-maker, appear to have provided him with the additional income that he required, enabling him at least to make ends meet. The auction held the following March, for example, saw him clear 300 books, maps and pictures at Ashton. From there he travelled to Stockport, Rochdale and Bolton, holding auctions of books with varying degrees of success. Increasingly Harrold provided a service for others, selling books for Nathaniel Gaskell of Cross Street Chapel, for which he charged commission of five shillings a night. His success enabled him to buy collections – the books of Dr Seddon, Henry Hampson, Dr Birch – and to sell in Manchester and in neighbouring towns the collections of Mr Hyfield and Dr Walker among others. Furthermore, it was profitable enough for him to arrange for printed advertisements to be made for which he paid the sum of twenty shillings (25 December 1714).[26]

Although auctioning books seems to have brought considerable material rewards, it was not an unqualified success. The auction of Gaskell's books held in November 1714 proved particularly traumatic.

> Went on & had Compleated but for Generall Coopers going mad; he made An high Chrch Storm on us. I bless God for Enabling me to pform and Govern myself so well as I did, considering y^t I was so much Scofffed and Derided and Jeereed [by] ye mobb & other malicious p'sons, who offered to baffle me with aprobious words. Indeed, ye told of all my faults, and more y^n all, of drunkenness, foolishness,…and was very abuseive, Especially G Cooper; but I pray god forgive y^{ir} folly, and I do.

Whilst the diary provides important evidence of a trade in books that takes place outside the normal channels populated by the stationer and bookseller, it has additional, not to say exceptional, value because of what it tells us about Harrold's own reading habits. For the most part Harrold traded in books that he himself read, and his chosen subject, not surprisingly, was theology. His favourite authors include William Sherlock (1641-1707), Master of the Temple, Dean of St Paul's and author of discourses concerning death and judgement, John Norris (1657-1711), the last offshoot of Cambridge Platonism, the puritan Thomas Sparke (1548-1616), Thomas Comber (1645-99), Dean of Durham, and William Beveridge (1637-1708), Bishop of St Asaph. These were invariably read to provide moral lessons; indeed the written word was used in exactly the same way as the sermon, as a way of encouraging moral improvement. Printed sermons were every bit as attractive as those he heard in church. Throughout the diary Harrold accompanied his account of the trade in books with comments on their usefulness or application. 'B[ough]t Bp. Beveridge on Restitution to read; Cost 1^s. I've Read it twice over, it's a good sermon and practicall' (10 July 1712). On 4 November, following an argument with Whitworth, Harrold went to bed only to be scolded by his wife for being drunk. He then got up and read a sermon by Norris, which he found 'very pertinent to my case and thoughtful'. Thus he felt comforted, even though his wife still made him spend the night on the couch.

Although his knowledge of sixteenth- and seventeenth-century puritan divines was extensive, he was at least aware of other Christian writers, notably Luther, a book of whose he sold to Parson Worsley for twelve-pence even though he would have accepted half the price (17 November 1712); and on one occasion he transcribed passages from some of the early church fathers, including Ignatius, Polycarp, Dionysius the Areopagite, and Justin Martyr. Furthermore, he appreciated secular authors and appears to have enjoyed books on history. On 1 August 1712 he read 'ye History of ye principality of Orange, & how it has been harrassed by Lewis 14 and how he's persecuted ye protestants.' Clearly the book had an intense personal effect on the diarist: 'it just made my heart ake to hear of his Actions to them'.[27] Other subjects referred to include geography and mathematics, whilst for lighter reading Harrold resorted to songs, poems, and a history of the most eminent cheats of both sexes. News was received from London newspapers and journals, which he read monthly, and from proclamations and pamphlets.

In addition to providing an account of what he read, the diary provides important evidence of the contexts of reading: how, when, where and under what circumstances books were used. For the most part it appears that Harrold read at night following the completion of his working day, and before he wrote his diary. Much of his reading took place at home following his evenings socialising, but there is considerable evidence that books were studied at work, when trade was slack. 'I'm at page 369 now about Humility (Very dull to day as to business) I've Read left at ye Institution of ye Sacrament' (27 September 1712). Occasionally reading had to take second place to other interests. Thus a series of entries in July 1712, for example, read as follows: '[23] came home, Read some in Sherlock and did w[i]f[e] new fash[ion]… [27]…came home, Read some of Sherlock, went to bed and did w[i]f[e] new fash[ion]: 'tis most convenient at this time. Fell asleep.' Books were read at times of personal crisis. When his daughter Esther was ill with the smallpox, Harrold managed to scan the book the *Complete Geographer*, whilst carrying his fevered child around the room (13 Oct 1712). Books could be used to bring about events; reading having the power to determine one's future state. When Harrold embarked on a mission to find a bride, he attempted to turn the thoughts of his prospective partner Mary Hill to marriage by giving her a book to read on the subject. This could be said to have had the right result, although not for Harrold. When he returned to see how she had got on, he discovered she was engaged to another. Undaunted he lent the very same book to another candidate, again with no success.

Harrold was a voracious reader, and often had several books on the go at one time. The entry for 14 November 1714 records, for example, 'Reading Dr Sherlock of a future state, Bp. Dawes against Atheists, and Patrick's Psalms'. Whenever one book was finished another was immediately started, and some books were read over and over again. His conversations with his closest friends, which were usually held in inns, were invariably about books. On one occasion, when he remained sober, he read out to his lodgers Dr Rigby's poem, 'The Drunkard's Prospective' (4 March

1713). On another, when, following a particularly heavy binge, he found himself incarcerated in Salford gaol, he used the opportunity to finish a piece he was reading on the coronation of King George (19, 20 October 1714). On release he resorted to writing out his thoughts on imprisonment. References to writing are few. Occasionally short passages from books were transcribed: on one he copied out Pythagoras's Golden Verses (16-18 December1713), and once he produced a discourse of friendship, which he read to Mr Thorp in Grantham's shop (15, 19 June 1714). These entries, however, are the exception; for the most part it appears that books were read without notes being taken.

In the diary of Edmund Harrold we have detailed evidence of the value attached to books by this obscure provincial tradesman. Books were, of course, important commodities, and for a trader and dealer their financial value could not be overlooked. But above and beyond their material worth is an emphasis on their personal and spiritual worth; their capacity to provide comfort, instruction, enlightenment and amusement; their power to bring about change and reform. Harrold's diary, at its best, offers us a constant and consistently positive view of the power of the written and spoken word.

The evidence that it provides of a trade in books in pre-industrial Manchester is both extensive and detailed. Harrold operated as a dealer in books, an auctioneer and trader, buying and selling, supplying books on order to customers. He was more than a mere hawker of books, but clearly not a formal member of the bookseller's profession. His barber's shop appears to have been used to store and most likely to distribute books, and he made wide use of credit facilities, indeed he recognised the importance of both personal and business credit.[28] Moreover, the diary demonstrates that he did not operate alone. Whilst the bookseller John Whitworth is involved in many of the transactions of books, there was a host of other persons, both men and women, who were buying and selling and who would not lay claim to the title of bookseller. It is clear that during the period that is covered by this diary, there was a substantial trade in secondhand books in Manchester, a trade that in the case of Harrold and some of his contemporaries operated alongside their other forms of employment. Books could be bought and sold as easily in an inn or in a barber's shop as in a bookshop and the diary points to ways that the trade in books relates to other service trades, those of the inn-keepers, shoemakers, gardeners, confectioners and tobacconists who made their living in the pre-industrial market towns.[29] It is doubtful that this type of trade in books is unique to the Manchester of the second decade of the eighteenth century and it may well point to an aspect of the book trade that could be investigated in other parts of the country and at other times. We may well find that the evidence given in the diary of Edmund Harrold is exceptional and that the historical record simply does not exist to support the view of a widespread activity in books that to some extent operates outside what we take as the normal channels and apart from the normal personnel. There is perhaps no other form of historical source than the diary which can help elucidate this trade in books and to identify traders such as Harrold. After all, if Edmund Harrold had not bothered to keep a record of daily events for a few years as a way of leading him to live a more godly life, we would have no idea that he ever existed as anything other than a barber and wigmaker, a husband and father, the barest outline of a life that can be gleaned from parish registers.[30]

NOTES

1. *The Book Collector*, 50, 1 (2001), 135-137.
2. John Harland [ed] *Collectanea Relating to Manchester and its Neighbourhood at Various Periods...*, vol. 2 (Manchester: Chetham Society, O.S., 72, 1867), 173-208.
3. J E. Bailey, 'The Diary of Edmund Harrold, of Manchester, Barber Surgeon, 1712-1715', given to the Manchester Literary Club, on February 11 1884. A manuscript draft of the lecture is in Chetham's Library, Bailey Collection, Mun. C.7.20(5).
4. Ralph Houlbrooke [ed] *English Family Life, 1576-1716: an Anthology from Diaries* (Oxford, 1988).
5. Report of a lecture, 'Book auctions in Manchester in the eighteenth century', in *Transactions of the Lancashire and Cheshire Antiquarian Society*, 27 (1909), 189-201.
6. Michael Powell and Terry Wyke, 'At the fall of the hammer: auctioning books in Manchester 1700-1850', in Peter Isaac and Barry McKay [ed] *The Human Face of the Book Trade: Print Culture and its Creators* (Winchester, 1998), 171-89.
7. Chetham's Library, Mun. A.2.137. A partial transcript of the work is in Chetham's Library, Bailey Collection, Mun. C.7.20(5). All quotations are taken from the original manuscript.
8. Chetham's Library, Bailey Collection, Mun. C.7.20(5).
9. Donald Read, 'John Harland: "the father of provincial reporting" ', *Manchester Review*, 8 (1957-59), 205-212.
10. Alan Crosby, *'A Society with no Equal': the Chetham Society 1843-1993* (Manchester: Chetham Society, 3rd ser., 37, 1993), 41.
11. Crosby, *'A Society with no Equal'*, 42.
12. D R Woolf, *Reading History in Early Modern England* (Cambridge, 2000), 103, n. 63.
13. Information on Harrold's family is taken from Chetham's Library, Bailey Collection, Mun. C.7.20(5).
14. The figure is based on a survey carried out by the Bishop of Chester in 1720. See F R Raines [ed] *Notitia Cestriensis, or Historic Notices of the Diocese of Chester by the Right Rev, Francis Gastrell, Lord Bishop of Chester* (Manchester: Chetham Society, o.s., 8, 19 21, 22, 1845-50). See also C B Phillips & J H Smith, *Lancashire and Cheshire from AD 1540* (London, 1994), 66-67.

15. Celia Fiennes, *Through England on a Side Saddle in the Time of William and Mary* (London, 1888), 186-87, quoted in L D Bradshaw, *Visitors to Manchester: a Selection of British and Foreign Visitors' Descriptions of Manchester from c.1538 to 1865* (Manchester, 1985), 10.
16. Daniel Defoe, *A Tour Through the Whole Island of Great Britain* (London, 1971), 544-46.
17. The best account of Manchester's government remains Arthur Redford, *The History of Local Government in Manchester*, 3 vols (London, 1939-40).
18. J P Earwaker, 'Notes on the Early Booksellers and Stationers of Manchester prior to the year 1700', *Transactions of the Lancashire and Cheshire Antiquarian Society*, 6 (1888), 1-26.
19. Houlbrooke, *English Family Life*, 5. For an incisive account of diary-keeping at this time see John Brewer, *The Pleasures of the Imagination: English Culture in the Eighteenth Century* (London, 1997), 108-112.
20. Harrold records sermons by some thirty-six preachers.
21. For introductions to wig-making see Francois Alexandre Pierre de Garsault, *The Art of the Wigmaker: comprising: the shaping of the beard; the cutting of hair; the construction of wigs for ladies & gentlemen; the renovator of wigs and the bath and hot room proprietor ... First published in 1767*, translated and edited by J Stevens Cox (London, 1961); J Stevens Cox [ed] *The Wigmaker's Art in the 18th Century: A translation of the section on wigmaking in the 3rd edition (1776) of the Encyclopedie of Denis Diderot & Jean d'Alembert* (London,[1965]); Janet Arnold, *Perukes and Periwigs* (London, 1970).
22. The names of the other barbers as recorded by Harrold are William Cook, Thomas Jenkinson, Thomas Sydall and Peter Cottrall.
23. First published in 1674 (Wing A2952), *The Compleat Works of that Eminent Minister of Gods Word Mr. Isaac Ambrose, consisting of these following treatises, viz. prima, media et ultima: or, the first, middle and last things*, was a work of some popularity.
24. John Whitworth succeeded his father Zachary as bookseller from 1697 at their shop in Smith Door. He died on 2 August 1727 and was succeeded by his son Robert. R W Procter, *Memorials of Manchester Streets* (Manchester, 1874), 183.
25. One of the most curious entries in the diary is that for 1 October 1714 where Harrold records that he was given a book for sucking Mrs Wiseman's breast: 'the greatest cure I ever did'.
26. It is not clear whether these were advertisements in newspapers or handbills.
27. Other history books mentioned include Knowles's History of the Turks (21, 25, December 1713). See Woolf, *Reading History*, 103.
28. On the importance of credit see Adrian Johns, *The Nature of the Book: Print and Knowledge in the Making* (Chicago, 1998), 113-14.
29. For a full account of retailing see Lorna Mui and Hoh-cheung Mui, *Shops and Shopping in Eighteenth-Century England* (Montreal, 1989); Ian Mitchell, 'The Development of Urban Retailing 1700-1815' in Peter Clark, *The Transformation of English Provincial Towns 1600-1800*, (London, 1984), 259-83.
30. Edmund Harrold died at the age of forty-two and was buried at the Collegiate Church on 4 June 1721. He was survived by his eldest daughter Ann.

Whitehaven, September 5, 1738.
PROPOSALS,
For Printing by SUBSCRIPTION,
A PROSPECT of the Town and Harbour of
WHITEHAVEN.
Conditions.

1st. THAT the said Prospect shall be neatly Engraven at LONDON, on Copper by an able Hand, with proper Decorations and Embellishments, and Printed on two Sheets of Royal Paper; in Length 3 Feet 5 Inches, and in Breadth 2 Feet 6 Inches.

2d. That the said Prospects shall be ready in *January* next, after which time none shall be disposed of but at an advanced Price.

3d. That the Price to Subscribers shall be Three Shillings, one Half to be paid at Subscribing, the other upon delivery of the Prospects.

4th. That such as Subscribe for Six shall have a Seventh *Gratis.*

SUBSCRIPTIONS, taken in by Mr. *John Spedding*, Mr. *George Crowle*, Mr *Carlisle Spedding*, Mr. *Robert Bowman*, and Mr. *Anthony Ponsonby* in *Whitehaven*, Mr. *Michael Falcon* in *Workington*, Mr. *Dixon* at the *Globe* in *Cockermouth*, Mr. *George Railton* in *Carlisle*, Mr. *Thomas Bacon* in *Dublin*, and in *London* by Mr. *Anthony Nicholson* at Mr. *Harris's* in *Maidenhead Court St. Thomas Apostle's*, Mr. *John Mathews* in *Queen's Court St. Katherine's* near the *Tower*, and by Mr. *James Spedding* at Sir *James Lowther's*, Bar^t. in *Queen's Square Holburn.*

REceived the *31* day of *October* 1738 from *the Revd Arch Deacon Fleming* — — the Sum of *Nine Shillings* being the Subscription Money for *Six Copys* of the above mention'd Prospects according to these Conditions.

by Geo: Railton

Whitehaven : *Printed by* Thomas Cotton.

The earliest surviving example of Whitehaven printing
Reproduced by permission of Cumbria Record Office (Carlisle)

Books in Eighteenth-Century Whitehaven

BARRY McKAY

ON 3 OCTOBER 1696 William Gilpin, steward to Sir John Lowther of Flatt Hall, Whitehaven, wrote to Lowther to complain that:

> We are at a loss here for a bookseller. There is one Henry Pattinson at Carlisle (whom I heretofore recommended to Mr Lowther being a voter for him) who binds tolerably well, and used to sell common books, and had thoughts of setting up that trade here if he could have got a tidewa[i]ter's place to have helped him.[1]

This passing reference in Gilpin's letter, which is otherwise largely concerned with financial and commercial matters in Whitehaven, is the earliest reference we have of any attempt to introduce the book trade into the growing town on the north-west coast of England.

An engraving of 1642 shows a small settlement consisting of a chapel and a number of houses clustered together near the shoreline. That it already had a small harbour is suggested by the presence of several ships in the harbour and a quay.[2] In actual fact the 'town' was still little more than a hamlet although perhaps one which already possessed aspirations towards being something grander having been granted a market charter during the Interregnum, that was confirmed following the Restoration. The engraving shows a lengthy ropewalk extending to the north-east, and a string of packhorses making their way towards the town, all of which leads one to suspect that there was some commercial and industrial activity in terms of shipbuilding (or refitting) and mining, as the packhorses are probably carrying coal from the nearby mines to the harbour for export to Dublin.

The area that was to become the town was owned by Sir John Lowther, and it was due largely to his vision and drive that Whitehaven expanded in the 1680s, to become one of the first post-mediæval planned towns in England. As Member of Parliament, who regularly attended the House, Lowther is likely to have been present at the debates concerning the rebuilding of London after the great fire. He was also a Fellow of the Royal Society of Arts where he could have come into contact with Sir Christopher Wren and others.[3] All these were contributory factors to his conviction that the town should be carefully planned. He wrote to Gilpin in April 1698 stating that 'uniformity is best when a town spreads from the centre to the circumference ... the best way of all is to mark out several streets ...'[4]

Although possessed of a good natural harbour, which over the years was extended and improved by the addition of more quays and moles, the town was otherwise difficult to reach by land. Its position in the shelter of the Cumbrian mountains with a small, lightly populated hinterland was perhaps the major contributory factor in its failure to reach the size and importance which Lowther doubtless envisioned for it. In 1699 Celia Fiennes complained that travel was 'tedious' due to the 'illness of the way' while Robert Molesworth writing in 1704 from Doncaster to his wife in Ireland warned her not to 'think of sending anything by Whitehaven. It is almost 100 miles from us, filthy way, ten times worse than hence to Chester.'[5] Despite there being no bookseller in the town, it was not without books, or familiarity with the processes of creating and obtaining them. Nor was there a problem with access to significant texts. Following the preaching of a consecration sermon by Thomas Smith, Bishop of Carlisle, in July 1693, Gilpin wrote to Lowther to state that he had:

> ... desired to know of his lordship if a request to print his sermon would be grateful. He made a modest reply, but I took encouragement by it, to cause the town to address him to that purpose, and he has complied with our desire. The copy is to be sent to Mr Addison[6] at London, who is to attend your honour for directions about the printing it. I suppose it would be civil to the bishop to leav [sic] him to the choice of his bookseller, but yet (that there may be no risk run by him) that wee undertake for so many copies as will defray the charge of the press, and that wee take care to have a good corrector.[7]

The Gilpin–Lowther correspondence provides a fascinating insight into many matters concerning the town and its growth. We learn for instance that in 1696 'the mathematick master ... has books but is not very well provided with mapps.'[8] In February 1697/8, Lowther wrote from London to Gilpin to enquire 'whether any at Whitehaven can paste maps upon cloth as those were I sent, or if pasted here, if they can do them well upon straining frames; also how Mr Pattinson doth bind books, or if any can doe it in town besides himself.' [9] The phrasing of this part of the letter suggests that Pattinson had been sufficiently encouraged to move from Carlisle to Whitehaven, but if so there is no further evidence for his presence in the town.

However, in terms of identifying the books that were already present in the town in the closing years of the seventeenth century, no document is more important than a four-page list entitled 'A Catalogue of St John Lowther's Books at Flatt, Septembr 3: 1697.' [10]

This catalogue of 170 titles contains a broad cross-section of reading matter, in English, Latin and French, covering history and topography (Camden's *Britannia* 'in English', *A Help to English History*,...), theology, politics (*Speeches in Parliament*, *More Speeches in Parliament*,...) the classics (Plutarch, Livy, &c), several bound volumes of plays, and a number of German and French grammars and dictionaries. However, the meat of this library – and I use the word library advisedly – so far as the town and its inhabitants are concerned are the books devoted to architecture, surveying and similar matters: Wootton's *Elements of Architecture*, Palladio's

Architecture in English, Vitruvius's *Architecture*, Smith's *Art of Gauging*, and Moxon's *Mechanick Exercises* '1 and 2d Volume'.

The architectural volumes were presumably included as 'model books' for Lowther's planned town; the Moxon and other titles, were there for equally practical purposes. Some time ago I discussed with Julian Roberts the possible conceptual difference between a gentleman's 'collection of books' and his 'library'. I posited, and Roberts agreed, that the former was perhaps intended for personal use, whilst the latter was envisaged as being made available for the use of others. There is, I submit, evidence in the Lowther letters that this idea obtained at the Flatt library, and that both Gilpin and Lowther tried to ensure there were such books as would aid the former in fulfilling the latter's aims and aspirations. Some titles were obviously of use in trade (not least the aforementioned grammars and dictionaries). England's wars with France, the Jacobites in Ireland, and later the American colonial rebels were seen in Whitehaven as little more than tiresome interruptions of the town's trade with those places.

Gilpin wrote in October 1697 requesting several titles which would assist in the exploitation of locally mined minerals. '...you will please to send by the return of this carrier such books as may be assistant therein. Such as the *Natural Histories* of Dr Plott. Dr Brown, Sir John Pettus's *Fleta*, etc., some parts of the *Philosophical Transactions* (for the whole set is not needful, and will be too dear).' [11] In February 1698 he requested 'Morden's *Geography*' (not included, or perhaps not yet identified, in the Flatt library catalogue) which would be useful to those involved in the Baltic Trade as it 'gives us an account of coyns, weights, etc.' [12] Lowther had written to Gilpin in August 1697:

> You have herin also the list of books sent last moneth by S. Briggs [13] Evelyn's *Sylva* is what you seem to want. Some others ther are of gardening that no thing may be wanted on that subject. The 3 volumes of sermons you may lend to Mr Yates[14] and Mr Stainton,[15] as you may any thing of navigation to Mr Pelin, being publick persons and making a mine therof, and if lent for a limited time they wil profit more by them in that manner than otherwise, but to any others, except Mr Gale,[16] I would not have you lend any for a practice of that kind would make every one expect it, and I would have their account answered by a library if we can get it.[17]

A century was to pass before Whitehaven was able to boast any sort of 'library'.

One of the names mentioned in this letter can be regarded as the town's first bookseller. Andrew Pellin (or Pelin) was an Irish serge weaver who might have been in Whitehaven in the 1680s. What can be said with some conviction is that by the early 1690s he was resident there and practising as a surveyor and teacher of mathematics. Lowther commissioned him to draw up several plans of the town that show a grid-pattern moving inland from the harbour area towards the countryside with broad main thoroughfares crossed at right angles by slightly narrower residential and service streets, a pattern still clearly visible in the town centre today.[18]

John Gale wrote to Lowther in February 1697: 'Mr Peling [sic] has hetherto don very well. He keeps books, mapps and instruments to sell, I beleeve has good incouragement.'[19] And again a fortnight later:

> as for Mr Pellin he teacheth at his owne house in towne, and has now but a few schollers, about 3 or 4. I suppose the most forward and skillful are gone to sea in the Virginian fleet ... He very well knowes what books instruments, mapps draughts, or other requisites are necessary for his practice and keeps such correspondence as constantly supply him with the newest of every sort, and sells them to his schollers or any other person.[20]

From the late seventeenth century to 1800 the available records reveal the names of eighteen chapmen, pedlars, hawkers and newsmen of Whitehaven, ranging from Robert Dixon, a chapman licensed in 1689, to John Pele, newsman, *fl* 1787 to 1800 (and possibly beyond). Some of these ghostly individuals must have played a role in distributing print from the growing town to its surrounding hinterland and beyond. What the town lacked was its own printer–bookseller. There had been a steady growth of what we may now term service industries throughout the first half of the eighteenth century. Sir John Lowther, and following his death in 1706 his son Sir James, made over 500 grants of plots of land in the town and appear to have actively encouraged – perhaps with occasional financial assistance or favourable rents to desired tradesmen. By 1720 a 'habadasher of hardware' had a shop, by 1732 a gunsmith, in 1738 a baker was 'willing to set up a great bakehouse...for bread and biscuits' and a whitesmith was also anxious to establish a business.[21] But the most significant development, so far as the book trade was concerned, occurred in November 1736 when Thomas Cotton moved to the town.

Cotton had previously printed in Dublin, Cork and Waterford [22] before establishing the first press in Kendal, Westmorland in 1730. In Kendal he had printed the county's first newspaper *The Kendal Courant,* copies of which together with what we may now recognize as a printer's keepsake used as a bookplate, and one book *The Directions to Surveyors of the County of Westmorland,* 1733, constitute all the surviving evidence of the first printer in present-day Cumbria. Cotton's enterprise in Kendal was short-lived, for in 1731 Thomas Ashburner, a local man also set up as printer, bookseller, stationer and newsagent. Ashburner presumably took the bulk of such trade as there was, for by 1736 Cotton was in some financial difficulties. John Spedding, Lowther's agent in Whitehaven, advanced Cotton a loan of ten pounds to clear his debts in Kendal and enable him to move to Whitehaven where he intended to keep a stationery shop and establish another newspaper.[23]

Cotton established his press in Whitehaven in 'an office with an outside stone staircase '... in James Street two doors to the east side of the Presbyterian Church', a site now occupied by the car park of the church.[24] His first priority appeared to be the establishment of a newspaper, the *Whitehaven Weekly Courant*, for which Sir James Lowther promised to send relevant news from London to be included in the paper.[25] Alas, no copies appear to have survived; however, some issues at least were still extant in the late nineteenth century as a contemporary writer records that it was:

> a small sheet measuring sixteen inches by twelve inches, three columns to a page, and it had four pages. It had not a scrap of local news, save half-a-dozen lines of shipping, and it had but one advertisement on the back page, which set out 'Doctor Daffy's Elixir, the most famous cordial in the world, truly prepared in London, and appointed to be sold by Thomas Cotton, at his printing house in James Street.' [26]

The *Whitehaven Courant* seems to have soon established a circulation of about one hundred copies per week, which, given the doubtless keen but restricted market amongst the merchants and tradesmen of the town, would seem a reasonable figure. However, the reported lack of advertisements would seem to indicate that it enjoyed a less than dramatic commercial success. Whether or not the lack of advertisements was a result of want of initiative on the part of Whitehaven's traders, or if 'it was thought mean and disreputable in any tradesman of worth and credit to advertise the sale of his commodities in a public Newspaper',[27] we cannot, at this remove and lacking the evidence of copies of the *Courant*, know.

No examples of book printing from Cotton's Whitehaven press have survived. In the British Library there are two broadsides, without imprint or date, which may be attributable to his press, and he doubtless printed a number of tradesman's bills and notices. Other than one piece, nothing has been located which can be definitely shown to be from, or confidently attributed to, his press in Whitehaven. The sole surviving example of the first Whitehaven press is a small folio broadside prospectus issued by Cotton on 5 September 1738: *Proposals, for Printing by Subscription, a Prospect of the Town and Harbour of Whitehaven...*[28] (see page 50). Of the thirteen persons named as taking in subscriptions only one of eight from Cumberland may perhaps be identified as belonging to the book trade. That single instance is George Railton, possibly the same Mr Railton, bookseller of Carlisle, who appears named in an advertisement for patent medicine in the *London Evening Post* of 25 December 1755. One other, Thomas Bacon of Dublin, is perhaps the auctioneer, and later bookseller, of Bacon's Coffee House (*fl* 1736-42).[29] The others whose names can be recognized, were all friends or business acquaintances of Lowther. The 'prospect' being subscribed for was an engraving by W Parr of Matthias Read's birds-eye painting of the town and harbour.[30]

How long Cotton's newspaper survived is not known. It has been suggested that his publication had ceased by April 1739 when, from its inception, the *Newcastle Journal*, had an agent, one Mr Birkett, in Whitehaven.[31] The Newcastle press certainly regarded Cumberland and Westmorland as within their sphere of influence for advertisements and official notices from both counties continued to appear in Newcastle newspapers even after John Ware had established the *Cumberland Pacquet* in 1774; therefore I suspect that too much has been read into this suggestion.

Cotton died in July 1743 and for a few years book trade activity in Whitehaven becomes unclear. The town first appears in the imprint of the Carlisle divine Erasmus Head's *Sermon Preached at the Ordination at Rose-Castle ...* (London: printed for J. Clark, [and three Cumbrian booksellers] 1746).[32] Of these Cumbrian booksellers, two are known from other sources: W Hodgson of Carlisle and John Thomlinson of Wigton.[33] Only one bookseller from Whitehaven is named: J Stretch, about whom nothing else is known.

The next major figure in the town's book trade is William Masheder (*fl* 1724-62), originally a teacher of mathematics and navigation, who was resident in Whitehaven in 1738 when he subscribed to a copy of Samuel Fearon & and John Eyes, *A Description of the Sea Coast of England and Wales from Black Comb ... to the point of Linus in Anglesea* (Liverpool, 1738). He seems to have retired from business shortly after 1757 and was still resident in the town, occupying the front of a property in Carter Lane in 1762. His name appears in the imprint of several titles, initially as a bookseller of Ann Fisher's *Grammar ...* of 1750; and as the printer of two theological works: the twelfth edition of Richard Steel's *The Christian Hero* (1756) and, of rather more local moment, Philip Moore's *Sermon Preached at the Funeral of ... Thomas Wilson... Bishop of Sodor and Man...* ([1755]). Three other books by him are of rather more interest: the local schoolmaster Abraham's Fletcher's *The Universal Measurer*, in two parts (1752-3) and in 1757 *The Youth's Companion* which Masheder may also have compiled. The *Universal Measurer* contains an advertisement that includes a list of books he offered for sale. This advertisement contains several theological works as well as a number of titles likely to appeal to the local navigators, merchants and mining engineers. Masheder's advertisement concludes with a catch-all list of subjects including 'a great variety of School Books, Books of Navigation, Sea Charts for all parts of the World, and Stationery Wares of all Sort.' However, his most significant publication was his own *The Navigator's Companion: or, Mariner's Compendious Pocket Book* (1754), which is the only one of his publications to have a lengthy list of other booksellers in the imprint. This shows that he had trading connections in London, Bristol, Liverpool, Newcastle, Berwick and Dublin.

Whether Masheder was himself a printer or only a bookseller–stationer must remain a matter of conjecture. It is likely that he employed the services of a journeyman printer, and if so then it is possible that his printer was William Shepherd who was active in the town under his own name from 1757. Contemporary with Shepherd was John Fell, another of those rather shadowy figures in which the Cumbrian book trade abounds. Fell was active as a bookseller in 1758 when he subscribed two copies of Baskerville's edition of Milton's *Paradise Lost,* and was still in Whitehaven in 1762 when he appears as one of three booksellers in the imprint of William Richardson's *Essays on Several Divine and Moral Subjects...* The other two booksellers were Thomas Ashburner of Kendal and William Charnley of Newcastle, both of whom are also present on the edition of 1756. William Shepherd printed and sold two editions of Locke's *Elements of Natural Philosophy,* 1764 and 1766, the year of John Fell's death. Shepherd also appears as one of a lengthy list of provincial booksellers on William Cockin's *Rational and Practical Treatise of Arithmetic* (London, 1766). Is it possible that, following Masheder's retirement, John Fell took over the bookselling side of his business and William Shepherd the printing? If so it would be extremely convenient, and unusually tidy, for by 1762 Whitehaven had become comparatively rich in members of the book trade. A census taken in that year reveals that William Shepherd (printer) was in the Market Place, John Dunn (stationer) was a few doors away, John Copeland (stationer) was in King Street, and William Copeland (printer) in Sandhills Lane. No 'booksellers' are recorded; doubtless Professor John Feather's assertion that the terms stationer and bookseller were almost synonymous in the eighteenth century was agreed with in Whitehaven. Furthermore no John Fell is recorded. The Copelands or Couplands have not been located in any imprints and are only known from the 1762 census and parish register entries. The other man recorded on the 1762 census, William Shepherd, died in 1768 and was succeeded by his wife Mary who continued to trade until 1774.

In conclusion, one other figure is worthy of note: Allason Foster, a native of Cumberland whose ancestors hailed from Crosthwaite near Keswick. He traded in the town from 1771 until some time before his death in November 1816. Only six titles are recorded with his imprint, four of which may be termed useful books (the other two being local sermonizing and poetasting): Draper's *Young Student's Pocket Companion* (1772), *The Navigators Vade-Mecum* (1773), and Chambers' *Universal Navigator* (1774). The fourth is the work of a Whitehaven writing-master and accountant, Edmund Fitzgerald, *An Epitome of the Elements of Italian Book-Keeping* (1771). A lengthy list of subscribers shows that 554 copies were taken up: 253 in

Whitehaven, 280 in four other Cumbrian towns (none, perhaps significantly, in Carlisle!), eight copies went to subscribers on the Isle of Man, seven to Scotland, mainly around Dumfries, five to Ireland and one to Yorkshire; a healthy, but decidedly localized, circulation. Amongst the subscribers to the *Epitome* we find the name of J Ware junior (who took only one copy) and who, together with his father published in the same year an edition of Thompson's *The Accomptants Oracle*. Was Ware looking at what the opposition was doing?

The Wares were to dominate the west-Cumbrian book trade for the next half century giving the town, and indeed the county, its first really good and significant newspaper, *The Cumberland Pacquet*. From their foundation of the *Pacquet* in 1774 they seem to have all but crushed all other serious opposition in the production of important texts, albeit of largely local significance. Although there were isolated glories still to come, Ware's editions of the *Bible* and *Common Prayer* in Manx for instance, one cannot escape the conclusion that Whitehaven's book trade had, like the town itself, passed its zenith.

Thus, as I hope I have shown in this paper, the Whitehaven book trade sought to fill the needs of its customers, both by obtaining books from London and elsewhere and by producing several significant mathematical and navigational books written to meet the needs of its seafarers and merchants. The book trade in the town can therefore be seen to have both fed the needs of its community and in turn itself fed, for some part of its products, off that community. It was clearly a two-way traffic, as all good business should be.

NOTES

1. D R Hainsworth [ed] *The Correspondence of Sir John Lowther of Whitehaven 1693-1698; a provincial community in wartime*, (London: British Academy, 1983), 312.
2. Reproduced in J V Beckett, *Coal and Tobacco; the Lowthers and the economic development of west Cumberland, 1660-1760* (Cambridge: Cambridge University Press, 1981) frontispiece, and Mary E Burkett and David Sloss, *Read's Point of View; paintings of the Cumbrian countryside, Mathias Read 1669-1747* ([Kendal?]: Skiddaw Press, 1995), xvi.
3. Beckett, *Coal and Tobacco*, 181.
4. Lowther to Gilpin 19 April 1609, Cumbria Record Office (Carlisle) D/Lons/W: Sir John Lowther's Letter Books.
5. Beckett, *Coal and Tobacco*, 172.
6. Presumably Thomas Addison (b.1641), iron smelter, merchant and Lowther's partner in the Baltic trade.
7. Gilpin to Lowther 16 July 1693, Hainsworth, *Correspondence*, 50.
8. Gilpin to Lowther 24 February 1696/7, Hainsworth, *Correspondence*, 355.
9. Lowther to Gilpin 1 February 1697/8, Hainsworth, *Correspondence*, 494.
10. Cumbria Record Office (Carlisle), D/Lons/W WhTown 80.
11. Gilpin to Lowther 9 Oct 1697, Hainsworth, *Correspondence*, 438.

12. Gilpin to Lowther 9 Feb 1697/8, Hainsworth, *Correspondence*, 499.
13. Samuel Briggs of Kendal, carrier from Kendal to and from London.
14. Francis Yates (occasionally Yeats), a clergyman possibly of Dissenting persuasion.
15. Richard Stainton (*d*1734) curate of St Bees, a small village several miles south of Whitehaven in which parish the 'town' was at that time situated.
16. There were several male members of the Gale family prominent in the town's affairs; the one referred to here is almost certainly John Gale the elder, a substantial merchant and one-time steward of Lowther's colleries.
17. Lowther to Gilpin 28 August 1697, Hainsworth, *Correspondence*, 423.
18. Sylvia Collier with Sarah Pearson, *Whitehaven 1600-1800; a new town of the late seventeenth century: a study of its buildings and urban development*, (London: HMSO, 1991) particularly chapter 1: 'The Topographical Development of the Town.'
19. Gale to Lowther 14 Feb 1696/7, Hainsworth, *Correspondence*, 352.
20. Gale to Lowther 28 Feb 1696/7, Hainsworth, *Correspondence*, 357.
21. Beckett, *Coal and Tobacco*, 185.
22. R L Munter, *A Dictionary of the Print Trade in Ireland 1550-1775* (New York: Fordham University Press, 1988); *A Hand-List of Irish Newspapers 1685-1750* (Cambridge: Bowes & Bowes; Cambridge Bibliographical Society Monograph 4, 1960); M Pollard, *A Dictionary of Members of the Dublin Book Trade 1550-1800; based on records of the Guild of St Luke the Evangelist, Dublin* (London: Bibliographical Society, 2000).
23. Beckett, *Coal and Tobacco*,188.
24. 'Chancellor' [Richard S] Fergusson 'On the Collection of Chap-Books in the Bibliotheca Jacksoniana, in Tullie House, Carlisle, with some remarks on the history of printing on Carlisle, Whitehaven, Penrith, and other north country towns; in *Transactions of the Cumberland and Westmorland Antiquarian and Archæological Society* [Old Series] Vol XIV, Part I, (1896), 30.
25. Beckett, *Coal and Tobacco*, 188.
26. Ferguson, *Collection of Chap-Books*, 30.
27. *Liverpool Chronicle* 6 May 1757, quoted in R M Wiles, *Freshest Advices; early provincial newspapers in England* (Ohio State University Press, 1965), 150.
28. Cumbria Record Office (Carlisle) D/Sen/Fleming/145.
29. Munter, *Print Trade*; Pollard, *Dictionary*.
30. *East Prospect of the Town and Harbour of Whitehaven*, Richard Parr, *sculpsit*, reproduced in Burkett, *Read's Point of View*, 100.
31. Beckett, *Coal and Tobacco*, 188-9.
32. ESTC t001413.
33. For an account of John Thomlinson and his problems regarding the illegal importation of books see Barry McKay, 'John Thomlinson of Wigton, Bookseller and Illegal Importer of Books' in *Quadrat; a periodical bulletin of research in progress on the British book trade*, 11, (2000), 9-14.

(20)
Of the LAMIA.

THE Lamia, Emblem strong of Sin,
  Does all her Charms employ;
To draw th' unwary Trav'ller in,
  And then the Wretch destroy.

The

Page from *A Pretty Book of Pictures, for little masters and misses*
London: printed for Newbery and Carnan, 1769.
Private Collection, produced with the owner's permission.

From George III to Queen Victoria: a Provincial Family and their Books

DAVID HOUNSLOW

ALTHOUGH LYDIA HASKOLL (*née* Heaton) was born in 1756 and died in 1826, a decade before Victoria came to the throne, to label her as *Georgian* would be inhibiting. This paper could just as easily have *From Charles II to Elizabeth II* as its title, for some of the books she read had their roots in the seventeenth century and the books she owned as a child were enjoyed by her great-great-great-great grandchildren when they were small. We need only look at a photograph of her youngest son William to know that if we must label her, she is a 'Mother of Victorians'.

Lydia, living a circumscribed existence from choice, in what could be seen as a provincial backwater, not only collected and read books thoughout her life, but also shared them with her children and her grandchildren. She added to her own library of children's books as a young woman in the years preceding her marriage, bought books for her family and gave some of her own obviously treasured possessions to Margaret Elizabeth and Emily, the daughters of her son Thomas James Haskoll. But she was also a child of the times. In 1781, when I believe she and her future husband had reached some kind of understanding, they jointly inscribed a number of books, all of them pocket editions published by John Cooke, and most required reading of the day. She was an admirer of the Evangelical Anglicans, her memorandum books are peppered with quotations from the works of Hannah More and Sarah Trimmer and she owned several of the *Cheap Repository Tracts* and a set of Sarah Trimmer's *Family Magazine* (1788-9). Her children and grandchildren were given similarly monitorial works: for the children, *Virtue in a Cottage* (attributed by Sarah Trimmer to one of the Kilners, but it could have easily come from her own pen) and for her grandchildren, volume two of the Taylors' *Original Poems for Infant Minds*. In the final year of her life, she is borrowing books from friends, making notes of new books she might wish to read and being asked by an author to subscribe to his forthcoming book. If we should even doubt for a minute that Lydia was a committed reader throughout her life, a quotation from Hannah More found in her memorandum book of 1826 will quickly dispel that:

> Reading! Thou source of instruction and information, how I venerate thee! From my youth up, I have been partial to thee; nor will age, I trust, damp my affection. Thou has [*sic*] furnished with a massive entertainment my solitary walks, and enabled me to pass in innocence the vacant hour.

Lydia Heaton was born in Brading on the Isle of Wight, the youngest child of Martin and Jenny Heaton, the family having moved from Yarmouth shortly before Lydia was born. Jenny's first husband had been a shoemaker and the surviving evidence suggests that Martin too was from a humble background. It may be that, like Jenny's first husband William Munt, Martin was a shoemaker by trade. He is listed in 1752 as a recipient of a donation of ten shillings from the charity known as *Lord Holmes's Gift,* which states that the charity was for the benefit of, 'such poor of the said town [Yarmouth] who should receive no alms from the parish.' Martin, however, was a householder, paying quarterly rates of two shillings, and a churchgoer, paying seat rental for himself and his wife in the parish church, so he was not destitute, but one of the 'deserving poor'.

Jenny Heaton died in 1765, when the child was nine years old. In her memorandum book Lydia describes herself as being left an orphan, but Brading parish records refer to Jenny as the wife, not widow or relict of Martin. It is possible Lydia is using the term *orphan* in its older sense, that is the loss of a single parent rather than both, but surviving evidence suggests that by 1768 Martin Heaton was also dead, for we know the child went to live with a Martha and William Legg in Newport in that year. The most likely explanation for the move is that she was being sent there as a 'parish apprentice'. At twelve, she would be too young to be left to her own devices and the overseers of the poor would not wish her to become a permanent charge on the parish. For only two or three guineas and a new set of clothes for the little girl, the overseers would have discharged their obligations and the child would receive training in domestic duties and a religious education.

It is most likely Lydia met her benefactress Mrs Margaret Holmes (1700-83) at the Leggs's. Margaret was one of the daughters of Captain Henry Holmes, governor of Yarmouth Castle and MP for the town, and heir to one sixth of his substantial estate. Margaret and Lydia were certainly living there when the former died in 1783 and in Margaret Holmes's will there are legacies for her servant, Lydia who is described as her companion, and Martha Legg. It was also Margaret who probably paid for Lydia's schooling. In 1768 Margaret Holmes was already quite an elderly person by the standards of the day and at sixty-eight her thoughts must have turned towards the infirmities of old age and the help she would need. What better than a little girl who could be trained up from scratch?

It was probably while living with Martha and William Legg that Lydia met her future husband, Thomas James Haskoll. Like Lydia he was an orphan, being cared for by his uncle James Haskoll, a brewer and maltster. Thomas was eventually to inherit his uncle's business. By 1780 it is likely that Lydia's thoughts had turned towards marriage and by 1781 they may have reached an understanding, with each other and with Margaret Holmes. They married by licence in 1783, a few weeks after the old lady's death, and their first child, Margaret Holmes Haskoll, was born in 1784. At first the couple lived in Newport and all their remaining children were born there: Joseph in 1785, Thomas James junior in 1786, Mary Lydia in 1789, James in 1791 and William in 1792.

In 1795, Thomas James bought the Hermitage and proceeded to extend and modernise the house. Set in the south of the island, it is high up in the lee of St Catherine's Down, looking north towards Newport, and must have been a paradise for children. From there, the boys went to school on the mainland and Margaret Holmes Haskoll, at least of the girls, probably went to school in London. This was now a prosperous family. The Hermitage remained the family home until 1809, when some kind of disaster struck and Thomas James and Lydia moved back to Newport. It is likely that Thomas James senior was taken seriously ill and this was the reason for the move. In 1817 he made the long journey, by land and sea, to the spa town of Harrogate in north Yorkshire where he died. Lydia lived on for a further fifteen years, probably with her daughter Margaret as her companion.

Although much of Lydia Haskoll's life has been recovered from obvious sources, it is the inscriptions in her books which have often provided essential leads. Lydia regularly placed marks of ownership in her books, most often a signature with an accompanying date and, more helpfully, notes of significant events in her life and the names of people who had some sort of impact on her as an individual. There are, also, clusters of dated inscriptions for January through to March 1770, for 1780 and 1788; the first cluster, I believe, is preparatory to going away to school, the second when she was thinking seriously about marriage and the third when she was teaching her first and favourite child to read. From an early age, she was also adding quotations to some inscriptions.

In her copy of *The Whitsuntide-Gift...* (1767), Lydia wrote, 'I came to Mrs. Leggs March 25th 1768' and 'Lydia Heaton Febuary [sic] 4th 1770'. Later, some four or five years after her marriage, she added 'Peggy Haskoll'. In her memorandum book for 1806 Lydia recorded Martha Legg's death, 'Tuesday April 29th 1806. Died Mrs Legg, aged 91 years; teach us to number our days, that we may apply our hearts unto wisdom.' Another book, *A New History of England from the Invasion of Julius Caesar to the Present Time* (c1766), also bears a number of inscriptions which shed light on the child's life. On the front free endpaper she has inscribed 'Lydia Heaton Januery [sic] the 18 1770': on the rear free endpaper, 'Let me go were so are I will England shall have my best wishes still Lydia Heaton Febry 18th 1770' and 'Who to forbidden joys would rove That knows the sweets of virtuous love.' There is one other partial inscription in Lydia's juvenile hand at the front of the book and,

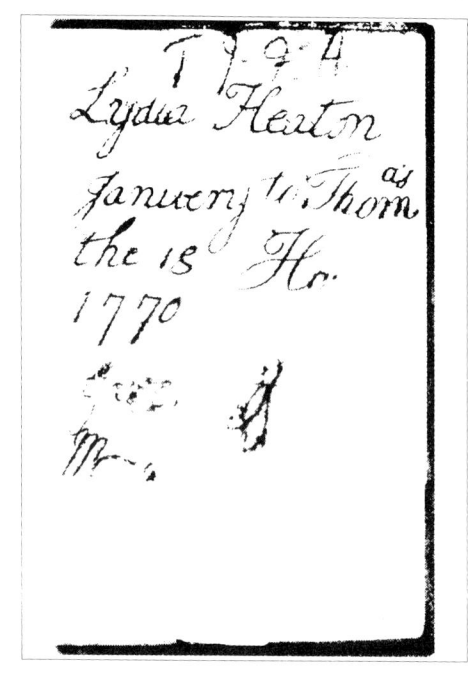

Front free endpaper of Lydia Heaton's copy of *A New History of England from the Invasion of Julius Caesar to the Present Time* printed for J Newbery, c1766

although part of the leaf is missing, enough survives for us to see that she gave the book to Thomas Haskoll. The book bears the initials of Thomas James Forbes Haskoll, Lydia's great-grandson, and has remained in the family's hands up to the present day.

Yet another, *Moral Lectures ...By Solomon Winlove Esq.* (1769), carries multiple inscriptions; firstly, 'Lydia Heaton her book march 28th 1770. Tis education forms the Minde. Just as a Twig is bent the Trees Inclined', and then in a different hand:

> The gods said Hesiod have placed labour before virtue the way to her is rough difficult but growes more smooth and easey the farther you advance in it with steadiness and resolution will in a little time find that her ways are pleasantness and that all her paths are peace.

Below is a partly indecipherable tongue-twister in the same hand signed, 'Elizabeth Bentley Hughes'. Again in her memorandum book for 1806 Lydia records the marriage of a Miss Maria Morley, adding that, 'The above young lady is the daughter of Miss Maria Hughes, who was my schoolfellow', which suggests Lydia did take some of her books to school and that Elizabeth was probably Maria's sister.

In 1780 Lydia, now twenty-four years old, placed marks of ownership in another small clutch of children's books; *Juvenile Sports and Pastimes by Master Michael Angelo* (2 ed, 1776); *The Cries of London* (nd); *The Poetical Flower Garden* (1775); *The History of Good Lady Kindheart* (nd) and Christopher Smart's *Hymns for the Amusement of Children* (3 ed, 1775). Of these all but *Juvenile Sports and Pastimes* would have been suitable for both boys and girls. *Juvenile Sports...*, however, is very much a book for small boys and there are no girls present in any of the woodcut illustrations. The text is avowedly masculine in tone, beginning with an account of the pseudonymous author's upbringing and education, continuing with explanation of the rules for hockey, cricket and marbles and instructions for making bows and arrows and a section on 'the art of dump-making' – a cast leaden counter used in a juvenile version of the extremely nasty 'throwing at a cock'. Lydia Heaton has retained her love of children's books and is perhaps looking forward to sharing them with her own infant sons and daughters sometime in the future.

The last group of books are all inscribed for Margaret Holmes Haskoll (1784-1843) in 1788 when the child was four years old. These include *The Cries of London* (1784); *Little Robin Redbreast; a Collection of Pretty Songs for Children* (1782); *Juvenile Rambles Through the Paths of Nature* (1786); *The Pious Child's Delight* (nd), an abridgement of Isaac Watts's catechisms; Watts's *Divine Songs...* (1784) and *The Easter Offering* (nd). Additionally several of the books owned by Lydia when she was a child are inscribed for Margaret and dated 1788. This does not, however, indicate a transfer of ownership, or that the books inscribed for Margaret alone were the child's sole property. For example, *Letters between Master Tommy and Miss Nancy Goodwill* (1770) has multiple inscriptions including two in Lydia's immature hand, one dated 1770, and two for Margaret dated 1788 in two separate places in the book. In *The Young Moralist* (3 ed 1782) Lydia again has inscribed in two places, 'Margt H. Haskoll July 10 1788' and, 'Margaret Holmes Haskoll July 12th 1788'. Part way through volume three of Lydia's copy of Sarah Trimmer's *Family Magazine*, on the reverse of one of the plates, we again find Margaret's name inscribed and dated 1789, suggesting that the mother is reading to, or with, the child and recording the event, perhaps at Margaret's request. There is a similar inscription for Mary Lydia Haskoll (b1789) in *The Curiosities of London and Westminster Described* (1791) dated April 13th 1793. It is unlikely, in either event, that such small children would be given what are effectively adult books, unless they were extremely precocious, and there is no evidence for this.

The constant inscribing of books, for whatever reason, would help explain why Margaret seemingly owned two copies of Watts's *Divine Songs*, one published in 1784 by H. Turpin and inscribed 'Margt. H. Haskoll October 28 1788', and the other published by Piercey in Coventry about 1785 and inscribed 'M. H. Haskoll 1787', with the further addition of a roan label reading, 'Miss Haskoll, St. Catherine's Hermitage 1797'. The family also owned two editions of *The Cries of London*, one published before 1780 and inscribed by Lydia in that year, and another published in 1784 and inscribed by Lydia, 'M. H. Haskoll 1788'. All this suggests that inscriptions in children's books should be approached with great caution. In the case of the

Haskolls, this is not helped by Lydia's particularly idiosyncratic figure eight, which can be mistaken for a nine.

Thanks to this plethora of inscriptions, some of the books once belonging to the family are easily identified and as succeeding generations of Haskolls in turn placed marks of ownership in the books, we know the line of inheritance of much of the family library. Even though books were given by Lydia to her two granddaughters, these at some stage became the property of their younger brother Joseph (1819-71). Similarly, a few books belonging to William Haskoll ended up in Joseph's hands as well. From Joseph, many of the books passed to his oldest son Thomas James Forbes Haskoll (1857-1914), who sold thirty of them to the Bodleian Library in 1882, retaining roughly the same number. These were passed on to one of his younger sisters, who in turn bequeathed them to the present owner. This can be explained in part by the fact that many of Lydia's female descendants never married.

However, there is evidence that this is not the full extent of the library and it is clear that some of the family's books have been sold piecemeal over the years. The Opie copy of *The Twelfth-Day Gift* seems to have been acquired before Peter Opie began systematically keeping his accessions dairies in 1962; there are two books in the Cotsen Collection in the USA and a further two which once belonged to Marjorie Moon. These two last were acquired by Moon from separate sources, a bookseller in 1986 and at auction in 1987. There are persistent rumours, too, of other books having been on the open market.

Of the books inscribed by Lydia Heaton in 1770, sixteen bear the imprint of one or other of the Newbery clan, of which two also carry the imprint of Benjamin Collins, who was a publisher, book wholesaler and the proprietor of the *Salisbury Journal*. Two carry the joint imprint of Richard Baldwin and Benjamin Collins and one that of H Roberts, J Wilkie and L Tomlinson. Another, *The Careful Parent's Gift*, bears no imprint at all, but is likely to have been published by Richard Marshall in Aldermary Churchyard. Those published by Baldwin and Collins and Newbery and Collins were regularly advertised in the *Salisbury Journal*, as were some of those published by John Newbery alone. In the 1760s, as many as 3000 book advertisements were printed in the paper annually. Of those in which Collins had an interest, an Isle of Wight bookseller was generally named as one of his agents, in the 1760s most often Peter Milligan of St James's Square, Newport. So it is entirely probable that most, if not all, of the books owned by Lydia in 1770 were bought from a bookseller on the island.

By 1780 there were other booksellers trading in Newport, including John Sturch (*fl.* 1776-94) and members of the Wise family, one of whom was still trading in the mid 1790s. Of the five books inscribed by Lydia in 1780, three were published by

John Newbery's stepson Thomas Carnan, one by Newbery's nephew Francis and one by Richard Marshall, the erstwhile chapbook publisher and business associate of Cluer Dicey.

A much larger number of books was inscribed by Lydia between 1787 and 1789 and these reflect the further expansion of the children's book market and give some idea of the reach of provincial booksellers. One of the two editions of Watts's *Divine Songs* owned by the family was published by Piercey of Coventry and two books, *The History of Sir Richard Whittington* and *The Pious Child's Delight*, by the better known Coventry bookseller Mary Luckman. Two others were published by a London bookseller, Homan Turpin, but by far the greater number are books published by Elizabeth Newbery, with three from her main rival John Marshall (*fl* 1783-1828).

Of the remainder of the books, inscribed by Lydia and her daughter Margaret between 1792 and 1829, it is Elizabeth Newbery who dominates the imprints, followed by John Marshall with four books; the Dartons, two; Mary Luckman, one; and one simple little booklet published by John Evans fairly early on in a career which spanned almost half a century. Elizabeth Newbery sold out to John Harris in 1801, and as one of the books inscribed by Lydia for one of her granddaughters in 1819 has a dated imprint of 1799 and three others inscribed at the same time were all probably published in the 1790s, it is clear Lydia did not always place marks of ownership in the family's children's books when the books were first bought.

It is clear that Lydia Haskoll was an avid reader throughout her life, but she seems also to have treasured her books as material objects. Those sold to the Bodleian in 1882 are generally in a fine condition and others have been carefully repaired at an early stage. One extremely rare title, *A Little Lottery-Book for Children*, was intended for use as an educational toy and the lack of early editions (it was probably first published in 1756) suggests that the book was heavily used by child owners, both as it was intended, and probably as a source of illustrations for the game of 'pick-a-pin'. Lydia's copy, the 'sixth edition' of 1767, is not only in remarkably good condition, but is the earliest surviving copy. It is also distinguished by the quality of the illustrations and I suspect this is what made the book desirable in Lydia Heaton's eyes.

This may also provide an additional explanation why the family owned two copies, both in excellent condition, of the Newbery *Cries of London*. The earlier of the two, undated, but inscribed by Lydia in 1780, is not recorded by Roscoe and is in remarkably good condition for an early children's book. It has been well looked after and there are no other marks of ownership. The same can be said of the later 1784 edition, which was inscribed in 1788 for Margaret Holmes Haskoll. Lydia also owned another book of cries published by Thomas Carnan in 1770 and once more the book is not only in fine condition, but is also the seemingly sole surviving copy.

Thanks to Lydia and her descendants, early editions of a number of books have survived through to the present day. For a long time hers was the earliest known English edition of Christopher Smart's *Hymns for the Amusement of Children* and was used for the Luttrell Society reprint and the Muses' Library edition of Smart's works. The family's copy of *Juvenile Sports and Pastimes* is the earliest survivor. Her copy of *The Orphan; or, the Renowned History of Little Gaffer Two-Shoes* is the only surviving perfect copy and her *Top Book of All*, issued sometime after 1764, seems to be another unique survival, although there is a probable earlier edition in the British Library.

However, it is the sum of the parts which should concern us most, not individual items – no matter how rare. The collection reflects changes in publishing for children, but it also demonstrates the longevity of titles way beyond their publishing histories. The Haskoll collection shows that the history of children's literature is not simply a stately progression from *Goody Two-Shoes*, through *Holiday House* and *Alice* to *The Wind in the Willows*, or Perrault to the Grimms and Andersen, but rather that some children, at least, held on to the books they loved. Books, which to modern eyes have no literary merit and are merely quaint, survived and were read by succeeding generations.

There is continuity too in the subject matter of many of the Haskoll family books, with Lydia giving her children and grandchildren books on subjects which interested her both as a child and as adult. This is best illustrated by reference to the children's books which can be loosely described as being on the 'Natural World' and later adult books which reflect an attitude towards the spiritual and earthly worlds which John Clare called 'the religion of the fields'.

The earliest of these, owned by Lydia, inscribed by one of her great-granddaughters and still in family hands, is the tenth edition of *A Pretty Book of Pictures, for Little Masters and Misses: or, Tommy Trip's History of Beasts and Birds* (1769). First published in 1752, the book has a text in both prose and verse with woodcuts, for the mammals at least from the same hand, accompanying each animal described. The bird illustrations, on the other hand, are clearly from miscellaneous sources and vary wildly in quality. The source of the mainly descriptive prose text is *A Description of Three Hundred Animals* (1 ed 1730), which in turn derives from Edward Topsell's *A Historie of Foure-Footed Beastes* (1607) and John Ray's *The Ornithology of John Willughby* (1675). The verses are in two pairs of rhyming couplets and here the author indulges in a degree of anthropomorphism and social comment.

The animals described include native wild birds and beasts, domestic animals, the more exotic such as the rhinoceros, which is accompanied by a passable copy of

Durer's woodcut and one mythical beast, the lamia of which the author tells his child readers, 'As to man, it allures him by its snares; for lying on its belly, and concealing all but its face [of a beautiful woman] and breasts, tempts his approach, till seizing on him by surprize, it tears him to pieces, and then devours him.' Elsewhere the book repeats, or makes oblique references to, common misconceptions such as the relationship between the lion and the jackal, the robin and the wren, and the swan singing at the point of death. It concludes by reprinting essay number sixty-one from *The Guardian* on cruelty to animals. The result is an undoubtedly attractive book, which must have proved popular with children for it was reprinted many times, but there is an overall uncertainty of touch which suggests that Newbery was still feeling his way in 1752, recognising that a market for books of entertainment was developing, but not entirely sure how to cater for it. Later, in *Jackey Dandy's Delight; or, the History of Birds and Beasts, in Verse and Prose*, a booklet inscribed for Margaret Holmes Haskoll in 1788, we see the form repeated, with the text and some illustrations bearing more than a passing resemblance to *A Pretty Book of Pictures...* Published by John Marshall, this little book was pirated by small provincial printers.

But between 1769 and 1788 publishing for children had moved on considerably and this is reflected in several others of the family's books. *The Poetical Flower Garden* (1775), using suitably florid language, is more earnestly didactic with an introductory *Poetical Essay on Flowers*, which are described as 'the favourite work of the eternal Lord.' Although the flowers are used emblematically, and the sentiments are trite, the book is a reflection of the growing interest in gardening for pleasure and the ever-widening range of inexpensive plants which were becoming available in the latter part of the eighteenth century. It is more confident in structure than *A Pretty Book of Pictures...* and comprehensive in coverage, with small workmanlike illustrations of the flowers accompanying each poem. Lydia retained a liking for this kind of simple versifying, copying out poems on snowdrops, robins and swallows into her memorandum books as an adult.

One of the children, probably a granddaughter, also owned an equally unassuming little book, *Spring Flowers; or Easy Lessons for Young Children,* published by John Harris in 1816 and once again theirs is a previously unrecorded copy. The prose text and verses are simple, with very little sentiment attached, and the illustrations are typical of the period and what we have come to expect from this particular publisher. Suitable for a three or four year old it would have been an appropriate book to give to a beginner and entirely compatible with Lydia's taste in children's books.

Sometime before 1802, when some of the children were still at home, the family acquired, either by lease or purchase, Fairfield, a farm a mile or so from Hermitage. From a surviving letter, we know they owned a herd of cows and produced their own milk and cheese, so the children were almost certainly aware of the fate of surplus calves and where the chicken on the table came from. If they were not, then another of the family's books, *Juvenile Rambles Through the Paths of Nature* (after 1786) would have left them in little doubt. Robust and generally unsentimental about animals, the book is an out-and-out piracy of Mrs Trimmer's *An Easy Introduction to the Knowledge of Nature, and Reading the Holy Scriptures* (1780), a fact which upset the good lady more than a little. Mrs T's religious message is considerably diluted and the section on human death omitted, as are the sections on philosophy and physics, but her descriptions of the fate of calves and lambs under the butcher's knife are left in. That the book is based on lessons she gave her own children is confirmation that parents did sometimes tell their children the unvarnished truth. Children were after all frequently reminded of their own mortality and that even 'cordial sleep' was 'to death akin'.

This uncompromising attitude towards domestic beasts does not mean that unnecessary cruelty to animals was condoned. Hunting with dogs and horses was condemned, but the shooting of fox and stag was acceptable. Cruelty towards beasts of burden was totally beyond the pale and creatures which seemed to serve no useful purpose were not to be harmed, for these were a part of God's inscrutable plan and it was not right for a mere human to interfere. Robbing nests and torturing wild animals had no place in this small book.

The background to all of these books is explicitly rural or suburban, but this environment extends to many of the others in the library. *Goody Two-Shoes* is a farmer's daughter and starts out running a hedge school; Sir Toby Thompson, one of the central characters in *The Renowned History of Giles Gingerbread* (1769), lived as a child in 'a little hut upon the green' and his patron is Mr. Allgood, a London merchant who owns a country house; *The Little Moralists* are 'the pretty little shepherd and shepherdess of the vale of Evesham'; *Good Lady Kindheart* lives in 'Hospitable-Hall, near the village of Allgood' and Virtue is found in a cottage. Added to this, most of the illustrations in the books have rural or suburban backdrops and the little shepherd and shepherdess are dressed 'after Watteau'. The rural idyll is alive and well.

It would, of course, be surprising if it were otherwise, for all this is representative of the debate on the relative merits of living in the town or the country. For a significant number, the town represented all the follies and vices of mankind and the country the virtues and a greater closeness to God. The orphan Tommy Two-shoes is attacked and arrested on a London street and some of the vendors in *London Cries* are exemplars of human depravity. In Lydia's *The Cheats of London Exposed* (c1769), a book expressly aimed at young people and the unsophisticated country visitor to London, the message could not be clearer:

> ...the vitiated state of the town, I call it vitiated, because people in general, delight either in the state of obscenity, or nonsensical operas, farces &c. which tend to corrupt and enervate the minds of the rising generation. ... The country life must as far exceed that of the town as health is preferable to sickness, the mind to the body, pleasure to pain, or substance to shadow.

Seen in this light, the choice of an isolated house, high on the downs and an hour or more from Newport, is not merely a statement about social status, but also about finding the right kind of environment for children to grow up in and a way to a more godly life as far as possible from the fleshpots of the town. There is a great deal in the memorandum books to confirm this, in personal statements of intent:

> July 11th 1806: This day 23 years since, I was married, and I hope I can say, with strict truth, that I have endeavour'd to make a good wife and mother, by staying at home, and instilling into the minds of my children the principles of virtue, and religion, what I profess, I have taught them.

and in the books she is reading and copying passages from.

One of these books we know the family owned, but it would be wrong to assume Lydia did not regularly borrow others and that some extracts were not themselves extracted from other books. There are, for example, two very short quotations from Sturm's *Reflections...* and from Catherine Talbot and Elizabeth Carter; all authors she was likely to read, but, unlike much longer entries, Lydia does not mention a specific source.

With this in mind, it is obvious that we cannot reconstruct a library simply from the entries in the manuscript books, but there are several which occupied her over days and even weeks and take up a great deal of space in the memorandum book compiled between 1806 and 1808. One such is Robert Nelson's *A Companion for the Feastivals [sic] and Fasts of the Church of England* (1 ed. 1700 and reprinted many times throughout the century) with one extract taking up twenty pages and another, Richard Lobb's *Contemplative Philosopher* (1800), with fifteen. Lobb's book is very much in tune with Lydia's known interest in natural science and religion with sections typically called 'Reflections on the Modern Art of Gardening', 'Reflections on the Divine Wisdom and Power in the Minuter Parts of Creation' and 'On the Chains of Beings in the Universe'.

Lydia's memorandum books need further study and it is to be hoped that others may eventually come to light, for it is likely that she kept such books throughout her adult life and it is possible she started the practice as a teenager. There are surviving examples of children keeping simple 'moral accounts', and John Newbery produced a little diary for recording good and bad deeds called *The Important Pocket Book* and which was puffed heavily in books owned by Lydia as a child.

As she has been mentioned regularly throughout, it seems fitting to end with Mrs Trimmer and *The Family Magazine*, for its pages encapsulate much that was close to Lydia Haskoll's heart. Published for only a short time, the magazine bears a more than passing resemblance to the *Cheap Repository Tracts* both in content and intention, which was 'to counteract the pernicious tendency of immoral books, &c, which have circulated of late years among the inferior classes of people. To the obstruction of their improvement in religion and morality.' Published in monthly parts, each issue contains poems, a moralising tale usually with a rural background, suitable readings for a Sunday at home, maxims, recipes and gardening hints. All grist to the Haskoll mill. We know Lydia inscribed Margaret's name in the book, so we will leave them, with the child on Lydia's knee or at her feet, reading an improving tale by Sarah Trimmer.

This paper is dedictaed to the memory of David Haskoll
a good and kind friend and true bookman.

NOTES

In preparing this paper the following books have proved most useful:

Leonore Davidoff and Catherine Hall, *Family Fortunes. Men and Women of the English Middle Class 1780-1850* (London: Routledge, 1987).

C Y Ferdinand, *Benjamin Collins and the Provincial Newspaper Trade in the Eighteenth Century* (Oxford: Clarendon Press, 1997).

Michael Mascuch, *Origins of the Individualist Self. Autobiography and Self-Identity in England, 1591-1791* (Cambridge: Polity Press, 1997).

Keith Thomas, *Man and the Natural World. Changing Attitudes in England 1500-1800* (Harmondsworth: Penguin Books, 1984).

Amanda Vickery, *The Gentleman's Daughter. Women's Lives in Georgian England* (New Haven and London: Yale University Press, 1998).

Thanks are due to the following people: Richard Smout and his colleagues at the County Record Office, Newport, Isle of Wight; the staff of the CRO, Trowbridge, Wilts; Clive Hurst, Head of Special Collections, Bodleian Library, Oxford; Colin Harris and his colleagues in room 132; Andrea Immel, Curator of the Cotsen Collection; Win and Trudy Haskell; and finally Heather and David Haskoll and Pamela Martin for their many kindnesses, their generous hospitality and the loan of Haskoll family material.

Print, Privilege and Piracy in the Book of Common Prayer
DAVID N GRIFFITHS

FOR RATHER too many years, I have been trying to work out the bibliography of the *Book of Common Prayer*, that well-known devotional manual which first appeared in 1549, and is still in print 450 years later. The only gaps were for five and a half years in the reign of Queen Mary I, and another fifteen years following the English Civil War. Only in two or three other single years did any new prayer book fail to appear, but with those minor exceptions a continuous series of editions and impressions extends back to the early days of printing.

It was some time before I began to see this as a personal challenge, and even then I came to it in a roundabout way. In the early 1960s my day job concerned overseas religious publishing and I became fascinated by the way in which this most English of books had for various reasons come to be translated into over 200 languages and dialects. The only published work on the subject had come out fifty years before and was seriously out of date. I started to write a new one, but by the time it was nearing completion there was no commercial market for so abstruse a subject. I turned my book into the thesis for a research degree and offered it to the Department of Printing and Graphic Communication at Reading University.[1]

Meanwhile my day job had changed twice and finally faded away. All I had was a modest pension, an unmarketable thesis, and what at first appeared to be endless time. Why not go back to 1549 and work through the English editions as well, so that every printing of the *BCP* (English or foreign) could be recorded within the same pair of covers? The translations had yielded about 1200 books in 200 languages; it was hard to know how many English editions there would be and whether much could be discovered about them beyond the physical evidence of the books themselves and the algebra which could be generated from their descriptions.

The early editions (English and foreign) are already well documented in the latest edition of the *Short Title Catalogue*. Its various extensions cover the next two centuries, but they are progressively less detailed and less complete. I needed some kind of framework to indicate what books ought to exist and how they related to one another.

The arithmetic seems to work out like this:
                1549-1640   350
                1641-1700   230
                1701-1800   850

LIGHT ON THE BOOK TRADE

1801-1860   1180
1861-2000   1000 *
Translations 1200
TOTAL   4810

The figures in the table are estimated numbers of separate issues (whether editions or impressions), and the asterisk * for the final period of English-language books reflects the difficulty of recording undated copies. All these figures include a total of at least 1000 American publications from the (Protestant) Episcopal Church and its sister churches in Brazil and elsewhere (say 950 English-language books and 50 translations). It is probably simpler and safer to reckon on some 5000 'issues' all told.

The records of the two privileged university presses proved to be surprisingly accessible. The relevant archive portions really only began late in the eighteenth century and they took time to interpret. Once an Australian bibliographer had helped me to sort out the eighteenth century, I gradually gained some idea of all the Cambridge and Oxford prayer-book editions from the earliest times until the present day. Many of them have still not come to light, but most of the missing books are impressions from long-running editions which are already known from other examples.

This is less of an achievement that it sounds, because the two universities came on the scene relatively late, when the Kings' and Queens' Printers had already been at work for nearly a century. Fortunately, that period was already well covered by STC, and there are many relevant entries in the successor volumes – but there are no surviving archives – and worse still, no file copies. This used to worry me more than it does now. The Queen's Printers were never a great corporation comparable to the university presses, despite John Baskett's ambition as King's Printer to absorb both Oxford and Cambridge (and even Scotland as well) into a single mighty empire. Cambridge never succumbed, and then after Baskett's death the empire fell apart.

In 1770 the third generation of the Baskett family sold the office of King's Printer for £10 000 to Mr Charles Eyre of Clapham, a Wiltshire gentleman who was not himself a practical printer. Charles Eyre then sold a third share in the patent to William Strahan (Samuel Johnson's printer) for £5000, and also appointed him manager at an annual salary of £300. William's third son Andrew succeeded his father in 1785, and in the King's letters patent of July 1799 the King's Printers are named as John Reeves, George Eyre, and Andrew Strahan. Reeves was an active partner and his was the name that appeared on twenty prayer-book imprints between 1801 and 1815.

Reeves was a publisher rather than a printer, and such firms as Whittingham's Chiswick Press exercised his privilege by proxy. His unconventional prayer books were unlike the publications of a privileged press, in that a commentary was added and some of the contents rearranged. Reeves seemed to be modelling his books on the unofficial editions which were then competing with the official versions. Meanwhile Eyre and Strahan began again to print bibles, and in 1815 they resumed the printing of traditional prayer books. When Strahan retired from active business in 1819, he was succeeded by his nephews Andrew and Robert Spottiswoode. Reeves died in 1829 and Robert Spottiswoode in 1832, after which the firm became Eyre and Spottiswoode, and continued to hold the royal warrant as Queen's Printers until about twelve years ago. They were then taken over by Methuen and finally absorbed by the ominously–named Octopus Group, handing over to Cambridge their nominal status as Printers to the Queen. It all sounds a sad come-down from the occasion in 1894 when Eyre and Spottiswoode lavishly entertained their country cousins from the two universities to a convivial lunch in their London board room. There the three presses agreed on a series of typographical adjustments to standardize the notorious variations between their prayer-book texts. Only seven years later there was a big row when the Lord Chamberlain sent a revised Accession Service to the King's Printers and overlooked the other two (upstart?) presses.

The truth seems to be that, insofar as there was competition among the three presses, the King's Printers had dropped out of the race after John Baskett's death in 1742. First Cambridge, and later Oxford, forged ahead, until in 1774 Eyre and Strahan ceased to print either bibles or prayer books. We have already discussed the partial revival under John Reeves. Eyre and Strahan themselves had resumed prayer-book production in 1815, and in 1849 the firm (by now Eyre and Spottiswoode) even began printing *American* Anglican prayer books for export to the United States. (Oxford and Cambridge do not seem to have begun until 1867 and 1889 respectively.) However, this was all small beer compared with the heroic days before the English Civil War. The then King's Printers (Robert Barker and the assigns of John Bill) had their best year ever in 1639, with sixteen issues, whilst their second best was 1704 with ten. Throughout the nineteenth century their successors were usually a poor third to the two university presses. Cambridge's best year was 1839 with twelve issues, whilst Oxford peaked in 1851 with twenty (which compares with a surprising fifteen Oxford issues as long before as 1682).

There is a possible fallacy here, in that these figures take no account of print runs. Did Eyre and Spottiswoode perhaps print longer runs of fewer books? There is a partial answer to that question, because a parliamentary select committee examined all the privileged presses (including Scotland and Ireland) in 1837. Their reports[2] give comparative tables for all five presses over most years between 1821 and 1836. The output of Eyre and Spottiswoode varied between 33 500 prayer-book copies in 1825 and only 5000 two years later. Cambridge varied between 68 000 copies in

1830 and a mere 10 000 in 1849. Meanwhile Oxford's maximum had been 315 000 prayer books in 1836, as compared with their minimum of 105 000 in 1830.

As to the size of editions, the Stationers' Company had decreed[3] as far back as 1587 that grammars, prayer books, and catechisms might have four impressions annually, each of 2500 or 3000 copies, instead of half those numbers for ordinary books. The full entitlement was not always printed, and it has been suggested that in any case these (fairly generous) preferential limits were intended to apply only to very small books. On the other hand, the tract *Scintilla* of 1641[4] referred specifically to impressions of 'London Common prayers in 24' as being in impressions of 4000, and to folios, quartos, and sixteenmos, all in 3000s. There must have been a startling change in course of the next century because exactly one hundred years later the Cambridge Syndics authorised a printing of 6000 nonpareil prayer books, plus 12 000 services-only to be bound up with bibles.[5] These production figures were to quadruple before the end of the eighteenth century, both at Oxford and at Cambridge, and the advent of the Stanhope press made for another increase that was more noticeable at Oxford than at Cambridge. Thus the number of issues from the three English privileged presses increased from (a statistically convenient) one hundred in the decade 1801-10 to 155 twenty years later and 239 for the 1850s, reducing by about half to 121 in the decade 1861-70. Meanwhile the number of unofficial editions had been rising from eleven in 1801-10 to a peak of forty-four in 1841-50.

Across the Atlantic, the increase began later because the Anglo-American War of 1812 delayed the introduction of stereotypes by about ten years. The corresponding figures from the Episcopal Church rose from twenty-six issues in 1801-10 to 175 in 1841-50, followed again by a falling-off. The world peak year for English-language prayer-books turns out to have been 1850, since when production has steadily declined. In the more esoteric world of foreign-language translations, the peak came as late as 1889, when no fewer than fifteen new versions were published. Other good years were 1876, 1912, 1914, and (surprisingly) 1916, each with fourteen new versions, besides the usual reissues of old ones.

Granted that the text itself has changed little over the centuries, it takes some kind of family tree to demonstrate how far the Book of Common Prayer has mutated in the course of that time, and each national mutation has a history of its own. In terms of sheer numbers, the English text of 1662 has dominated the field, but it has usually been bound up with other material (such as bibles, metrical psalters, and devotional manuals) which has varied from time to time.

The two revolutionary innovations of the original Book of Common Prayer were first that the services were all printed in English (and soon afterwards in such vernacular languages as French and Welsh), and secondly that it contained all the essentials of Christian worship within a single pair of covers. All the essentials but one. Even though about sixty per cent of the words in the prayer book are themselves direct quotations from holy scripture, a bible is still needed for many of the services, especially the daily offices of mattins and evensong (morning and evening prayer). There were no proper composite volumes until 1561, when extracts from Queen Elizabeth's liturgy of 1559 were reissued as prelims to a new edition of the Great Bible of King Henry VIII. These sections were unmentioned on the title page itself, and that same formula was repeated over twenty times, until the first proper 'bible version' was issued by Christopher Barker in 1586.

There is a difference between these early 'composite bibles' and the 'bible versions' which flourished from 1586 until 1906. A bible version is a complete prayer book with its own title page and all the usual contents except for the eucharistic lections of epistles and gospels. References are given so that worshippers can find the scripture passages for themselves in the attached bible, just as they would have had to find the lessons at mattins or evensong. Bible versions were at first printed in quarto, but they soon diversified. In the 1639 *annus mirabilis* of the King's Printers, fifteen out of the sixteen prayer books issued that year were bible versions, of which two were folios, four quartos, six octavos, and three duodecimos. Never again was there to be such a spectacular flowering, although bible versions were a genre that continued to flourish for many years. The last formal bible version was issued in 1833 by the Oxford press in a long-running series in nonpareil octavo, officially described as *prayers* and *Tate for ruby bible* and it ran with minor changes (such as dropping Tate's metrical psalms) until 1879. The plates were scrapped in 1906. Combined volumes continued to appear until well within living memory, usually on an *ad hoc* basis as office books for the clergy. One Oxford example comprised a ruby 32mo bible with a bourgeois bold-face prayer book bound between the Old Testament and the apocrypha; all printed on india paper.

I promised you some idea of the stylistic changes. One way in which compiling a bibliography differs from cataloguing a library is that very few of the books can be in front of you at any one time and you must depend on your notes, only to find that the earliest ones were made before you knew what questions to ask. Thus there have been many missed opportunities, especially over typography. The earliest editions were all printed in black letter, and the first use of roman type was in 1586. Black letter dominated larger formats until after the Restoration and then faded away (last appearing in 1709).

Dates usually appeared on title pages from 1549 until after 1860, but the first time that arabic numerals appeared there was in 1620. On the other hand, the early editions of 1662 had the psalms numbered in arabic, and afterwards reverted to roman figures until the end of the nineteenth century. In principle it might have been possible to work out the dates (or ranges of dates) when the 'long s' was abandoned or catchwords disappeared, but each transition may well have taken so long that the information would be of little use.

There was a curious reluctance to number the pages of the text. Two possible reasons suggest themselves, either or both of which may be true. One is that printers liked to issue abridged editions, and the other is that they also liked to remedy gaps in the text by using sheets from other editions (usually of smaller type) where the paper was compatible and of roughly the same size. This was especially true of large formats, which were made up for churches on an almost bespoke basis. Whatever the reason, the absence of pagination makes editions harder to describe and leads to vague entries in library catalogues.

Even within the prayer book itself the contents have never been immutable. The services for Gunpowder Treason, King Charles the Martyr, and the Restoration of the Royal Family (commemorated on 29 May or 'Oak Apple Day') were included from 1662 until 1859, although never strictly part of the prayer book. Nor is the table of kindred and affinity, which was someone's bright idea in 1681, and is still included. The traditional service of 'touching for the King's Evil' dated back to King Edward the Confessor. It did not appear in the prayer book until 1706 (headed *At the Healing*) but disappeared in 1732 because the Hanoverian monarchs were unsure whether the requisite spiritual gifts had descended to their branch of the royal family.

Then there were (indeed, are) such items as the various Acts of Uniformity and *The Constitutions and Canons of the Church*, usually omitted from the smaller formats. The ordinal (or ordination of bishops, priests and deacons) had always existed but was only formally included in the prayer book in 1662. It disappeared from small and medium-sized prayer books because such services only took place in the private chapels of bishops. One by-product of the Oxford Movement was that ordinations became great public occasions which ought to be seen and understood by lay church people. Similarly, the unofficial editions in particular tended to reflect eighteenth-century custom by playing down the importance of holy communion. It was either printed in small type, like the commination service and the churching of women, or divided into two parts with (say) long primer type up to and including the creed, and nonpareil thereafter, corresponding to an iniquitous custom whereby the choral part of the service ended then, when the choir and all but a holy few marched out. That custom disappeared when the unofficial editions went into decline.

There is a surviving catalogue of Cambridge books for March 1838, on the very eve of their peak year for prayer-book production. It lists twenty-one items, ranging from a diamond fortyeightmo to double pica folio. Closely examined, these entries shrink to seventeen basic prayer books, slightly multiplied by the sizes and qualities of paper used for the same setting of type. There are one or two Oxford catalogues dating from the very early nineteenth century and then nothing until 1883, by which time prayer-book publishing was in the doldrums. Oxford 1883 appears to offer twice as many basic items, inflated again by a generous choice of qualities and bindings, but the true range is much the same as Cambridge 1838. The only difference is that most of the Oxford list was on offer with or without red rubrics. None was formally listed by Cambridge in 1838, although they certainly existed for copies in great primer.

Within the history of the Book of Common Prayer, the term 'rubric' does not appear to have been taken literally (to mean that liturgical directions were printed in red) until an Oxford eighteenmo of 1826. Earlier editions had been 'rubricated', meaning simply that parts of the title page and prelims had been picked out in red, either printed or added by pen and ink. Oxford in 1883 was offering a choice of thirteen formats printed in red and black (ranging again from diamond fortyeightmo up to double pica folio) and nineteen formats in black-only, covering the same size-range with more stopping-places. These were supplemented by a wide variety of special books such as proper lessons and church services in various formats, with or without borders in red. Much of this list might well have been made up with surplus stock left over from the boom years which faded away after 1861. Perhaps that is why the privileged presses gave up dating their title pages in the mid-1860s. It is only possible to place undated prayer books very roughly if they came out between (say) 1865 and 1870, when they were still issued as they had been since 1801, in the name of the 'United Church of England and Ireland'. (Irish disestablishment dissolved that union, and for the next thirty years there were no changes in the prayer for the royal family.)

Irish disestablishment also ended the involvement of the Queen's Printer General for Ireland, and in due course the new Church of Ireland prayer book was issued first by the (Irish) Association for Promoting Christian Knowledge (APCK), and later by the Church itself. For most of the eighteenth century, the Irish BCP had been printed in Dublin by successive generations of the Grierson family, who were still in office as King's Printers at the time of the first parliamentary enquiry in 1832. This recorded a range of formats from thirtytwomo up to quarto, issued in small impressions of 3-5000 copies, and at the leisurely rate of one new impression every other year. Four new impressions were said to have been in the press at the time of the enquiry. In the absence of detailed figures it is hard to be sure, but the surviving copies from earlier years seem to show that this was an average to good rate of Irish production, even if it failed to achieve the occasional folios and bible versions of the previous century.

These two parliamentary enquiries had arisen because of mounting complaints about the King's Printers for Scotland, Sir David Hunter Blair and John Bruce.[6] Most of these complaints concerned their monopoly of Scottish bible printing, which had become unduly expensive. Their prayer books were also thought to be expensive. The range of formats was wider than their Irish counterparts, but not all were in print. Their royal letters patent (for both bibles and prayer books) were due to expire in 1839, and perhaps the prayer-book privilege alone might have been renewed but for an unfortunate mishap in 1830. The printers had very properly reissued their pica octavo prayer book with state prayers for the new king and queen, William IV and Adelaide of Saxe-Coburg Meiningen, but they forgot to replace the royal warrant for King George IV which continued to appear at the opposite end of the book.

There was certainly no suggestion that the select committee ever acted with undue haste. In seven years they issued two reports and collected many useful statistics, no doubt feeling in those days of the 1832 Reform Bill that it was time not only to respond to specific grievances, but also to review the effectiveness of ancient and profitable monopolies. Nothing happened to affect the English privileged presses, nor to the Queen's Printer for Ireland. The Scottish appointment was however put into commission, when the crown issued letters patent to a new body known as the Bible Board. This consisted of the Lord Advocate and the Moderator of the General Assembly of the (Presbyterian) Church of Scotland, together with a handful of nominated members, who collectively held the appointment of Her Majesty's Sole and Master Printers for Scotland.

These master printers printed nothing at all, but anyone who wished to print a bible, a Book of Common Prayer, or even a catechism for use in Scotland had to submit each edition to be licensed by the Bible Board, which demanded sample copies and then examined them line by line with Caledonian rigour. In its early days, several firms regularly applied for licences to print the BCP; the former Queen's Printers did not apply. The number of applicants dwindled after 1867 and had altogether ceased by 1881. In 1890 the prayer book was removed from the list of works that required licensing. Thus it is slightly surprising to discover that well before that date, in 1862, William Collins of the firm now known as Harper Collins, had begun to style himself 'Queen's Printer for Scotland.'[7]

No one thought this odd in the topsy-turvy world of Scottish church publishing, where Presbyterian dignitaries had royal authority to approve or reject Anglican liturgies. Nor did it seem odd that the books at issue were not specifically Scottish liturgies at all but copies of the old familiar English Book of Common Prayer. The historic Scottish liturgy did exist and had in fact been adopted by the American Episcopal Church, but it was not in regular Sunday use among Scottish episcopaleans until after 1929.

Small wonder then that Scottish printings of the English prayer book tended to seep across the border and undercut the more stylish and expensive products of the three English privileged presses. No one really minded their circulating in Northumberland and Cumberland, but the seepage caused grave offence when it reached the streets of London. Since this source was better funded and organised, it was probably more of a threat to the establishment than all the pirate publications of English provincial presses. I discovered this fascinating byway of prayer-book history about two years ago and I have only tracked down a few of the Scottish bible-board editions that came out between 1840 and 1890. The others are certainly not in the National Library of Scotland, but might well be in the libraries of Scottish universities and provincial cities, not to mention second-hand bookshops. It is a sound rule that any book can turn up anywhere at any time, but there does seem to be a direct correlation between mileage from London and the likelihood of finding something interesting and affordable on bookshop shelves. Even so, there are fewer old prayer books around than when I began, and I can't make out whether the appearance of a bibliography will coax more treasures out of granny's attic on to one's own shelves, or drive them away via the sale rooms into the bank vaults of millionaires.

Peter Isaac kindly gave me space in two successive issues of *Quadrat*[8] to try out a draft list of those eighteenth and nineteenth century private-enterprise editions of the prayer book. Various helpful suggestions have come along, and amendments to my list might justify a future mini-article summing up the additions and subtractions. Most of the subtractions are removals of putative dates which turned out to be wrong. There is no better way of creating ghost entries in a bibliography than taking up the theoretical dates put forward over the years for books that were either undated from the start or lost their title pages through excessive wear and tear.

I began by trying to define the unofficial editions. It seemed best to exclude publications by the King's Printers for Scotland and Ireland, and by nominees of the King's Printers for England (frequent between 1800 and 1820); Welsh editions printed in Shrewsbury and elsewhere; antiquarian versions of (say) 1549 and other early editions, and prayer books in shorthand. I also omitted those editions reformed to the *plan of the late Samuel Clarke,* which was an Unitarian variation on the prayer-book theme. There were still 216 books on the list, and one or two categories began to stand out. One is the number of editions (dare I say 'like the one by William Davison of Alnwick'?) produced by well-loved provincial printers to show that they were capable of something more demanding than the jobbing work that was their normal bread and butter. There are also such titles as *A New and Correct edition... of the Book of Common Prayer... in which certain alterations and amendments are most humbly offered by a priest of the same church.* You have to read with close attention to discover what the amendments were *for*. Was the compiler a crypto-Unitarian or a crypto-Methodist, or an orthodox Anglican who merely thought that the existing book could be made more user-friendly by a bit of rearrangement or simplification?

Nothing dismissive was implied by the exclusion of 'antiquarian versions of other early editions' for they later came to be of special significance. The first flurry of interest in Anglican liturgical history occurred between the last days of Oliver Cromwell and the appearance of the 1662 prayer book. For many years the only comparative study of the earlier books was that written in 1659 by Hamon L'Estrange, *The Alliance of Divine Offices*, even though L'Estrange died almost at once and no one bothered to bring his book up to date in any of the three subsequent editions. It was perhaps another by-product of the Oxford Movement that in 1844 William Pickering published an authoritative modern luxury edition of seven historic English prayer books, ranging from 1549 to 1662, including Merbecke's *Book of Common Prayer Noted* (1550) and the Scottish Book of 1637. This seemed to open the floodgates and after that scarcely a year passed without some scholarly or quasi-scholarly edition of past liturgies from the Reformation onwards.

Just about then, the ancient but dormant Convocations of the Church of England revived and began to transact actual business; Canterbury in 1852 and York in 1861. Within another ten years they had successfully introduced one or two modest adjustments to make church services less tedious. Daring spirits who had read the historic liturgies were beginning to rediscover the forgotten glories of past worship and to realise that even the 1662 prayer book had its limitations. By the end of the nineteenth century, when the demand for cheap unofficial prayer books was being more easily satisfied from Scotland rather than English provincial presses, prayer-book reform began to sound both desirable and even feasible. Not only had the American Episcopal Church produced its own version of the prayer book as recently as 1790, but it was planning to issue a centenary revision in 1892. Anglo-Catholics, Evangelicals, and Modernists all wanted to influence future liturgical reform. However, the Church of England would first need some degree of self-government.

This appeared to have come in 1920 as an unexpected by-product of the disestablishment of the church in Wales. The new Church Assembly spent several years reviewing the possibilities and finally adopted a conservative revision of 1662. However, it was to be another fifty years before the Church Assembly (or rather, its successor the General Synod) could legislate for worship without the need for specific parliamentary approval of every detail. The new book was rejected in 1928 by an alliance of non-Anglican Members of Parliament with evangelical allies from within the Church of England. They had taken particular exception to changes in the service of holy communion, especially the provision for reservation of the blessed sacrament for the communion of the sick.

By that time the Americans had revised their book yet again, and the Canadian and Scottish churches had launched new books of their own. All that the poor English bishops could do was agree to ignore Parliament and *deem* the new book to have been passed, so that in practice (and with due safeguards) parishes could act as though it were. This Gilbertian compromise eased the constraints of the 1662 prayer book for another two generations, and into what was effectively a new world.

After 1965, Vatican Two had opened up new ways of worship to a far larger and even more conservative world church than any of part of the world-wide Anglican Communion, and the repercussions affected Christian worship everywhere. The time for antiquarian models was past, and it was already too late for cosmetic amendments to 1662. The cry for radical reform was influenced by quite other models, including non-liturgical worship and fresh interpretations of holy scripture. Within the Church of England its results were seen first in the *Alternative Service Book* of 1980 and more recently in *Common Worship* 2000 (which at least includes a few prayer-book services). The only solace for traditionalists is that the Book of Common Prayer is still protected by Act of Parliament to the limited extent that it remains what might be called 'legal tender' in Anglican worship and is still issued by the two surviving privileged presses.

NOTES

1. W J Muss-Arnolt, *The Book of Common Prayer Among the Nations of the World* (London: Society for Promoting Christian Knowledge, 1914).
2. House of Commons, *Report from the Select Committee on King's Printers' Patents, with the minutes of evidence* and *appendix, session 1881-2* (718). Appendix D, 335-345. *Report from the Select Committee appointed to inquire into the nature and extent* of *the King's Printers' Patent in Scotland, session* 1887 (511), 52-56.
3. Marjorie Plant, *The English Book Trade* (3 ed. London: Allen & Unwin, 1974), 92 and following.

4. A S Herbert, *Historical Catalogue of Printed Bibles* (London: British and Foreign Bible Society, 1968), 185.

5. David McKitterick, *A History of Cambridge University Press,* vol. 2 (1698-1872) (Cambridge: University Press, 1998), 184 and following.

6. Leslie Howsam, *Cheap Bibles: Nineteenth-Century Publishing and the Bible Society,* (Cambridge: University Press, 1991), 112 and following. See also note 2 above.

7. David Keir, *The House of Collins; the story of a Scottish family of publishers* (London: Collins, 1952), 169 n1.

8. Peter Isaac [ed] *Quadrat; a periodical bulletin of research ...on the British book trade,* 12 and 13 (2001).

John Gregory and the 'Leicester Journal'

JOHN HINKS

THE EIGHTEENTH-CENTURY provincial press has been reassessed in recent years and its amateurish 'scissors-and-paste' image has given way to a more positive view. Many editors, at least prior to the political polarisation of the press in response to the French Revolution, worked with considerable professionalism, selecting appropriate items from the London news and designing their papers with some care in order to reflect, and sometimes also to shape, public opinion on national and local issues. The economic position of the larger provincial papers has also been reconsidered:

> It seems likely that producing a paper capable of securing a readership large enough to make a profit was no easy task, but one which demanded entrepreneurial flair combined with a sensitivity towards local opinion.[1]

One provincial editor of considerable skill and success was John Gregory, founder of the *Leicester Journal*, the town's first newspaper.[2] He was not the first printer in Leicester but he was apparently the first to print books in the town and was certainly its first newspaper publisher.[3]

John Gregory was born in Derbyshire in 1727 and probably came to Leicester in 1752: he was made free on 26 May of that year as a 'stranger'.[4] He perhaps saw his move to Leicester as a significant business opportunity, realising that Leicester was lagging behind other comparable towns in not yet having its own newspaper.[5] In the nineteenth century James Thompson, the local historian and newspaper publisher, lauded the *Journal* as one of the 'improvements' which had benefited Leicester in the middle years of the previous century. Noting the huge growth in the town's population (it had doubled in fifty years from 4500 to more than 9000) Thompson observes that Leicester

> rapidly emerging from the dullness and slowness of the small market town to a state more important... had established a kind of fire brigade, erected a new exchange and new assembly rooms, attempted to procure a lighting and watching act, and was promoting the formation of turnpike roads; it next encouraged Mr. John Gregory to commence a weekly newspaper. On May 12, 1753, he accordingly issued No. I of the *Leicester Journal*...[6]

Although early issues of the *Journal* no longer survive, it is fortunate that James Thompson had access to them.[7] He records that the first issue (12 May 1753) contained only four advertisements and was priced at two-pence. In common with most early newspapers, the *Journal* claimed to be politically neutral but in reality took a Tory line and was usually, though not invariably, pro-Corporation.

Thompson describes it as an average provincial newspaper, using rather 'quaint' language and containing mostly London news although some local news was reported:
> It helped, however, to bring to light some of the smaller incidents happening in the town and neighbourhood, which would be considered beneath what is called 'the dignity of history'.[8]

On 8 November 1755 the *Journal* carried the following notice:
> John Gregory of Leicester, and Samuel Cresswell of Nottingham, Printers: take this Method of acquainting the Public that by the Advice of their Friends, they have lately enter'd into Partnership in the Mystery of Printing, and that they are determined to publish this Weekly Paper early every Saturday Morning, at their respective Shops in Leicester and Nottingham... [9]

The paper, now entitled *The Leicester and Nottingham Journal*, was run by Gregory and Cresswell in partnership until the latter withdrew in 1769. Despite continuing as *The Leicester and Nottingham Journal* until 1787 it had in reality always been a Leicester paper, carrying little Nottingham news or advertising.[10] The *Journal* is known to have circulated in Nottingham before the partnership between Gregory and Cresswell was set up: in September 1753 Samuel Cresswell was summoned before the Nottingham magistrates for selling the *Leicester Journal*.[11] Without such independent evidence, it can be difficult to ascertain the circulation areas of individual papers; their claims to wide circulation may have been exaggerated in order to attract advertising. In the early part of the eighteenth century the few provincial newspapers circulated over wider areas than later when there was more competition, though the quantity distributed far afield may always have been relatively small. The circulation of the *Northampton Mercury* (founded in 1720) declined in this way: 'It reached its peak about 1740, but then was challenged by the *Cambridge Journal*, the *Coventry Mercury*, the *Oxford Journal* and the *Leicester Journal*.'[12]

> Provincial newspaper circulation did not follow a neat pattern showing individual newspaper 'spheres of influence', but an extremely complicated arrangement. In the Midlands at least, no paper could lay claim to an area which was not encroached upon significantly by other papers and did not itself trespass upon the territory of its neighbours.[13]

This is certainly true of Leicester, where other newspapers circulated before and after Gregory commenced the *Journal*. The *Cambridge Chronicle* for example was distributed by newsmen to Leicester, to other towns in the Midlands and East Anglia and as far afield as York, Newcastle and Carlisle.[14] Leicester people wishing to read the news had an alternative source of supply: they could subscribe to the London papers. In 1777 the *Journal* carried an advertisement for a Mr A Norman 'at Mr.

Leece's' in Sweeting's Alley, Cornhill. He could supply a range of newspapers to subscribers, for example the *Daily Advertiser* at £3.18s.0d. per annum on credit (£3.5s.0d. for ready money), the *Westminster Gazette* at £1.16s.0d. (£1.10s.0d.), weekly papers at 18s. 0d. (15s.0d.), even the *Courier de l'Europe* at £2.15s.0d.[15]

The distribution of a newspaper across a wide area involved agents in a number of towns and a rare piece of evidence for this practice survives in a 1770 copy of the *Leicester and Nottingham Journal* in the collection of Nottingham City Library. Along the bottom of all four pages an agent has added closely-written notes to Gregory. The agent is not identified but was probably a Mr Saunders who traded in Derby and Ashbourne. He complains, not for the first time, about an incorrect invoice:

> Mr. Gregory, Sir... I must again earnestly caution ag[ains]t the carelessness of your Servants. I rec[eive]d 45 stamped Papers & only one blank. I wish you would direct that Mr. Bladon's Papers be <u>always sent open</u> with mine as it is less trouble to me to take account of them so when separately packed. P[lease] to observe this.

He also refers to the practice of subscriptions being collected by agents:

> You will not advise me about unsettled Customers. Why will you not? I rec[eive]d an Additional Subscriber yesterday at Ashborne & promise of another soon so that my Quarterly Customers are now increased to 25. You must charge me for 26 instead of 25 Papers yesterday, by which you see I have 3 remaining, the present one and two others...

The distribution of papers through a network of agents in distant places must often have been as troublesome as this piece of evidence indicates. Another of the marginal notes suggests that meetings between Gregory and his agents were infrequent 'We agreed to meet at Loughboro' the beginning of August which is near, if you have any intention to do so pray signify it in your next.' Yet another of the notes in this issue of the *Journal* indicates that agents also passed on complaints and comments from other book-trade people: 'Mr. Roome has intimated that the Price of Arnold's Psalms which is 4s. only in the Cat. sh[oul]d be 4:6... Please inform your Brethren of this and alter the list accordingly....' In a more positive vein, the agent adds:

> It is with singular pleasure that I transmit to you the following short Advertisement for which I have rec[eive]d 3s 6d and [ask] you to put it in the most conspicuous place of your next paper – To be sold, a Tobacco-Engine, A Press, A Good Iron Screw, A Flatting Mill, and Thirty Two Boxes, all in Good Condition... [16]

At the same period, Gregory requested that advertisements should reach the printing office by 4 p.m. on Fridays, adding that those from Nottingham, Derby, Sheffield or towns further north, if given to his agents or 'put into the Post Office' by Thursday, would be inserted in that Saturday's paper. He also planned to expand the paper's circulation northwards by appointing agents and attracting advertising in the Sheffield area where the *Journal* already sells 'several Hundreds' of copies.[17] The area of the *Journal*'s circulation is indicated in a typical issue from 1787 which informs us that advertising and other material was accepted by agents who delivered the paper in several Leicestershire towns, in Nottingham (two), Derby (two), Sheffield, Rotherham, Bakewell, Chesterfield, Mansfield, Wirksworth, Tideswell, Ashbourne, Uttoxeter and Burton, and also

> by the printers of the other country papers and by the news-men who distribute this paper. Also in London at Peel's, London, and Chapter Coffee Houses, and by Mr. Tyler, Warwick Court, St Paul's Churchyard.

The same issue also notes that 'Every Saturday a Newsman sets out from the Printing Office in Leicester for Hinckley, Nuneaton and Atherstone, where this paper is delivered early on that day.'[18]

There is no certainty that Gregory originally printed the *Journal* himself as earlier issues bear the imprint 'Printed for J. Gregory....'. Although he was certainly printing by 1755, the *Journal* dated 7 January 1758 is the first to carry Gregory's own imprint: 'Printed by J. Gregory in the Market-Place, Leicester'.[19] It is not known who printed the *Journal* before Gregory.[20] Although Gregory's printing capacity must largely have been taken up with the weekly production of the *Journal*, plus some jobbing work, he did print a number of books of which a dozen or so survive. He certainly advertised himself as a printer: the imprint of the *Journal* usually included words such as 'printing in general executed with neatness and precision'.[21] Gregory also offered a binding service, advertising in 1763: 'At J. Gregory's bookseller in Leicester is constantly kept a bookbinder, a very good workman where gentlemen may have any business of that kind done completely and expeditiously.'[22]

John Gregory is significant as Leicester's first known printer of books, his earliest extant book dating from 1755.[23] Gregory's books are competently printed and represent the standard fare of the eighteenth-century provincial printer: poll-books, sermons, essays and devotional works, mostly by local authors, as well as the libretti of some of Handel's oratorios, probably in connection with local performances.[24] He also printed his own book-sale catalogues, of which three have survived.[25] Gregory had close links with the local author John Throsby (1740-1803) who wrote and illustrated several important works on Leicestershire history and topography.[26] Gregory was also involved in the publication of the second edition of another work on Leicestershire, William Burton's *The Description of Leicestershire, containing matters of antiquity, history, armoury and genealogy*, published in 1777.[27] In the same year, Gregory was involved in an abortive attempt to publish a new edition of Thoroton's *The History and Antiquities of Nottinghamshire*.[28]

Gregory's own advertisements in the *Journal* are a rich source of evidence for his goods and services. The range of his stock is typical of a provincial bookseller of the latter half of the eighteenth century: books on a wide range of subjects, part-publications, maps, printed music, almanacs, periodicals, lottery tickets, stationery and other goods. The popularity of the theatre in eighteenth-century Leicester is reflected in the periodicals he sold, including several which printed a complete play in each issue, such as the *Theatrical Magazine*.[29] The fiftieth issue of *New English Theatre* included a play entitled 'The City Wives' Confederacy' as well as a portrait of David Garrick and other engravings, all for sixpence.[30] Like many booksellers, Gregory sold, and may have printed, theatre tickets. Theatrical performances, concerts and recitals were advertised frequently in the *Journal* with Gregory often named as a supplier of tickets. Although willing to make money from selling theatrical periodicals and tickets, he disapproved of such 'frivolities' – the *Journal* was severely critical of 'theatricals' and recommended, as an alternative to the vulgar habit of theatregoing, a fencing master for men and a dancing master for ladies.[31] Other forms of entertainment such as cockfighting were sometimes advertised: in 1777 the *Journal* carried an announcement from a gentleman who was planning to 'fight a main of cocks'. Although he wished not to be named, 'any real gentleman, on application to Mr. Gregory the printer will be informed who the person is', which suggests that he was trusted to appraise enquirers.[32]

The typical eighteenth-century provincial bookshop sold a wide variety of goods and the columns of the *Leicester Journal* abound with Gregory's advertisements for household items, agricultural products and a huge range of patent medicines.[33] Stationery features infrequently in Gregory's advertisements, though in 1769 he advertised that he intended 'to sell in the future all kinds of stamp paper, parchment &c. Also the Licences upon exactly the same terms as the stamp office'.[34] A composite advertisement for various goods includes patent ink cakes and black, red and white lead pencils, all at sixpence.[35] As well as advertising the various goods he sold, Gregory also publicised a wide range of services in the *Journal*. Employment advertising was prominent, both situations vacant and wanted, though advertisers' names and addresses were seldom disclosed, leaving Gregory to act as an intermediary, providing further details of vacancies or putting applicants in touch with employers. It is possible that Gregory carried out an initial appraisal of enquirers on behalf of his advertisers: if they were unwilling to disclose their names in the columns of the *Journal* it is unlikely that they would have permitted their details to be given out to any casual enquirer at the printing office without some degree of vetting. The range of employment advertising is typical of the period: apprentices and journeymen in various trades, curacies and a range of domestic service. Advertisements placed by people seeking work were far fewer than those for vacancies, though young clergymen advertised quite frequently. One, optimistically seeking 'a curacy or two', preferably with a house, wished offers be addressed to 'A.B' at Gregory's printing office. The printer could supply details of a young man 'bred a grocer' who was seeking work, while a youth of fifteen advertised for a master 'in any creditable business' though, having some knowledge of Latin, he preferred a surgeon or apothecary.[36]

Military recruitment advertising was carried by the *Journal* from time to time, for example:

> Wanted: a sightly young fellow to serve in a marching regiment of foot, now in England – Twelve guineas will be given to any young man approved of for this service, and one guinea will be given exclusive to any person bringing such a man to the printer of this paper.[37]

Again it is possible that Gregory vetted potential recruits and paid those introducing them. In any case he must have been involved in some paperwork, at least keeping a record of each applicant and his introducer to pass on to the regiment. Whatever his role as an agent in any way for advertisers, Gregory surely gained a decent income from the abundant employment advertising placed in the *Journal*. Advertisements for real estate – houses, inns, shops etc., for sale and to let – appeared from time to time with details sometimes obtainable from Gregory. Charitable appeals publicised in the *Journal* included a case in which Gregory took a personal interest in 1777: the child of a poor woman who had died following a caesarean. The baby, named Julius Caesar, was healthy but funds were needed for his care:

> The child is placed under a careful nurse and the donations of the charitable will be received by the printer of this paper for his use, who will also see that they are properly applied... Many thanks are due for subscriptions already received, particularly to a lady who was so kind as to send a guinea.[38]

Gregory was able to announce two months later that six and a half guineas had been subscribed.[39] From time to time, 'lost and found' advertisements appeared in the *Journal*, such as a lost £20 banknote ('whoever brings it to the printer of this paper shall receive two guineas reward') and Gregory was even prepared to take in a lost dog: anyone finding a white pointer answering to the name of Sancho would receive a reward of five shillings upon delivering him to the printing office.[40] On the delicate matter of 'concealed pregnancy' Gregory could supply the address of a London surgeon, Mr J White, whose services were 'worthy the perusal of ladies whose situation requires a temporary retirement'. The 'man-midwife' was located in St Paul's Churchyard (better known as a centre of bookselling!) though his exact address was obtainable from Gregory only upon payment of a shilling.[41]

John Gregory ran a sizeable and thriving business, advertising from time to time for both apprentices and journeymen; twelve apprentices were bound to him at various times.[42] One of Gregory's apprentices, Francis Hodson, went on to become an important printer and the publisher of the *Cambridge Chronicle*. Upon being made free in 1762 Hodson went to Cambridge, where he seems to have traded until he died in 1812, his son taking over the business.[43] John Gregory's elder son, also John, inherited his father's business when he died in 1789. The later history of the *Journal* has been told elsewhere and is merely summarised here.[44] The younger John made the paper more overtly Tory than it had been in his father's time and when he died without issue in 1806 his brother-in-law, John Price, already a partner in the *Journal*, became sole proprietor, making the paper even more politically extreme. Price changed its title to *The Leicester Journal and Midland Counties Advertiser*, perhaps in the hope of improving circulation and advertising revenue. The *Journal* appears by this time to have been a freestanding enterprise and there is no further evidence for the other parts of the bookselling and printing business established by John Gregory. He also had a younger son, Joseph, who became vicar of St Martin's and All Saints, Leicester, and a daughter, Fanny, who married John Price. Joseph's sons, Thomas and John, both became printers, the latter being apprenticed to his uncle, the younger John Gregory, after his father died in 1802.[45]

It has been suggested that provincial newspaper proprietors tended not to become part of the urban élite until the mid-nineteenth century.[46] However it is clear that John Gregory was one of Leicester's leading eighteenth-century citizens and businessmen: he served for many years on the Corporation, became an Alderman and served a term as Chamberlain and a year as Mayor.[47] Gregory devoted himself zealously to the interests of the town and was instrumental in the foundation of the Leicester Infirmary, of which he became Treasurer. He died while in London for discussions on 'the navigation and commerce of the Town of Leicester'.[48]

John Gregory dominated the book trade in Leicester from the mid-eighteenth century until the 1770s when competitors began to establish bookselling and printing businesses of comparable size. There is ample evidence that he ran a successful and diverse book-trade business, the largest that Leicester had seen up to his day, but his chief contribution to the town was perhaps his introduction of its first newspaper. Gregory's prominent role in the affairs of the Borough and his various charitable activities, not least his tireless work for the Leicester Infirmary, suggest that he was a man of considerable ability and good character. John Nichols wrote of Gregory:

His behaviour through life, as a tradesman, husband, father, and as a magistrate, he discharged with such openness of heart and upright conduct, that his loss will be long felt and regretted by a large circle of friends and acquaintances.[49]

ACKNOWLEDGEMENTS

I am very grateful to Diana Dixon for her helpful comments on a draft of this chapter, which has its origins in my doctoral research at Loughborough University on the book-trade history of Leicester to *c*1850. I wish to record my thanks also to Professor John Feather for his thorough and inspirational supervision of my PhD studies.

NOTES

1. Hannah Barker, 'Catering for provincial tastes: newspapers, readership and profit in late eighteenth-century England', *Historical Research*, 69 (1996), 42-61, (43). Dr Barker is an advocate of the 'revisionist' approach to the provincial press. See especially her *Newspapers, Politics and English Society, 1695-1855* (Harlow, 2000); also chapter six of Jeremy Black, *The English Press 1621-1861* (Stroud, 2001).

2. In the interests of brevity, Gregory's newspaper is referred to throughout as the *Leicester Journal* or simply the *Journal*, although it was entitled the *Leicester and Nottingham Journal* between November 1755 and February 1787. In common with other provincial papers of the period, the *Leicester Journal* was a weekly paper; there would not be a daily paper in the town until the *Leicester Daily Post* commenced in 1872.

3. Printing arrived slightly later in Leicester than in many other comparable provincial towns. Matthew Unwin, a small-scale bookseller, stationer and printer, introduced printing in 1740 or 1741 and traded until his death in 1750. He is not known to have printed any books other than a single extant book-sale catalogue dated 1743. (ESTC: t119047, British Library 1607/2597.)

4. John Nichols, *The History and Antiquities of the County of Leicester* (1815, reprinted Wakefield, 1971), 1 (pt. 2), 587-8. Henry Hartopp [ed] *Register of the Freemen of Leicester 1197-1770, including the Apprentices sworn before successive Mayors for certain periods, 1646-1770* (Leicester, 1927), 287.

5. By 1750 a number of provincial towns of less importance than Leicester had their own newspapers as did several Midlands towns: Nottingham since 1712 (two during the 1730s), Stamford (1713), Northampton (1720), Derby (1732), Coventry and Birmingham (both 1741). R M Wiles, *Freshest Advices: early provincial newspapers in England* (Columbus, Ohio, 1965), Appendix B (chronological chart).

6. James Thompson, *The History of Leicester in the Eighteenth Century* (Leicester, 1871), 82.

7. The British Library file commences with issue number 297, 6 January 1759. The Record Office for Leicestershire, Leicester and Rutland has a microfilm of the BL file and does not hold any earlier copies of the *Journal*.

8. Thompson, *History of Leicester*, 83.

9. *Leicester Journal*, 8 November 1755.

10. The issue dated 3 February 1787 reverts to the title *Leicester Journal* and has a redesigned masthead. The *Leicester and Nottingham Journal* aimed to compete with the *Weekly Courant* which had commenced in Nottingham in 1712.

11. The cause of offence was that the *Journal's* vigorous resistance to the Jewish Naturalisation Bill was deemed by the magistrates to be in opposition to the Government. G.A. Cranfield, *The Development of the Provincial Newspaper* (Oxford, 1962), 146; Wiles, *Freshest Advices*, 58-9.

12. Cranfield, *Provincial Newspaper*, 205.

13. Barker, 'Catering for provincial tastes', 55.

14. *Cambridge Chronicle*, 27 November 1762. Quoted in Cranfield, *Provincial Newspaper*, 202.

15. *Leicester Journal*, 15 February 1777.

16. *Leicester Journal*, 28 July 1770. Copy in Nottingham City Library Local History Department. The manuscript notes are partially lost where the edge of the paper has crumbled. Bladon was Gregory's agent in Uttoxeter; Roome was a bookseller in Derby.

17. *Leicester Journal*, 3 March 1770.

18. *Leicester Journal*, 10 February 1787. The Leicestershire agents were in Loughborough, Ashby de la Zouch, Market Harborough, Hinckley and Lutterworth.

19. *Leicester Journal*, 7 January 1758.

20. W H Allnutt, 'English Provincial Presses', *Bibliographica*, 7 [1900/01], 276-308, (303), states that the *Journal* was said to have been originally printed in London. This suggestion is not attributed and no evidence to support it has been found.

21. This example: *Leicester Journal*, 3 February 1787.

22. *Leicester Journal*, 1 January 1763.

23. The earliest surviving book printed by Gregory is the anonymous political work *Faction Unmask'd...*(1755). ESTC: t186068. Bodleian Library: Vet.A.5.e4385.

24. *Messiah* (1760?), *Esther* and *Judas Maccabeus* (both 1761), *Jephtha* (1774).

25. *A Catalogue of the Genuine and Curious Library; of the late Reverend Mr. John Jackson...* (1764), ESTC: t164114, Munby Collection, Cambridge University Library: Munby d.5^6. *A Catalogue of Books, now selling at the prices printed, at the shop of J. Gregory...* (1779), ESTC: t074573, British Library: 128.K.10 (3). *A Catalogue of the Library of the late Dr Richard Bentley, Rector of Nailstone...* (1786), ESTC: t187280, Bodleian Library: Mus. Bibl. III 8° 296.

26. Jess Jenkins, 'John Throsby: "a man of strong natural genius",' in John Hinks [ed] *Aspects of Leicester*, (Barnsley, 2000), 39-54. Much of Throsby's research was used by John Nichols in the compilation of *The History and Antiquities of the County of Leicester*, published in 1815. Throsby traded for a time as a stationer, bookseller and printer.

27. The first edition had been printed in London but the imprint of the second 'enlarged and corrected' edition reads: 'Lynn: printed and sold by W. Whittingham; R. Baldwin, Pater-noster Row; T. Payne & Son, Mews-gate; Benjamin White, Fleet Street; H. Gardner, Strand, London, and J. Gregory, Leicester. MDCCLXXVII'.

28. Gregory announced in the *Journal* on 8 November 1777 that he proposed to print this work in association with Whittingham of Lynn and Cresswell of Nottingham. On 29

November the *Journal* carried two large advertisements side by side describing rival proposed editions of Thoroton: one by Cresswell and George Burbage, also of Nottingham, and one by Whittingham, who claimed that Cresswell and Burbage had suppressed his advertisement in their paper while announcing their own cheaper edition. On 27 December Gregory declared in the *Journal* that he had never intended to publish a new edition of Thoroton. His part in this strange affair is unclear. Although he originally proposed to publish with both Whittingham and Cresswell, they ended up on opposite sides and Gregory had apparently withdrawn. Neither proposal was realised although Whittingham issued a few copies of the first instalment in 1781. A new edition was published in 1796 by John Throsby. See Adrian Henstock, 'Nottinghamshire Historical Writing, 1677-1997', *The Thoroton Society: a commemoration of its first 100 years* (Nottingham, 1997), 7.

29. *Leicester Journal*, 25 January 1777.
30. *Leicester Journal*, 19 July 1777.
31. Thompson, *History of Leicester*, 123.
32. *Leicester Journal*, 10 May 1777.
33. In addition to the range of patent medicines retailed by Gregory, he was an appointed wholesaler for several, including Vandour's Nervous Pills, Dr Walker's 'Jesuit Drops' and 'Specific Purging Remedy'. *Leicester Journal,*, 25 January and 28 June 1777.
34. *Leicester Journal*, 7 October 1769.
35. *Leicester Journal*, 26 May 1787.
36. *Leicester Journal*, 1 March 1777, 24 August 1777, 7 April 1787.
37. *Leicester Journal*, 15 November 1777. There is a similar type of advertisement for the Marines in the *Leicester Journal*, 6 December 1777.
38. *Leicester Journal*, 25 October 1777.
39. *Leicester Journal*, 27 December 1777.
40. *Leicester Journal*, 1 November 1777, 6 September 1777.
41. *Leicester Journal*, 17 February 1787.
42. For example in 1760 Gregory required a journeyman printer and in 1765 he sought an apprentice and a journeyman bookbinder. *Leicester Journal*, 16 February 1760, 20 April 1765.
43. John Nichols, *Literary Anecdotes of the Eighteenth Century* (1812-15), 8, 481; Michael Murphy, *Cambridge Newspapers and Opinion: 1780-1850* (Cambridge, 1977), 16-19, 24-25, 33, 35.
44. Derek Fraser, 'The Press in Leicester c1790-1861', *Transactions of the Leicestershire Archaeological and Historical Society*, 42 (1966-67), 53-75.
45. Hartopp, *Register of Freemen*, 523. On 16 March 1803, John Vowe Gregory (aged 13 years and 9 months) was bound with effect from 30 September 1803. A £30 grant was given by the Sons of the Clergy. There is no record of his freedom.
46. Black, *The English Press*, 118.
47. Henry Hartopp [ed] *Roll of the Mayors of the Borough and Lord Mayors of the City of Leicester: 1209-1935* (Leicester, 1935), 167.
48. Hartopp, *Roll of the Mayors*, 167.
49. Nichols, *Literary Anecdotes*, 3, 678.

Literary Institutions in the Lake Counties
Part IV: Catalogues

JOHN GAVIN

PREVIOUS STUDIES[1] have examined the distribution and chronology, social setting and purpose of a range of early libraries in the old Lake Counties of Cumberland, Westmorland and Lancashire North-of-the-Sands. This paper, the fourth in the series, reports on a pilot study to examine the content and arrangement of the catalogues that have survived. The aim is to show what books were available and how they were chosen and, in due course, to provide a survey of libraries in Cumbria.

The local archives of Cumbria contain records of the parochial libraries from the eighteenth century, and earlier, to the free public libraries of the late nineteenth century. The few early catalogues which survive are simple printed lists, with the books either numbered in order of accession or arranged by size and storage arrangements. Later examples progress into more complex alphabetised and classified arrangements. The early libraries in Cumbria frequently had close connections with members of the local book-trade. The local bookseller, as well as being the main source of the books, often held office as librarian or committee member, occasionally stored the library on his premises and, should he also be a printer, produced the catalogue.

The smallest institutions had a book of rules which generally, following a pattern in similar classes of library, covered membership, subscriptions, and borrowing arrangements as well as the selection and acquisition of stock; often with a request scheme for members. Typically the officials were listed, and sometimes the members, and the printed catalogue often formed part of this membership booklet. A regularly updated catalogue was an essential requirement from the early days of informal book clubs; where they exist, these are often the only record to indicate that a library flourished and the list of books (when included) is all that remains to imply the interests of its readers. The records of actual borrowings rarely survive. The methods of organisation into classes offer evidence of a growing sophistication and also of changing interests. It is clear that practical advice was available, most probably through book-trade connections.

In his article *The Community Library,* Paul Kaufman [2] provides useful models for analysis with: 'A Descriptive Outline of Circulating Library Catalogues' and 'A Descriptive Census of Subscription Library Catalogues' and also cites some examples of Cumbrian libraries. I have adapted his method to tabulate Cumbrian library data for a wider range of categories and added a classification system. Elsewhere, he makes the point that while a catalogue may provide a broad indication of the reading tastes of the library's regular users, it does not indicate which books were read and which were not. Popular books were probably read to death; and stock that survives has simply not been subject to the same degree of wear and tear.[3]

The most basic catalogue is a simple numbered list. This may be in a complete sequence, or incomplete where based on an accessions register of new books purchased and old stock auctioned off. The list is sometimes arranged in storage groupings; *i.e.* convenient arrangements for finding books by size and/or by shelf location. Until well into the nineteenth century, such lists included the number of volumes and occasionally date and cost.

Larger libraries changed to alphabetical methods of sorting, which were sometimes random groupings under the initial letters ('not fine sorted'); and it took a while for methodical systems to evolve. There are many problems with early catalogues. Titles are often abridged and it can be difficult to identify the subject matter as fact or fiction. Confusion applies not only to where a particular book belongs, but also to the identity of authors. Compilers switched between lists of titles (with or without authors) and authors in a random fashion before conforming to the standard alphabetical author, title sequence. Hence, in the system of catalogue symbols below, modifiers are used for mixed sequences or when author's names are missing or incomplete. Considerable research is required to identify anonymous or pseudonymous authors and the earlier and more obscure authors can be impossible to identify.

The listing of titles presents its own problems. They can (and often do) begin with the article or a choice of permutations, e.g.: *'The History of the Admirable Crichton'*; or *'Crichton, The History of the Admirable'*; or even *'Admirable Crichton, The History of...'*

Table 1. Catalogue Types

Catalogue	Symbols
List; Numbered; in Sequence 1 to n	L; /N; seq: 1 - n
Books: by size-folios, etc.; Shelves, stacks	–F; –S
Volumes; date; price	+v; +d; +pr
Alphabetical: not fine sorted	^A
Alphabetical: mixed titles/authors	/Am
Title; Author + title; Authors incomplete	t; at; a-
Alphabetical: titles; authors and titles	/At; /Aat
Classified; Dictionary	C; D

The next stage in the cataloguing progress is a division into classes. Initially these were broad groupings, but they later became more precise. These provide an insight into changing interests and fashions as well as contemporary issues. The dictionary catalogue comprises authors, titles and categories in one alphabetical list. The system of symbols adopted is an attempt to codify the catalogues for purposes of comparison. It goes from the simple list [L] to the classified subject list of authors and titles [C/Aat] or the even more comprehensive Dictionary catalogue [D].

1. Parochial and other Religious Libraries

The libraries administered by the parochial authorities comprised, for the most part, religious works intended for the use of the incumbent, other local clergy, and sometimes a select group of parishioners. Dr Bray's fund provided a standard, usually numbered, set for the use of an incumbent in the poorer parishes. These books were checked on a change of parson and at other intervals.

William Nicolson, Bishop of Carlile [*sic*], made a routine visit of inspection in 1703. He notes that Cammerton Church had a Bible 'of the old Translation: For here we met with the *Ballat of Ballats* (instead of ye *Song of Solomon*).' He was highly critical of Ainstable and its Vicar:

> the onely thing that appear'd to my first View, which pleas'd me, was a decent Repository for the Books given by B. *Oley*... But—the Birds were flown. The Vicar, Mr Hodgson (with an assurance peculiar to himself) protested they were all in his own possession, and in good Condition; presumeing that I would have relyed on ye Credibillity of his Evidence without making any further Enquiry. ... persisting in my Demands to see them, after a tedious Expectance, he brought me Thirteen of the Sixteen. These were more in Number than I look'd for: But they were all in the abused condition yt I expected to see them in. ... At the Visitation a further Enquiry ought to be made; and the Vicar obliged to purchase (*de novo*) those that are lost.[4]

The purpose of some of these libraries changed over time to widen their readership. Parish libraries for the local inhabitants were established from the middle decades of the nineteenth century, as one aspect of the philanthropical movement for educating the working classes.[5] A proportion of simple sectarian institutions persisted to the end of the nineteenth century.

Carlisle Cathedral library was available to non-clerics and has loan registers from the eighteenth century. The content was mainly 'theological, ponderous folios of obsolete divinity' [6] and although Coleridge used it the library did not attract many borrowers. The manuscript *Catalogus Librorum in Bibliotheca Carl: repositorum ordine Alphabetico digestus* [not fine-sorted] was the primary source but *A Catalogue of the Library of the Dean and Chapter of Carlisle* was printed in 1783 for external 'Gentlemen' borrowers.

Documents relating to the Kendal Friends Book Society (1821-1939) were recently discovered in the Friends' strong room.[7] The books were allowed to circulate twice among the group before being auctioned off at the Annual General Meeting. Among the papers are the revised Rules for 1846. These include: '... if on reading a Work, any Member think it unsuitable for circulation, he shall send it for adjudication to the President; [and] ... If any Member incline to make a remark in any Book, it shall be done in pencil, and the initials of the marker affixed.' The Quakers may be unique in encouraging comments in their library books.

Table 2. Sample Records for Religious Libraries

Institute: [Rel. Lib]	Est.	Cat.	Pp.	Titles	Vols	Mem.	Content:
Beetham Parish Library	1795	1795	3	180	500	Lim.	Bibles, theology, dictionaries.
The gift of Wm Hutton and 'for the use of the Vicar & Curate, the School Master & the Church Wardens. The last to examine the Books by the Catalogue every Easter Monday.'[8] Also More's *Utopia*, Bodleian's Books catalogue, Gibbons *on Women*, 2 Vol., Pliny *Nat. Hist.*, Linnaeus & Mophuet *on Insects* & Puffendorf's *Law Nat.*							
Cockermouth Parish Library	1762	1815	14	351	700	Lim.	Bibles, theology, sermons.
Associates of the Late Dr Bray and augmented by late Dr. Keene... intended to be a lending library for the use and benefit of such Clergymen as shall be nominated thereto by the Trustee... the Rectors of Workington, Brigham, Moresby, Dissington, and Cockermouth. The Trustees were to appoint a Librarian and sign the catalogue each retaining a copy. Bray's Bibliothica Parochialis, Pufendorf's Law of Nature in Folio and Quarto (Pufendorf *de Jure Naturae*), Pope's *Homer*, Aesop's *Fables*, Greek and Latin, Terence's *Comedies*, Ascham's, *Schoolmaster*. [Pr. Thomas Bailey] Fol 1-43+3; 4to 44-64; the rest 8vo.							
Kendal Zion Chapel		1859	16	340	350	Subs	Religious and Moral teaching
Bunyan's Works, Religious Revivals, *Uncle Tom's Cabin*, by Mrs Stowe, Young's *Night Thoughts*...							

2. Gentlemen's Libraries

The majority of 'gentlemen's libraries' had a frequently changing stock and books that had passed around the membership were disposed of at regular sales. The proceeds of these sales, together with the subscription revenue, provided the funds for the new purchases; often 'new' only in the sense of recently published. Numbering was a continuing accession sequence in the stock-book. The records of the Dalton Book Club, founded in 1764, show an initial purchase of twenty-seven books at a cost of £4.8s.6d for the seventeen members plus a 'Catalogue of Books for 60 years past' which cost a further sixpence. The books included *The Annual Register* for 1763, which contained literary articles.[9]

The Whitehaven Subscription Library was founded in 1797, funded by a Proprietor's joining fee and an annual subscription.[10] The first Librarian was Thomas Nicholson. John Ware, appointed secretary, was a local bookseller and printer and printed the first catalogue in 1797. The General Regulations include: 'III - Each Subscriber shall have a catalogue of the books, and a Ticket which must be paid for.' Regulation IV allowed for member's choice: 'Any subscriber may propose books for admission, by writing the title, the price, the number of volumes, and a reference to their character if possible, in a book kept for that purpose in the library room: every recommendation of a book must be signed by the proposer.' Later members were asked for a review reference to its character.

Table 3a. Sample Records for Gentlemen's and Subscription Libraries

Organisation	Est.	Cat.	Pp.	Titles	Vols	Mem.	%fict
Cockermouth Book Club	1785	1794	8	229	483	59	1%

(Called Cockermouth Library in *Rules and Orders*). Alphabetical, highly representative of eighteenth century, with distinct liberal cast; only fiction, *Man of Feeling* and *Sentimental Journey*, but several plays. A notable inclusion is 'Wordsworth's Poems' (between 'Williams Letters from France, 4 vols.' and Wollstonecraft's *Rights of Woman*), a very rare entry of Wordsworth in any community library before 1850.[11]

Whitehaven Sub. Library	1797	1797	212	315	600	101	Small

Books arranged in groups: Gp 1: a mixture of History, science, travels, poetry, religion & agriculture in a numbered sequence: 1 – 80; Gp 2: Plays numbered 81-169; 6 Operas; 37 Tragedies, including Aphra Behn's *Oroonoko*; 46 Comedies, including *She Stoops to Conquer*. A sample of titles goes from HISTORY *of Irish Bishops*, Boyle's *Lectures*, 4 vols, Life of Mahomet, Trowell's *Husbandry*, Gibbon's *Roman Empire*, 6 vols, Dixon's *Voyages to the South Sea*, Voltaire's *Maid of Orleans 1st Canto*, Johnson's *Lives of the Poets*,4 vols, and *The Devil in England*, 6 vols. Gp 3 Misc. 170-205; Woodfall's *Parliamentary Reports, [1796 and 1797]*, English *Philosophical Transactions for 1796*, *Gentleman's Mag.*, Smith's *Wealth of Nations*, & Gisborne's *Duties of the Female Sex* (*nb* a later catalogue has his ...Male Sex). Gp 4 contains Addenda, printed and hand-written, to no. 315, Jan 1798. The % of Fiction small. Subscribers [p11] include 11 women.

Kendal Library	1794	1798	28	300	1000	110	10%

Members included 32 ladies. Johnson's, *English Poets* 75 vols; *British Theatre*, 22 vols. The *Encyclopaedia Britannica* among the 10% of Miscellaneous; 28 books on Travels; 28 History; 19 Memoirs, biography; 10 Agriculture; some on Science, Education and Verse.

Table 3b. Sample Anaylsis of Classes

Lib	Name	Date	Class	Notes 1
GL*	Cockermouth	1794	/A	See Kaufman.
GL*	Whitehaven	1797	Gp/Nseq: 1-315	In 4 Groups. Limited fiction
GL*	Kendal Library	1798	/N^Am+v	Novels lack authors. West's Guide.
GL	Whitehaven	1801	-F/Nseq: 1-315^Am+v	Note reorganisation.
GL	Carlisle Library	1827	C/N^At +d	Est. c1785. Novels

3. Circulating Libraries

Circulating Libraries, which originated in the early eighteenth century, are a source of information on 'popular' works. The general perception is that they catered for largely female consumers and they certainly sustained many female writers from the 'Gothic' to the 'Courtship' novel. A 1797 pamphlet *The Use of Circulating Libraries Considered; with Instructions for Opening & Conducting a Library upon a large or small Plan,* suggested a stock of 1500 books which was 80% fiction: 1050 'novels' and 130 'romances'.[12]

Table 4a. Sample Records for Circulating Libraries

Proprietor	Est.	Cat.	Titles/vols	% Fiction	Other
John Soulby, Ulverston	1795	1809	250/1000	90%	Travels, memoirs
Soulby ordered new books recommended by any lady or gentleman giving them the first reading. Mainly 3-volume novels. Among recent publications are Elizabeth Hamilton's *Cottagers of Glenburnie* (1808); Madame de Stael's *Corinna* and Miss Anna Maria Porter's *Hungarian Brothers* (1807); Walter Scott's *Lay of the Last Minstrel* and Harriet and Sophia Porter's six-volume *Canterbury Tales* 1805. Other recently published novels include best sellers such as Miss Jane Porter's *Thaddeus of Warsaw* and Maria Edgeworth's *Belinda*. [Dates?]; earlier authors: Mrs Amelia Opie, 'Monk' Lewis, Ann Radcliffe, Fanny Burney and Clara Reeve and the recognised eighteenth-century classic, Fielding's *Joseph Andrews &c*. The non-fiction includes Travels and Voyages: Mungo Park, Anson, Boyle and Cook; the Memoirs & Biography feature Lackington and Swift; there are two histories and one book of songs and poetry.					
J Braithwaite	1785	1814	595/1785	95%	10 Plays
Of Kent-Lane, Kendal. Est. 1785. Catalogue c1814 on internal evidence. Some magazines and non-fiction. Pr. J S Lough, Kendal. Contemporary publications but works from 17th and through 18th C.					

Table 4b. Sample of Classes

Lib	Name	Date	Class	Notes 1
CL	Soulby, Anthony	1808	/N^Am+v	Pr AS Penrith, <fiction
CL*	Soulby, John	1809	/Nseq: 1-997 ^A m+v	Pr JS Ulverston,
CL*	Braithwaite, J	1814	/Nseq: 1-595^Am+v	JS Lough, pr, Kendal. West's Guide
CL	Thurnam, Chas	1827	Nseq: 1-2278+/At+v	Carlisle, lists: Standard novels, etc.

4. Working Men's Institutions

Working men's libraries largely, and necessarily, were established philanthropically with the aim of self-improvement. There is little evidence for genuine artisan involvement in management of these enterprises in the early years.

Table 5a. Sample Records for 'Working Class' Libraries

Institution	Est.	Cat.	Pp.	Titles	Vols	Mem.	Content:
Carlisle Lit. Sc. & MI	1824	1833	16	200	400	Subsc.	Lit. Sc. General
A false start in 1824 – nearly failed 'owing to a stagnation of trade.' Meetings held by 'persons who felt an interest in the education of the working classes' and the money subscribed to rescue it. The Committee, chosen by ballot, included professional and tradesmen. The collection of books is mainly trades oriented, but with pure sciences and some poetry and literature that justifies the Institution's name.							

Institution	Est.	Cat.	Pp.	Titles	Vols	Mem.	Content:
Cockermouth Rel. LL	<1839	1839	16	400+	410+	Subsc.	Lives, religious tracts,

Religious Lending Library: Subscribers could borrow one book every fortnight for a penny a month. The library was managed by the Committee of the Cockermouth Religious Society and the books kept by Daniel Fidler as Librarian (and Printer). The 1845 Catalogue (containing over 600 books) had a new Rule 'That no books of a *Professedly Controversial* character, be admitted into this Library except such as relate to the Evidences of Religion.' Titles: *Advice to Cottagers*, Bunyan's *Pilgrim's Progress, Travels*, and *Missionary Records* in South Africa, Chinah [sic], Burmah, Ceylon, India North America, Tahiti and Society Islands; John Wesley's *Life*. Fiction minimal.								
Bromfield Parish Library	1853	1853	44	950	1000+	Subsc.	Classified Range-see below	
Distinguished donors, Committee: Patron, The Lord Bishop of Carlisle. The aim was 'not only to open to the Parishioners at large the sources of innocent gratification which properly directed Reading is capable of affording, but also to offer the means of self-instruction …' all leading 'to a more intelligent and devotional reading of the Book of Books, —the Bible. Works by De Foe, Sir Walter Scott, Dickens, Miss Martineau. Poetry by: Cowper, Dryden, Goldsmith, Gray, Pope, Milton and Hannah More. Also: *Alcoholic Liquors, Use and Abuse of*, Hannah More's (Moral) *Stories for the Middle Ranks*, and Hildreth's *The White Slave*.								
Penrith Workhouse	1840	1860	8	350	600	-	Classified Range-see below	
The content suggests a preponderance of children. There are school texts and books for the young but also a *Manual for the Aged*. There is an emphasis on preparing for a life of service – *My Station and its Duties, Self-Improvement, Going to Service, Lads of the Factory*. There are however some worthwhile (rather than worthy) books that encourage one to hope that the young had some stimulating literature. *Black Giles, The Poacher* and *Idle Dick* probably all came to a bad end but titles include: *Uncle Tom's Cabin*, Gay's *Fables*, and books of poetry including Cowper's verse; there is also a *History of Penrith*.								

Table 5b. Sample Analysis for 'Working Class' Libraries

Lib	Name	Date	Class	Notes [Est]
WM*	C. Lit, Sc. & MI	1833	/N/Am+v	Carlisle, [1824-31; 1833-]
WM[R]*	Cockermouth RLL	1839	/N/Am+v	Religious Lending Library.
WM	Penrith RR	1845	/N/At+a+v	Good Library, Reading Room.
WM	Cockermouth	1852	C/N/Am+v	MI [1845]. Wordsworth's Poems 6 v.
WM[R]*	Bromfield PL	1853	C/N/Am	Parish Library; Juvenile section.
WM*	Penrith Work-house	1860	C/At	Juvenile literature. A few authors
WM	K. WM Institute	1881	C/Nseq/Am+v	Kendal, [1844]. Seq. 1-1773 books.
WPubL	C. Public Library	1900	C/Aat	Carlisle, Code system: EKLM…

5. Categories of Books

The record of borrowings from the Bristol Library in the late eighteenth century was a unique survival and Kaufman's analysis is a valuable contribution to library history. He comments that the arrangement of the titles and the nine classes of the titles and nine classes of subjects in the 1782 Catalogue is 'of value in reproducing the pattern of thinking then prevalent in library "Science" at least in Bristol.'[13] There are overall figures for borrowings by subject categories (he uses the term 'tabulation') which can be used as a basis of comparison from Cumbrian library holdings.

The Kendal catalogue, undated but mid-eighteenth century, offers 'Choice Books, New and Old, in Divinity, Philosophy, History, Poetry, Law, Physic, Classics &c.'

Table 6a. Comparison of Categories of the Kendal, Bristol and Carlisle Libraries

Kendal c1750	Bristol Library 1782 [P. Kaufman]	Thurnam's CL 1827
Divinity	Theology and Ecclesiastical History	
History	History, Antiquities &Geography: *283 titles.	History; Voyages; Travels
Law	Jurisprudence	
	Philosophy [includes Economics]	
Philosophy	Mathematics, etc. [all physical sciences and technology]	
Physic	Medicine and Anatomy	
	Natural History and Chemistry	
Poetry	Belles Lettres [incl. novels]: ** 236 titles.	Novels and Romances
Classics &C.	Miscellaneous	Miscellanies; Reviews
		Adventures
		Biography
	Total borrowed-13496; Titles-900; ratio-15.0	

No borrowing records survive of the Cumbrian libraries, but they may be comparable to the Bristol borrowings. These show that the most popular category was 'history, antiquities and geography' where the 283 titles saw 6000 borrowings, mainly of books of travels and voyages. Second most popular was 'belles lettres' where 236 titles saw 3313 borrowings, mainly of novels. The 1827 catalogue of Thurnam's of Carlisle shows a predominance of novels and romances, and also contains periodicals: literary, philosophical, sporting, and reviewing magazines.

The earliest Cumbrian bookseller's catalogue, from 'The Printing Office, Kendal', though probably intended as a stock-list rather than a library catalogue, has subject headings similar to those found in early library catalogues and they roughly equate with those of the Bristol Library. Divinity includes: seventeenth-century *Sermons* and William Sherlock's *Against Popery*; Philosophy includes locally-born Ephraim Chambers' *Cyclopaedia or Dictionary of Arts and Sciences* and Boyle's scientific essays. The Poetry includes Pope's *Works* and Quarel's [sic] *Sonnets*. Arrangement of the titles, following contemporary practice, is by size under Folio and Quarto editions.

The Cumbrian libraries show a broad agreement in categories. Bromfield has a religious bias and caters for juveniles as a separate class, while all the classes in the Penrith Workhouse catalogue contain a majority of books for young readers.

LITERARY INSTITUTIONS IN THE LAKE COUNTIES

Table 6b. Comparative Categories of Two Cumbrian 'Working -Class' Libraries

Bromfield, Wigton 1853 (Religious)	Penrith 1860 (Work-house)
History and Biography	History, (General)-1p. Biography-½p.
+ Voyages and Travels-5pp.	Geography, Voyages, & Travels-½ p.
National Customs and Topography –4pp.	
Agriculture, Gardening, Botany, Natural History –2pp.	Natural History, Botany & Zoology for Schools (Science)-1/2p.
Arts and Sciences-1p.	
Natural Theology, and Christian Evidences-1p.	Religious Works-2pp.
Misc. Divinity, Sermons &c-4pp.;	
Moral and Religious Tales, Allegories, &c-1p.	
General Fiction, Poetry and the Drama-2pp.	Poetry, Tales, and Anecdotes-1½p.
Miscellaneous Literature-3pp.	Miscellaneous-½p. Magazines, &c.- ¾p.
Juvenile Literature-3pp.	
Books lent to the Library-mainly 'Travels.'	Social and Domestic Economy-1p.

Kaufman's analysis of the Bristol Library included an ordered list of books in particular demand with a record of borrowings. Sixteen titles were in the range of 100-200 borrowings; thirty titles were borrowed 50-100 times (including: Marmontel, *Moral Tales*, 1766, 79 times) and 137 titles borrowed 20-49 times (including Vicesimus Knox, *Essays, Moral and Literary*. 2 vols. 1779, 47 times and Le Sage, *Adventures of Gil Blas*, 1773, 28 times), 119 titles were only borrowed once. This data provides a potential yardstick for comparative studies of late eighteenth-century catalogues which one might label: 'Kaufman's Reading Vogue Index'. How many of the ten popular books shown in Table 7 are included in other contemporary catalogues? How does the range of categories and proportion of titles compare with that of the Bristol Library? As can be seen from these classes, the continuing popularity of certain books is clearly evident.

Table 7. The Ten Most Popular Titles Borrowed from the Bristol Library

Hawkesworth, John	Voyages, 1773	201
Brydone, Patrick	Tour Through Sicily	192
Chesterfield, Earl [Stanhope, PD]	Letters to his Son 1774	185
Hume, David	History of England, 1754	180
Goldsmith, Oliver	History of the Earth	150
Raynal	European Settlements	137
Robertson, William	History of Charles Vth, 1769	131
Sterne, Laurence	Tristram Shandy	127
Lyttelton, George	Henry II	121
Fielding, Henry	Works (chiefly his novels)	120

Barrow Free Public Library

There was a considerable delay before the Public Libraries Act of 1850 was implemented in the Lake Counties. Barrow, a new industrial town with a growing work force, opened the first Free Public Library in Cumbria in 1881. It was an important stage in the town's evolution. The 1884 Chairman's Report of Barrow's Free Library, detailing the second year of its operations, is an encouraging document. He notes a large increase in lending particularly marked in the Reference Department. He suggests that the Reference and Lending Departments were becoming better known and the selection of books approved. Catalogues were provided for the readers and the range of statistical information covers every aspect of the library's facilities and use. Coded systems were used in the Free Public Libraries with a letter identifying the class and a number the item.

Table 8. League Table of Borrowings in 1884 (297 days)

	Class	%	Vols. In Lib.	Issues	Times issued
1	Fiction	54.0	1494	36411	24
2	Juvenile Literature	20.0	833	13273	15
3	History and Biography	6.5	1708	4329	2
4	Geography and Travels	5.5	765	3703	4
5	Literary Miscellany	3.0	558	2070	3
	Total	89.0	5348	59786	11

The Lending Department report of 26 September 1884 shows a daily average of 225 books issued by the Department with a grand total of 59 786 for 1884. Seasonal differences were noted: August saw a drop in borrowing including Fiction and Juvenile Literature; Philosophy and Theology were more popular in the winter months together with Useful Arts. Medical books peaked in October and November; Geography and Travels with History and Biography from January to March. Fiction and Juvenile Literature were hugely popular accounting for 74% of borrowings and placing these holdings under pressure.

Of particular interest, as it concerns the readers rather than the books, is the table of the occupations of nearly 2000 borrowers.[14] A tentative analysis suggests that a large group, at approximately 35%, were the 'working-class': labourers, artisans and workers from a range of occupations. Some portion of the 442 'unidentified' (22%) could well have belonged with this group. There was a noteworthy 17% of juveniles who made excellent use of the Free Library's 'sound and healthy literature, suited to their years, thus developing a taste for the prosecution of a more matured course of reading, besides obviating the danger incurred by the perusal of light, trashy,

Literature.' Presumably this refers to 'Penny Dreadfuls', no doubt much enjoyed by these apprentices, office, errand- and shop-boys and scholars. The 'Professionals' and other middle-class occupations, with many sub-groupings, came to about 26% of the library's users. The report is an important source for library history and the series of Barrow Reports from 1883 to 1900 and those of the other Free Public Libraries merit a thorough analysis.

Thomas Kelly comments that cataloguing is a subject about which the layman does not think enough, and the librarian is apt to think too much. The basic principles are simple:

> The primary task of a library is to serve its readers, and the first task of the librarian is to arrange his books in such a way as to make them as readily available as possible both to himself and (if the readers are given access to the shelves) to the readers. ... The second task of the librarian is to provide a catalogue as a guide to the collection.[15]

Over forty years ago Dr Paul Kaufman was promoting the study of library book stocks as evidence of their use. He described and examined both extant catalogues and surviving library books; bookplates can supply interesting details. He refers to studies that have shown how changing social forces create new reading publics and how new publics shape literature. His research was motivated by 'the belief that the rising tides of social and political movements were stirred and shaped to a marked degree by the rapid spread of the several types of community lending libraries'.[16]

Forming a library involved the selection of books for a particular group of readers and was a complex operation that embraced changing and widening interests and aspirations. The eighteenth and nineteenth centuries were undoubtedly times of considerable social and industrial change in the northwest as elsewhere. There was also a significant local contribution to literature and other publications during the period considered. The distribution, timing and content of the regional libraries may well point to developments within the region and the effectiveness of communications with the wider world.

NOTES

1. See: John Gavin, 'Westmorland Literary Institutions to 1850', *The Bibliothek*, 20 (1995),144-54; 'Literary Institutions in Cumberland to 1860' in M T Richardson [ed] *Branches of Literature and Music. Proceedings of the Thirteenth Seminar on the History of the Provincial Book Trade* (Bristol: 2000), 47-63; and 'Cumbrian Literary Institutions: Cartmel & Furness to 1900' in Peter Isaac & Barry McKay [ed] *Images &Texts: their production and distribution in the 18th and 19th centuries* (Winchester: St Paul's Bibliographies & New Castle, DE.: Oak Knoll Press, 1997), 53-64.

2. Paul Kaufman, 'The Community Library a chapter in English social history', *Transactions of the American Philosophical Library* NS57 Part 7 (1967), 5-65.

3. Paul Kaufman, *Libraries and their Users* (London: Library Association, 1969), 193.

4. William Nicholson, *Miscellany Accounts of the Diocese of Carlile*. R S Ferguson [ed] (Carlisle: 1877), 85, 110.
5. See the section on Working Men's Institutions.
6. B Botfield, *Notes on the Cathedral Libraries of England* (London: 1849), 50 quoted in T Kelly, *Early Public Libraries* (London: Library Association, 1966), 63.
7. I owe thanks to Mrs Eva Hopwood for this information.
8. William Hutton, 'The Beetham Repository, 1770', J Rawlinson Ford [ed] *Transactions Cumberland & Westmorland Antiquarian & Archælogical Society*, 1906, 157-9.
9. Ernest H Boddy, Dalton Book Club: a brief history, (Dalton, 1982) 3.
10. The Motto *Non quot, sed quales* [Not how many, but of what sort.]
11. Comment in Kaufman, *Libraries*, 211. My research so far corroborates Kaufman's comments on the surprising rarity of Wordsworth's works in Cumbrian catalogues.
12. Bodleian Library, Oxford, quoted in H M Hamlyn, 'Eighteenth Century Circulating Libraries in England', *Library* Ser 5 vol 1, (1947), 197-222.
13. Paul Kaufman, *Borrowings from the Bristol Library 1773-1784; A Unique Record of Reading Vogues* (Charlottesville, VA.: 1960), 7-11, 188, 193-4, 210. He notes the number of women readers.
14. See Barrow-in-Furness Public Lending Library *Report 1883-4*, Table IV.
15. Kelly. *Early Public Libraries*, 171.
16. Kaufman, *Borrowings*, introduction.

Influential and Mysterious:
The Career of Septimus Prowett
Bookseller, Publisher and Picture Dealer

MARGARET COOPER

Introduction

MUCH OF THIS RESEARCH was undertaken for Howard Hanley, Professor of Chemistry at the University of Colorado, and a collector interested in the painter John Martin. Hanley's curiosity was particularly aroused by the unknown publisher who in 1824 offered Martin 3500 guineas to illustrate Milton's *Paradise Lost* in a style he knew would be radically different from that of any previous edition. Who was this Septimus Prowett – a name Dickens himself might have conjured up – and what financial source enabled him to dig so deep? It is interesting that sixty-five years ago an anonymous contributor to the short-lived *Bibliographical Notes & Queries* (2 [May 1936] 11-12) was similarly curious about Prowett and his finances. There was no reply in the remaining volumes.

Very little was known about Prowett. The British Library catalogue lists twenty of his published titles, the first four in Worcester, the rest in London, but others from different sources have been located during this research.[1] The references are few and include one contemporary comment – unfortunately, from a writer who seems to have fallen out with most people; three useful trade announcements in *The Literary Gazette;* and some inaccurate details in a piece by Martin's son written much later in the century. None contains anything about Prowett's origins (beyond the idea that he was American).

The investigation aimed to lift Prowett from obscurity and to account for his sudden disappearance in 1830; and the more the records revealed about him the more it became appropriate to comment on his significance within the early nineteenth-century book trade. It seemed best to begin with the earliest known references in Worcester.

A Smart Start

You could say Prowett got off to a 'smart' start in the 'faithful city'. He surfaces in 1820 when he published three local, but substantial, books by John Chambers: *A General History of Malvern; A General History of Worcester;* and *Biographical Illustrations of Worcestershire.* They were first published in 1817, 1819 and 1820 respectively by William Walcot who had moved into William Smart's shop at

88 High Street when the latter, a very prosperous bookseller and said to be the country's leading collector of Baskervilles, retired in 1811.[2] Baskerville was, of course, a local man, son of an old Worcestershire family. Prowett's arrival seems to have marked Walcott's demise and it looks as though he moved into Walcott's premises as well as taking over some of his titles. The latter, listed in the *Worcestershire General and Commercial Directory for 1820*, does not appear anywhere again.

That same year Prowett also published a sermon by Samuel Lee, orientalist, master of eighteen languages and a Bristol canon. But preceding these four publications, still in 1820, was an item which came to light only days before this conference, an eighty-eight-page catalogue of just under 3000 wide-ranging titles, each one priced.[3] A little over 20% are foreign language texts, mainly Greek, Latin and French; and the fact that there are no Walcott or Prowett titles suggests this may well have been the opening shot on arrival in Worcester. But how did the young bookseller (he was just about twenty-three) acquire such an extensive stock?

Prowett's stay in Worcester was brief. He was already in London by the time the Worcester bookselling business of R & S Prowett was listed in *Pigot and Co's London & Provincial New Commercial Directory* (1822). No other local records searched contained any references to him or his activities in the city or suggested any local connections. Before following him to the capital, however, a quick but crucial encounter with some basic records revealed that a Robert Prowett, son of John and Mary, was christened at Caterham, Surrey, on 25 May 1788, along with two brothers, David in 1786 and James in 1790. Were these relatives, and in particular was Robert the 'R' of 'R and S Prowett'? The locating, shortly afterwards, of a death certificate and a will in the General Registry Office showed that Septimus was seventy when he died in 1867 and was thus born in 1796 or 1797; and that Robert Prowett was his brother and sole executor. A framework of a life was beginning to emerge – but Septimus was unobligingly absent from the Caterham parish registers. At this point an article in an 1899 edition of the *Newcastle Weekly Chronicle*, in which Martin's son, Leopold, claimed that Prowett was an American, proved a little puzzling, but the attack on the usual sources was continued: biographical, bibliographical, professional, topographical and trade, together with some contemporary newspapers and journals and some private papers relating to a possible connection with an important landed Staffordshire family.[4]

What subsequent searches established was that in 1821 Septimus was moving not *on* to London to spread his wings, but *back* to London. Parish registers record that the three eldest sons of John Prowett, grocer, and his wife Ann – John (1780, died in infancy), John (1781) and William (1782) – were born in Aylesbury; a sister, Susanna (1783), in Smithfield; and the next four brothers in Caterham: David (1786), Robert

(1788), James (1790) and Charles (1792). Not long afterwards the family moved again and the three youngest Prowetts were born in Southwark; Elizabeth (1795, died in infancy), Septimus (1797) and Edward (1801). Septimus was born on 27 February and baptised two-and-a-half months later in the parish church, Christ Church. In 1818 Prowett & Son are listed as grocers and tea dealers in Great Surrey Street, Blackfriars Road, and by this time the business could well have been in the hands of the eldest son, John, two of whose children were born at that address.

So the appropriately named Septimus, neither an American nor, strictly speaking, a Londoner (since Southwark still lay in Surrey), was the seventh surviving son of nine surviving children. The Census for 1851 suggests that his siblings were all comfortably off. A few of the older ones, including his sister, appear to have lived off unearned income. Trade directories, however, show that the five younger Prowetts all did some sort of work: Robert was a dentist, James a stockbroker, Charles a clergyman and Edward, the youngest, may have been in the legal profession. It is hard to be more precise about Edward because although for many years directories list him at an address in the Strand he is not given an occupational title and there were journalists and translators as well as barristers and solicitors at the same address.[5] Only Robert and Edward had some direct link with the career of their brother.

A Pioneering Decade

Septimus was back in London by the autumn of 1821.[6] On 2 October he was admitted as a freeman of the Coopers' Company, just as his brother James had been five years earlier, and straight away he published an anonymous book, *Impressions... from a set of Silver Buttons*.[7] This proved to be a deceptively low-key start to the second phase of his career which turned out to be a decade of considerable achievement. Between 1821 and 1830 Prowett published over thirty titles. For the first two or three years he was still in partnership with Robert, but from 1824 onwards only his name appears in the imprints. Until 1825 he was still selling books but by 1826 Septimus confines himself to publishing.

He had probably always been on his own in the business. In the 1830s, 40s and 50s Robert must have been a very successful dentist, living and working among the titled and other successful medical men at fashionable addresses in Spring Gardens, Berkeley Square and Cavendish Square.[8] He was in his thirty-second year when the Prowett name first appears in Worcester. It seems unlikely he would have packed up whatever he was doing to accompany a much younger brother into the provinces; and it is just as difficult to imagine him being able to start from scratch on a new career at the age of thirty-six when 'R & S' became 'S'. More plausible is the theory that he was always the sleeping, perhaps senior, partner, providing a variety of brotherly support, including finance.

Septimus Prowett's output as a publisher was very varied. It included 'reliables' such as *The Canterbury Tales*, and *The Life of Izaac Walton*; and translations including four volumes of Thomas Roscoe's *Italian Novelists* and two works of Schiller by John Payne Collier. Publication of Collier's *The Poet's Pilgrimage* was part of the Schiller agreement but by all accounts the poetry was so dreadful that not even 'one of the shrewdest book dealers of his generation' managed to sell it.[9] There were a number of plays that revived reputations and at the same time caused friction between publisher and editor; and two self-help books, *The Art of Improving the Voice and Ear* and *The Art of Improving the Hair*, written by James Rennie, a surgeon, and popular enough to justify new editions the following year.

Prowett's best years were between 1824 and 1828. In 1824 the first of his three major books appeared, *The Works of Antonio Canova*, in small folio and large paper folio. The speed with which Prowett identified an opening and acted on it is evidence not only of his genuine interest in illustrated books but also of his entrepreneurial skills. Canova, arguably the best-known sculptor of the neo-classical movement, died in late 1822. Prowett commissioned Henry Moses to copy the engravings in the Countess of Albrizzi's book, issued in Pisa between 1821 and 1824, and arranged for translations of the Countess's text and a biography of Canova published the previous year. This two-volume edition of Canova's work up to 1819 was published in 1824 and followed by an updated three-volume set issued between 1824 and 1828. All five volumes displayed the highest production standards.[10]

Prowett's second outstanding work, and his most well known, was the particular stimulus for this research. In the previous century the Tonson family, Jacobs I, II and III, had enjoyed a forty-year monopoly on Milton's poetry, and had made a great deal of money from it. After the business ceased, following the death of the third Jacob in 1767, Milton's contract (the original one with Simmons, drawn up in 1667) had apparently got lost. In 1824 it surfaced in the hands of a London tailor and Prowett snapped it up, together with some other Tonson papers, for £25.[11] We simply don't know whether he then proceeded to look round for a suitable illustrator or already had Martin in mind, but his decision to approach the painter is a measure of both his vision and ambition.

This was still the very busy year of 1824 and Prowett was still a comparative newcomer to the London scene. He was no longer, however, unknown. He now had a number of publications to his name, in particular the Canova which was getting good reviews, and Cruikshank's *Mornings at Bow Street*. So his approach to Martin would not have been lightly dismissed. And, besides, the huge sum of money might well have overcome any lingering doubts. Where did the 3500 guineas come from? There is no certain answer. Most of Prowett's publications had probably made some profit by this time; but Robert and other family members were the most likely source of funding. As a tribe the Prowetts didn't go in for marriage. Most had no families of their own to support and were clearly affluent, especially Robert to whom Septimus remained very close all his life.[12] It is also possible that Septimus had some inherited money by now because the family business disappeared not long after 1818 and by 1821 129 Great Surrey Street was occupied by Edward Jones and family.[13] Perhaps John, the eldest, had sold what may well have been a lucrative grocers and tea-dealing business and money had been distributed. Perhaps it was that money which enabled Septimus to set up in Worcester in the first place.

John Martin was known for his dramatic biblical scenes including the celebrated *Balshazzar's Feast*, first exhibited in 1821, and was enjoying great popular and critical acclaim. Prowett, knowing that this artist would produce something fundamentally different from the illustrations of previous editions, must have been looking to publish a *Paradise Lost* that could speak to a new age. The result was a set of plates in which Milton's characters are dominated, overwhelmed by the sheer scale and drama of natural and man-made landscape. Prowett must also be credited with being the first publisher generous and shrewd enough to give the name of the illustrator equal prominence with the author on the title page of *Paradise Lost*.

Between 1825 and 1827 at least two editions were published in twelve monthly parts. An announcement in the *Literary Gazette* on 19 March 1825 (page 191) shows that Prowett was a meticulous publiciser of Martin's work, although with the size of the commission one would expect nothing less than a maximum promotional effort. He presents to the public 'the most splendid and beautiful form in which that immortal Poem has ever yet appeared' and for the first time, he continues, Milton's descriptions have been 'treated with a boldness and grandeur kindred to the mighty imagination which created them.' A special note for 'the Connoisseur' also explains something of Martin's method on this particular book. The illustrations, writes Prowett, represent the artist's first conception and possess 'the spirit and finish of the Painter's touch' because 'Mr Martin, by a rare effort of art, has wholly composed and designed his subjects on the Plates themselves'. Prowett, originally intending to publish just an Imperial quarto edition, announces an additional Imperial octavo edition for which Mr Martin has redone the engravings to the appropriate scale. This presumably accounts for the fact that Martin's commission was advanced in two parts, 2000 guineas and 1500 guineas.[14]

Prowett must have met John Payne Collier not long after he returned to London, if, that is, he hadn't known him before. Collier, who provides the only known contemporary comment on the publisher, seems to have been a proud and tetchy man, ready to find fault with others while guilty at times of overrating his own literary output.

Prowett had difficulty with him over *The Poet's Pilgrimage* which he issued as part of the agreement on the two Schiller titles that Collier translated in 1824 and 1825. The latter, handsomely produced by the publisher, 'probably made money', but the 'rather prosy' English translation 'did not help Collier's reputation as a poet'. More damaging still was *The Poet's Pilgrimage* which did not sell and caused Collier to write later that Septimus Prowett 'didn't understand business', presumably unaware that the quality of his literary effort may have had something to do with it.[15]

There were also arguments over the omission of some plays in *Dodsley's Old Plays*, originally published in 1774 and re-issued by Prowett in 1824 and again between 1825 and 1827. Collier, who was introducing and annotating the plays, persuaded Prowett to publish an extra volume but was then unhappy at not being given the chance to proof it, claiming the 'mangled' book was full of errors and had damaged his reputation. Whatever the truth about all this, the publication marked the revival of four dramatists unread for two centuries, Robert Greene, Thomas Nash, Thomas Lodge and George Peele; and Prowett was cajoled by Collier into publishing cheap editions of four more long-forgotten titles in 1828 and 1829, by Henry Chettle, Nathaniel Field, Thomas Hughes and Anthony Munday.[16]

None of the plays was particularly successful in commercial terms and publication took much longer than planned.[17] But at the same time, in 1828, and despite the tensions, Collier and Prowett were co-operating on what proved to be a huge bestseller. Collier must have mentioned he had written down the dialogue, scenes and a description of the Punch and Judy performance when he was a teenager and, according to his own account, Prowett sent his younger brother Edward to ask him to write up his notes and add a few pages on the history of the entertainment. There is a suggestion that Edward may have been assisting Septimus for some time, a view supported by Collier's tantalising diary entry: 'Edward Prowett was a young man I wished to oblige.' Collier says he was told George Cruikshank's etchings were already done and was given just three weeks to provide the text.[18] Cruikshank's story is a little different. He describes how he visited Mr Piccini, the Punch and Judy man, at his lodgings in a 'low public house' off Drury Lane, to arrange a special 'morning performance' for Prowett, Collier and himself, and how the play was stopped from time to time for sketching and note-making purposes.[19]

Punch and Judy was a great success. Within a week or two it went into a second edition and, during the next hundred years, into dozens more. The irony is that Collier sold his manuscript for £50, probably because he was unwell and in need of money since *The Morning Chronicle*, his main source of income for many years, paid only for work done. Professional pride may also have been at play: writing in his diary some seven years later Collier explains that he had insisted on anonymity because although the manuscript might have satisfied the Prowetts it hadn't satisfied him.[20] Perhaps he was right. In the opinion of Cruikshank's recent biographer, Patten, Collier's 'prosy introduction and intrusive footnotes' are totally eclipsed by Cruikshank's illustrations which 'almost jump off the page with vitality'.[21]

Prowett had already enjoyed a successful connection with Cruikshank over the publication of the third edition of John Wright's *Mornings at Bow Street*, at the end of 1824 (but postdated 1825). And this is a further example of Prowett's shrewdness and energy. The book had been published earlier in 1824 by C M Baldwyn and reprinted in the summer. When Baldwyn died in October Septimus immediately obtained the rights for a third edition and had it out in time for Christmas.[22]

During the 1820s both imprints and Pigot's 1822 directory put Prowett at a number of different addresses: in Sweeting's Alley, then the Strand, Old Bond Street, Paternoster Row and, finally, Pall Mall. This movement does not necessarily add up to an unstable business. Such short-term arrangements, commercial and/or domestic, were far from unusual: Prowett's own parents had at least four different addresses during child-bearing years, and his brother, Robert, practised as a dentist from four different premises. One might, on the other hand, argue that Septimus Prowett did get carried away at one point in his career. In 1825 he had a lot on. He added seven or eight new titles to his list, and was managing the part-work publishing of *The Works of Antonio Canova* and *Paradise Lost*, as well as *Dodsley's Old Plays* and its difficult author. On the surface, therefore, it seems to make sense that he chose this year to give up bookselling in order to concentrate on publishing; but dropping 'bookseller' from his title was not all it appeared to be. His agenda was rather different.

On 28 January 1826 he took almost a complete column in the *Literary Gazette* (page 64) to announce the establishment of the London Literary and Publishing Society, housed, as it happens, at his own address. The opening couple of lines reveal all: 'The very high prices of new Books, whether original works or reprints, have long been a subject of just complaint with the Public...' and Mr Prowett intends to set about 'remedying an evil calculated to prevent... the diffusion of knowledge, and moral improvement of society'. In other words, he's cutting out the booksellers, amongst whose ranks he had so recently moved, by selling direct to the public. There are a couple of interesting details in the rationale for such a scheme. New books, he explains, have passed through several hands before they reach the buyers and 40-50% is added to their original price. By dealing direct and in 'ready money' the public will benefit. Yet the example he immediately gives – an eight- or nine-shilling book will be available from the society for only five shillings – represents savings of between 37.5% and 45.5%; significant, of course, but also providing a bit more for the publisher. One of the results of this move will be the reprinting of valuable works, in demand but too expensive to publish under the present system. Lower prices will attract a larger circle of buyers. Though the society has been formed 'with the auspices of several literary and patriotic men' Prowett is clearly in charge: 'Mr. Septimus Prowett has the management of the entire publishing department.' Despite the sizeable puff, however, the scheme doesn't appear to have taken off. Nothing more is heard of it.

In 1829 Prowett published just four titles and in the following year only one, *The Poetical Works of Thomas Campbell*. It may have been his last because Septimus Prowett then disappeared.

The Disappearance

The only certainty was that he was still alive, somewhere. The suggestion that he got into financial difficulties comes in Charles Tilt's announcement of the second octavo edition of *Paradise Lost*, in late 1832.[23] It is headed 'Martin's Milton' (a piece of shorthand which underlines its success) and Tilt, publisher and bookseller, adds in an explanatory footnote that in 'consequence of the failure of the Proprietor of this splendid Work, and with a view to a very extended circulation [he is offering it] at less than half its original price'. It is deeply ironic that Tilt should be so dramatically reducing the price of a title published by the man who failed to do the same sort of thing a few years earlier. But Prowett's financial failure isn't an entirely convincing theory. During the 1820s he had published some solid work and some enormously popular titles, like *Paradise Lost*, *Mornings at Bow Street*, and *Punch and Judy*; and no notice of bankruptcy has been found. On the other hand, if he did run out of money his family would have been in a position to prevent any unseemly public proceedings.

Having failed to find Septimus in any of the obvious places throughout the 1830s the possibility of a mid-career change was explored. He was finally located in 1842 when he is listed for the first time in the *London Post Office Directory* as a picture dealer. This makes sense: his published list betrays his interest in visual art (though getting rid of Martin's mezzotints in 1832 is surprising). He may have found his true métier by now. He remained a picture dealer until his retirement in 1864; all of those years, the same directory shows, in Regent Street except for the last three when he operated from Wigmore Street.

The End

The Prowetts were a close-knit family. Four unmarried members lived in the same area of London. Susanna and James shared a house and were next door to David; not far away were Edward and even Cecilia, the youngest daughter of Sir William Wolseley of Staffordshire and Charles's widow.[24] Censuses show that for at least fifteen years – and probably much longer – Septimus lived with Robert at his fashionable West End houses and, finally, at Grove House in Chiswick, an impressive early eighteenth-century mansion set in extensive grounds and leased by Robert from the Duke of Devonshire.[25] Septimus died from old age and dropsy three years after retirement, leaving in his will a modest estate worth less than £1000 together with a number of pictures. He asks his longstanding friend, Robert Underdown, a gentleman hatter, to help brother Robert dispose of them.

Cruikshank's biographer, Patten, is a little wide of the mark in describing Prowett as 'a minor theatrical publisher'.[26] He turns out to be much more significant than that. He seems to have combined vision, energy and ambition with high standards. For the most part he filled the gaps he detected in the market with worthwhile and, in some instances, major titles that sold, he wasted no time in putting plans into action, and he engaged some of the best artists of the day: Henry Moses, a highly skilled and distinguished engraver, John Martin, at the peak of his career in the 1820s and 30s, George Cruikshank, the celebrated illustrator and cartoonist. Septimus Prowett was certainly 'one of the shrewdest book dealers of his generation' but, more importantly perhaps, he was among the first publishers to commission illustrators of the highest calibre, to allow them ample scope to express themselves, to give them full credit on the title page and to promote their work with vigour.

Mr Prowett, then, has been 'placed' – in a family, in two cities, in two careers. His short spell in Worcester and the 'missing' decade remain mysteries, at least for the present.

NOTES

1. Details of these and Prowett's other published titles appear in a preliminary list at the end of this paper.

2. *Dictionary of National Biography*. 1,1284.

3. *Catalogue of Books, in Various Languages and Classes of Literature, now on sale, at the prices affixed to each article, by R & S Prowett, High Street, Worcester 1820*. Birmingham Reference Library, ref. A0174.

4. Supplement, *Newcastle Weekly Chronicle*, 31 March 1889, 1.

5. *London Post Office Directories* 1842-66.

6. Early enough to be included in the 1822 edition of *Pigot & Co Commercial Directory for London*.

7. Guildhall Library MS 5634/3-4.

8. *London Post Office Directories* 1833-61.

9. Dewey Ganzel, *Fortune and Men's Eyes: the career of John Payne Collier* (Oxford: Oxford University Press, 1982), 30, 35.

10. In this section I am largely indebted to Professor Hanley's evaluation of the achievement of the artists engaged by Prowett. For more detailed discussion of Prowett's *The Works of Antonio Canova, Paradise Lost* and *Punch and Judy* see Howard J M Hanley,

Margaret Cooper & Susan Morris, 'The mysterious Septimus Prowett: Publisher of the John Martin Paradise Lost', *British Art Journal*, 2, no.1 (2000), 20-25.
11. J W Good, *Studies in the Milton Tradition: the publication of Milton's Works* (Illinois: University of Illinois Press, 1915), 29.
12. Robert Prowett died in Richmond in 1881 leaving an estate worth around £40 000.
13. *Kent's Original London Directory 1818*; London Metropolitan Archives, 1821 local census of part of Southwark, ref: Mf X15/158.
14. *Illustrated London News*, 17 March 1849, 177.
15. Ganzel, *Fortune and Men's Eyes*, 35.
16. Ganzel, *Fortune and Men's Eyes*, 35-37.
17. Ganzel, *Fortune and Men's Eyes*, 37.
18. John Payne Collier, *An Old Man's Diary, Forty Years Ago, 1832-1833* (London: Privately published by Thomas Richards, 1871-2), Part 4, 77-78.
19. Quoted in W Blanchard Jowett, *The Life of George Cruikshank* (London: Chatto & Windus, 1894), 118-19.
20. Ganzel, *Fortune and Men's Eyes*, 37; Collier, *Old Man's Diary*, 78.
21. Robert L Patten, *George Cruikshank's Life, Times and Art 1793-1835*, 2 vols (London: Lutterworth, 1992-96), 1 (1992), 321.
22. Patten, *George Cruikshank's Life*, 280-82.
23. *Literary Gazette*, 17 November 1832, 734.
24. Colwich Parish registers, 1780-1812. Cecilia married Rev Charles Prowett on 30 June 1812.
25. *Victoria County History of the Counties of England: A History of Middlesex*, C R Elrington [ed] (Oxford: Oxford University Press, 1982), 76-77.
26. Patten, *George Cruikshank's Life*, 320.

TITLES PUBLISHED BY SEPTIMUS PROWETT:
A PRELIMINARY LIST

All are London: Septimus Prowett, unless otherwise stated.
1. John Chambers, *Biographical Illustrations of Worcestershire* (Worcester: R & S Prowett, 1820)
2. John Chambers, *A General History of Malvern* (Worcester: R & S Prowett, 1820)
3. John Chambers, *A General History of Worcester* (Worcester : R & S Prowett, 1820)
4. Samuel Lee DD, *The duty of submission to the ordinances of man...* (Worcester: R & S Prowett, 1820)
5. *Impressions ... from a set of Silver Buttons* (London: R & S Prowett, 1821)
6. Geoffrey Chaucer, *The Canterbury Tales of Chaucer*, 5 vols (London: W Pickering; R & S Prowett, 1822)

7. Thomas Zouch, *The Life of Izaac Walton* (1823 [?25])
8. *Museum Worsleyanum; or, a collection of antique basso ...* (1824)
9. John Wright, *Mornings at Bow Street* (1824)
10. J C F von Schiller, *Fridolin*, tr. by John Payne Collier (1824)
11. *The Works of Antonio Canova in Sculpture and Modelling*, 2 vols (1824)
12. *The Works of Antonio Canova in Sculpture and Modelling*, 3 vols (1824-28)
13. J C F von Schiller, *Fight with the Dragon*, tr. by John Payne Collier (1825)
14. Thomas Roscoe, *Italian Novelists*, 4 vols (1825)
15. George Wood, *The Subaltern Officer. A Narrative* (1825)
16. James Rennie, *The Art of Improving the Voice and Ear* (1825, new ed. 1826)
17. James Rennie, *The Art of Preserving the Hair* (1825, new ed. 1826)
18. Thomas Amory, *The Life of John Buncle, Esq*, 3 vols (1825)
19. John Milton, *The Paradise Lost of Milton*, 2 vols, quarto (1825-27)
20. John Milton, *The Paradise Lost of Milton* 2 vols, octavo (1825-27)
21. Alexander Dyce, *Specimens of British Poetesses* (London: T Rodd & S Prowett, 1825)
22. I Reed, *A Select Collection of Old Plays*, ed. by John Payne Collier (1825-27)
23. J P Collier, *The Poet's Pilgrimage* (?1825 & 1828)
24. *Punch and Judy* (London: S Prowett, 1828, 2 ed. ?1828)
25. Anthony Munday & Henry Chettle, *The Death of Robert Earl of Huntingdon*, (1828)
26. Thomas Hughes, *The Misfortunes of Arthur* (London: S Prowett, 1828)
27. A Devonshire Freeholder, *The Catholic Question* (?1829)
28. Nathaniel Field, *Amends for Ladies* (London: S Prowett, 1829)
29. Nathaniel Field, *A Woman is a Weathercocke* (London: S Prowett, 1829)
30. George Cumberland, *Outlines from the Antients ... Greek and Roman Sculpture* (1829)
31. Thomas Campbell, *The Poetical Works of Thomas Campbell* (1830)
32. *Ancient Baptismal Fonts* (No other details)
33. *Ancient Greek Coins* (No other details)

Figure 1. The Yorkshire Joint Stock Publishing & Stationery Company Limited. An engraving by John Storey, Leeds c1866.

Typography in Nineteenth-Century Children's Readers: the Otley Connection

CAROLINE ARCHER
SUE WALKER AND LINDA REYNOLDS

THE YORKSHIRE Joint Stock Publishing & Stationery Company was a small provincial printer active in the middle of the nineteenth century. One aspect of its trade was reading books for young children ranging from ABC books to primers. Some of these books are typographically very different from other readers being produced in the United Kingdom around the same time, and it is these that form the basis of this paper.

The 'Typographic Design for Children' Project

Our interest in the reading books produced by the Yorkshire Joint Stock Publishing & Stationery Company arose during an Arts and Humanities Research Board-funded project looking at typographic design for children.[1] One of the aims of this project was to look at the characteristic features of and typographic changes in children's readers from the 1830s to the 1950s. This involved noting the typographic attributes of over 350 readers from this period, and the recording of these attributes in a database. We recorded the physical characteristics of the book (its size and orientation, the number of pages, whether there are page numbers, whether it is printed in black or a colour, whether the paper is rough, smooth, white or off-white); the typeface (serif, sans serif or script, whether infant characters have been used, whether the type has the appearance of being medium, light or bold); type size (the height of the small letters, the height of the capital letters, the height from the top of the ascending strokes to the bottom of the descending ones); use of vertical space (baseline to baseline distance between rows of type); horizontal space (space between letters and words); treatment of the line (line length, number of characters per line, whether the text is justified or ragged right, whether hyphenation is used at the ends of lines). In carrying out this work it became evident that the publications from the Yorkshire Joint Stock Publishing & Stationery Company were typographically different from other books included in our survey.

Beatrice Warde remarked in 1950 that children's readers were 'the books that nobody saw'. Since then, however, there has been considerable interest taken by scholars and others concerned with the teaching of reading, although the visual aspects have received little attention.[2] One problem in such studies is that of definition – what is a children's reader? Ian Michael's *The Teaching of English; from the sixteenth century to 1870* provides a comprehensive listing of the material used for the teaching of English in this period. He also defines and categorises the material into ten groups including spelling books, grammar books, books dealing with language, rhetoric, punctuation and so on. Our survey reflects four of Michael's categories: elementary reading books; anthologies, single author texts, readers not in series; books primarily for home reading, but which may have been used in school; and readers in series.[3] The books included in our survey were mainly intended for children in the early stages of learning to read: beginners; those who are relatively fluent, but still decoding; and those who are fluent and reading for meaning. We excluded 'subject readers' which have the teaching of reading as a secondary function to the teaching of geography, history, science and so on.

Most of the books we surveyed came from the British Library, the Renier Collection at the Bethnal Green Museum of Childhood, and the Parker Collection at the City Reference Library, Birmingham.[4] How representative the books in these collections are of children's readers published in the United Kingdom in the nineteenth century is difficult to determine. The books may have been saved by reason of their popularity, or they may have survived only as examples of less popular books which did not suffer the damaging effects of over-use. It could be that few early readers have survived because they were often flimsy in manufacture, subjected to prolonged use and, for reasons of economy, read until they disintegrated.[5]

The publication of children's readers in the provinces

In the nineteenth century, the provincial producers of children's readers did not have publishing as their sole business; the issuing of books was just one of many allied services that they provided. Their main concern may have been printing, or the manufacturing of stationery and account books, or book binding. They may also have produced school equipment or engaged in bookselling.

Readers were relatively cheap to produce as they customarily had few pages, and were printed in a single colour on cheap paper of an inferior quality. The text for the readers was often written by a 'mother', a 'lady', or the local schoolmaster, such as an edition of *The Only Method to Make Reading Easy, or, child's best instructor* (1839) published by Emerson Charnley of Newcastle and written by T Hastie, School-master, of Newcastle. Some texts were produced as stereotype editions, such as William Mavor's *The English Spelling Book* and William Markham's *An Introduction to Spelling and Reading English,* which were both frequently reproduced by various publishers throughout the nineteenth century. Either way, acquiring text for the locally-produced reader was inexpensive. The consumers of these books could be found both locally and nationally, and in some instances even internationally,[6] but wherever the books were sold, it was to a steady and constant market which gave the regional publisher a reasonable return on his money.

Our survey covers only a fraction of the readers produced at the time, but it does reveal some trends in output that may reflect a more general pattern. Many readers were produced in, and issued from, the three major publishing centres of London, Edinburgh and Glasgow. Publishers included Bell & Daldy, Blackie & Sons, W & R Chambers, Cundall & Addey, Darton & Harvey, Longman's, Green & Co, Macmillan & Co, and Oliver & Boyd. A significant number of children's readers were also produced by publishers in regional towns and cities around the United Kingdom. The names our survey noted from the 1830s are: R Elliott, Hereford; Thomas Melrose, Berwick-on-Tweed; William & John Bell, Newcastle-upon-Tyne; and their rivals, Emerson Charnley. By the 1850s and 1860s, children's publishing in the regions appears to decline slightly, but we noted the following names: I I Humphries, Caernarvon; Edward Pite, Woodbridge, Suffolk; William Walker & Sons Ltd, Otley; Webb Millington & Co, Leeds and Otley; and their successors, the Yorkshire Joint Stock Publishing & Stationery Co. By the end of the nineteenth century, the vast majority of children's books were produced in London, and the number of children's readers published in the United Kingdom provinces seems to have dwindled. In the 1890s our survey reveals John Heywood of Manchester as the only business publishing children's books outside London, Glasgow and Edinburgh. The decline in children's readers produced by provincial publishers appears to coincide with the introduction of the Revised Code of 1862 when the Board of Education issued a syllabus for reading, writing, and arithmetic arranged in six standards. Standard One was based on monosyllabic words; Standard Two on words of more than one syllable; and Standard Three on a short paragraph.[7] As this syllabus was compulsory, it meant a certain uniformity was adopted in producing books for primary schools. Provincial publishers no longer had the flexibility to produce children's readers when and how they wanted.

The Yorkshire Joint Stock Publishing & Stationery Company

In the middle of the nineteenth century, some of the most notable provincial children's readers were produced by three companies based in Otley, West Yorkshire. Otley, a small market town in rural Wharfedale, became home to an innovation in printing technology when two local joiners and cabinet makers, William Dawson and David Payne, joined forces to invent the Wharfedale stop-cylinder printing press.[8] This was a high-quality and durable machine which met the increasing demands for cheap printed literature in expanding British and colonial markets. The printing industry employed 2000 people in Otley, and by the end of the century there were ten individual printers' engineering firms producing iron presses which were being exported around the world. But even before the advent of printers' engineering, Otley had a small but lively printing and publishing industry. Three Otley firms are notable for the printing and publishing of children's books: William Walker & Sons Ltd, Webb, Millington & Co and the Yorkshire Joint Stock Publishing & Stationery Company.

William Walker & Sons Ltd established its printing office in Otley in 1811.[9] It was a general printer, bookbinder, stationer, a fine colour printer of artists' prints and also a newspaper office which published the *Wharfedale and Airedale Standard*. William Walker & Sons Ltd was a company of a significant size which had a nominal capital of £28 000 by the end of the nineteenth century. The company first employed William Dawson to serve his time with simple printing technology and acted as the original distributor for Dawson's printers' engineering equipment. William Walker & Sons Ltd was still trading in Otley in the 1980s.

Webb, Millington & Co of Leeds and Otley was founded by William Webb (bookseller) and Jesse Millington (printer) in the 1830s.[10] Its full trade directory description was 'printers, publishers, wholesale stationers, booksellers, and bookbinders, copperplate and lithographic printers, and stereotype founders'. It was also an agent for the distribution of William Dawson's cutting and ruling machines. Webb, Millington & Co was a large company which, by 1851, employed fifty-four people in a very large building in the centre of Otley. On 29 August 1862 the printing, publishing and stationery business of Webb, Millington & Co was sold to the Yorkshire Joint Stock Publishing & Stationery Company, also of Otley.

The Yorkshire Joint Stock Publishing & Stationery Company was established for the sole purpose of purchasing Webb, Millington & Co.[11] It commenced trading with a nominal capital of £50 000 divided into 5000 shares of £10 each. William Walker & Son Ltd and Webb, Millington & Co. were local businesses operated by local people. The Yorkshire Joint Stock Publishing & Stationery Company, on the other hand, was owned by a consortium of eleven businessmen from around the country.[12] Ten years later, the initial group of seven shareholders had increased to forty-five. The Company managers were William Webb and Jesse Millington (from the original firm of Webb, Millington & Co), and the works manager was Samuel Taylor. The Company had its main offices in Otley, and branches in Bond Street, Leeds, and Broad Street, Birmingham. Dean & Son of Ludgate Hill were its London agents. In the Yorkshire Joint Stock Publishing & Stationery Company's first catalogue (c1864) it announced itself as a 'wholesale, warehouse and manufactory of valentines, perfume packets and poetry cards, ledgers, day books, cash books, metallic books and general stationery'. This announcement only advertised a fraction of all that it produced; the company also offered a stereotyping service for both type and woodcuts, and was an agent for Dawson & Payne & Co's printing, cutting and ruling machines. The Yorkshire Joint Stock Publishing & Stationery Company traded for fifteen years before it went into voluntary liquidation on 5 December 1876, and finally ceased trading two years later, on 20 December 1878 (Figure 1, see page 118).

The children's readers issued by the Yorkshire Joint Stock Publishing & Stationery Company were typographically quite different from those being produced elsewhere in the provinces or the main centres of publishing. In order to appreciate the books produced in Otley, it is necessary to summarise the characteristics of other readers being produced at the time. The organisation of children's readers was often as complex as that in books for adults. Most books opened with a half-title page followed by a title page on which was often displayed an extraordinary amount of information set in miscellaneous Victorian types: the title, author, publisher, date and place of publication, a list of contents, advertisements for the book, and an affidavit declaring the book to be the best, the easiest, or the only method of learning to read. Obviously aimed at the instructor, the title page made an intimidating introduction to the book for the child. However, nineteenth-century children's readers were not intended to be read by unsupervised children, and certainly not for pleasure. In many schools, books were regarded as existing primarily to be read aloud after the text had been learned by rote.[13] It was, therefore, not considered necessary to make any typographic accommodation for children.

Most nineteenth-century children's readers were small in format to suit small hands[14] as can be shown from the following examples of books produced by provincial printers: *The English Primer,* R Elliott: Hereford (*c*1830) 140 x 88 mm; *The Only Method to Make Reading Easy,* Emerson Charnley: Newcastle-upon-Tyne (1839) 140 x 88 mm; *The Child's First Book,* Edward Pite: Woodbridge, Suffolk (*c*1860) 146 x 98 mm. The size may have been determined by the maximum sheet size the local printer could print, or because small books were easier and lighter for the travelling salesmen to carry.

The small format inevitably meant the books were printed in a small size of type seldom exceeding 12 points, a size that would now be regarded as too small for beginner readers. The most widely-used type in nineteenth-century children's readers was a Modern Face, characterised by a strong contrast between the thick and thin strokes, and hair-line serifs. Another common feature was the justification of all lines of text, a practice which often resulted in excessive and inconsistent word and letter spacing which can have done little to improve the legibility of the texts. Typically, the pages were densely-packed pages of text with minimal interlinear space.

The nineteenth-century Modern Face is a style of type which is often light in appearance and is easily damaged, and many of the children's readers of this time are printed with type which is worn and broken. As a result the legibility of the text is diminished. The problem of legibility was compounded by the use of poor quality paper which allowed an unacceptable degree of show-through. Damaged type and rough paper impeded clean and even press-work, and there is often great variation in printing quality between the pages of an individual book. The books were seldom printed in colour and for reasons of economy the use of illustrations was often limited to engravings taken from the printer's collection of stock blocks.

Examples of the 'Otley Readers'

The early publications of William Walker & Sons Ltd consisted of a series of highly coloured artists' drawings of horses and cattle. By the middle of the nineteenth century the company was also producing art catalogues, religious tracts, school text books and classics of English literature on behalf of such London publishers as Thomas Allman, Simpkin & Marshall and Smart & Allen. It was also a publisher in its own right, issuing a wide range of material for children, including a charming collection of miniature readers: the 'Natty Series', the 'Dainty Series', the 'Midget Series' and the 'Tiny Tots First Books'. Unusually, these readers were delightfully illustrated and highly coloured. Alongside William Walker & Sons Ltd, Webb, Millington & Co printed and published a wide range of reading material including grammars, religious and moral tracts, biographies, local interest books and school textbooks including 'Dr Bedford's Elementary School Series'. But it was Webb, Millington & Co's successors, the Yorkshire Joint Stock Publishing & Stationery Company, that produced the most notable children's readers.

The Yorkshire Joint Stock Publishing & Stationery Company produced a range of educational books, many of which were aimed at young readers. Its *Trade Catalogue of Books, Prints, Stationery &c., Published and Sold by the Yorkshire Joint Stock Publishing & Stationery Co. Limited* (c1864) includes 'Children's Toy Books', 'Packets of Books', 'Reading Easies' or 'Primers'. Other readers, which may also fit into the categories listed above, are listed as individual titles.

Although many of the texts of these books reverberate with nineteenth-century moral strictures, the typography, at least, appears to have been selected with a view to its readership. Most of the Yorkshire Joint Stock Publishing & Stationery Company's publications have fewer pages and a larger format than the average reader (*The First Step to Learning, Easy Readings for the Young* and *Picture Lessons for Little Children* are all 211 x 137 mm and have eight pages; *My First primer*, 180 x 106 mm, has twelve pages).[15] The larger format allowed the texts to be set in a dramatically larger size of type. *The First Step to Learning* was set in a type with an x-height of 7.1 mm (equivalent to a type size of around 40 points); *My First Primer* used a combination of two type sizes, equivalent to 26 points and 16 points; and *Easy Readings for the Young* and *Pictures Lessons for Little Children* both used three sizes: 24, 16 and 14 points.

Not only are the readers printed in a larger size of type, the typefaces used were different from those used in other readers of the period. *The First Step to Learning* was set using Figgins Condensed No 2 from the English foundry of Stevens Shanks. This is a Fat Face, similar to a Modern Face, but with an exaggeration of the contrast between thick and thin strokes. The type is big, black and bold, and well printed in contrast to many other readers of the same period (Figure 2).

My First Primer uses two typefaces and two type sizes. It is divided into ten

Figure 2. Page from *The First Step to Learning* (Otley: Yorkshire Joint Stock Publishing & Stationery Company [c1860s]), 211 x 137mm. Set in a large size of Figgins Condensed No 2.

lessons of progressive difficulty. Lessons 1–5 are set in Antique No 5 from Stevens Shanks with an x-height of 4.6 mm (equivalent to a type size of around 26 points). Antique No 5 is a condensed, almost monolinear slab serif type; it was very popular in the nineteenth century, and used on a wide range of material. The more difficult lessons 6–10 are set in a smaller Modern Face.

Easy Readings for the Young is particularly interesting for its choice and use of typefaces. Divided in to seven lessons, it opens with the alphabet and simple words

EASY READINGS.	EASY READINGS.
LESSON 1.	
A B C D E ant boy cat dog elk	
F G H I J fish girl hare ibex jay	**LESSON 4.**
K L M N O kite lamb man nag owl	How pleasant it is to ride in the train! how fast it runs along. When we arrive at the end of our journey we must not get out until the train stops.
P Q R S T pig quail rook snail toad	
U V W X urus viper wolf —	Railways enable us to visit distant places in a very short time, they are also of great use to us in carrying merchandise from place to place.
Y Z yew zebra	

Figure 3. Page from *Easy Readings for the Young* (Otley: Yorkshire Joint Stock Publishing & Stationery Company Company[*c*1860s]). 211 x 137mm. Lesson 1, set in Latin Expanded No 2, with an early use of the infant form of the small letter 'g'.

Figure 4. Page from *Easy Readings for the Young* (Otley: Yorkshire Joint Stock Publishing & Stationery Company Company, [*c*1860s]). 211 x 137mm. Lesson 4, set in Antique No 5; it is well printed but has inconsistent word spacing.

set in Stephenson Blake's Latin Expanded No 2, which shows an early use of the infant form of the lower case 'g'. Lessons 2–4 use Antique No 5, a Modern Face is used for Lesson 5, and Antique No 5 is again used for Lessons 6 and 7. The size of the type decreases as the lessons become more difficult. Although it appears to be a conscious decision to reduce the size of type as the text increases both in difficulty and length, the change of typeface may have been dictated by what was available in the type racks, as much as by reasoned choice. A similar pattern of typeface and type size usage can be seen in *Picture Lessons for Little Children*. This approach appears to be paving the way for the children to progress to a smaller size of type and a face which would have been used in books for adults (Figure 5).

Increasing the size of type, and choosing a face which was strong and bold, was an assistance to infant readers not offered in many other children's books of the period.

It also meant that far fewer words appeared on a page – another aid to the young reader. However, large type together with a short line length caused some erratic word spacing within the line, particularly before and after punctuation. As the lessons progressed in difficulty and more text appeared on the page, less space was allowed between the lines of text and the pages start to look over-full and rather solid. However, the impression of the type on the page is good, and the letters appear crisp and undamaged. This alone is a vast improvement on many other reading books of the nineteenth century.

The small collection of extant readers issued by the Yorkshire Joint Stock Publishing & Stationery Company offers a tantalising glimpse of some children's books which were well-planned and carefully printed, using typography that was in advance of its time. It can only be hoped that there exists a more extensive collection of this company's work, so a fuller assessment of its contribution to children's typography might be made.

figure 5. Page from *Picture Lessons for Little Children* (Otley: Yorkshire Joint Stock Publishing & Stationery Company Company, [c1860s]). 211 x 137mm. Lesson 6, set in a Modern Face, is well printed but has inconsistent word spacing and tight interlinear spacing.

NOTES

1. 'Typographic design for children' was funded by the Arts and Humanities Research Board (AHRB) from 1999 to 2001. It was directed by Sue Walker and Linda Reynolds, and the Research Assistant was Caroline Archer. The project was based at the University of Reading in the Department of Typography & Graphic Communication. We are grateful to the AHRB for their support, and we would like to thank librarians and archivists at the various libraries and museums we have used in the project.

2. Ian Michael, *The Teaching of English: from the Sixteenth Century to 1870* (Cambridge: Cambridge University Press, 1987) is a key text for anyone working in this area. Michael includes a comprehensive bibliography that includes many kinds of 'reader'. A useful, if short, summary of key readers and reading schemes from 1870 is given by P Horner, 'The Development of Reading Books in England from 1870' in G Brooks and A K Pugh, *Studies in the History of Reading* (Reading: University of Reading and UKRA, 1984), 80–84. In the same

volume J M Morris provides a good account of the development of phonic-based reading schemes in the twentieth century. Issues of the Textbook Colloquium's journal *Paradigm* contain a number of articles about reading textbooks, for example, P M Heath, 'Mrs Trimmer's school readers', *Paradigm*, 2 (March 1990), 2–3; H Price, 'Lo, it is my Ox!: reading books and reading in New Zealand schools 1877–1900', *Paradigm,* 12 (December 1993), 1–14; P W Musgrave, 'Readers in Victoria, 1896–1968: II The Victorian Readers', *Paradigm*, 16, (May 1995), 1–12.

3. Michael, *Teaching of English,* 9.

4. Bethnal Green Museum of Childhood was home to the Renier Collection which contains over 80 000 children's books, toys, games and printed ephemera dating back to 1585. Most subject areas are represented including educational books – easy readers, grammar and comprehension books, pre-school picture books and graded reading schemes. The collection has now moved to the National Art Library at the Victoria and Albert Museum. Birmingham City Reference Library, Arts, Literature and Languages Department is home to the Parker Collection of nearly 12 000 children's books and games. The original collection was based upon the acquisitions of Mr and Mrs J F Parker of Bewdley who collected children's books published from 1830 to the end of the nineteenth century. In the 1950s the collection was donated to Birmingham Library and it now contains fiction, educational textbooks and picture books dating from 1538 to the present day. The British Library has numerous children's readers from both the nineteenth and twentieth centuries. In addition, and particularly relevant to this paper, Otley Museum holds a substantial collection of material published and printed by William Walker & Sons Ltd and other Otley printers. Amongst this material is a collection of children's books.

5. See, for example, R D Morss, 'The Neglected Schoolbook' (*The Monotype Recorder*, 34 (2) (1935), 3–13 and Ian Michael, *Early Textbooks of English* (Reading: Colloquium of Textbooks, Schools and Society, 1993), 9.

6. A large number of children's readers published by the Otley firm of William Walker & Sons Ltd has been found in Europe, America and the Commonwealth. These books were not published with a foreign market in mind, and it is not known how they travelled so far from home (from information supplied by Paul Wood of the Otley Museum).

7. Board of Education, *Report of the Consultative Committee on Books in Public Elementary Schools* (1928), 1–27.

8. See P Wood, *Otley and the Wharfedale Printing Machine* (Otley: Otley Museum, 1985).

9. Public Record Office, Kew. File number BT/31/9175/68024.

10. We are grateful to Paul Wood, former keeper of Otley Museum, for information relating to Webb, Millington & Co.

11. Public Record Office, Kew. File number BT/31/664/2810. Remarkably little seems to be known about what was a significant Otley firm. We found no material relating to the Yorkshire Joint Stock Publishing & Stationery Company in Otley, Leeds or Birmingham libraries or museums.

12. The names and addresses of the seven subscribers who formed the company were: George Meek (embosser), 2 Crane Court, Fleet Street, London; R. Holme (gentleman), 30 Park Street, Camberwell, Surrey; George Edward Meek (embosser), 2 Crane Court, Fleet Street, London; George Alfred Henry Dean (publisher), 11 Ludgate Hill, London; James Granger (pencil case maker), 40 Islington Street, Birmingham; John Bayly (grocer), 19

Thomas Street, Woolwich, Kent; Charles Bansfield (ink maker), 9 Long Lane, Smithfield, London.
13. Board of Education, *Report...* (1928), 1–27.
14. B Warde, 'The making of children's books', *The Times Literary Supplement*, 24 November, 1927. Reprinted in part in *The Monotype Recorder*, 44, 1, (1970), 39.
15. None of these publications is dated, but it is likely they were produced in the 1860s.

Reproduced by permission of The British Library, shelfmark 1882.d.4.(15)

Baker's Juvenile Circulating Library in Sydney in the 1840s

WALLACE KIRSOP

IN THE THREE DECADES that followed 1820 the British colonies in Eastern Australia – New South Wales and Van Diemen's Land – moved from rudimentary and largely makeshift arrangements for the provision of books to a tolerable degree of literary civilization.[1] In the early days of the penal colonies the flow of printed matter was in the hands of the government through the medium of its official presses, of the chaplaincy aided by evangelizing and missionary societies or of private individuals who made their own dispositions to import the books they needed. Borrowing and the beginnings of a free auction market were the only other resources available to those who could not rely on their own prior accumulations, on the help of friends in the British Isles or on satisfactory contacts with London booksellers. In the 1820s this started to change in a number of ways that were to contribute considerably to the colonies' literary and intellectual infrastructure. The first regular bookshops and circulating libraries were established. That they were dangerously dependent on exclusive sources of supply – trade or denominational – in the United Kingdom or on what happened to turn up as speculative consignments to Australian ports was for the moment irrelevant. The freeing of the newspaper press, achieved against the autocratic tendencies of governors trained to command soldiers, brought into being vigorous and often rancorous organs of opinion. Institutions of all kinds were created and sometimes flourished, notably a wide selection of Christian and other religious organizations. These were pluralist societies, soon eager to rid themselves of the burden and the stigma of convict transportation and to promote autonomy through a range of local initiatives. Secondary schools came to join those engaged in elementary instruction. By 1850 the first universities had been mooted and were soon to become a reality. The mechanics' institute movement arrived quickly and took hold in a fashion that was later quite astonishing.[2] Nascent scientific societies, a growing array of courts of law, the first steps towards independent legislatures, all of these developments were in evidence, not least through the collections of books that they began to form and some of whose printed catalogues have been preserved.

Ferguson's *Bibliography of Australia*, which is in theory all-inclusive up to 1850 and even lists items attested by advertisements only, notes amongst others:[3] *Rules and Regulations for the Conduct of the Australian Subscription Library and Reading Room* (Sydney: Robert Howe, 1826; F1060); *Observations on the Establishment of the Wesleyan Library, at Hobart Town, Van Diemen's Land. With the Rules and Regulations; a List of the Books Collected; and an Appendix* [on Wesley] (Hobart Town: Andrew Bent, 1826; F1098a); *Catalogue of Books and Tracts in the Repository of the Australian Diocesan Committee* (Sydney: J Tegg & Co, Atlas Office, 1838; F2427); *List of Books and Tracts in the Depository of the Society for Promoting Christian Knowledge, in New South Wales* (Sydney: Stephens and Stokes, 1834; F1767); *Catalogue of the Books belonging to the Hobart Town Book Society (corrected to Oct. 1828)* (Hobart Town: James Ross, 1828; F1198b); *Catalogue of the Sydney Law Library Instituted 17th August 1842* (Sydney: E Alcock, 1843; F3734); *The Rules and Regulations of the Commercial Reading Rooms and Library. Established 1841* (Sydney: Kemp and Fairfax, 1842; F3382); *Rules and Catalogue of the Sydney Jewish Library and Hebraic Association* (Sydney: 1848; F4924a); *Index to the Legislative Council Library, 12 May 1849* (Sydney: W W Davies at Government Printing Office, 1849; F5129). If one adds a substantial number of book auctions in the 1840s for which printed lists as well as newspaper advertisements have survived,[4] it is easy to see that half a century after the First Settlement of 1788 opportunities for buying, borrowing and reading books were notably better for those who – voluntarily or involuntarily – found themselves in the Australian colonies.

It is in this context that one has to situate the Circulating Library for Juveniles that William Baker opened at his Hibernian Printing Office and General Stationery Warehouse, 10 King Street East, Sydney, on 1 January 1843. The catalogue, which was not known to Ferguson and which even escaped Elizabeth Webby's net, survived not because a subscriber kept it, but because it was reused for the auction sale of the library in February 1847 by John Moore.[5] A copy eventually found its way into the great collection of Sir William Dixson, now in the State Library of New South Wales. This document[6] is what needs to be examined, but, before proceeding to this analysis, it is appropriate to look at what is known of Baker's career and at other efforts in the 1830s and 1840s to provide reading matter for the children of the colonies, especially in Sydney and Hobart.

By far the most comprehensive account of William Kellett Baker (c1806-57) is contained in Richard Neville's article in *The Dictionary of Australian Artists. Painters, Sketchers, Photographers and Engravers to 1870.*[7] The *Dictionary*, edited by Joan Kerr, is no mere compilation like so many works of this kind that have had the favour of publishers in recent years, but genuinely based on new and original research. Neville concentrates, naturally enough, on Baker's work as an engraver. Here it is more important to stress his activity in the book trade in general and as a publisher.

Baker can best be introduced through the self-portrait he wrote for *Heads of the People*, the illustrated journal he produced in two volumes that ran from April 1847 to March 1848.[8] The periodical was about to go under, and the number of

25 March 1848 contained some rather melancholy reflections on the difficulty of publishing literature in colonial New South Wales:

> It is acknowledged on all hands that there is talent in the country, but few speculators can be found bold enough to engage it, and, with the exception of an occasional clever newspaper article, a sparkling bit of poetry or a piquant paragraph, there is nothing to distinguish the literary world of Sydney from the realms of dulness.

He then continues:

> We will now turn from a theme productive of many sad reflections to add a few words respecting the subject of this week's illustration, Mr. William Baker, the projector, proprietor, and publisher of the Heads of the People. He is a native of Dublin, and arrived in the colony in 1835, with the intention of carrying on the business of lithography and copper-plate engraving; but, finding that the time was not sufficiently ripe for the successful prosecution of these pursuits, he accepted the situation of Clerk to the Deputy Inspector General of Hospitals, which he retained till 1845, when he had the misfortune to break his leg. This accident laid him up for 12 months, and ultimately compelled him to resign the appointment; although he still holds that of Clerk to the Medical Board. He first turned his attention to publishing in 1842, when he commenced a reprint of Charles O'Malley in a cheap form, which met with a large and ready circulation. In three years afterwards he engaged in bringing out Mr. Callaghan's Acts of Council; the Australian Atlas, containing an account of every portion of the colony, and other charts and maps. In 1846 he published the Australian Medical Journal, which was edited by George Brookes, Esq., Senior Colonial Surgeon: this publication he disposed of to Mr. Aaron, who, however, was not fortunate enough to obtain the support of the medical profession, and the work was consequently discontinued. At the time of parting with the Medical Journal Mr. Baker commenced the Heads of the People, which he has carried out with enterprize and spirit through a period of gloom that would have deterred a less indefatigable and enterprising man.[9]

What is most apparent is the somewhat improvised character of this part-time career in the trade. At present we know nothing of Baker's training in Dublin, and he does not figure in the files being compiled and edited by Charles Benson. The Sydney years were soon to end, because the Irishman moved to Victoria in the early 1850s at the time of the Gold Rush. William Howitt, in his *Land, Labour and Gold,* remarks in his extended account of Bendigo:

> There is a lending library close to the camp, with this emblazonment in great letters all along its side – 'Baker's gold-diggers' Go-a-head Library and Registration Office for New Chums.' It must be American. [10]

The 'Go-a-head' nickname derived from Baker's time in Sydney,[11] but it may have been deemed particularly appropriate for a rumbustious camp settlement. More soberly, surviving *Bendigo Advertiser* numbers from 1854 show 'Mr Baker, Library, View Point' as a subscription agent. As George Mackay noted,[12] Bendigo had a 'number of circulating libraries' by 1853. Some of them paid for notices in the *Bendigo Advertiser*, for example

'Porter's Yankee Circulating Library, View-place, Near the Church' on 6 October 1854.[13] In the end such businesses were as ephemeral and mutable as the gold fever itself. More durably Baker's name was attached to premises in Melbourne, indeed well beyond his death in the Maitland district of New South Wales in January 1857. One has to assume that the firm was maintained after that date by the widow and one or more of the seven surviving children. There is, in any case, a certain continuity of interests, as the publishing list shows. More particularly, and maybe not fortuitously, there is the circumstance that William Baker, whose main shop was at 71 Swanston Street, was the immediate predecessor of that other Dubliner Samuel Mullen at 67 Collins Street East. There is no Victorian probate record for him, so that his achievement as a publisher is the most accurate indicator of what he was about.

Thanks to the work being done by Ian Morrison and Maureen Perkins to catalogue nineteenth-century Australian almanacs – a predictably prolific genre – and to the former's invaluable *The Publishing Industry in Colonial Australia. A Name Index to John Alexander Ferguson's* Bibliography of Australia 1784-1900,[14] we now have a reasonable idea of Baker's involvement in the colonial industry. Several of the almanacs are known only from advertisements. They were issued from Sydney, Bendigo and Melbourne: *Baker's Sydney Almanac and Pocket Companion*, 1842 (F3355); *Baker's City of Sydney Almanack*, a sheet almanac, 1844-1845 (F3781, F3978); *Baker's Pocket Diary*, 1845 (F3979); *Baker's Miniature Almanac and Diary*, 1846-1849 (F4226, F4706a); *Baker's Pictorial Sheet Almanac*, 1846 (F4227, F4228); *Baker's Go-A-Head, Victoria Golden Almanac* (for 1854) (see page 130);[15] *Baker's Miniature Almanac and Diary*, 1854 (Morrison & Perkins 243); *Melbourne Almanac*, 1853 (Morrison & Perkins 340).[16] Beyond this persistence in a presumably profitable vein we see a certain variety based initially on the Irishman's special skills. As early as 1836 he printed and published William H Fernyhough's series of twelve profile portraits of the Aborigines of New South Wales (F2122). In 1842 he began publishing in parts and by subscription an Australian edition of Charles Lever's *Charles O'Malley, the Irish Dragoon*, with the two volumes consolidated appearing in 1843 (F3438 & F3647). Perhaps because the parts are not known to have been preserved, this parallel to Dowling's 1838-1839 Launceston edition of *The Pickwick Papers* has had much less attention from collectors and bibliographers.[17] Between 1843 and 1846 Baker's 'Hibernia Press' brought out the twenty-one maps of his *Australian County Atlas* (F3560). In 1843 he also issued *J.S. Kercht's Improved Practical Culture of the Vine*, a work that was, according to Ferguson, discounted two years later (F3641). Commissions were also received from the Governor and Council of New South Wales, as witness the *Court of Requests Act Amendment Act* of 1843 with a coloured plan of the County of Cumberland (F3671).

As time passes one notices the opportunism it is reasonable to expect from a 'go-a-head' publisher. In 1845 Baker's address, along with that of Falkner of London, appeared on a song sheet, *Leichhardt's Grave: an Elegiac Ode*, words by Robert Lynd, music by Isaac Nathan (F4088). From August 1846 to April 1847 the Dubliner was responsible for producing the *Australian Medical Journal*, the first of its kind in the colony (F4222). Leichhardt's triumphant return from the dead gave rise in 1846 to *Journal of Dr. Ludwig Leichhardt's Overland Expedition to Port Essington in the Years 1844-5* (F4327) and to *Lectures delivered by Dr. Ludwig Leichhardt, at the Sydney School of Arts, on the 18th and 25th days of August, 1846* (F4329). The following year Baker turned his attention to George W Ellis's *Synopsis of Phrenology* (F4502a) and to *Heads of the People* (F4533).

The Melbourne years were to exhibit another direction again. The imprint on Rev Edward Hoare's *Baptism as taught in the Bible and Prayer Book* announces that the small book is 'Sold by W. Baker at the Church of England Book Depot, Swanston Street' (F10455a). The Anglican connection, a prefiguration of one of the roles Mullen was to play in Melbourne in obvious succession to Baker, is represented again by the distribution of the *Melbourne Church of England Messenger* (F5450) in the early 1850s and the publication of two sermons and of a charge to the clergy of the diocese by Charles Perry, Bishop of Melbourne, in 1851 and 1852 (F14039-41). Later in the decade Baker the illustrator brought out Evan Hopkins' *On the Geology of the Gold-bearing Rocks of the World, and the Gold Fields of Victoria* (F10533a & b) and, from his 'Bible Depot' in Swanston Street, a lecture, *The Dangers & Duties of the Young Men of Victoria*, by the noted Presbyterian divine, the Rev Dr Adam Cairns (F7779). It is difficult to escape the impression of a pragmatic diversity, from which children were noticeably absent despite already existing precedents for the publication of juvenile literature and textbooks.

As early as 28 June 1834 David L Waugh in Sydney was writing to his brother in Edinburgh that 'No books sell here except School Books and a few Fashionable new publications'.[18] The charge is fair enough insofar as books of a recondite character were much more likely to crop up at auction than in the booksellers' planned importations or in the speculative consignments of London merchants, who had no very high opinion of the intellectual quality of colonial society. However, it is worth spending a moment to look at what was being offered for sale.

The pattern adopted for setting up bookselling businesses in nineteenth-century Australia was not unlike that being studied by Warren McDougall for the United States fifty years earlier. In other words friends, associates or family members were sent out to obtain a foothold and were, in theory at least, assured of regular supplies from a reliable source. The most spectacular example of this trend was the arrival in Sydney in the mid-1830s of two sons, James and Samuel Augustus, of Thomas Tegg of Cheapside. James confined his operations to Sydney whereas his brother eventually moved to Hobart and Launceston in Van Diemen's Land. Ultimately the venture failed, or was not continued, so that the name Tegg had disappeared from the Australian scene by the middle of the century.[19] Others, like Robertson and Mullen, were to shape and profit from the different circumstances of the 1850s and 1860s. Although there are at present no known surviving business records for the Teggs, there are advertisements and catalogues. In particular, *A Catalogue of the Most Extensive and Valuable Stock of Books Ever Imported into Australia, now first arranged and completed for the inspection of the public, and on sale by James Tegg, at his Repository, George Street* (Sydney: printed at the *Atlas* Office, by James Tegg & Co, 1838)[20] represents effectively the remainders and cheap reprints or piracies that were so important a part of the stock-in-trade of the elder Tegg. In some fifty-one pages one has an extensive selection of titles for both adults and children. A main alphabetical sequence (p3-32) is followed by a supplement (p33-51). A slant towards juveniles is evident in such items as 'Abbott's Works, 10 vols. in a case', 'Bonnycastle's School Books, by the Revd E. C. Tyson', 'Boys' Own Book', 'Bunyan's Pilgrim's Progress, abridged for Young Persons, by the Rev. Thomas Smith, with 28 engravings on wood', 'Child's (Mrs.) Girl's Own Book, an Account of Studies, Amusements, and Employment for Young Ladies, with 144 wood engravings', 'Don Quixote abridged, with 12 engravings', 'History of Sandford and Merton, 2 vols.', 'Juvenile Scrap Book, a Collection of Interesting Tales for Young Persons, plates', 'Juvenile Instructor, a Collection of Religious and Moral Poetry and Prose, 6 vols.', a half-page list of specifically identified 'Juvenile Works', the numerous works of Mrs Hofland, 'Looking Glass for the Mind; or, Intellectual Mirror: an elegant Collection of delightful Tales, chiefly translated from "L'Ami des Enfans," 65 Engravings on Wood', 'Mangnall's Historical and Miscellaneous Questions, new edition, brought down to the present time, by G. N. Wright', 'Murray's School Books, new editions improved, by Tyson', 'Nursery Library, containing Barbauld's Hymns; Mamma's First Step to Learning; Uncle John's Moral Stories; Instructive Lessons for Children, 2 parts, in a case', 'Peter Parley's Tales', a page of 'Reward Books and Presents, handsomely printed', 'Sargant's Tales for Young Ladies on their Entrance into Life, comprising Ringstead Abbey, Temptation, and Consistency', ditto 'Life of Archbishop Cranmer, for the use of the Young', 'Tales for Young Ladies' and 'Uncle Philip's Conversations with Children about the Trades and Tools of Inferior Animals'. The supplement has long series like 'Diamond editions (for presents)', 'Pinnock's Catechisms' and 'School Books'. The same, or similar, titles can be found in the single sheet *Just arrived per 'Statesman', new and valuable books, to be sold at London prices, James & Samuel Tegg, George-street, opposite Bridge-street, Sydney*,[21] which also announces 'School Copy Books' and 'Children's Toy Cards'.

If one pushes beyond the catalogues, the evidence becomes sparser. However, the happy survival of the first day-book used by Major J W H Walch and his sons when they took over the Hobart shop of S A Tegg at the beginning of 1846[22] gives us greater insight into a juvenile market fed by school stationery supplies and by toys as much as by tailor-made books or magazines. Large invoices sent from Tasmania to booksellers in Adelaide, Melbourne and even Auckland contain – as indeed one would expect – familiar titles from the Tegg stock. Later, the return to reliance on speculative consignments exposes the fragility of the supply line. Superior offerings, like the sale of a 497-lot catalogue from Edward Lumley of London in Launceston on 23 and 24 January 1849 (F4933a),[23] did not ignore Mangnall, Parley and Pinnock, but for shops and private buyers the pickings in specialized fields could be meagre. As the Walches recognized at about the same moment in the next decade as George Robertson, it was high time to set up London buying-offices and to make the trade independent of the whims and vagaries of people who knew little about Australian circumstances.

The trouble with Baker's Circulating Library for Juveniles was that it belonged to the period when the Australian trade was still struggling to achieve its equilibrium and that it would therefore find it difficult to escape a certain adhocery and improvisation. It may have been a first for the Australian colonies, but it is hard to believe it did not have antecedents elsewhere in the English-speaking world. In any case it did not stand alone, but was attached to a general circulating library, as the initial announcement makes clear:

W. BAKER

Respectfully announces to his friends and the public in general, that, at the solicitation of many influential supporters, he will, on the 1st day of January, 1843, open a Circulating Library, at the Hibernian Printing Office and General Stationery Warehouse, 10, King Street East, for which he solicits a share of public patronage.

Among the books selected by W. B. for this purpose, will be found all the standard novels, together with the most recent productions of English literature, to which will be added, from time to time, every work of merit published in the united kingdom.

W. B. will also open on the same day a Circulating Library for Juveniles, to which he begs to call the attention of parents and heads of schools, as being of incalculable advantage in forwarding the education of children. The leisure time of the present season (Christmas Holidays) affords a happy opportunity to young people to call and see this valuable and amusing treat.

Catalogues and rules will be ready in a few days, to which W. B. respectfully begs leave to invite public attention.

Hibernian Printing Office and General Stationery Warehouse,
No. 10, King Street East,
26th Dec., 1842.

Although there was a different set of rules for the general as opposed to the juvenile library, procedures were not markedly different.

> RULES AND REGULATIONS TO BE OBSERVED AT BAKER'S
> JUVENILE LIBRARY, HIBERNIAN PRINTING OFFICE:
>
> I. Every person joining this library shall be required to pay a deposit of seven shillings and sixpence.
>
> II. One book only to be given at a time, for which one penny per day will be charged.
>
> III. No book to be detained longer than three days under a penalty of two-pence for every subsequent day, and threepence per day if detained longer than seven days.
>
> IV. No person shall lend, or suffer to be lent, out of his own residence any book belonging to the library under a penalty of one shilling for each transgression.
>
> V. For any book damaged or destroyed the parties to forfeit their deposit money; and if desirous of continuing members, will be required to renew the same, previous to their receiving any more books.
>
> VI. Every member joining will be furnished with a card, which must be produced on the demand of any other book.
>
> VII. Every book to be paid for on its being returned to the library (agreeably to the above rules) prior to others being issued.
>
> VIII. Every member will be at liberty to demand his deposit money, which will be returned to him, provided he has complied with the foregoing rules.
>
> *The Library will be open from 8 a.m. to 10 p.m.*

There is nothing surprising in any of this. What needs to be tested is the extent to which an effort was made to provide an authentically distinct and appropriate bookstock.

When Baker's library was offered for sale in 1847, the advertisement claimed there were 800 volumes, undoubtedly from both sections. The initial list of the 'JUVENILE LIBRARY' – covering two-and-a-half pages in two columns – has 281 items. Since we do not have the general catalogue at present, it is impossible to make any guesses about its contents, except to note that the Derwent Circulating Library the Walches took over from S A Tegg in 1846 was preponderantly fiction, as were the other collections of this kind recorded for the Australian colonies before 1850. Older novels – '50 St. Clair of the Isles', '79 Joseph Andrews', '137 Roderick Random, 2 vols.', '147 Paul and Virginia', '160 The Castle of Otranto' – were not absent, perhaps because of their presumed classic status. There were some local publications: '178 A Mother's Offering', *i.e.* Charlotte Barton's book printed in Sydney in 1841 and hailed as Australia's first children's book,[24] and '186 Maclehose's Picture of Sydney'. Otherwise there are numerous titles one can recognize from the Tegg and Walch catalogues or lists of books for sale – Abbott, '57 Sandford and

Merton' and the rest – and enough works of clearly juvenile intent, like '9 A Good Grandmother', '11 Alicia and her Aunt', '28 Poetry for Children', '45 Anna and her Doll', '63 Mrs. Marcett's Book for Young Children' and '241 Juvenile Letter Writer', to justify the label the library had assumed. However, there are also more worrying inclusions, like '49 Byron's Don Juan' and '264 Analogy of Religion', which lead one to suspect that, given uncertain supplies in remote Sydney, stock was filled up in opportunistic and ultimately inappropriate ways.

We have no list of borrowers or register of what they signed out. However, the Walch records for the five years or so they continued in this branch of the business they took over suggest reasons for the rapid decline of many libraries of this kind. There had to be capital – think of Baker's accident in the mid-1840s – and a constantly renewed stock. The history of circulating libraries can all too easily deviate – through concentration on lists and titles alone – into a study of 'Borrowers of the Mind', to adapt a phrase of Don McKenzie.[25] The sad end of Baker's venture no doubt has to be understood in this context.

ACKNOWLEDGEMENTS

My thanks are due to the Mitchell and Dixson Librarians of the State Library of New South Wales for allowing me access to the basic materials for a study of Wiliam Baker and of his circulating library. Charles Benson in Dublin confirmed that Baker is at present missing from the record. Des Cowley, Tom Darragh, Ian Morrison and Richard Overell reminded me once again how well served and advised book-trade researchers can be in Melbourne.

NOTES

1. For a more detailed account of the developments outlined in this paragraph see Wallace Kirsop, 'Bookselling and publishing in the nineteenth century,' in *The Book in Australia: Essays towards a Cultural & Social History*, [ed] D H Borchardt & W Kirsop (Melbourne: Australian Reference Publications in association with the Centre for Bibliographical and Textual Studies, Monash University, 1988), 16–42, 174–181, and Wallace Kirsop, *Books for Colonial Readers — the Nineteenth-Century Australian Experience* (Melbourne: The Bibliographical Society of Australia and New Zealand, 1995), esp. chapter I 'The four phases of Australian book-trade history', 1–15, 77–83.

2. Victoria, officially separated from New South Wales at the beginning of 1851, was to have over 1000 mechanics' institutes. See Pam Baragwanath, *If the Walls Could Speak: a Social History of the Mechanics' Institutes of Victoria* (Windsor, Victoria: Mechanics Institute Inc, 2000).

3. John Alexander Ferguson, *Bibliography of Australia* (Sydney: Angus and Robertson Ltd, 1941–1969, 7 volumes; reprint: Canberra: National Library of Australia, 1975). See also *Bibliography of Australia, John Alexander Ferguson. Addenda 1784–1850 (volumes I to IV)* (Canberra: National Library of Australia, 1986). Titles cited from the 'Ferguson' period (pre-1901) are given F numbers in what follows.

4. See Elizabeth Webby, 'A Checklist of Early Australian Booksellers' and Auctioneers' Catalogues and Advertisements: 1800–1849', *Bibliographical Society of Australia and New Zealand Bulletin*, 3 (1978), 123–148; 4 (1979), 33–61, 95–150.

5. See *BSANZ Bulletin*, 4 (1979), 103: 'S.M.H. [= *Sydney Morning Herald*] 16 February Moore 19 February Stock of Mr William Baker's Library 800 [volumes]'. 35 volumes remaining were sold by Moore on 8 October of the same year (ibid., 105).
6. Shelf mark: Dixson 84/505.
7. (Melbourne: Oxford University Press, 1992), 39–40.
8. See Richard Neville, *Faces of Australia: Image, Reality and the Portrait* (Sydney: State Library of New South Wales Press, 1992), 16, 46–47, 78–79, and *Heads of the People: a Portrait of Colonial Australia*, [ed] Tim Bonyhady & Andrew Sayers (Canberra: National Portrait Gallery, 2000), 3–4, 38–53.
9. *Heads of the People*, II, 176.
10. William Howitt, *Land, Labour and Gold; or, Two Years in Victoria: with Visits to Sydney and Van Diemen's Land* (London: Longman, Brown, Green, and Longmans, 1855, 2 volumes), II, 38.
11. See Frank Melthorpe, 'Other Days: Sydney Litterateurs in '48', *Sydney University Magazine* (October 1878), 30–38, esp. 37–38.
12. *Annals of Bendigo. 1851–1867* (Bendigo: Mackay & Co, [1912]), 17.
13. 3 f.
14. (Melbourne: BSANZ, 1996).
15. (Bendigo: William Baker, Hibernian Press, 1853). The only known copy of this sheet almanac – held in the British Library – is discussed in Maureen Perkins, *Visions of the Future: Almanacs, Time, and Cultural Change 1775–1870* (Oxford: Clarendon Press, 1996), 174–175, 188. An advertisement for Baker's library in the *Bendigo Advertiser* of 24 January 1855 (1g – requesting the return of books for stocktaking) announces the arrival of the next edition of 'Baker's Go-a-head Golden Almanac' and celebrates this event with eleven four-line stanzas of doggerel.
16. One senses that the titles recorded — to which must be added two others produced in Sydney in 1865 and 1873 under Baker's name by his heirs and successors (F6549 & F6550) — are the tip of an iceberg of demagogic, but none the less utilitarian, publishing.
17. See Clifford Craig, *The Van Diemen's Land Edition of* The Pickwick Papers. *A general and bibliographical study with some notes on Henry Dowling* (Hobart: Cat & Fiddle Press, 1973).
18. Mitchell Library, Sydney: MS A 827 (microfilm CY 812).
19. See James J Barnes & Patience P Barnes, 'Reassessing the Reputation of Thomas Tegg, London Publisher, 1776–1846', *Book History*, 3 (2000), 45–60, and Victor Crittenden, *James Tegg, Early Sydney Publisher and Printer* (Canberra: Mulini Press, 2000).
20. Not in Ferguson. See Elizabeth Webby in *BSANZ Bulletin*, 3 (1978), 148.
21. Loc. cit.
22. See chapter IV 'Bookselling in Hobart Town in the 1840s' in W Kirsop, *Books for Colonial Readers*, 59–76, 93–6.
23. On Lumley's activities see chapter III 'Edward Lumley and the consignment trade' in W Kirsop, *Books for Colonial Readers*, 39–58, 88–92.
24. See Marcie Muir, *Charlotte Barton* (Sydney: Wentworth Books, 1980). The original (F3158, with a wrong ascription) is available in facsimile: *A Mother's Offering to Her Children by a Lady Long Resident in New South Wales*, [ed] Rosemary Wighton (Milton, Queensland: The Jacaranda Press, 1979).
25. See, for further remarks on this subject, Wallace Kirsop, 'Bendigo's Nineteenth-Century German Library', *BSANZ Bulletin*, 18 (1994), 169–172.

Staying the Course: the Edinburgh Cabinet Library, 1830-1844

IAIN BEAVAN

FROM THE LATE 1820s the advertising columns of the British newspaper press reflected the vogue for (relatively) cheap non-fiction publication within sets or series. The pages of the *Scotsman* in autumn 1830 are entirely typical in this respect, with advertisements for the Family Library, for titles within the publishing programme of the Society for the Diffusion of Useful Knowledge (SDUK), and for Longman's Cabinet Cyclopaedia and Cabinet Library. Also present were prominent announcements for the new edition, at five shillings per volume, prepared by Scott himself, of the Waverley Novels, and published in Edinburgh by Robert Cadell.

Within these columns was an advertisement for yet another non-fiction series, the Edinburgh Cabinet Library, from the firm of Oliver & Boyd.[1] The appearance of the series was both a new departure and a natural progression for the firm. The firm's early imprints and stock lists suggest they relied heavily on educational and school texts, along with chapbooks, song books and other cheap works. Their *c*1823 catalogue included sixpenny editions of the perennial *Goody Two Shoes,* the *Death of Cock Robin, Mother Bunch's Fairy Tales,* the Little Warbler (a series of song books), spelling books, and guides to penmanship, English and Latin grammars, and 'cheap and accurate' editions of the most popular performances in their New British Theatre.[2] This catalogue also demonstrates Oliver & Boyd's dalliance (largely during the 1820s) with the idea of becoming a literary publisher, in carrying announcements of James Hogg's *Mountain Bard* and *Winter Evening Tales,* with which, during the same decade, the company published some of Galt's novels, and a translation, by Carlyle, of Goethe. But their interest in literary publishing was not sustained, and never supplanted their more reliable, if less immediately exciting, investments in the production of children's books and school texts.[3]

By the early 1830s Oliver & Boyd had added the SDUK and the Society for Promoting Christian Knowledge to the list of major publishers for which they acted as wholesalers in Scotland, from which position the Edinburgh firm was ideally placed both to judge the success of books aimed at the 'useful knowledge' market, and also to contribute to it, in acting as agents for the Family Library (published by Murray, and with whom Oliver & Boyd had worked since 1819) and also for the SDUK's Library of Useful Knowledge and Library of Entertaining Knowledge. They were also able to appreciate the success of Cadell's edition of the Waverley Novels, which proposed to deliver a volume every month.

The prospectus (printed in the spring of 1830) for the Edinburgh Cabinet Library repays attention, for within it we find Oliver & Boyd trying to position their series in a crowded market. The firm essentially attempted to differentiate its new series from the Library of Useful Knowledge and Library of Entertaining Knowledge, both of which were heavily criticized as irrelevant and relentlessly serious,[4] by proposing a set of newly commissioned texts on travel and discovery with appropriate details of natural history that would provide a 'foundation of useful knowledge' which reflected the 'realities of nature and of human life' and concluded that 'the story... of those adventurers who first traversed the expanse of stormy oceans... is diversified by scenes as eventful and affecting as can be created by the effects of the most brilliant fancy'.[5]

In the 'Completion of the... Library', a statement included in the *Travels of Marco Polo* (1844), the publishers listed all twenty-six discrete titles produced in thirty-eight volumes, and reiterated (p.1) their major aim to have constructed, 'from varied and costly materials not easily accessible to the general reader, a popular Work... devoted to those branches of knowledge which most happily combine amusement with instruction', and continued by reflecting the impulse of commercial expansion and the imperative to save souls, as the titles within the series were to 'bring before the eye of the British reader regions interesting as the scenes of colonial or missionary enterprise'. It is unsurprising, then, that descriptions of Canada, parts of Africa, and New Zealand figured significantly in the series.

The Edinburgh Cabinet Library was published as a small octavo, with engravings, at five shillings in cloth boards, and was due to be published (though it never was) at a rate of one volume every two months. The prospectus tells us that the series was to be 'printed uniformly with the beautiful edition of the Waverley Novels now in course of publication'.[6] This is somewhat unusual, in that emulation – in this instance with a fiction series – was adopted as part of the marketing tactics.

Oliver & Boyd may have argued that the texts would be subtly different in approach, yet simultaneously claimed that the Edinburgh Cabinet Library 'from its size, may, if desired, be bound up as a companion to Dr Lardner's Cabinet Cyclopaedia, the Family Library or to the Library of Entertaining Knowledge'. The company clearly calculated that close (physical) likeness – if not, in a very real sense, total absorption – in the common cause of supplying useful knowledge would offer the prospect of better sales than outright competition. It is certainly the case that all the series referred to in the prospectus are very similar in size. It is almost as though the small octavo shape had become an accepted, perhaps expected, part of the successful sales formula for many monographs and monographic series of the time. In late 1829, Hugh Murray, the geographer, who was busy writing up the first of his many compilations for the Edinburgh Cabinet Library, consulted George Boyd on a project of his (previously rejected by Longman) to have been called 'General Review of Living and Contemporary Poets', and continued, 'The work would make I think a pretty close printed volume of about 400 pages in small octavo to correspond with the Specimens of Ellis, Southey, & Campbell; or in any other shape you might think more saleable'.[7]

The series did not get off to its promised start. The first volume was to have been on the modern history of Greece; and Sir William Hooker, later Director of Kew, was supposed to have supplied the whole series with botanical notices, but neither plan came about. Others had misgivings about being associated with the series. Sir John Leslie, mathematician and physicist, and holder of the chair of Natural Philosophy in Edinburgh, wrote to George Boyd,

> I rather inconsiderately assented to your proposition to give my name to your proposed work. Some of my friends have since remonstrated with me for this facility & have urged that the public will view it as a lowering of my credit. They state that if I make such a sacrifice, I should receive an handsome pecuniary reward besides the payment for such articles as I contribute... The London booksellers purchase the countenance of known names at a high price.[8]

The matter was presumably resolved amicably, as Professor Leslie's name appeared as one of the authors in the first of the series, *Narrative of Discovery and Adventure in the Polar Seas* (1830).

The major writers for the series were predominately Scottish. Many were educated or taught at a Scottish university (usually Edinburgh), or else were members of the various learned societies of the time. It would be an exaggeration to describe the contributors as a coterie, but they certainly moved in overlapping circles. In one instance, the authors were related by marriage: Patrick Fraser Tytler and James Baillie Fraser were brothers-in-law and both were established writers. Tytler, who also wrote for Murray's Family Library, had been called to the bar, had already undertaken some serious historical studies, and was a candidate for the post of Historiographer Royal for Scotland.[9] Fraser had written on India, Nepal and Persia, and used these experiences as a basis to produce a few novels under Colburn's imprint.[10] James Wilson,[11] zoologist, who contributed to the growth of Edinburgh University Museum, and who comes across in his correspondence with Oliver & Boyd as an obliging but very busy man, offered George Boyd considerable advice on the early volumes of the Library, and acted as intermediary between the publisher and Audubon, when the ornithologist was on one of his periodic visits to Edinburgh, to try and persuade him to prepare a volume for the series. However, Audubon, fearful lest such a commitment might jeopardise his other publishing plans, declined the invitation.[12] William MacGillivray, also an ornithologist, and who collaborated with Audubon on other publications, had been an assistant to Robert Jamieson, mineralogist, and Professor of Natural Philosophy at Edinburgh. Both Jamieson and MacGillivray were to contribute substantially to the Edinburgh Cabinet Library. James Nicol, the geologist, had also studied under Jamieson, and was to follow MacGillivray into the chair of Civil and Natural History at Marischal College, Aberdeen.[13]

George Boyd's contracts with his authors were tightly drawn. James Fraser's book on Persia finally appeared in 1834, though the contract had been agreed in March 1832. Boyd wrote to Fraser:

> We would propose to illustrate the work with a correct map and seven or eight wood engravings including a Vignette for the title page... As we have several works in preparation, the one proposed will be in good time if the Manuscript is finished in twelve or fifteen months from this date. We may again repeat that we cannot afford to exceed 400 pages on the same size and page and type as the other vols of the Edinburgh Cabinet Library being exactly 12½ sheets. For the entire Copyright of the work we will agree to give you ten guineas per sheet.[14]

Fraser, with over £130 on offer, was treated more favourably than William MacGillivray who was yet to establish his reputation, and who was offered only £75 for the copyright for his work on Humboldt.[15]

Arrangements occasionally went sour. Boyd might later have wished he had approached someone other than Christian Johnstone to compile *Lives and Voyages of Drake, Cavendish and Dampier* (1831). An established author, and later senior editor for *Tait's Magazine*, Christian Johnstone knew the literary and publishing world extremely well.[16] She was also married to John Johnstone, a printer and publisher in his own right.

Boyd's offer to Christian Johnstone of £80 for the copyright of *Drake* was very badly received. John Johnstone wrote to Boyd on his wife's behalf, and warmed to his theme:

> I really cannot think of taking £80 for the volume of Lives which Mrs Johnstone at your special request wrote for the Cabinet Library... At the time I mentioned to her that you would never pay the volume less than £100 – I certainly never dreamt that you would, after having often heard you say that you were to engage none but first-rate writers for the Library...you forget that I can calculate to a pound what this volume costs you – and I know that after paying the writing as it should be paid you will have a handsome profit even upon the first Edition, as well as the entire gain on all that may come after.[17]

Specialised knowledge often demanded expert writers. Hugh Murray, the major author of the three-volume *Historical and Descriptive Account of China* (1836), sent Boyd the article on commerce, prepared jointly by John Crawfurd and his literary secretary, Peter Gordon, and commented on the expected fee: 'as to remuneration he [Crawfurd] said that it was equal to <u>two</u> sheets of the Foreign and Westminster reviews, which paid out at the rate of <u>Ten</u> Guineas <u>per sheet</u>'. Boyd evidently agreed that the contribution was indeed worth 20 guineas, and paid out for 48 pages or 1½ sheets precisely £21.[18] The text on China was being prepared at a time when interest in extending commerce and trade with that country was high, with the East India Company about to lose its trading monopoly. Murray wrote to Boyd, 'The subject [of the tea trade] will now be of preeminent importance, since there seems to be no doubt that the trade will be thrown open', and went on to argue that the writer of the commercial sections on China, would have to be 'strictly neutral, and not take any part against free trade which is the popular side...he should study to communicate every information which can be useful to the free traders'.[19] Crawfurd carried out his task robustly. Starting with tea, he led the reader through discussions on the commercial possibilites of silk and sugar, but saw the opium trade as presenting real opportunities, and argued that

> if the Chinese government impose absurd rules... if they make laws which they have no power to enforce... they must take the consequence of their own folly... With respect to the deleterious quality of the drug, we consider this opinion to be a mere prejudice... It is, in fact, not the use but the abuse which is hurtful.

On trade contacts with China, Crawfurd suggested that 'We may take possession of an island on the coast with a good harbour...and there form a commercial emporium' through which 'an active contraband trade might be maintained'.[20] The overall message was of course clear: nothing was to stand in the way of British commercial power and expansion.

Revd Michael Russell, installed Episcopalian Bishop of Glasgow in 1837, but whose earlier ministry was in Edinburgh, was a voluminous author who, overall, made the single largest contribution to the Edinburgh Cabinet Library. As well as his own compilations within the series, he frequently acted as editor, and reader, advising Boyd on manuscript submissions and proofs. Russell was almost invariably considerate in his comments on the writing of others, indeed at times he could be somewhat apologetic: on being sent a copy of *Narrative of Discovery...in Africa* (1830) for comment, he wrote, 'you will think me a traitor & a deceiver & every thing that is bad, for returning the slips uncorrected. But the real truth is I <u>cannot</u>. Any attempt to alter would spoil the whole, by changing the train of thought [and] ...doing an incalculable injury both to Mr Murray & to his work'.[21]

In April 1831, Dr John Memes offered an elaborate outline of a projected work on Italy. Memes, who had yielded to an unacceptable degree of discursiveness, should have known better, as he had previously written for Constable's *Miscellany*. The synopsis was sent to Russell who, uncharacteristically, became exasperated with it, and suggested to Boyd that 'the work may be easily comprehended in one volume not exceeding 400 pages, provided Dr Memes will consent to leave out all the <u>details</u>

of his <u>excursions, walks & journeys</u> & simply give the result under proper heads'.[22] A contract with Memes was subsequently signed, presumably accepting the need to keep the work down to 400 pages, but after the author failed to come up with the manuscript in due time (May 1832), George Boyd's patience eventually cracked.

In December 1834 he wrote to Memes, then living in Ayr, ending the contract, stating that 'we farther intimate that we hold you liable in damages to us for your breach of engagement, which has produced to us not only great inconvenience, but considerable pecuniary loss', and continued, ' We request you will return the books we lent you, to Mr Dick, who has our Authority to receive them'. John Dick, bookseller in Ayr, was requested by Boyd to call on Memes, and retrieve those works that had been lent to the author to help with the writing of the volume on Italy, and was advised, 'We wish you to be peremptory in your application to Dr M, and not allow yourself to be put off with any of those promises of which he is so liberal'.[23]

Memes was not at all unusual in being lent background reading to enable him to undertake the commission, though none of the other authors appears to have had the impudence to retain the books. And there is some irony in the fact that of the books he retained to provide the background for his text, one at least was from Lardner's Cyclopaedia, one from the SDUK's publishing programme, and one from Murray's Family Library.[24] And the manner in which Memes – and others – went about their work raises a cluster of wider, more general, and as yet largely unanswered questions, bearing on the extent to which popularising texts digested and incorporated the thinking and presentation of other such works in a given subject area.

Most authors struggled successfully through their tasks. In December 1835, Andrew Crichton, historian, and biographer, having seen his *History of Arabia* appear in the series in 1833, subsequently laboured with his book on Scandinavia (which eventually appeared in 1838) and apologised to Boyd 'for being so long in finishing it, but it has proved a more serious task than I had anticipated',[25] largely because of a lack of immediately available background information. James Baillie Fraser became totally disenchanted with his *Mesopotamia and Assyria* (1841). In October 1839 he wrote to Boyd, 'I can with truth say that I have spared neither time nor pains to make it complete, and that it has cost me more in labour and mental exertion than anything I have had before to do... I scarcely know any bribe that would induce me to undertake another similar work'. That, unfortunately for Fraser, was not the end of the matter. By January 1841, the work had gone to the compositors, at which time a shortfall in the quantity of text (equivalent to 16 to 20 pages) was discovered. Fraser was asked to make up the deficiency. He made Boyd aware of his feelings:

Now I must say that this seems hardly treating yourselves or the work, not to say myself, very fairly - You press me in the first place to compress as much as possible - you cut out, you squeeze in, and...abridge & curtail the work when in your hands - and at the eleventh hour when more than half printed you call upon me for more matter![26]

It was not only Michael Russell who contributed more to individual titles than might at first appear. Other writers did likewise: James Nicol, still at the beginning of his career as a geologist, prepared a volume on Iceland (1840) for a copyright purchase of £70. Nichol's name, it may be noted, never appeared on the title page. But behind the scenes, Nicol had been earning money from Oliver & Boyd by assisting Andrew Crichton in translation work (presumably working on *Scandinavia, Ancient and Modern*), and on preparing an article on the climate and geology of Scotland for the publishers' *New Edinburgh Almanac*.[27]

It obviously suited Michael Russell to contribute to the Edinburgh Cabinet Library: even after his appointment as bishop, he wrote up the volumes on *Polynesia* (1842) and *Voyages Round the World from the Death of Captain Cook* (1843), prepared additional, updated matter for the fourth edition of *British India* (1843) and the third edition of *China* (1843), and revised the proof sheets of William Spalding's *Italy and the Italian Islands* (1841) and Fraser's *Mesopotamia* (1841). Russell himself was criticised for taking on so many varied commissions, and being prepared to write on subjects about which he had no first-hand knowledge. There is no evidence that Russell ever travelled outside Britain, so that no element of his geographical or topographical writings on *Ancient and Modern Egypt* (1831), *Palestine* (1831) or the *Barbary States* (1835) could have been based on personal experience. To be fair to Russell, though, his writings for the Edinburgh Cabinet Library and other series may have been a means to a greater end, as it has been suggested that a major reason why he continued to devote time to such writing was to raise funds to assist the publication of his more scholarly religious publications.[28]

It could also be said in Russell's defence that his volumes for the Cabinet Library proved some of the most popular: his *Palestine, or the Holy Land* went through at least four editions, and over 10 000 copies were sold. And Russell, the cleric, was also prepared to expose the wider reading public to new geological ideas. In his *Nubia and Abyssinia* (1833, p384) he refers (ambiguously) to 'a celebrated theory of the earth...[in which] all the land now above water will be swept into the sea, to be re-formed into new continents, and in due time raised above the surface, as the abode of future generations'. By the time of *Polynesia, including New Zealand* (1842) Russell was prepared to make explicit reference to Sir Charles Lyell's massively influential *Principles of Geology* (1830-33), which offered a uniformitarian interpretation of geological activity and processes, and which effectively challenged attempts to render the scientific account somehow consistent with the Biblical record of earthly creation.[29]

The Edinburgh Cabinet Library prospectus noted (p3) the 'avidity manifested for every species of useful knowledge'. The meaning and significance of the phrase differed according to almost individual circumstance, though in so far as it was applicable to aspects of the texts in the Cabinet Library series, it had much to do with aspirations of self-reliance, respectability, and financial security. The first volume, on the Polar Seas, drew attention to what were seen as opportunities in the whaling industries, the facts about which Boyd was careful to confirm as best he could, by corresponding with Forbes Frost, a bookseller in Aberdeen, who, in turn passed on relevant information from 'Messrs Catto, who are intensive ship owners & managers for a whale fishing company'.[30] The volumes on British America offered advice to emigrants on how best to clear and manage the land; and, in the interests of a growing Empire, the volumes on India included advice on how to travel comfortably, what exercise to take, and how to maintain good health.

The volumes in the series were printed and published in Edinburgh, but their overall production demonstrates the interdependence of the various elements of the book trade. First editions appeared in impressions of between 2500 and 6000 copies, a proportion of which was sent down to sent down to Simpkin, Marshall (Oliver & Boyd's wholesale agents in London) immediately after publication. In November 1836 Simpkin, Marshall persuaded the London trade to subscribe to c530 copies of *Circumnavigation of the Globe...to the Death of Cook*; and, some weeks later, had on hand a further c170 copies. And of the earlier works in the series (*i.e.* up to volume 20) Simpkin, Marshall had in stock a total of c1250 copies.[31]

The paper for the Edinburgh Cabinet Library was throughout supplied by John Dickinson, from his mills in Hertfordshire. Dickinson was on friendly terms with Boyd, and his letters to Edinburgh often carried news from the London book trade. In October 1834 he commented that Murray's Family Library

> will I understand finish at Vol 50, this entre nous, - It will leave rather a better field for yours, tho' I don't think your sale depends much on these sort of circumstances, your books are good & cheap & when the set is complete according to your prospectus, I think it will be generally & permanently regarded as a family desideratum.

Dickinson then drifted off into a discussion on stamp duties.[32] But a few weeks later he wrote to Boyd in more serious tones: business was in temporary trouble.

> The mills are almost at a stand, for we have had the greatest drought ever known in our country. We have been put to all manner of shifts for paper & have no stock...[and] I am unable in consequence to send you an invoice for any portion of your last

order...We now have rain & every appearance of a change of weather, & if we can get a supply of water I mean to get up a large stock of your dble fCap.[33]

The wood engravings, also, were executed in London, where, at first, they appear to have been printed up and shipped back up to Edinburgh for binding in the volumes. The engravings for the earlier volumes were purchased from Vizetelly, Branston & Co., with whom George Boyd rapidly became uncomfortable over prices, and had to be firmly reminded:

> On referring to the charge for the Impressions in 8vo foolscap from the Woodcuts there does not appear to be any clerical error, tho' the price (18/- Per Thousand) perhaps may, without explanation, appear rather high...We have almost daily instances in which the making ready of a cut occupied twice as much time as the printing of the impressions afterwards.
>
> In order to do the fullest justice to work of this sort we pay the pressmen extra wages, and their progress is after all so slow that we seldom get more impressions worked off in a day than you would expect in an hour...Mr Branston desires me to say that it is desirable for your Artists to give as little sky as possible as that is a part of a landscape which it is very difficult to give proper effect to, on wood.[34]

Oliver & Boyd soon adopted a different approach and turned to John Jackson who evidently sent the wood engravings themselves up to Edinburgh.[35] At the time, the quality and fidelity of the engravings were admired, especially so in the context of a relatively cheap series: Robert Jamieson, on receiving a copy of MacGillivray's *Humboldt's Travels*, noted that 'the engravings - excepting however the map which is very bad - are excellent - the Jaguar alone is worth 5 Sh-'.[36]

The last volume was published in 1844, though the series had been sinking for some time before then. When in early 1843 George Boyd died, and Thomas Oliver retired, the business was taken over by Boyd's brother and nephews, who early decided formally to discontinue the Cabinet Library. As wholesalers, they would have recognised that other 'useful knowledge' series were ailing or had already folded, and that the demand for such material was diminishing. Altogether it was an unsettled time. Back sets could not be shifted, and were offered at reduced prices. Retail underselling was not uncommon.[37] Attempts to discover markets abroad came to nothing: their own titles had beaten them to it, and they were advised by Carey & Hart of Philadelphia not to try sending copies of the Edinburgh Cabinet Library to America, 'as nearly every work in the series have been republished by Messrs Harper & Brothers in New York in their Family Library 150 Vols at 2/- per volume, and are now reissuing the Work at 1/- sterling per Vol.'[38] In order to try to revive sales, Oliver & Boyd halved the price per volume. But in spite of making a modest profit at this lower retail price, and in the knowledge that some at least of the volumes were still worth reissuing,[39] a decision was made in 1849 to dispense with the titles, and so the series, or at least the remainder of the stock and stereo plates, passed out of Oliver & Boyd's hands, and were sold on to Nelson & Co.[40]

George Boyd appears to have been a tough but fair businessman, and seems usually to have had a good working relationship with his writers.[41] He may also have been too preoccupied with business for the comfort of his friends and acquaintances. Dickinson's letters to Boyd are full of earnest requests for information on his health, and pleadings to take life easier. After hearing reports of Boyd's suffering intestinal troubles, Dickinson warned him to forego spirits and stick to wine only, and added

> Beware of the other sex, its a tempting amusement, but won't do when a man is not in robust health - Business also must be taken in moderation [as] there's no great advantage after you're lodg'd in the Kirk yard in having people say "he was the cleverest & most indefatigable man of business in Edinburgh, but he made himself a slave to it & it killed him".[42]

ACKNOWLEDGEMENTS

Acknowledgements are due to the following for permission to quote from the Oliver & Boyd papers: Pearson Education Ltd; National Library of Scotland. Thanks also to Napier University for a 1999 MacCaig Visiting Fellowship, allowing me opportunity to work on this business archive.

NOTES

The Oliver & Boyd papers, deposited in the National Library of Scotland, are cited throughout as Acc 5000.

1. *Scotsman*, 18 September 1830.
2. Catalogue, Acc 5000/1411.
3. I am grateful to David Hounslow for raising the intriguing question as to whether didactic texts prepared for a juvenile market (e.g. some of Rev Isaac Taylor's compilations published by John Harris) influenced the style and illustration of useful knowledge series (primarily intended for an adult readership).
4. J A Roebuck, 'Useful Knowledge', *Westminster Review*, 14 (1831), 365-94.
5. Prospectus in Acc 5000/1423.
6. First noticed by Jane Millgate, *Scott's Last Edition: a study in publishing history* (Edinburgh: Edinburgh U.P., 1987), 141. See also chapter 7 for the publishing influence of Cadell's 1829-33 edition of Scott. Even John Murray thought that sales of his new edition of Byron could be helped by comparing it with Cadell's edition of the Waverley Novels. See his advertisement in the *Scotsman*, 23 November 1831.
7. Letter, 4 December 1829. Acc 5000/195. On 12 August 1829, Hugh Murray wrote to Boyd that 'the finished copy of Africa...will, I think, exceed the agreed extent of 350 pages...but you will perhaps find it expedient to enlarge somewhat the page to make it equal to the Family Library'. Acc 5000/195. Hugh Murray prepared, alone or as the major author, volumes on the Polar Seas (1830); Africa (1830); British India (1832); China (1836); British America (1839); United States of America (1844); Marco Polo (1844).

THE EDINBURGH CABINET LIBRARY

8. Letter, 18 April 1830. Acc 5000/195.
9. Tytler contributed to the Edinburgh Cabinet Library a *Historical View of...Discovery on the More Northern Coasts of America* (1832), and biographies of Raleigh (1833) and Henry VIII (1837).
10. *Narrative of a Journey into Khorasan* (London: Longman, 1825) preceded *The Kuzzilbash: a tale of Khorasan* (London: Colburn, 1828).
11. His eldest brother was John Wilson, Professor of Moral Philosophy at Edinburgh, and famous as the pseudonymous Christopher North of *Blackwood's Magazine*.
12. Letters, Wilson to Boyd, 18 and 28 January 1831. Acc 5000/196.
13. See *DNB* for most of the Cabinet Library's authors.
14. Letter of 11 March 1832. Letter Book, 1814-47. Acc 5000/140, 351-54.
15. Acc 5000/140. Letter, 1 July 1831. MacGillivray's work on Humboldt appeared in 1832. A subsequent commission, to prepare a multi-volume biography of naturalists, was reduced to a single-volume *Lives of Eminent Zoologists* (1834), on which MacGillivray became uneasy over the 'altogether absurd' changes made at proof stage. A little earlier, MacGillivray was concerned that George Boyd might contractually constrain him from writing another (similar) zoology book that might interfere with the sales of the one published in the series. Thus MacGillivray to Boyd: 'If I were to write a little book on zoology, it would be as absurd in me to promise not to write a large one on the same subject, as for a tailor who had made a coat for a customer to promise not to make one of the same kind, or a better one, for any other person'. Letters, 19 February 1833 and 1 April 1834. Acc 5000/197.
16. Also well known as Meg Dods, under which name she wrote *The Cook and Housewife's Manual*, which went through many editions under Oliver & Boyd's imprint.
17. Letter, 1 December 1831. Acc 5000/196.
18. Murray advised Boyd, 'On considering the important question of the commerce...the best person is John Crawford...for several years governor of Sincapore [sic].. He was examined at great length before the house on the subject of the China trade and most of the articles on the oriental trade in Mcculloch's Dictionary were communicated by him'. Letters, 18 April and 6 August 1834. Acc 5000/197. Boyd's payment is recorded in the firm's Cost Book, 1834-94. Acc 5000/22. Calculation of payment by type-set page seems to have been commonplace. James Wilson discussed the payment for his natural history contributions to the new edition of the *Encyclopaedia Britannica*. 'For the other 480 pages or 60 sheets of new matter I am allowed Five Hundred Guineas which I think is about £8. 15s. a sheet.' Wilson then went on roughly to equate 16 pages of the Edinburgh Cabinet Library with a $4°$ sheet of the *Encyclopaedia*. Letter, 27 May 1830. Acc 5000/195.
19. Letter, 31 May 1833. Acc 5000/197.
20. Hugh Murray and others, *An Historical and Descriptive Account of China...*3 vols (Edinburgh: Oliver & Boyd, 1836), III, chapter 2, especially 64, 88-89.
21. Letter 14 June 1830. Acc 5000/195.
22. Memes's synopsis of May 1831, Acc 5000/196. For Russell's comments see letters of 2 and 5 May 1831, Acc 5000/196.
23. Copy letters, 31 December 1834, to Memes and Dick, Acc 5000/197.
24. The list of books with Dr Memes as at 24 June 1836 included Smedley's *Sketches from Venetian History*, vol. 1 (Family Library, 20), 1831; Simonde de Sismondi's *A History of the*

Italian Republics (Cabinet Cyclopaedia: History), 1832; a volume of *Pompeii* (Library of Entertaining Knowledge), 1831. Acc 5000/198.
25. Letter, 20 December 1835. Acc 5000/197.
26. Letters, 1 October 1839, Acc 5000/200; 27 January 1841, Acc 5000/201.
27. Payments of 10 January 1838 recorded in Acc 5000/140, 460.
28. William Walker, *Three Churchmen: Sketches and Reminiscences*...(Edinburgh: Grant, 1893), 53-55.
29. Robin Gilmour, *The Victorian Period: the Intellectual and Cultural Context of English Literature, 1830-1890* (London: Longman, 1993), 118-21.
30. Letter, Forbes Frost (of the booksellers, Alexander Brown & Co.) to George Boyd, 20 January 1830. Acc 5000/195.
31. Letters, Simpkin, Marshall to George Boyd, 8 and 26 November 1836, Acc 5000/198.
32. Letter, 30 October 1834. Acc 5000/197.
33. Letter, 31 December 1834. Acc 5000/197.
34. Letter, 2 November 1830. Acc 5000/195.
35. Jackson is perhaps best known for his work on the *Penny Magazine*. For the engravings in *British America* (1839) Jackson charged just under £20, though that did include seven guineas for the view of Halifax, N.S. Postal charges were split between Jackson & Boyd. Acc 5000/22.
36. Letter, 10 December 1832. Acc 5000/196.
37. See, for example, the letter of Simpkin, Marshall, 8 April 1846, and the letter of Thomas Nelson of 4 November 1846. Acc 5000/203.
38. Letter, 25 February 1845. Acc 5000/203. No form of reciprocal copyright agreement with the United States then existed.
39. The sixth edition of Russell's *Egypt* appeared in 1844, and MacGillivray's *Travels of Humboldt* described as '11th thousand' in 1848.
40. Profit and Loss Book, Acc 5000/58, records the profit on the Cabinet Library between 1843 and 1849 as £2949.
41. Hugh Murray and Michael Russell worked for him up to his death; others, like James Nicol, turned to Oliver & Boyd to publish some of their later works.
42. Letter, 21 October 1831. Acc 5000/196.

Paths Through the Wilderness: Recording the History of Provincial Newspapers in England

DIANA DIXON

IN THE NINETEENTH CENTURY Cornelius Walford wrote: 'Periodical literature may be compared to a vast wilderness, without form and void, its extent unknown, its ramifications unfathomed.'[1] In this paper, I intend to explore some of the sources necessary to find out about the provincial press in England. I have deliberately avoided discussing the situation in Scotland, Wales and Ireland where their national libraries have been energetic in recording information about newspapers. My comments are based on my own experiences with press history in Huntingdonshire, Northamptonshire, Leicestershire, and Middlesbrough and also on the work that preceded the publication of *The Nineteenth Century Periodical Press in Britain: a bibliography of modern studies*[2] which Lionel Madden and I compiled in the 1970s, and my own efforts to update this and keep abreast of recent publications on newspaper history.

The first stage in any investigation of the publishing history of provincial newspapers is to discover what, if anything, has already been written on the subject. This may range from an in-depth study in the form of a PhD or a published monograph, to reminiscent jottings by a former newspaper reporter, or a few lines in a commemorative supplement. There are a number of bibliographies that will prove useful and although I do not wish to go into much detail, it is useful to mention some of the leading players. The most comprehensive, though by no means exhaustive for the provincial press, is *The Newspaper Press in Britain* by David Linton and Ray Boston[3] and this should be the starting point for any enquiry. It is necessarily selective but it will lead the enquirer to some bibliographies of secondary sources although it is deficient in its coverage of local antiquarian journals.

A number of bibliographies are restricted to a particular period. A good example is William Smith Ward's *British Periodicals and Newspapers, 1789-1832: a bibliography of secondary sources*.[4] I have already mentioned the Madden and Dixon bibliography of twentieth-century writings about the nineteenth-century periodical press in England which was updated by Larry Uffelman[5] in 1992. We tried to cover as much material as we were able to locate in provincial libraries as well in the national collections. Nonetheless, it is restricted by period, and omits a large number of important nineteenth-century publications, including the two major press histories by Fox Bourne[6] and James Grant,[7] as well as numerous interesting snippets of information contained in publications such as *Northampton Notes and Queries*. Currently, two annual bibliographies attempt to record recent writings about newspaper history: these are in *Victorian Periodicals Review* and in *Media History*.[8]

If the researcher is fortunate, the search through bibliographies may yield golden nuggets, as in the case of Middlesbrough[9], where a local printer faithfully recorded information about the history of newspapers, or in Loughborough where a former editor provided some interesting information about the early days of the *Loughborough Echo*. From this we learn that its founder

> Mr Deakin did the whole thing single-handed. He wrote the news canvassed for advertisements and set the type which, when ready he trundled in a cart to the premises of Alfred Clarke in Baxter Gate where the paper was printed. Later he carried the sheets back to the lean to office, folded them and supervised their delivery throughout the town by boys.[10]

Both are unique and informative manuscripts and are a useful starting point for any research as long as caution is exercised in trusting their veracity. They may have their own agendas and prejudices, which prevent them viewing the history of rival publications with complete impartiality.

Secondary sources on press history are as varied as the newspapers themselves. They range from scholarly and reputable general press histories such as those by Jeremy Black[11] and Alan Lee[12] to the anecdotal and unreliable. For the early eighteenth century the works of Geoffrey Cranfield[13] and Roy Wiles[14] are essential reading.

A large proportion of studies of newspaper history focus on the period before 1855 and this is because after the repeal of the Stamp Act in 1855 the number of newspapers mushroomed. The sheer quantity of nineteenth-century newspapers meant that it was no longer possible to write the sort of general overview that Cranfield, Wiles and Black had done. Most sizeable provincial centres could boast five or six competing titles at any one time, and with the advent of the provincial evening newspaper in the 1880s this number increased further, so that even towns the size of Kettering boasted two rival evening papers. To give some idea of the magnitude of the newspaper press, in 1884 the *Newspaper Press Directory* advertised 275 new newspaper and magazine titles. In 1895 it claimed there were some 2304 newspapers flourishing in the British Isles. For this reason, many historians have concentrated on newspapers within a given locality, and within that, often on a particular period. Major studies, often based on research for higher degrees, have been produced. Examples are: K.G. Burton's 'The Early Newspaper Press in Berkshire';[15] Maurice Milne's thesis on 'The Press in Northumberland and Durham'[16] which became the basis for a monograph,[17] or Aled Jones's thesis on 'The Press and the Labour Movement, Wales, the Potteries and the Black Country'.[18]

Rarer are monographic studies of the history of the press in an area: welcome exceptions are Murphy's work on Cambridge newspapers 1880-1850[19] and Challen's work on radical newspapers in Hull.[20] Occasionally, an important anniversary of a paper prompts publication of a monograph: this was the case with the centenary of the *Whitehaven News* in 1952[21] and the Nottingham *Evening Post* in 1978.[22] Most studies of provincial newspapers are considerably less substantial although not necessarily less scholarly. They appear as chapters in books and in a range of periodicals, scholarly and popular. Many, as, for instance, the articles by Herbert Norris on newspapers in Huntingdon in *Notes and Queries*,[23] are detailed and informative, as is Derek Fraser's 'The Press in Leicester c1790-1830' in *the Transactions of the Leicestershire Archaeological and Historical Society*.[24] Modern studies of printers and printing in a locality yield useful information on newspapers: as for example, Derek Nuttall's work on Chester printers,[25] or Peter Isaac's on William Davison[26] which throws light on the *Alnwick Mercury*. Local histories also contain interesting information on the press, as for example Olney's chapter on the 'County press' in a work on Lincoln politics,[27] or the volume of the Victoria County History Essex[28] which describes newspapers. Finding this information is made easier in cases where libraries compile extensive indexes to their local studies collections.

Unfortunately, however, much of the information about the provincial newspaper in England has to be gleaned from much slighter resources. One of the best sources of information often is the commemorative supplement produced by the paper to mark a milestone anniversary in its publishing history. Centenary supplements were common in the twentieth century and rarely a month went by without one appearing. Nowadays some newspapers are celebrating longer anniversaries and bringing out supplements, such as that celebrating 250 years of the *Northampton Mercury* in 1970. The information they contain has to capture the interest of modern readers and is couched in journalese, often making extravagant claims. Examples include 'From printer's devil to the computer age' in the *Slough, Eton and Windsor Observer* centenary supplement; 'W K Morton, our founder, could be described as the complete Victorian' in the *Horncastle News* centenary supplement; or, 'Tea table news for working class folk' in the *Eastern Evening News*.[29] They can be valuable for their historical information on rival publications over the years as in the Nottingham *Evening Post's* centenary supplement.[30] Often they supply a facsimile at least of the first page of the first issue, and they may contain photographs of premises, presses and editorial staff.

The difficulty for the researcher (and bibliographer) of press history is tracking commemorative issues down. Current press directories, such as Benn's and Willings', may give claimed starting dates for newspapers but these must be used with a degree of caution, as often all is not what it seems. Unless one is prepared to write to a newpaper office shortly after a special supplement has appeared, or to travel to a local library to see it, there may be a considerable delay in gaining access to it. The British Library Newspaper Library does not usually microfilm its provincial newspapers until a couple of years after publication and they will not be available there for considerably longer.

Clearly, the main source of information has to be the newspaper itself because its pages will reveal who printed it, where it was distributed, its editorial policies and changes over the years. Often the first issue of a newspaper sets the tone: in its first issue, the editor of the *Loughborough Echo*, Joseph Deakin, stated

> permit me to inform the reader the Echo is produced purely as an advertising sheet. Party interest Liberal or Conservative will be studiously avoided. But what strikes me as of interest to the borough and district will be welcomed. Voters don't want the Echo to pose as a mentor in politics.[31]

Editorials within the paper may show political allegiances and often contain attacks on rivals. In 1832 the *Leicester Herald* commented on the death of the editor of its main rival, the *Leicester Chronicle*,

> Tommy Thompson here doth lie,
> Who oft did lie before,
> His Chronicle was full of lies,
> But here he'll *lie* no more.[32]

The main problem for the would-be researcher is locating where, if anywhere, copies exist. In Britain by far the largest and most comprehensive collection of British and foreign newspapers is held at the British Library Newspaper Library at Colindale. Although its holdings are impressive, there are some serious gaps in coverage, especially of British provincial newspapers before the middle of the nineteenth century. Holdings prior to 1830 are sparse and it is generally safer to assume that titles will be in local public libraries. However, it is important to recognise that public libraries only came into being in the mid-nineteenth century and that parish libraries rarely retained newspapers, so that survival of eighteenth-century newspapers is at best fortuitous. Additionally, eighteenth-century newspapers were not regarded as worthy of collection and Muddiman[33] atttributed two reasons for the incomplete coverage: 'the somewhat unaccountable neglect with which they were treated and second the maleficent results of the Stamp Acts' which he suggested led to an enthusiasm for collecting the stamps, thus mutilating the periodicals. The British Museum only collected newspapers systematically after the Copyright Act of 1842 and even then many publishers only deposited them a year after publication, by which time many short-lived titles had disappeared without trace. Colindale suffered serious bomb damage in World War II and 15000 volumes were destroyed, especially from the years 1874, 1876, 1896-1900, 1908-1912. Its catalogue is now available on the British Library OPAC [34] and can be searched both by place and also by title.

Besides Colindale, impressive holdings of newspapers are held in the British copyright libraries of Oxford and Cambridge universities, the National Libraries of Wales and Scotland, and major academic libraries. Their OPACs are available via the Internet. It should also be remembered that many North American libraries, especially Yale and the Huntington Library, have rich holdings of English provincial newspapers, some of which are the only surviving copies. Many eighteenth-century newspapers are in the Burney Collection which is available on microform in the British Library at St Pancras. Also, the major local studies collections in public libraries hold significant runs of local titles and these are often much more comprehensive than those held in the Newspaper Library. Thus, collections in Liverpool, Birmingham, Bristol and Nottingham will yield many more titles than a glance at the Colindale catalogue reveals. Although 90% of Leicestershire titles are available in Colindale, only 52% of those for Huntingdonshire are. Newspapers may be held in local museums as in the excellent Norris Museum at St Ives, the Royal Institution of Cornwall in Truro, the Newcastle Literary and Philosophical Society, the Devon Atheneum or the Framlingham Museum, to name but a few. They may be held by newspaper offices, such as the *Loughborough Echo* and, as they are private property, access may be politely discouraged or less politely prohibited.

As all researchers using nineteenth-century newspapers are aware, tracing a title in a bibliography is no guarantee that the newspaper is in a fit state to permit browsing of its pages. Indeed, the condition of many is so precarious that it is no longer possible to read them at all. I have found to my cost on several occasions that newspapers may not be accessible. In one case, I wanted to consult the 1870 file of the *Gateshead Observer* in Newcastle Central Library. It was brought to me in a brown paper parcel but when I started to open the parcel, the newspaper poured out in the form of grey crumbs. In other cases, microfilm has been so poor that it has not been possible to read it because the print was so blurred. This was true of the *Loughborough Monitor* for 1860, so I went to Colindale to consult the original only to find that the print quality was so indistinct it was impossible to get a clear image. Worse is when you ask for a paper listed in a bibliography, only to find, after some delay, a red-faced librarian having to admit that no one can find it.

The British Library's NEWSPLAN project audited the physical state of all British provincial newspapers and made recommendations for their microfilming for posterity. NEWSPLAN covers the British Isles, including the Republic of Ireland, and is based on ten regions, all of which published a separate NEWSPLAN report.[35] Researchers can now trace holdings of newspapers in local libraries, record offices and newspaper offices throughout the British Isles and also be aware of their physical condition. Many of these reports are now available on the Internet and others are being up-dated.

Many local bibliographies were produced in the nineteenth century, listing newspapers circulating in the county or region at the time with brief historical notes. Good examples are *Bibliotheca Dorsetiensis*[36] and *Bibliotheca Buckinghamiensis*.[37] However, a glance at some of these reveals just how many titles appear to have disappeared without trace and are no longer available anywhere. A recent check through a a pamphlet entitled *The Newspaper Press and Periodical Literature of Liverpool* demonstrated just how true this is, with several titles having disappeared completely. In this case the bibliographer indicates this and gives additional information

> *The Leverpoole Courant*, being an abstract of London and other news. Printed and published by Samuel Terry, Leverpoole. This is undoubtedly the first newspaper issued in Liverpool. No copies are extant at the present time, but a copy of No 18, from Tuesday, July the 15th to Friday July the 18th, 1712, was seen and used by Mr. Brooke when writing his history of Liverpool.[38]

Many public libraries publish lists of their local papers: examples exist for Surrey, Devon and Hertfordshire newspapers, and Derbyshire has just published the fourth edition of its list of local newspapers.[39] However, complacency about the whereabouts of listed titles is misplaced. Sometimes newspaper files are disposed of in an arbitrary manner. Only recently the Suffolk local studies librarian was alerted just in time that the Beccles Town Hall was about to jettison its newspaper holdings. In the 1970s Middlesbrough public library, faced with shelves of deteriorating original newspapers, disposed of unique files of its earliest papers, after having them microfilmed, to a private collector, who allows no access to them. Because the quality of the microfilm is poor some papers are no longer readable.

Before publication of the ten NEWSPLAN volumes, bibliographic control of the provincial British press was both incomplete and patchy. By no means all provincial titles, especially short-lived nineteenth-century titles, found their way into the British Library Newspaper Library at Colindale. The *Bibliography of British Newspapers*[40] currently covers eight English counties but it is still woefully incomplete, with many parts of the country still awaiting investigation. If you want a selective list, with a facsimile of a page of the paper, John North's monumental *Waterloo Directory of*

English Newspapers and Periodicals, 1800-1900 [41] has the advantage over other listings in that wherever possible it gives the name of the proprietor, printer and editor, plus additional information. The disadvantage is that it is highly selective and by no means all the titles for a given locality appear.

Cataloguing newspapers is fraught with problems and bibliographies are littered with the results of shoddy work and the failure to impose consistency. Should cataloguers list the first known or the last known title with cross references? The papers themselves do not make things easy. Title changing was frequent. If you wish to raise a shudder at Colindale just mention the *Walthamstow Guardian* and its numerous title changes, with each local edition having a different title. Sometimes proprietors purchased rights to a defunct title that by linking it to a predecessor's heritage claimed a longevity the new title did not possess. Other titles have inserted spurious claims in the *Newspaper Press Directory* claiming links to distinguished but defunct titles.

The problem is that newspaper publishing was extremely volatile and many newspapers had extremely short lives. If the first issue of a title is not there to prove conclusively that it first appeared on a given date, it is hard to date it with any real accuracy. It is perhaps appropriate in Worcester to raise the question of longevity and the oldest known English provincial newspaper. In 1940 *Berrow's Worcester Journal* proudly celebrated two hundred and fifty years of publication. However, it is impossible to substantiate that it first saw the light of day in 1690 and the dating of the *Lincoln, Rutland and Stamford Mercury* is equally contentious. This title claims continuous publication back to 1695 but the earliest surviving copy dates from 27 August 1713. It seems likely that the myth was perpetuated by its proprietor in 1826 claiming that by working backwards from the issue of 7 July 1826 the paper had been in existence for 6833 weeks, which brought it to 11 February 1695. Later the *Newspaper Press Directory* accepted this as fact and the myth continued. Similarly, printers sometimes enhanced the numbering to suggest the paper had a longer life than it did. Rosemary Wells[42] cites the example of the *Exeter Gazette* that numbered its first issue 1024 in June 1792. Sometimes it may simply have been a typographical error as when the *Wellington News* for 11 May 1983 was volume 125, number 19 and the next issue was volume 105 number 20. Other pitfalls may include problems with numbering: for instance in 1948 in order to obtain a greater paper ration, the proprietor of the *Gateshead Times* which had reached its seventy-fifth number purchased rights to the *Gateshead Weekly Pictorial Post* and continued the paper as the *Gateshead Post* running from number 15.

Eighteenth century newspapers altered the frequency of publication sometimes appearing twice weekly, or fortnightly, making it impossible to determine starting dates.

Newspapers, however humble, are the product of human endeavour but information about the proprietors, printers and reporters is often surprisingly elusive. Last year while researching the history of the newspaper press of Middlesbrough, I was anxious to flesh out the information I had on the proprietor of the Middlesbrough *Evening Gazette,* Hugh Gilzean Reid. Despite his distinguished career as a newspaper proprietor and as a politician, standard biographical sources were surprisingly evasive about the history of his early career in Scottish newspapers. The centenary supplement was vague and this was perpetuated in Gifford's *Encyclopedia of the British Press.*[43] Fortunately, I was given a lead in *Scottish Notes and Queries* and able to flesh out the facts. Often the only source is the local newspaper or periodical, obituaries in the local press, directories, or biographical compilations such as *Boase*, or the county by county biographical series of *Eminent Edwardians*. A helpful discussion was provided by John Catt, who reviewed sources for the history of local newspapers in the 1970s.[44]

If locating biographical sources is frustrating, how much more so is finding archives. So few newspapers retain their archives and recent years have seen even major national dailies condemning archives to the skip. It is always worth consulting the National Register of Archives web site which does have information on newspaper archives and how to search for them and for people associated with the newspapers themselves. It is recognised that there is an urgent need to survey what newspaper archives still exist and their location, and ownership both of existing companies and their predecessors. Lack of funds has meant that this has been directed to the Business Archives Council. It would have been impossible to record the turbulent history of newspapers in Westmorland and Cumberland in the early nineteenth century without recourse to the Lonsdale papers. County Record Offices or Local History Centres often contain correspondence and prospectuses of newspapers. The prospectus where it exists is a useful indication both of the political allegiance and intended readership of a newspaper.

Newspapers also advertised themselves through the press directories of which the two main ones are *Mitchell's Newspaper Press Directory* and *May's*. Not all titles are listed and claims regarding circulation and longevity may be exaggerated. Nonetheless where a paper is featured it often gives us useful background information, thus the 1888 *Newspaper Press Directory* advertised *Payne's Leicester Advertiser*, as it

> advocates the interest of agriculture. It is well circulated among the aristocracy, gentry and clergy in the county as a business and family newspaper thoroughly identified

with cause of political progress and social improvement in the districts through which it circulates.

We must remember that advertising puts the product in the best possible light:
From its commencement the HERALD and GAZETTE took the foremost position in the district as a newspaper and its circulation is greater than the combined issues of its local contemporaries. It is printed at the rate of 12.000 copies per hour.[45]

Since Cornelius Walford wrote there have been great advances in controlling 'this almost unexplored region' but the historian of the provincial newspaper still needs to be something of a detective to ensure that pieces of the jigsaw are not overlooked. However, the commitment of the British Library Newspaper Library to the NEWSPLAN project, and to making its own resources more widely known, means that there is more than a glimmer of light at the end of the tunnel.

NOTES

1. Cornelius Walford, 'The Outline of a Scheme for a Dictionary of Periodical Literature', *The Bibliographer* (1883).

2. Lionel Madden and Diana Dixon, *The Nineteenth Century Periodical Press in Britain: a bibliography of modern studies, 1901-1971* (Toronto, 1975).

3. David Linton and Ray Boston, *The Newspaper Press in Britain: an annotated bibliography* (London, 1987).

4. William Smith Ward, *British Periodicals and Newspapers, 1789-1832: a bibliography of secondary sources* (Lexington, KY, 1972).

5. Larry Uffelman, *The Nineteenth Century Periodical Press in Britain: a bibliography of modern studies, 1972-199* (Evansville, IL, 1992).

6. H R Fox Bourne, *English Newspapers: chapters in the history of journalism*, 2 vols (London, 1887).

7. James Grant, *The Newspaper Press: its origin - progress - and present* (London, 1872).

8. 'Annual Review of Work in Newspaper and Periodical History' in *Media History* from 1998. This follows on from bibliographies in *Journal for Newspaper and Periodical History* (1984-1994) which became *Studies in Newspaper and Periodical History* (1995-97). The list aims to be comprehensive for Britain and selective for the rest of the world. The *Victorian Periodicals Newsletter* (1969-78) later *Victorian Periodicals Review* (1979-) carries an annual checklist of criticism on Victorian periodicals including newspapers.

9. J Jennings, 'Early press of Middlesbrough'. Undated manuscript in Middlesbrough Public Library.

10. P J Rippin, 'Brief History of the *Loughborough Echo*'. Unpublished typescript.

11. Jeremy Black, *The English Press in the Eighteenth Century* (London, 1987).

12. Alan J Lee, *The Origins of the Popular Press in England, 1855-1914* (London, 1976).

13. G A Cranfield, *The Development of the Provincial Newspaper, 1700-1760* (Oxford, 1962).

14. R McK Wiles, *Freshest Advices: early provincial newspapers in England* (Columbus: OH, 1957) and R S Crane, and F B I Kaye, *A Census of British Newspapers and Periodicals, 1620-1800* (Chapel Hill, NC, 1927).
15. K G Burton, 'The Early Newspaper Press in Berkshire' (MA thesis, Reading, 1952).
16. M Milne, 'The Press in Northumberland and Durham 1855-1906' (MLitt thesis, Newcastle, 1969).
17. M Milne, *The Newspapers of Northumberland and Durham:a study of their progress during the golden age of the provincial press* (Newcastle, 1971).
18. A Jones, 'The Press and the Labour Movement, Wales, the Potteries and the Black Country' (PhD thesis, Warwick, 1981).
19. M Murphy, *Cambridge Newspapers and Opinion, 1780-1850* (Cambridge, 1977).
20. C Challen, *The Quarrelsome Quill: Hull's radical press from 1830* (Hull, 1984).
21. J R Williams, *Whitehaven News Centenary: an outline of 100 years* (Whitehaven, 1952).
22. G M Denison, *The Evening Post: the story of a newspaper and a family* (Nottingham, 1978).
23. Herbert Norris, 'St Ives, Huntingdonshire, Booksellers and Printers', *Notes and Queries* 10 series V (1909), 201-2.
24. D Fraser, 'The Press in Leicester c1790-1830', *Transactions of the Leicestershire Archaeological and Historical Society* , 42, (1966-7), 53-75.
25. D Nuttall, 'A History of Printing in Chester', *Journal of the Chester Archaeological Society* (1967) 37-96.
26. Peter Isaac, *William Davison of Alnwick: printer and pharmacist* (Oxford, 1968)
27. R Olney, *Lincolnshire Politics 1832-1885* (Oxford 1973).
28. 'Newspaper Publishing', *A History of the County of Essex* Vol 2 (London, 1907), 472-3 (Victoria County History of the Counties of England).
29. *Evening Chronicle* Centenary Special (1980) 4; Centenary Souvenir *Slough, Eton and Windsor Observer*, 6 May 1983, 2; Centenary Supplement, *Horncastle News*, 5 September 1885, 4-7; Centenary Supplement;, Eastern Evening News , 4 January 1982, 4-10.
30. 'Nottingham Newpapers Through the Ages', *Nottingham Evening Post*, 2 May 1978,.18-19.
31. 'Editorial', *Loughborough Echo*, 7 November,1892, 1.
32. *Leicester Herald,* 5 December 1832.
33. J G Muddiman, Introduction, *Tercentenary Handlist of English and Welsh Newspapers, Magazines and Reviews,* (London, 1920) (facsimile reprint, 1966) 14.
34. www. bl.uk/collections/newspapers
35. The ten reports published by the British Library provide a comprehensive listing for the whole of the British Isles of the main files of UK and Irish local newspapers which remain in existence with details of their extent, gaps, condition and location: Ruth Cowley, *NEWSPLAN report of the project in the North* West (1990); Selwyn Eagle, assisted by Diana Dixon, *NEWSPLAN report of the project in the London and South East* (1996); Ruth Gordon, *NEWSPLAN report of the project in the East Midlands* (1989); Beti Jones, *NEWSPLAN report of the project in Wales* (1994); Alice MacKenzie, *NEWSPLAN report of the project in Scotland* (1994); Andrew Parkes, *NEWSPLAN report of the project in Yorkshire and Humberside*

(1989); David Parry, *NEWSPLAN report of the project in the Northern Region* (1990); James O'Toole, *NEWSPLAN report of the project in Ireland* (1992); Tracey J. Watkins, *NEWSPLAN report of the project in the West Midlands*(1990); Rosemary Wells, *NEWSPLAN report of the pilot project in the South* West (1986).
36. C H Mayo, 'Newspapers', *Bibliotheca Dorsetiensis* (London, 1885), 74-87.
37. 'Local Newspapers', *Bibliotheca Buckinghamiensis* (Aylesbury, 1890), 69-70.
38. J Cooper Morley, *The Newspaper Press and Periodical Literature of Liverpool* (Liverpool, 1887), 4.
39. W Myson, *Surrey Newspapers: a handlist and tentative bibliography* (London, 1961); Lorna Smith, *Devon Newspapers: a finding list* (Torquay, 1973); M F Thwaite, *Hertfordshire Newspapers 1772-1955: a list compiled for the County Bibliography* (Welwyn, 1956) and *Local Newspapers in Derbyshire* (4 ed Matlock, 2001).
40. R K Bluhm *Wiltshire* (1975); W Bergess et.al., *Kent* (1982); F Manders, *Northumberland and Durham* (1982); M Brook *Nottinghamshire* (1987); A Mellors and J Radford *Derbyshire* (1987); I Maxted *Devon and Cornwall* (1991) all published in London.
41. J North, *The Waterloo Directory of English Newspapers and Periodicals, 1800-1900* (Waterloo, Ont., 1997).
42. Wells, *NEWSPLAN* 1986. 24.
43. Denis Gifford, *The Encyclopedia of the British Press, 1492-1992* (London, 1992), 483.
44. John Catt, 'Sources for Local Newspaper History', *Local Historian* 16 (1985), 479-82.
45. This relates to the *Loughborough Herald and North Leicestershire Gazette* (NPD 1888), 236.

Yours
most truly
James Everett

James Everett
and the Sale of Adam Clarke's Library, 1833:
a Newly Discovered Manuscript

BRENDA J SCRAGG

WHILE LOOKING THROUGH the booksellers' and auction catalogues of the nineteenth century in the John Rylands Library I came across a previously unrecorded manuscript of the Methodist preacher and bookseller James Everett. The manuscript is bound in the front of the sale *Catalogue of the Valuable and Extensive library... of the late Adam Clarke...which will be sold by auction by Mr. Evans at his house No.93 Pall Mall on Monday February 18th and nine following days... 1833.*[1] and contains a wealth of interesting information. It was printed by T S Clarke, 45 St John's Square, Clarke's younger son, and was sent to Everett with the compliments of Theo. Sam. Clarke, Clarke's elder son. The catalogue came to the Library in 1903 when Mrs Rylands purchased from R Thursfield-Smith a large collection of Wesley material which became known as the Rylands Wesley Collection. This should not be confused with the Methodist Archives, also housed in the John Rylands Library from 1977, on permanent deposit by the Methodist Church in Great Britain.

The lives of both Everett and Clarke are well-known to Methodist historians but outside theological circles little is common knowledge. Both have lengthy entries in the *Dictionary of National Biography*. Adam Clarke was born about 1762 in the parish of Kilcronaghan in Co. Londonderry. After attending a local school his education was completed at the Methodist-established Kingswood School near Bristol.[2] In 1778 he became a Methodist and a great admirer of John Wesley. He began preaching with little formal training and, as was the custom of the time, held positions in a number of widely separated places in Ireland, Scotland and the Channel Islands. He was stationed in Manchester 1791-92, 1803-04 and 1817-19, but from 1805 he was based mostly in the London area.[3]

Not having shown great learning at school he afterwards became an assiduous scholar. The languages and literature of the Orient held a special attraction for him and he became fluent in Hebrew, Syriac, Arabic, Persian and Sanskrit and gave much help in these areas to the British and Foreign Bible Society. He was honoured by the University of Aberdeen in 1807 with an MA and in 1808 was made a Doctor of Laws. Such academic distinctions were rare among Methodists and this accorded Clarke a unique position of respect amongst Wesleyans. He became one of the most

Adam Clarke

Drawn by DERBY Engraved by COCHRAN

influential British Methodists in the generation following Wesley's death and is considered to have been in great measure responsible for holding the Connexion together. He served three times as President of the Wesleyan Conference. Clarke was a prolific writer on many aspects of Biblical interest, his most important work being a commentary on the whole books of Scripture published in eight volumes from 1810-26. The books he collected for his own library reflected his many and varied interests and his collection was extensive. Clarke died of cholera aged seventy-two on 26 August 1832 and his death was noted in *The Times* of 28 August. James Everett contributed an extensive obituary to the *Manchester Times* of 15 September 1832.[4]

James Everett was born in 1784 at Alnwick in Northumberland. In 1803 he became a Methodist and began preaching, becoming a Minister in 1806. His first circuits were in Sunderland, Shields and Belper. From 1815-16 he was appointed to the Manchester circuit. From 1825-1833 he was again in Manchester, though not as an active minister.[5] In 1821 a throat complaint made him no longer able to undertake the rigours of being a minister. He was, however, still active as a preacher. Early in his life he had made a point of writing his impressions of literary and notable people whom he met. Some of these were later published. He also began assembling notes for the *History of Methodism in Sheffield*[6] which was published in 1823. He had served as a Minister there from 1819 to 1821. A similar *History of Methodism in Manchester* was published in 1825.[7] Having gained some insight into the business of bookselling by working for a time in Paternoster Row and as an assistant to the Steward of the Methodist Bookroom, the Methodist Publishing House, when he was no longer able through ill-health to be a full minister he started a bookselling business on his own account, initially in Sheffield and moving to Manchester in 1825. Richard Chew in his biography of Everett quotes Everett:

> I proceeded to Manchester with a view to look at a situation which was open for the stationery and bookselling business. I engaged premises in Merchant's Buildings, Market Street (taken down some years afterwards in order to form the new street leading from Newall's Buildings to Shude Hill.) The rent was to be £100 per annum, to commence on the 25th April 1825 and the lease was for 7 years.[8]

He lived at 3 Stanley Street, Red Bank, at a rent of nineteen guineas a year, later moving to 7 Sedgwick's Court, Deansgate. His shop also moved from No. 10 Market Street to 19 Market Street, presumably when the former building was demolished. He also edited and published a short-lived paper called the *Manchester Journal*, a weekly first issued on 7 March 1826. No surviving copy has been located. During his stay in Manchester Everett published a number of pamphlets and literary works including a eulogy addressed to Clarke on the completion of Clarke's commentary on the Bible in September 1826. He became a member of the Manchester Literary and Philosophical Society. By 1834 he had sufficiently recovered his health to be appointed to the Newcastle circuit. He made over his bookselling busines to his nephew and moved back to the northeast being appointed first to Newcastle and later to York. The later part of his life and ministry was taken up with controversies which do not concern this paper. He died at Sunderland on 10 May 1872.

Clarke and Everett were friends and Everett came to regard Clarke as his hero. In 1843-49 Everett published his three-volume monumental life of Clarke, *Adam Clarke Portrayed.* [9] In 1851 he published a new edition of Clarke's *Commentary on the Holy Bible.* [10] After Clarke's death his papers and notes became the property of his son, Theodore Sam Clarke. Given the friendship between Clarke and Everett and their mutual interest in books it is not surprising that Everett would take a professional interest in the disposal of Clarke's Library. Everett's copy of the Catalogue containing his notes about Clarke and the sale was sent to him 'With Theo. Sam. Clarke's respects'. The advertisments pasted into the front of the catalogue from an unidentified London paper and the *Manchester Guardian* stated 'Catalogues... may also be seen at James Everett's, printer, bookseller, and stationer, 61 Market Street, Manchester, who will be glad to execute commissions...'

> The manuscript opens with some general remarks on the content of the catalogue:
> In the following Catalogue, we have an account of only that part of Dr. Clarke's Library, etc. which the Family and Executors had agreed to bring to the hammer. The sale does not include
> —His Minerals and their Cases, of which he had a large collection, embracing many rare specimens.
> —His coins and medals.
> —His telescopes and various Astronomical Instruments.
> —His Apparatus for various Philosophical Experiments.
> —A variety of Antiquities and Natural Curiosities.
> —His collection of Plants, etc.
> —A number of Plans, Facsimiles of ancient Laws, etc.
> —His Persian, Hebrew, Greek, Chaldee, Arabic, Latin, and other Manuscripts, valued at a considerable sum – thousands of pounds, if I mistake not, he told me... His MSS. were left to his youngest son, the Revd J.B.B.Clarke...

The manuscripts were later sold by Sothebys in June 1836 and realised £1804. 5s. Everett calculates the number of volumes offered in the Catalogue, including bound volumes of tracts, to be 6725. Items not included are gifts to friends, items kept by the family, and the manuscripts. These would have increased the total of his Library to nine or ten thousand items. Also bound into the same volume is *A Catalogue of the Museum of the late Adam Clarke containing a valuable collection of Minerals... a collection of coins... which will be sold by auction by Messrs. Machin, Debenham, & Storr at their rooms 26, King Street Covent Garden on Friday, April 26, 1833.* This

THE SALE OF ADAM CLARKE'S LIBRARY

catalogue was a gift to Everett from John Wesley Clarke. The sale lasted two days. We do not know if Everett attended the sale as he has not annotated the catalogue.

Surveying the range of subjects covered in Clarke's library Everett continues :
We find <u>different</u> <u>editions</u> of the same work sometimes, exhibiting the Dr. in the character of <u>a collector</u>.

Viewing the number of <u>Classic</u> <u>authors</u>, especially those of <u>Greece</u> and <u>Rome</u>, in their original tongues, and also the works in <u>other</u> languages it may be pronounced to have been one of the most <u>scholar-like</u> <u>Libraries</u> of modern times – at least raised up within the last <u>fifty years</u>, by the efforts of a <u>single</u> <u>man</u>, in <u>far</u> <u>from</u> <u>affluent</u> circumstances, and in a situation equally unfriendly, in consequence of frequent removes from place to place, to an accumulated stock.

There is one thing, which cannot but force itself, on the perusal of the Catalogue, upon even an ordinary observer, and that is – The small proportion, for the Library of an English Divine, of <u>English</u> <u>Theological</u> <u>Writers</u>. The works of some of our most popular divines are not to be found. Of <u>Sermons</u> especially, there is a great dearth. The truth is, as to the latter, his own mode of sermonising was disimilar to that of most men, and it was neither by <u>prejudice</u> nor a <u>national</u> <u>divinity</u> that he was led. He was a child of liberty; he loved no fetters, that the pure Bible itself did not impose. But look the Catalogue over, and there will be found the pure **Word** of **God** in its original languages, and almost every other work, whether of <u>criticism</u>, history, or what else, that will tend to be its illustration. The <u>formation</u> and the <u>stream</u> are to be seen in every direction; the latter, not systemized in <u>Sermons</u> and <u>Bodies of Divinity</u>, but in the work of the greatest scholars and most <u>accurate critics</u>. The Dr. never appeared before his <u>hearers</u> or <u>readers</u> in the – systematic trammels imposed by his countrymen – never in the same shape costume that characterised the generality of English Preachers. His preaching partook of his Library, and was like his Commentary, – as unlike Benson, Henry, and others, as it was possible to be. Drawing perpetually from the fountain head – from original classic authors – and from his own original intellectual resources, he had ever and anon something <u>new</u>. He was always rich bold and varied.

It is not to be denied, that there are some works, such as Paine's "Rights of Man", Byron's "Don Juan", "Rabelais", and a few luscious ones on matrimony, which have not much divinity about them; but it is possible that a few of them might have found their way to his shelves, as much by accident as by choice, having been bought in lots, or through a desire to witness the <u>intellect</u> rather than the <u>depravity</u> of the authors, which could not be well separated from each other. The following lots may be pointed out: 952 [Paine's Rights of Man, 1792 and various others], 1142 [Rabelais: Works, 1750 Edited by Ozell, 5vols. Cuts.], 105 [Byron's Sardinapalies, Cain, etc 1821, Byron's Don Juan, 2vols., 1828.]

How with the slender means he had to start with, and the often straitened means at different periods of life, he became possessed of such a Library, many of the works in which appear to be <u>costly</u> and rare, is matter of astonishment to many, and may be curiosity to all! <u>First</u>, after he became an <u>author</u> his <u>pen</u> often furnished him with the

169

"needful". Secondly, He was always on the look out, and his itinerant life threw him often in the way of works, which by a fixed residence, he would have escaped. Thirdly His talents and character procured him many friends, and he had works occasionally presented to him. Fourthly, He was a warm friend of Wm. Baines, Bookseller, Paternoster Row, London;[13] Baynes felt it, and was in some instances his publisher; and being in the habit of visiting the Continent, and purchasing largely, and often cheaply valuable foreign works, he felt a pleasure giving the Dr. the first chance of selection, without being at all exorbitant in his charges. This was a mine in which the Dr. often dug, and dug successfully for love. The purchases of between forty and fifty years are sure to tell a tale in magnitude. I have been with him at Baynes's and have seen some of his purchases, as well as himself in all his glory, turning over the dusty tomes of the ancients. On being absent from the metropolis for a length of time he always manifested a restlessness of spirit, on the occasion of a visit, till he had satisfied himself by an examination of Mr Baynes's stock. During his residence at Millbrook, he had occasion to go up to town. On his arrival at Mr. Hook's his son-in-law, in the course of a visit, he immediately shaved, washed, and got brushed. When he came down the stairs the following conversation took place.

Mrs. C. "You are going to see Mr Butterworth, I suppose?
Dr. C. "I am going to Billy Baynes's for two-penny worth of Books".
Mrs C. "You really must go and see Mr Butterworth".
Dr. C. "He may come and see me, who have come so far".
Mrs C. "He is poorly and cannot".
Dr. C. "If he cannot walk, he has his carriage and horses at command".
Mrs C. "It may be hazardous for him to stir abroad?"
Dr. C. "I am going to Billy Baynes's for an odd two-penny worth of Books." Thus Billy Baynes commenced and Billy Baynes closed the business. The Dr. had no apprehension of immediate danger in the case of his brother-in-law; he could see him at another time; - there was a passion to gratify; - and a favourite book might be borne off by a purchaser in the interim. Billy Baynes had some of his earliest greetings.

Among other books kept back by the family from the sale, was a volume of Dr. Chambers's Sermons, the margin of whose pages was crowded with critical remarks in the hand-writing of Dr. Clarke – some of them extremely severe, both on style and sentiment. Mrs. Clarke was afraid lest it should have found its way into the sale catalogue, having been lost sight of for some time, and was happy when it was found in another place.

The sale of Clarke's Library produced a great deal of interest and many reports were given in newspapers and journals. Everett quotes the report in the *Christian Advocate* of 25 February 1833, 'The sale of the late Dr. Adam Clarke's Library commenced on Monday last. The works have generally realized high prices. A beautiful copy of the Biblia Sacra Polyglotta [Lot 401] produced £57.15.0d...' The catalogue

THE SALE OF ADAM CLARKE'S LIBRARY

describes this item as containing the rare advertisement to subscribers to the publication of the first volume. It was bought by J R Kay.

> ... another copy [lot 42 was purchased by Henry Bohn] £42. On the second day's sale, several Wesleyan ministers and gentlemen were present. The principal attraction with them appeared to be the Biblia Sacra Hebraica Gr. Et Lat. Munsteri, Vol.I (Genesis to Kings) Basil 1546. [lot 404 sold to Marriott.] This was the copy which had belonged to the Revd. Samuel Wesley, Sen., and was full of manuscript notes by him in his own hand-writing. It has also the autograph of J. Wesley. It was knocked down to Thomas Marriott, Esq.,[10] who, for his zeal in collecting the works and papers of the Wesley Family, together with those connected with the rise of Methodism, may be justly styled the Wesleyan antiquarian. This curious volume shows the labour of one of the greatest critics of his age. It has been several times collated with other versions. Each book is headed and concluded in Samuel Wesley's peculiar manner, with the dates when the notes were made, thus: In, Nom. Dom. Incept. July 30, 1724, [note] Fin. Aug. 26, 1724...

This volume is now preserved in the Methodist Archives in the John Rylands Library. On the front board in Adam Clarke's hand is written 'This vol. was once the property of Samuel Wesley Senr Rector of Epworth in Lincolnshire; & the MSS. notes & corrections are by his own hand A. Clarke.' Below is a note in the hand of James Everett, 'This volume appears to have fallen into the hands of John Wesley on the demise of his father. Mr Tegg purchased it of Mr Marriott whose writing is beneath that of Dr. Clarke, and afterwards presented it to me, on editing the *Miscellaneous Works* of Dr.Clarke for him. It was in bad rough calf binding when I received it; and covered in purple morocco, by Mr Sumner of York. James Everett, Newcastle-on-Tyne Nov. 1832.'

> ...We understand that Dr. Clarke has given a particular account of this work in the manuscript he has left (revised by himself) for a second and much improved edition of his "Wesley Family". Those who have inspected the Biblia Sacra, will fully corrobrate the remarks which Pope made in one of his letter to Swift respecting Mr. Samuel Wesley, "I call him what he is, <u>a learned man'</u>."

The *Morning Chronicle* of 26 February 1833 also carried a report of the sale which is once again quoted by Everett.

> <u>Dr. Adam Clarke's Library</u> The sale of the books of this very learned Wesleyan preacher commenced at Evans' on Monday week, and was numerously attended. The Complutensian Polyglott Bible, 6 vols., [lot 398 sold to Henry Bohn] brought 40 guineas; Walton's Polyglott Bible [lot 401] and Castell's Lexicon 8vols., sold for 55 guineas; Biblia Sacra Latina, 2 vols. Printed by Eggesteyn about 1535, imperfect, [Lot 609] sold for 60 guineas; the Byzantine Historians, 26 vols. 19 guineas; the Greek, Roman, and Italian Antiquities of Graevius, Gronovius, and Burmann, 80 vols., £55; Corps Diplomatique, 17 vols., in morocco, £30. The sale of the last week exceeded

£1,900 and it continues four days more, the produce will be considerable. – People are surprised that a Wesleyan Missionary was should have collected so valuable a library; but Dr. Clarke was one of the most learned men of the age; in extensive philological knowledge without a rival in this island.

The *Morning Chronicle* of March 4th 1833 carried a further report of the sale--
The sale of the Library of Dr.Adam Clarke terminated at Evans's on Thursday, and proceeded with equal spirit to its conclusion. The splendid volume of Chinese drawings [lot 2076] brought sixty-nine pounds...

These are described as one of the most splendid collections of Chinese drawings ever brought into this country. The brilliancy of them cannot be surpassed; many of them are heightened with gold.

...Holloway's engravings of the cartoons of Raphael, twenty-seven pounds [lot 2077 bought by Moore, Boyes & Greaves]; the Philosophical Transactions, fifty-guineas; Purchas's Pilgrims, twenty-seven pounds [lot 1664 bought by Cochran] Montfaucon's Monarchie Francaise, sixteen-pounds [lot 1528]; Mer des Histoires, 2 vols., 1498, sixteen-pounds [lot 1641 bought by Thorpe]; Roderici Speculum [humanae] Salutis, 1468, fifteen-guineas [lot 1813 bought by Thorpe, the Sir M.M.Sykes copy]; the Dead Christ in Mosaic, ten pounds. The whole Library produced three thousand two hundred pounds - an extraordinary instance of the unwearied diligence and perserving spirit of a Dissenting Clergyman, worth even of episcopalian imitation; but Bishops in our day are not <u>ardent</u> collectors of books.

On 1 March 1833 Everett received a letter from Thomas Marriott of Windsor Terrace, City Road, London[13] informing him that Marriott had

...purchased at the sale every thing which may be useful to the Work [Dr. Clarke's Wesley Family, left in manuscript to Marriott], and which may be requisite for reference, viz 'Biblia Sacra' with Samuel Wesley's notes, [John Wesley's father] – 'Wesley's Maggots' [lot 1898 14/6] – 'Dunton's post Angel' [lot 798 15/6]- 'The Letter on Heroic Poetry with Marlborough annexed' – 'Bonnel's Life' – 'Athenian Mercury or Gazette, etc' [lot 1029, 18/6]. I wish you could have spent a week before the sale in looking over the MS. Notes [of Dr Clarke] in his printed books. Many observations on the works were very striking. These notes generally enhanced the price. Bentley's *Proposals for a Greek Testament*, 1721 worth about 3 shillings, because of a statement in the Catalogue of a critical MS. Note by Dr. Clarke, sold for <u>3 guineas</u>. Of Dr. Mace's *New Testament, Greek and English*, he had written a most severe character. The motto on the title-page was 'If the light which is in you become darkness, how great is that darkness' under which the Dr. had written, '<u>This is strictly true of Dr. Mace the editor</u>.' There were many books on astrology and magic. I looked into one, entitled, and lettered 'Magical Tracts'. One of the three tracts related to Halifax, and the Dr. had written on the Fly leaf 'From Hell, Hull, and Halifax, Good Lord deliver us!' Everett suggests that Clarke was perhaps aware of a personal allusion, the Dr. having been rejected by the Halifax Society, when appointed by the Conference to the circuit, in the earlier part of his itinerancy. I am glad I secured Wesley's Notes on the Testament, though I gave a high price; but it is in many parts filled with MS. Notes of the Doctor's. The following singular note I have in one of the books I bought.

"Spoken by A.C. in a dream to Mr. C. Fox"-
'Within yon cavern'd rock old Kezzar dwells,
Who guards the fount of immortality.
If haply he the heavenly draught impart,
Then shall we never die.'

Everett continues his commentary on the sale

Mr. Arch, the bookseller, of Cornhill, gave £63 for the Bible of Miles Coverdale, though the two last leaves were supplied by MS., and several other defects. Tindale's New Testament Imprinted by Tylle, 1548, sold for £26.15.6 Erasmus's New Testament, Imprinted by Powell, 1547, sold for £10.15.0. It cost the Doctor 1/- as his son John told me. Mr. Offer, formerly a bookseller, who was present when the lot was sold, went immediately to a Bookseller who had another copy , and purchased it for 30/- The price, in many cases were perfectly arbitrary. Some as much too high, as other too low. I saw a curious Tract you had given the Doctor, on which he had written some notes, entitled 'The five wounds of Christ' - I laid out above £10, and, upon the whole, am very well satisfied with my purchases.

During the whole of the sale, there was great interest excited, when any book was noticed as having the autograph of the Dr. in it. One in particular was expatiated upon by the auctioneer, as having a critique upon it in the Dr.'s hand-writing. After working his auditors up to the highest pitch, and without any one apparantley attending to the character of the work, it was knocked down at a goodly price, when the purchaser found penned on a blank leaf, with the Dr.'s signature appended to it, a sentence to the following effect, 'This book is a tissue of lies from beginning to end.'

In 1833 Everett was still in business as a bookseller. He appears to have invested in some dozen lots from the sale and their varied subject matter, which did not include religious works, leads us to the conclusion they were stock for his shop. A number of lots in the catalogue are priced but without the buyer's name and some have no annotation at all. Several well-known booksellers are frequently represented: Thorp, Baynes, Hodgson, Bohn and Longman. Thomas Marriott the Methodist collector purchased many items. The names of other individuals have not been identified.

As already mentioned the London bookseller Baynes from whom Clarke bought many of his books also published some of his works. Baynes was the publisher of Clarke's *A Bibliographical Dictionary...1802-04*, six volumes in three. The third volume published in 1804 was printed in Manchester by R & W Dean & Co and the date corresponds with the time Clarke was minister in the Manchester circuit. Dean was also the printer of at least two other pamphlets in 1804 and 1805. James Everett printed and published several items while in business in Manchester but none by Clarke.

The Methodist Archives has a considerable quantity of original manuscript material by and relating to James Everett much of which has not been fully listed so it is possible that more information concerning Everett and the library of Adam Clarke may come to light at a later date.

ACKNOWLEDGEMENTS

The text of the manuscript is reproduced with permission of the John Rylands University Library of Manchester. I am grateful to Alan Rose for a number of suggestions and reading the final text.

NOTES

1. James Everett's copy of the Catalogue containing the manuscript. Library call number R22832. There is also a copy in the Methodist Archives. MAB/B190.

2. Kingswood School was founded in 1748 by John Wesley to educate the sons of Methodist families.

3. William Hill, *An Alphabetical Arrangement of all the Wesleyan Methodist Preachers missionaries...* (London:1827).

4. A copy is preserved in the Methodist Archives. PLP/26/8/6.

5. William Hill, *Alphabetical Arrangement*.

6. James Everett, *Historical Sketches of Wesleyan Methodism in Sheffield and its Vicinity* (Sheffield, 1823).

7. James Everett, *Historical Sketches of Wesleyan Methodism in Manchester and Vicinity* (Manchester, 1827).

8. Richard Chew, *James Everett: a biography* (London, 1875), 225.

9. James Everett, *Adam Clarke Portrayed, 3* vols (London, 1843-49).

10. The details of the negotiations have been covered by D W Riley, 'Tegg v. Everett: the publication of the second edition of Clarke's Commentary', *Proceedings of the Wesley Historical Society,* xliv (1984), 145-150.

11. Ian Maxted, *The London Booktrades, 1775-1800: a preliminary checklist of members,* (London, 1977). Baynes was in Paternoster Row from 1796-1841.

12. Thomas Marriott, 1786-1852. See John Vickers, *A Dictionary of Methodism in Britain and Ireland* (Peterborough, 2000).

13. Quoted by Everett but the original of this letter has not been traced.

Thomas Gee Senior

PHILIP HENRY JONES

FROM THE LATE 1840s onwards the Denbigh printer-publisher Thomas Gee (1815-98) became the most important Welsh-language publisher of his time, as well as playing a prominent role in radical-nonconformist politics, both directly in events such as the 'tithe war' of the later 1880s and also through his twice-weekly newspaper, *Baner ac Amserau Cymru*. His fame has tended to obscure the achievements of his father, after whom he was named. The biography of Thomas Gee by T Gwynn Jones, a masterly literary achievement, was, as I have shown elsewhere, heavily influenced by family pressures.[1] Since it was published in 1913 when the struggle over Welsh disestablishment was at its height, it (quite understandably) failed to recognise how many Anglican works the press printed during its first few decades. It also failed to give adequate recognition to the readiness with which clergymen and landowners supported Welsh culture by subscribing to Welsh publications during the 1820s and 1830s. A final – and equally understandable – omission was the recognition that in order to retain the custom of landowners and clergy Thomas Gee senior was sometimes compelled to resort to compromises and reticences.

Although the press is so closely identified with three generations of the Gee family, the business was not founded by a member of the family nor was it initially intended to be a profit-making concern. The object of its founder, Thomas Jones (1756-1820), was essentially a religious one. Jones, the wealthiest Calvinistic Methodist of his day in North Wales, reputedly spent some ten thousand pounds on producing Welsh-language publications, mainly of his own composition.[2] While some of this very considerable outlay was gradually recouped by sales, only one of his publications, his English-Welsh dictionary (*Geiriadur Saesoneg a Chymraeg*), first published in 1800, is believed to have made a profit.[3] In its disregard for commercial considerations Jones's publishing activities thus represented a continuation of the long tradition of providing subsidised works in the vernacular for the enlightenment of the monoglot Welsh and the salvation of their souls.

Between 1796 and 1802 most of Thomas Jones's publications were printed at Chester in the office of William Collister Jones.[4] Since the latter possessed at best a limited knowledge of the Welsh language, from 1798 onwards he employed as corrector of the press John Humphreys (1767-1829), a Calvinistic Methodist preacher and friend of Thomas Jones. In 1800 Humphreys began to publish a biblical dictionary. Thomas Charles became involved in this project at an early stage and, as his interest in the work developed, the expense and delay incurred in having it printed at Chester became increasingly burdensome to him.

It was therefore decided during 1802 to set up a press at Y Bala, trading as Jones & Co. Thomas Jones contributed £61 to the partnership, a third of the capital cost of acquiring a second-hand wooden press and a supply of new type (including Greek and Hebrew founts) from Caslon and Catherwood. The other members of the partnership were Sarah, the wife of Thomas Charles (he, as an ordained clergyman, could not engage in trade) and, quite probably, John Humphreys. The office began to print in May 1803. Its overseer was Robert Saunderson (1780-1863), formerly apprenticed to William Collister Jones, and Humphreys initially acted as corrector of the press. Although Thomas Jones had been one of its founders, the press printed only three of his works, partly because of geographical factors (Jones lived in Rhuthun, some eighteen miles from Y Bala), but largely because of the pressure of work. Even though a second press was acquired in September 1806,[5] the office was fully employed in printing works by and for Thomas Charles; according to Saunderson, it printed 'not less than about four hundred thousand school books' during its first decade.[6]

The Wesleyan Methodist mission to Wales from 1800 onwards was bitterly resented by the Calvinistic Methodists. Thomas Jones's attack on Arminianism, *Drych Athrawiaethol* (Doctrinal Mirror) which appeared in 1806, delayed by a year because of pressure of work at the Bala office,[7] led to his becoming engaged in a fierce theological debate with the Wesleyan champion, Owen Davies (1752-1830).[8] In mid-June 1807 Jones published another anti-Arminian work, over 450 pages in length, *Ymddyddanion Crefyddol* (Religious Dialogues). Within six weeks of its publication Owen Davies published *Drychau Cywir* (True Mirrors), a 408-page counterblast. The speed with which Davies produced his reply was remarked upon, since it was generally known that all his Welsh works were first composed in English.[9] Although Davies modestly ascribed his feat to the workings of Providence (*tro Rhagluniaethol*), it soon emerged that, in exchange for being liberally treated to drink, a disreputable printer at the Bala office had allowed Davies to see the proofs of *Ymddyddanion Crefyddol*.[10]

This stab in the back finally convinced Jones, who now had several substantial works in preparation, that he needed to have a press which would be under his own control. So, in October 1808, Jones set up his press in Well Street, Rhuthun, in a disused brewhouse behind the Antelope Inn.[11] Despite the town's importance as a market centre, this was the first press to be established there. On the recommendation of William Collister Jones, Thomas Gee was appointed as its overseer.

Gee, born in Chester in 1780, was apprenticed by his mother (widowed in 1785) to William Collister Jones and his partner Thomas Crane on 14 January 1796. During his apprenticeship he gained some experience of setting Welsh and, when his time was completed in 1803, he went to London to seek work as a journeyman printer. Nothing is known about his time in London but one might legitimately speculate that it was there that he developed his radical political views (he was, for instance, an early advocate of the secret ballot).

At Rhuthun Gee produced Thomas Jones's Welsh translation of the fourth part of William Gurnall's *The Christian in Compleat Armour*. The 416-page book took some seven months to set and print, being published in April 1809.[12] During the same month Thomas Jones moved to Denbigh, eight miles to the north of Rhuthun, taking the press with him.

Denbigh, with a population of 2391 in 1801, was the major commercial centre of the Vale of Clwyd, a fertile area where farms were large by Welsh standards and farmers had profited from the high grain prices of the Napoleonic Wars: in his reminiscences James Evans, one of Gee's apprentices, maintains that before 1815 'many farmers of the surrounding districts, when riding home from Denbigh markets, used to cry out 'Dal ati, Boni bach!' ('*Keep it up, little Bony!*').[13] Although Denbigh's craft industries, chiefly glove making and shoemaking, were in decline, its reputation as a healthy spot (until the cholera outbreak of 1832) had made it, in the words of a contemporary writer, 'more a place of genteel retirement than of trade'.[14] The town's wealthy residents, and occupiers of the 'numerous splendid seats and elegant villas, inhabited by opulent families'[15] in its vicinity constituted a numerically small but potentially lucrative market for fashionable English books and the latest periodicals.

Politically, Denbigh displayed the classic features of a pre-1830s borough. With two other contributory boroughs, Rhuthun and Holt, it constituted the Denbigh Boroughs constituency. By the early nineteenth century control of the constituency was contested by the Tory West interest based in Rhuthun and the Whig Biddulph interest which controlled Denbigh borough. Hard-fought elections were characterised by the large-scale creation of burgesses, lavish treating, and the intimidation of voters. From a printer's point of view, contested elections were welcome since they generated a considerable amount of jobbing work. Indeed, when the Denbighshire county seat was not contested in 1837, Gee expressed his disappointment: 'We have not been as busy as at former Elections – very little squibbing having occurred.'[16] But in the days of declaring one's vote on the hustings, partisanship in elections could threaten a printer's business. Although professing reformist views, Gee thought it best to abstain in the 1837 election to avoid losing the custom of local Tories.

Denbigh corporation itself generated a fair quantity of jobbing printing, a little of which has survived. The only evidence of its value is Gee's bill to the corporation for the year December 1843 to December 1844 for £4.16s.6d, which includes such picturesque items as printing '100 Bills of mad dogs'.[17]

In religion, the established church in Denbigh was beginning to lose ground by the early nineteenth century. Old Dissent had long been active there, although it was not until 1742 that the Independents built Denbigh's first Nonconformist chapel. The earliest Calvinistic Methodists experienced severe persecution: in 1752 Howell Harris spoke of the brethren 'in Denbigh and Dyffryn Clwyd being in constant Danger of their lives'.[18] During the 1790s, war with France created fresh problems as the politically quietist Methodists were accused of being Jacobin agitators and instigators, *inter alia*, of the Denbigh militia riots of 1795. Even so, the Calvinistic Methodists built their first chapel in Denbigh in 1793 and had been forced to expand it twice by 1813. Their Sunday School was also firmly established by the early nineteenth century, with no fewer than 500 pupils on the books by 1806.[19] Since they were all taught to read Welsh, they constituted an ever-expanding market for vernacular texts ranging from ABCs to expositions.

Finally, authors and scholars of the Vale of Clwyd had played an important part in Welsh literary and scholarly life from the fifteenth century onwards. Although the scholarly tradition gradually withered away during the later seventeenth century, the literary tradition still retained its vitality, producing figures such as the poet and writer of interludes, Thomas Edwards 'Twm o'r Nant', and Robert Davies 'Bardd Nantglyn'. During the later eighteenth century the area was linked to the lively cultural life of the London Welsh through the Gwyneddigion Society, which drew more of its membership from Denbighshire than from any other part of Wales.[20]

As well as influencing the output of Gee's press, all these factors made Denbigh an excellent centre for a printing business. But perhaps the greatest advantage enjoyed by Gee's press was the absence of local competition in the printing trade, his only rival in the Vale of Clwyd being the Rhuthun bookseller Robert Jones, who began to print in 1825. Older centres of printing such as Holywell, Mold, and Wrexham were all a considerable distance away. In bookselling and book binding (mainly English books for the 'county' trade) Gee faced some competition from Thomas Roden, established in Denbigh from about 1790 and, from 1818 onwards, from Roden's former apprentice, Thomas Vaughan. Following Vaughan's death, his successor David Jenkin sold the business to Gee in 1840. Gee's announcement that he had taken over Jenkin's book and periodical orders casts a little light upon his links with the London trade: 'Mr Gee receives a parcel from London regularly on the first day of every month, and also two or three times during the interval.'[21]

The printing office was initially located in Factory Lane. The first item to bear a Denbigh imprint was *Catecism Eglwys Loegr*, a Welsh translation by Thomas Jones of Alexander Nowell's *Catechismus sive Prima Institutio*. Since this 192-page work probably appeared in June 1809,[22] most of it must have been printed at Rhuthun before the move to Denbigh. An advertisement dated 23 September 1809[23] indicated what was to be the main task of the press for the next four years, the publication (initially in thirty-five shilling parts) of *Diwygwyr, Merthyron a Chyffeswyr Eglwys Loegr* (Reformers, Martyrs and Confessors of the Church of England). This 1182-page volume eventually became extremely popular: Thomas Jones's biographer noted approvingly that it became '*a favourite book in hundreds of Welsh families*' and that it '*did more to create and maintain hatred in the minds of the Welsh towards Popery than any other book published in the Welsh language*'.[24] Although it was reprinted twice in the course of the century, initial sales were disappointing, and following the death of Thomas Jones in 1820 his widow was left with a large number of unsold copies which she gradually disposed of during the 1820s and 1830s.

While the martyrology was in the press, Gee printed a number of items for Thomas Jones and others. The most substantial work printed for Jones was the second, greatly expanded edition of his English and Welsh Dictionary, comprising 500 pages in double-column, dated 1811 but probably appearing at the beginning of 1812.[25] This was an early indication of the importance of lexicography in the office's output. 1811 also saw the publication of two briefer works by Jones, a response to an attack by Owen Davies and a twelve-page pamphlet to celebrate the defeat in May 1811 of Lord Sidmouth's attempt to clamp down on itinerant preachers. Other works produced at this time included sermons by both Anglican and Dissenting clergymen, and a quantity of jobbing printing. As well as notices for Denbigh Corporation,[26] early jobs included the annual reports of the recently founded Denbigh Dispensary and, in 1810, 2000 copies of a popular Welsh-language treatise on hernia, which the Dispensary hoped its subscribers would lend out 'among their poor and afflicted neighbours'.[27] Since the Dispensary spent over £110 on printing and stationery in the four years between 1810 and 1813, it represented a regular and substantial source of income to Gee.[28]

As soon as the martyrology had been published, Thomas Jones sold the press to Gee. Gee's Declaration that he possessed a printing press and type (as required by 39 Geo III, c 79) has survived and is dated 16 October 1813. Jones also sold Gee a considerable quantity of paper, since Bersham-made paper watermarked 'Harris 1811', as used for the martyrology, was still being used by Gee for posters as late as 1817.

Since the output of Gee's office between 1813 and 1845 reflects to a considerable extent his interests and personality, we need to spend a little time examining his business interests and personal beliefs.[29] Unlike many Welsh printers, Gee came from a fairly affluent family, his father owning several houses in Chester. By January 1812 his prosperity, respectability, and status as a protégé of Thomas Jones were such that he could marry Mary Ffoulkes (1782-1838), the daughter of a well-off Vale of Clwyd farmer and a niece of the Independent divine, Edward Williams of Rotherham. Of their seven children, five were to survive infancy. The three boys, Thomas Gee (1815-98), Robert Gee (1819-91), and Edward Williams Gee (1821-81) all served apprenticeships in their father's office. Thomas Gee senior and his wife were members of the Church of England and, like Robert Saunderson of Y Bala, might have remained so had it not been for the influence of Thomas Gee junior, who joined the Calvinistic Methodists in 1830. His parents then followed his example.

During his early years in Denbigh Gee came to speak Welsh fluently and, although his spoken Welsh always betrayed that he had learnt the language, he participated enthusiastically in Welsh cultural institutions. By 1821 he was a member of the council of the Denbigh Cymreigyddion,[30] a society devoted to supporting the language and literature of Wales. In June 1824 he was one of three who offered the society a prize of three guineas for the 'best Welsh Anthem on our Saviour's Resurrection',[31] and subscribed a guinea to the 1828 Denbigh Eisteddfod.[32] During the 1820s he became increasingly friendly with the Welsh scholar William Owen Pughe, who finally took up residence at Nantglyn, a few miles from Denbigh, in 1825.[33] Although Pughe's scholarship was sadly defective by modern standards – like other Welsh scholars of his day he was an autodidact whose idiosyncratic views were unconstrained by membership of a broader scholarly community – his contemporaries considered him to be the leading authority on Welsh grammar and lexicography. Gee's friendship with Pughe – they even took a seaside holiday together – was to have a considerable influence on the output of the press and is well documented in Pughe's diary.

Like most provincial printer-publishers Gee pursued a number of those additional occupations that were integral to the success of any provincial printer. The usual trades of bookseller, bookbinder and stationer could involve some unexpected activities such as cleaning the Bishop of St. Asaph's library.[34] By 1840 Gee dealt in wallpaper,[35] encouraged doubtless by the abolition in 1836 of the duty on that commodity.[36] One might have expected him to have operated a circulating library, but since the only reference to one is in a bill-head from the early 1840s, he probably did not pursue this line of business for long. As well as selling tea, he was prepared to purvey dubious remedies for even more dubious complaints such as Solomon's Cordial Balm of Gilead (at eleven shillings per bottle a very profitable commodity) and Dr Boerhaave's Red Pill No 2.[37]

By the later 1820s, Gee was the Denbigh agent for the Phoenix Fire Insurance Company and subsequently added to this the agency for the associated Pelican Life Insurance Company.[38] Since these agencies involved finding substantial sureties, they indicate Gee's prosperity. A less usual – and more speculative – venture was mining. By 1816 Gee was one of the nine partners working a copper mine at Tanyrallt, near Trawsfynydd,[39] but his involvement appears to have been fairly short-lived. A leading figure in the enterprise was the land-surveyor John Matthew, whose grandson, John Matthews, was to marry Gee's grand-daughter, Sarah Gee, in one of those marriages which bound together the emerging Welsh radical-nonconformist elite of the later nineteenth century.

Up to 1813 Gee acted solely as a printer, working either for Jones or for others. Although Welsh-language title pages are often ambiguous (if not misleading),[40] it appears that as soon as he bought the press Gee ventured to publish at his own risk, beginning in 1814 with *Y Cyfrifydd Parod*, a 120-page ready-reckoner which would have been an expensive work to set and proof. Between 1813 and Gee's death in 1845 his press issued over a hundred and forty substantial items, as well as a mass of minor jobbing work. New items are still coming to light – the recent publication of the long-awaited supplement to *Libri Walliae* added several new items and confirmed the existence of others. We also know of several items which have still to be located: between 1829 and 1833 William Owen Pughe refers in his diary to translating or correcting ten items for Gee, none of which has yet been traced.

Over half the items printed by Gee were of a religious nature and about a quarter were purely secular, mainly practical or educational works. The religious works included such substantial items as the first diglot Welsh/English New Testament in 1824 and two editions of the Book of Common Prayer, the second in 1823, also a diglot publication. They also included devotional and controversial works by Thomas Jones and others, and Welsh translations of works by Isaac Watts and other popular English religious writers. The press did not publish religious works which conflicted fundamentally with Gee's beliefs: he is known, for instance, to have refused to publish a pro-Catholic Welsh-language work despite being offered a considerable sum to do so.[41]

Popular religious verse often appeared in the four- or eight-leaf format traditionally used for ballads. The commonest subjects were elegies or pieces celebrating the role of divine intervention in securing good harvests. When, as in 1816, the harvest had been poor, verses would explain why divine favour had justly been withheld. Several of the verse publications appearing from 1817 onwards were the work of Robert Jones, a compositor in Gee's office until 1830, who was equally inept as poet and craftsman.[42]

The secular titles fall into two broad categories. Those in Welsh – the great majority – were generally of a practical and popular character, while the few English works consisted mainly of scholarly or antiquarian works for the gentry and clergy. A few of the practical works, such as John Parry's *Arweinydd i'r Anllythyrenog* (A Guide for the Illiterate), were intended to provide basic literary skills. At a more advanced level, Robert Davies's *Ieithiadur* (Grammar) led its purchasers from the rudiments of grammar to the rules of Welsh strict-metre poetry. Gee printed the second (1818) and third (1826) editions of this popular work for the author, bought the copyright following his death in 1835, and published a fourth edition in 1839.[43] Gee also printed in 1816 the first book containing a Welsh system of shorthand, Robert Everett's *Stenographia*. The shorthand examples had to be individually written by hand in each copy, but the second shorthand manual produced by Gee, Thomas Roberts's *Stenographia* (1839), was a much more ambitious venture which included sixteen specially prepared copper plates. One of these came to light a few years ago under the floor of the Swan Lane building.

Aids for craftsmen and farmers were also in demand – works such as *Y Cyfrifydd Parod,* a ready-reckoner published by Gee in 1814, and *Y Mesurydd Tir a Choed* (The Land and Wood Measurer). No copy is known to survive of the first edition of 1813 of the latter, but in the introduction to the second edition, published in 1816, Gee stated that the number of examples had been restricted to keep its price down, in view of the trouble and expense of producing a book of this nature.[44] The relatively high price of two shillings and sixpence charged for a 154-page diglot ready reckoner for the buyer and seller of corn published in 1840 similarly reflects the cost of setting and proofing tabular work. Veterinary works were also produced, the first to be published by Gee being *Y Cyfarwyddyd Profedig i Bob Perchen Anifeiliaid* by John Edwards, a 384-page book published in parts between mid-1814 and early 1816.[45] Almost two decades later an ambitious attempt to publish a comprehensive treatise on horses, *Y March*, in five parts selling at a shilling each had to be abandoned for lack of support after only one part had appeared.

English-language material of a scholarly nature included *An Account of the Castle and Town of Denbigh* printed in 1829 for its author Richard Newcome, Warden of Rhuthun, and, in 1835, *The History and Antiquities of the Town of Aberconwy* by Robert Williams, Curate of Llangerniw. A major undertaking during the second half of the 1820s was the printing of the third edition of John Walters's *An English and Welsh Dictionary*, extensively revised by Walter Davies, Rector of Manafon, a leading figure amongst the 'hen bersoniaid llengar' (literature-loving parsons). The dictionary was published by Walters's granddaughter with the support of Colonel William Lewis Hughes of Kinmel Park. Subscriptions for the three-guinea work were being sought by the end of 1824,[46] and on 24 July 1826 Gee sent Walter Davies the first sheet, stating

> as I am employed as Miss Walters [*sic*] printer I consider it a duty incumbent to submit my first efforts either for your approbation or disapprobation [...] The typographical department, I shall endeavour to execute in a workmanlike manner; and in a way which I hope will be satisfactory to Colonel Hughes, Miss Walters, and yourself.[47]

Six hundred copies of the two-volume, 1250-page work were published.[48] 295 subscribers (including ten Oxford and Cambridge college libraries) ordered a total of 309 copies; it is possible that comparatively few of the remaining copies were sold since the work was regularly advertised in Gee catalogues for over sixty years.

As a companion to this massive English-Welsh dictionary, Gee then set about publishing a new edition of William Owen Pughe's Welsh-English dictionary. Pughe's diary notes that he discussed the project with Gee on 19 March 1828, and by 12 May 1828 he had started preparing copy.[49] Pughe inserted his additions and corrections in a copy of the first edition of 1793 which has fortunately survived.[50] The first of the projected twenty-four half-crown parts had appeared by November 1828,[51] and publication was completed by the autumn of 1832. Contemporaries were well aware of the scale of the venture and its significance in enhancing the prestige of the Welsh language; the Holywell Cymreigyddion Society, for example, toasted both Pughe and Gee at its 1830 Saint David's Day dinner.[52]

Since the early 1790s Pughe had wished to publish the text and his translation of the Mabinogi and Romances, important and hitherto unprinted middle-Welsh prose tales.[53] After many false starts and disappointments because of his failure to secure sufficient support, the London Cymmrodorion Society resolved in 1831 that the work be published in Denbigh under Pughe's 'superintendence'. Fifty pounds was to be advanced towards the expenses, '£25 to be paid to the printer when the work is in the press, and the further sum of £25 when the edition is printed off'.[54] The precise terms still remain unclear: Pughe's son hoped 'that Gee, our Denbigh printer, may undertake the work, allowing my Father some number of copies, a risk which may suit him better than us, on account of his connexions, & greater facilities in delivering the work'.[55] Pughe gave Gee the first part to set at the beginning of 1834 and worked hard at preparing the remainder until mid–May, when his health suddenly deteriorated and references to the project in his diary cease.[56] Some of the text was certainly set, since in mid-April 1834 Pughe noted 'cyweiriaw adbrawv mab. Pwyll'.[57] Since the word 'adbrawf' is defined in his dictionary as 'a second proof', the entry suggests that at least the first branch of the Mabinogi had been set and proofed.

Another scholarly venture which failed to gain sufficient support was a Cornish Dictionary prepared by the clergyman-scholar Robert Williams. Although proposals printed by Gee in 1840 stated that the work would be published in an edition limited to 250 copies, no more than seventy-four subscribers (including Southey) could be found, and it proved impossible to proceed with the work. Williams had to wait until 1865 before his *Lexicon Cornu-Britannicum* was published at Llandovery.

The office printed two substantial volumes of Welsh verse. In 1827 Gee printed *Diliau Barddas*, a 320-page collection of the work of Robert Davies 'Bardd Nantglyn'. Davies had issued proposals in the spring of 1825 for this fairly expensive book (costing four shillings and sixpence in paper-covered boards)[58] and eventually persuaded 998 subscribers to order 1198 copies. This led Gee to think well enough of its sales appeal to buy the copyright (with that of Davies's grammar) in July 1839 for £19.19s.6d,[59] though he never published a new edition. Davies's collection followed the traditional pattern, but the next volume of verse printed by Gee broke new ground. *Ceinion Awen y Cymmry : The Beauties of Welsh Poetry*, an anthology selected by T Lloyd Jones, included poems in the strict metres but added to these the work of contemporary Welsh poets and translations of contemporary English favourites. Pughe, to whom it was dedicated, prepared the volume for the press during November and December 1830.[60] Although at three shillings and six pence in boards the book was considerably cheaper than *Diliau Barddas*, it appears to have appealed to a far narrower readership with 365 subscribers ordering 436 copies.

The subscription lists published in many of Gee's books show that many of the gentry and clergy of North Wales were still prepared to support the publication of Welsh literary and scholarly works. Indeed the social pressure to do so was such that a *nouveau riche* newcomer to the area such as Joseph Ablett of Llanbedr Hall, who imposed a fine of a penny whenever Welsh was spoken in his servants' hall, subscribed to Gee's diglot New Testament (thirty copies), to *Diliau Barddas*, to Walters's Dictionary, and to Pughe's Dictionary (two copies of each), and offered to assist in the publishing of the Mabinogi.[61]

The varying standard of workmanship and quality of material used for Gee's publications indicate that he catered for two distinct markets. Most of the Welsh works concentrated on squeezing as much matter as possible into a minimum of space and were printed on cheap paper, but the more expensive works in both Welsh and English are very competent examples of good provincial printing. Some of the more expensive works used high-quality paper manufactured locally: for example, John Jones's *An Address, Wherein are Considered the Relative Duties of the Rich and Poor* of 1829 was printed on fine paper watermarked 'Afonwen 1829'.

Gee's interest in technological advances is shown in the letters he wrote to his son Thomas when the latter went to London in 1837 to broaden his experience of the trade and of fine printing in particular. Two themes recur, the lettering of the spines of cloth-bound books and the care of inking-rollers. Thus in June 1837 he wrote, 'Try to find out how the <u>lettering on the backs</u> of Cloth bound books is done – I wish we could manage this properly.'[62] He returned to the problem in late July, asking 'Can't you find out who letters them so from Tegg or Marshall.'[63] The fullest discussion of rollers is in an undated letter:

> Have you been able to ascertain, how the <u>Pressmen preserve their Rollers soft</u>. – I have turned Roller maker myself – and I believe have improved, by soaking the old ones in water before re-melting, by which process it <u>amalgamates</u> better in the boiling.[64]

These letters demonstrate that the geographical distance of some two hundred miles between Denbigh and London corresponded to a technology lag of some two decades.

In its early years the press employed very few hands. In 1892, reminiscing on the occasion of his golden wedding, Thomas Gee, junior, said that in 1830 the office (then in a building in a yard behind the Cross Foxes Inn, Hall Square)[65] occupied a single small room, and the workforce, apart from his father, consisted of one journeyman, two apprentices, and a pressman.[66] Although the working day ran from six in the morning to eight in the evening[67] (Gee senior being often there at five a.m.),[68] there was always more than enough to do: as an observer wrote in 1830:

> Mr Gee is at present so busy that he does not know where to turn [...] Since the big Dictionary, the Ceinion, the Mabinogion and various other masterly books are to be published, he will have [...] to be busy for a long time on great tasks.[69]

In 1832 the office moved to its present site in Swan Lane and the number of workers began to grow.

Thomas Gee junior had to return from London at the beginning of 1838 because his mother's health had deteriorated. He took over as overseer of the office, and it appears that his father's interest in it gradually declined following her death in October of that year. Some of the major publications of the first half of the 1840s such as the pioneering Welsh quarterly, *Y Traethodydd* (The Essayist), can be attributed to Thomas Gee junior though he was careful to stress that his father still had the last word. The clearest indication of this was the rejection in 1842 of a proposal that the office should publish a Welsh-language newspaper. Quite apart from the technical and financial problems, Thomas Gee junior pointed out the 'very great obstacle' that

> ... there is only ourselves in the trade in Denbigh, but were we to publish a Newspaper it would advocate Liberal principles of course, and in that case the Conservatives would conspire to injure us in bringing an opposition Printer to Denbigh – This would be worse than all – [70]

He was not made a partner until 1 February 1845, and then only, one suspects, to ensure that proper provision was made for his sisters and youngest brother. Thomas Gee senior died at his son Robert's house in Liverpool in November 1845. Under his son's leadership the press moved on to new ventures, its nature as a Welsh-language publishing concern being finally fixed after Gee lost his 'county' trade in books, periodicals, stationery, and insurance in a single week as a result of his prominence as an anti-Tory organizer in the 1852 election.[71]

NOTES

1. P H Jones, 'Saernïo'r gofeb: T. Gwynn Jones a *Chofiant Thomas Gee*', *Y Traethodydd*, 147 (1992), 183-210.
2. Jonathan Jones, *Cofiant y Parch. Thomas Jones o Ddinbych* (Dinbych, 1897), 453.
3. Idwal Jones, 'Thomas Jones o Ddinbych – awdur a chyhoeddwr', *Journal of the Welsh Bibliographic Society*, 5 (1937-42), 153.
4. For William Collister Jones, see Derek Nuttall, *A History of Printing in Chester from 1688 to 1965* (Chester, 1969), 35-6.
5. D E Jenkins, *The Life of the Rev. Thomas Charles, B.A. of Bala*, 2nd edn (Denbigh, 1910), III, 67, 69.
6. Quoted in Ifano Jones, *A History of Printing and Printers in Wales to 1810* [...] (Cardiff, 1925), 178.
7. Jonathan Jones, *Cofiant*, 153. The office charged Jones £24.12s.9d. for printing 2000 copies.
8. For a balanced discussion of this debate see R T Jenkins, *Hanes Cymru yn y Bedwaredd Ganrif ar Bymtheg* (Caerdydd, 1933), 35-7.
9. A H Williams, *Welsh Wesleyan Methodism 1800-1858* (Bangor, 1935), 140.
10. Thomas Jones (quoted in Jonathan Jones, *Cofiant*, 182) gave a trenchant account of these events, describing the printer as 'dyn nodedig am feddwdod, a llawer o anfoes' ['*a man noted for drunkenness and much immorality*'] whom Davies had treated excessively to drink 'i ormodedd, fel y gwelwyd arno'.
11. Jonathan Jones, *Cofiant*, xxii. The work contains a photograph of the building facing page 128.
12. The address to the reader is dated 27 March 1809.
13. National Library of Wales [hereafter NLW] MS 6180B, James Evans 'A retrospect of my past life'.
14. Quoted in A H Dodd, *The Industrial Revolution in North Wales* (Cardiff, 1933), 303.
15. Samuel Lewis, *A Topographical Dictionary of Wales* (London, 1833), art. 'Denbigh'.
16. NLW MS 8310D (Gee MS 6) (482) Thomas Gee senior to Thomas Gee junior, [1837].
17. I must thank Mr R M Owen of Denbigh for making available a copy of this document.
18. Harris's Diary, 23-25 March 1752, as quoted in E P Jones, *Methodistiaeth Galfinaidd Dinbych 1735-1909* (Dinbych, 1936), 43.
19. E P Jones, *Methodistiaeth*, 96.

20. A point emphasised in G J Williams, 'Traddodiad Llenyddol Dyffryn Clwyd a'r Cyffiniau', *Trans. Denbighshire Historical Society*, 1 (1952), 20-32 (31-2).
21. *Carnarvon and Denbigh Herald*, 19 September 1840.
22. The Address to the Reader is dated 31 May 1809.
23. This fragment, preserved in University of Wales Bangor Library, was described by Thomas Richards in 'Dinbych a'r Wasg Gymraeg', *Transactions of the Honourable Society of Cymmrodorion*, Session 1939, 133-4.
24. 'Daeth [...] yn hoff llyfr mewn cannoedd o deuluoedd Cymreig.' 'Gwnaeth fwy, [...] i greu a chadw atgasedd ym meddyliau y Cymry tuag at Babyddiaeth nag un llyfr arall a gyhoeddwyd yn yr iaith Gymraeg.' (Jonathan Jones, *Cofiant* 209).
25. The title page is dated 1811, but since the Preface is dated 20 December 1811 the book may not have appeared until January 1812.
26. The earliest yet seen is a list of the public officers for the Borough of Denbigh for the year commencing the second of November 1810 (Rhuthun, Denbighshire Record Office BD/A/68).
27. Printed slip attached to sig. $\pi 1^b$ of copy at NLW Wp 2583.
28. Figures based on those printed in Dispensary Reports from 1811 onwards.
29. The main sources remain – despite their inaccuracies – the article on Thomas Gee in the second edition of *Y Gwyddoniadur Cymreig*, X 614B-614D and T Gwynn Jones, *Cofiant Thomas Gee* (Denbigh, 1913), 9-19.
30. *Seren Gomer*, 4 (1821), 219-20.
31. *Chester Chronicle*, 11 June 1824.
32. *The Gwyneddion; or an Account of the Royal Denbigh Eisteddfod* [...] (Chester, 1830), 173.
33. Pughe had inherited the estate in 1806 but did not move from London to live there permanently until his wife and prominent followers of Joanna Southcott had died (Glenda Carr, *William Owen Pughe* (Caerdydd, 1983), 243-6).
34. NLW MS 8310D (472) Thomas Gee senior to Thomas Gee junior, 25 May 1837.
35. Advertisement, *Carnarvon and Denbigh Herald*, 19 September 1840.
36. A Dykes Spicer, *The Paper Trade: a Descriptive and Historical Survey* [...] *from the Commencement of the Nineteenth Century* (London, 1907), 114.
37. Advertisements in *Chester Chronicle*, 14 and 28 October 1825.
38. The 1844 edition of Piggot's Directory was the first to list the latter agency. For some reason, the billhead used by Gee in 1845 listed an agency for the Clerical & Medical Life Insurance Company but makes no mention of the Pelican.
39. University of Wales Bangor Library, Amlwch Papers 4 (25) Articles of Agreement dated 21 April 1817.
40. The formula 'Argraffwyd ac ar werth gan' ('*Printed and sold by*') normally – but not invariably – meant that Gee was the publisher of the work in question.
41. *Gwyddoniadur*, art. 'Thomas Gee'.
42. T Lloyd Jones wrote 'a chan nad oedd R. Jones yn Gysodydd hylwydd, nid oedd yn addas i'r gwaith arbenciav a ovynir ei gyvlawni.' ['*since R Jones was not a successful/swift compositor he was not suitable for the most specialized work that has to be undertaken*'] T Lloyd

Jones to R Lloyd Morris, 2 December 1830 as printed in J Jones, *Adgof Uwch Anghof* (Pen y Groes, 1883), 227.
43. The press subsequently brought out new editions in 1848 and 1862.
44. *Y Mesurydd Tir a Choed* (Dinbych, 1816), 4.
45. Publication of Part 1 was noted in *Seren Gomer,* August 1814; the address to the reader is dated New Year's day 1816.
46. Notice, front wrapper *Goleuad Cymru,* December 1824.
47. NLW MS 1805E (i) (Crosswood MS 165 (i)) Thomas Gee to Walter Davies, 24 July 1826.
48. NLW MS 8311D (Gee MS 7) Hannah Walters to T Gee, 2 August 1834.
49. NLW MS 13248B (Mysevin MS 28) 19 March and 12 May 1828.
50. NLW MS 866D (Ty Coch 52).
51. *Seren Gomer,* November 1828, wrapper [4].
52. *Y Cymro,* 1 (1830), 60.
53. Arthur Johnson, 'William Owen-Pughe and the Mabinogion', *National Library of Wales Journal,* 10 (1957-8), 323-8.
54. *Cambrian Quarterly Magazine,* 3 (1831), 253.
55. Aneurin Owen to A. J. Johnes' 15 February 1831 as printed in Marian Henry Jones, 'The Letters of Arthur James Johnes', *National Library of Wales Journal,* 10 (1957-8), 233-64, 329-64 (245).
56. NLW MS 13248B (Mysevin MS 28) 4 January 1834. The last reference to correcting the work is the entry for 17 May 1834.
57. NLW MS 13248B (Mysevin MS 28) 18 April 1834.
58. Robert Davies to Rev T Richards, Berriew, 9 March 1825, printed in J Jones, *Adgof*, 96.
59. NLW Thomas Gee MSS O2.
60. NLW MS 13248B (Mysevin MS 28), where Pughe records editing the work between 29 November and 6 December 1830.
61. William Tydeman, 'Ablett of Llanbedr; Patron of the Arts', *Trans. Denbighshire Historical Society*, 19 (1970), 141-87, (142, 165).
62. NLW MS 8310D (474) Thomas Gee senior to Thomas Gee junior, 9 June 1837.
63. NLW MS 8310D (476) Thomas Gee senior to Thomas Gee junior, 24 July 1837.
64. NLW MS 8310D (481) Thomas Gee senior to Thomas Gee junior, [1837].
65. Gee's speech at his golden wedding celebrations, *Baner ac Amserau Cymru* [hereafter *BAC*], 19 October 1892, 4.
66. *BAC,* 19 October 1892.
67. NLW MS 6180B James Evans 'A retrospect of my past life'. Hands were allowed to cease work at seven p.m. when there was a weekday chapel service.
68. NLW MS 8310D (482) Thomas Gee senior to Thomas Gee junior, [1837].
69. 'Mae Mr. Gee mor brysur yn bresenol mal nas gwyr yn iawn i ba van i droi [...] Trwy fod y Geiriadur mawr, Y Ceinion, Y Mabinogion, ac amryw eraill o lyvrau gorchestol, i'w hargraffu, rhaid iddo [...] vod yn brysur am yspaid maith o amser mewn gorchwylion mawr.' T Lloyd Jones to R Lloyd Morris, 2 December 1830 as printed in J Jones, *Adgof*, 226-7).
70. NLW, Thomas Charles Edwards Collection 1472 Thomas Gee junior, to Lewis Edwards, 6 October 1842.
71. T Gwynn Jones, *Cofiant*, 132.

False Imprints and the Bridger Specimen Books

R J GOULDEN

AN ACCOUNT OF SURVIVING Kentish specimen books was given in a paper[1] for the fifteenth seminar on the British book trade at Canterbury in July 1997. These specimen books are, firstly, two folio scrap-books compiled by Jasper Sprange, printer at Tunbridge Wells, the period covered being the late 1790s and the early 1800s; secondly, a loose collection of specimens printed by John Blake of Maidstone in the 1790s; and thirdly a fragment of a specimen book that had contained work by George Waters printing at Cranbrook, the three surviving specimens from it all dated 1826.[2] To these we can now add an irregular run of specimen books compiled by father and son, William and Frederick Thomas Bridger, both printers at Tonbridge. These specimen books do not constitute a full record of the Bridger printing output from 1834 as they cover only the years 1842-6, 1848-50 and 1867-9. There is in addition an envelope tucked into the volume for 1844. It contains miscellaneous printed items including two catalogues for auctions on 16 July 1838 and 31 March 1841. The volume for 1842 includes a number of items printed in December 1841. What these surviving Bridger specimen books hold is considerable. The specimen book for 1842 has 376 printed items. This suggests by extrapolation that the eleven specimen books may well hold around 3900 printed items, the majority not duplicated elsewhere.

The provenance of the Bridger specimen books is not complicated. The Bridger bookselling and printing concern was conducted firstly by William Bridger (1801-54) and then by his son Frederick Thomas Bridger (1824-93). In 1880 Frederick Thomas Bridger handed the firm over to his son Harry Stephen Bridger (1852-1926), who in turn passed on the business to his son Frederick Marston Bridger (1886-1963), who died intestate. Letters of administration were granted on 20 March 1964 to Frederick's son Stephen Dudley Bridger, also a printer. On 13 July 1967 Stephen Dudley Bridger wrote to Allen Grove of Maidstone Museum: 'Many thanks for your letter of 23 June regarding the volumes of old printing, as I wish to dispose of them as much as you wish to purchase them I am prepared to drop the price asked to £40 and hope this will satisfy your committee.'[3] Evidently the Museum committee was satisfied as the Bridger specimen books are now in Maidstone Museum.[4]

Early printers' specimen books are to the historians of the provincial eighteenth and nineteenth century book trade as gold-bearing rocks in virgin territories were to the eager pioneer-prospectors. Strenuous excavations are called for, perhaps in the end unprofitable, but the promise of treasure is hard to resist. Specimen books may throw light on the nature and working of the provincial book trade if they contain details on apprentices, journeymen printers and auxiliaries; on customers, commissions and market depth; on services and facilities offered such as the provision of newspapers, circulating libraries, reading rooms, binderies, and even insurance; and on the availability of specialized lines and forms: *inter alia* ledger books, forms of prayers, accounts of trials and executions, and law stationery. Specimen books may also enable one to assign printed material without imprints to particular printers. This is an important consideration. The Bridger specimen book for 1842, for instance, contains 376 printed items, of which only 125 bear imprints: in other words a startling 67% of the material would in all probability not have been identified as from the Bridger press had the 1842 volume not survived.

The Bridger specimen books contain a surprise: the inclusion of alien material. Pasted into the volumes are folio, quarto and octavo announcements, reports and advertisements from printers in Hadlow, Edenbridge and Westerham, all near Tonbridge, and the printers having no obvious connections, whether family or commercial, with the Bridgers of Tonbridge. It is easy to suggest that the Bridgers so admired the layout and styles of those productions that they admitted them into their own specimen books for use as samples for future work. A very different and much more intriguing explanation for the presence of the Hadlow, Edenbridge and Westerham broadsides and pamphlets emerges after a close scrutiny of both the alien material and the backgrounds of the printers involved.

Only a single piece, a poster, by the Hadlow printer is found in the Bridger specimen book for 1849, which also contains several items printed by John Wickenden of Edenbridge. The earlier specimen books before 1849 do not contain alien material. Examination of the type used by the Hadlow printer for the announcement that a Mr J Teodor, 'formerly a Romish archdeacon, of the diocese of Podlachia, in Poland,' will deliver in June three lectures on the downfall of the Church of Rome, reveals some damaged letters, especially a capital R which is chipped. This damaged capital R is also found in a Bridger poster announcing a cricket match on 11 September 1849. An announcement printed by Wickenden for the Edenbridge Book Society in October 1849 has a capital E with damage to its upper arm and a capital N with both up and down strokes broken. These damaged letters are both found in a poster announcing an auction on 4 March 1850. This poster was printed by Bridger and Son, and is in the specimen book for 1850. The same volume holds several items from a Westerham printer, George Puddefoot. His poster, *Crispin Bridge near Four Elms, Hever, … to be sold by auction, … on March the 25 [th], 1850 …*, has a capital N damaged at the top of the left stroke head. One is not now surprised to find a similar damaged N in another Bridger and Son poster, for an auction on 30 October 1850. Wherever one looks, the same damaged type is found in both the alien and the Bridger pieces.

The 1867-9 specimen books compiled by Frederick Thomas Bridger virtually tell the same story for the Edenbridge material. Another damaged capital E, found in a Bridger and Son auction poster of September 1850, is present in an announcement on '*a miscellaneous entertainment*' being held on 21 January 1867, the announcement printed by John Norman of Edenbridge. Another printer there, Agnes Humphreys, used a distinctive capital M in a poster for a musical entertainment on 10 January 1868, this M also used in a Frederick Thomas Bridger poster for the Tonbridge Dorcas Society's tea meeting on 16 December 1868. And so on. What are we to make of it all?

The circumstances of the Hadlow, Edenbridge and Westerham printers hardly encourage us to see them as actual printers. The imprint of the 1849 Hadlow piece is quite uncompromising: *Briggs, printer, Hadlow*. Documentary sources seem to suggest otherwise. The earliest Hadlow reference to Ferdinand Martin Briggs has him in 1847 as stationer and bookseller. By 1851 he was also a bookbinder and by 1855 Hadlow's postmaster. The Hadlow baptism registers between 1848 and 1849 have him as stationer and bookseller, and so does the 1851 Hadlow census. His family background was mercantile for his father, Benjamin, was a grocer, and Briggs himself was, before he came to Hadlow around 1846, in London as a draper.[5] As far as can be ascertained, there were no members of the Briggs family in the Kentish book trade before 1845. Ferdinand Martin Briggs left Hadlow in or before 1855 for his successor, Josiah Oliver, is noted in the *Maidstone Chronicle* of 20 December 1855 as of Hadlow, stationer and agent for the same newspaper. Josiah Oliver was, like Briggs, a bookseller, stationer, bookbinder and postmaster. He was also a chemist. Sources on Oliver do not refer to any printing done by him.[6] Oliver's successor, Edwin Shrivell, was a stationer and chemist.[7] The type evidence and documentary sources thus imply that Ferdinand Martin Briggs never possessed a printing press.

Edenbridge as the crow flies is nine miles from Tonbridge. John Wickenden of that smallish Wealden town (imprint: *Wickenden, printer, Edenbridge*) is represented by several broadsides in both the 1849 and 1850 Bridger specimen books. He was born in Edenbridge in 1808, the son of Nicholas Wickenden, carpenter, and married there in 1828. The earliest printed mention of his involvement in the Kentish book trade is in the 1851 Post Office directory, which describes him as ironmonger, insurance agent, stamp sub-distributor and stationer. The 1851 Edenbridge census records him simply as an ironmonger.[8] John Wickenden's involvement in the book trade ceased sometime between 1859 and 1862; his successor, Henry James Humphreys, was known *inter alia* as an ironmonger, stationer and *printer*.[9] It is unfortunate that there are no Bridger specimen books for the years 1862-6 for it would have been useful to check on Humphreys imprints before 1867. Henry James Humphreys was when he married in 1861 a draper at Cowden, his father William a carpenter. In Edenbridge by 1862 he was described in its baptism registers as an ironmonger. Humphreys died in January 1867, aged 35, and his widow Agnes continued the business. The Bridger specimen books of 1867-9 contain items bearing her imprint *(A. Humphreys, printer, Edenbridge)*; the first in February 1867. Documentary sources only note her as a stationer and ironmonger, never as a printer. When she ceased trading is not known; when she married for the second time, in August 1879 to a Maidstone grocer, she declared on the marriage certificate that she had no trade.[10]

Edenbridge's postmaster was also a stationer. John Norman, born in Newbold-on-Avon in Warwickshire around 1805, came to Edenbridge before 1859 from Hever, a few miles away, to take up the postmastership, and remained in Edenbridge until his death in 1879. The Post Office directories almost invariably have him as postmaster, bookseller and stationer. John Norman described himself in his will, made in 1876, as postmaster and stationer. His elder son, William Edward Norman, succeeded his father as postmaster in 1879 and was at that time described as a stationer. Probate papers for his mother and brother in 1886 and 1909, and his will made in 1910, give his occupation as postmaster. The bookselling and stationery business was carried on by John Norman's widow, Rachel, until 1886, and then by their daughter, Eliza Ann Norman, until her death in 1902.[11] Nary a mention of any press owned by the Normans, yet the Bridger specimen books for 1867 and 1869 contain pieces 'printed' by John and William Edward Norman.

Westerham, a little further from Tonbridge than Edenbridge, is a larger Wealden town, sufficiently capable of supporting a wide range of tradesmen. It had a proper printer working in the 1830s and 1840s, Henry George. He is the subject of a biography by James Moran who shows that Henry George was apprenticed in 1788 to James Dixwell, printer of London, and later worked in London as a compositor. His kinsman, Thomas George, settled in Westerham by 1820 as a grocer, and Henry George came to Westerham around 1830 to establish himself there as printer and bookseller. He printed the Rev Thomas Streatfeild's *Lympsfield and its Environs* in 1838. The Westerham churchwardens' accounts list invoices from Henry George from 1838 to 1844. In 1844 he launched a monthly periodical, *George's Westerham Journal,* which ceased in September of the same year. In the following November he was a bankrupt, his estate assigned to two men in the London book trade. Henry

George died before December 1848, exactly when is not known, but most likely in 1846.[12] His widow, Harriett, apparently sold only the bookselling and stationery part of the George business to Thomas Clare as he sold books and stationery at least from 1847, and was never a printer.[13] For the printing of their notices the Westerham churchwardens went to 'Mr. Payne', whose invoice was paid on 2 July 1846.[14] James Payne was a printer at Sevenoaks.

Thus from 1844 for a few years Westerham did not have a printer. The Bridger specimen book for 1850 contains pieces printed by a George Puddefoot. Like the Hadlow and Edenbridge 'printers' George Puddefoot appears to have no known expertise in printing. In 1830 a daughter was born in Westerham to Walter and Sarah Puddefoot. Walter was a hairdresser who may not have found Westerham congenial as his place was taken by his kinsman, perhaps brother, George Puddefoot by 1832. The Westerham baptism registers up to 1842 has George Puddefoot as hairdresser.[15] Then, in 1850, George Puddefoot made an announcement in an advertisement found in the Bridger specimen book for that year. The advertisement begins: *George Puddefoot, printer, bookbinder, bookseller, &c. Westerham, in returning thanks ... begs to inform ... that he has added the above branches to his business ...* The same Bridger specimen book has an invoice headed: *George Puddefoot, hairdresser and perfumer, printer, stationer, & bookbinder,* and a card in which Puddefoot announces that he has opened a drying house in Westerham for smoking and drying hams, tongues, and bacon. It is pertinent to ask why, if George Puddefoot was indeed the possessor of a press, these items should be in the 1850 Bridger specimen book as well as several notices with the Puddefoot imprint, usually worded as *G. Puddefoot, printer, bookbinder, &c., Westerham.*

George Puddefoot was still in Westerham in 1855 (as hairdresser, stationer and insurance agent)[16] and seems then to have left the town as he and his family do not appear in the Westerham registers from the late 1850s onwards. Westerham had to wait until the 1860s before it had a proper printer, Charles Hooker, who may have bought Puddefoot's stationery business as he was a stationer in Westerham in 1859.[17]

Frederick Thomas Bridger was careful to note on each item pasted into his specimen books the number of copies printed and the date of printing. He occasionally named the clients. On a broadside for the Edenbridge Young Men's Mutual Improvement Society's 'miscellaneous entertainment' on 21 January 1867 Frederick Thomas Bridger noted: '100. Jan. 10. 1867.' This piece was printed by John Norman. On Agnes Humphreys's pamphlet for the Edenbridge branch of the National Church School's annual account, 1865-6, Frederick Thomas Bridger minuted: '50. April 4, 1867.' The *State of Poll* sheet, meant to be completed in ink to indicate the progress of the voting during the election of 1868, is without imprint but has an interesting Bridger note: '1 doz. Nov. 11, 1868. Mr. J. Norman'. Practically all the Edenbridge pieces were annotated by Frederick Thomas Bridger.

To summarize: the damaged types found in the Hadlow, Edenbridge and Westerham broadsides and pamphlets are also found in pieces printed in Tonbridge by William Bridger and his son Frederick Thomas Bridger. The circumstances of Ferdinand Martin Briggs and the 'printers' of Edenbridge and Westerham do not suggest that they were familiar with the press nor that they possessed presses. The Edenbridge items in the Bridger specimen books of 1867-9 bear MS notes by Frederick Thomas Bridger on copies printed and when: would he have done so had the Norman and Humphreys pieces in fact come from presses in Edenbridge? The evidence inexorably leads us to the Bridgers as the real printers of the Hadlow, Edenbridge and Westerham pieces. We now need to ask ourselves the question: *why did the Bridgers conceal their printing, using false imprints*? After all, it would be perfectly reasonable for the Bridgers to state in their imprints that they were printing for the commissioning bookseller.

It may be that the Bridgers were attempting to expand their printing business by persuading stationers in smaller towns and larger villages both to be their agents and to channel printing commissions to them in return for either small rewards or discounts on stationery and books. But were the Bridgers to adopt the usual imprint mirroring the relationship between printer and bookseller or stationer: *printed by Bridger for xxx* [the bookseller], the Bridgers risked alerting rivals to these commercial arrangements, and it might be an easy matter for rival printers to approach their agents in order to offer even more favourable discounts, and so win over possibly profitable customers. To complicate matters, the stationers and agents might well learn to play the game and string along interested printers until satisfactory bargains were struck. In such situations it would not be easy for the Bridgers to win back their agents without further concessions. False imprints purporting to indicate that the 'printers' were indeed so could have been advantageous to these stationers in that local people would gravitate toward them, the 'printers', instead of going directly to urban printers. The stationers would then generate extra income by channelling printing orders to the Bridgers. Their customers placing the printing orders might well look around their shops and purchase stationery or whatever was on display: a bit more income there. One could also suggest that the stationers, by increasing their importance in the commercial life of their home towns, might hope for elevation to the higher ranks of society.

This hypothesis is difficult to prove, but may go some way in explaining the Bridgers' use of false imprints: to safeguard their quiet expansion of business by concealing the true relationship between the stationers of Hadlow, Edenbridge and

Westerham and themselves to prevent rivals from taking away new business; and the stationers in calling themselves 'printers' (as the Bridgers might well have told them) could hope for increased business and better social standing.

Since specimen books of the eighteenth and nineteenth centuries are decidedly uncommon, it may not be possible to discover further examples of false imprints. The deductions I have made where the Bridger false imprints are concerned may either be seen as cloud-castles or later by other historians rejected. But if further examples of false imprints used by provincial printers are in time to come discovered and explanations for these put forward, should these explanations be similar to my hypothesis, then we have an unexpected and delightful insight into how provincial printers tried to expand their business on the quiet.

NOTES

1. The paper was published as *Print Culture in the Kentish Weald* in Peter Isaac & Barry McKay [ed] *The Reach of Print; making, selling and using books* (Winchester: St. Paul's Bibliographies, and New Castle, DE.: Oak Knoll Press. 1998), 1-20.

2. The Sprange scrap-books are in Tunbridge Wells Museum; the Blake specimens in Maidstone Museum; and the Waters scrap-book fragment is in the Centre of Kentish Studies (henceforth CKS), Maidstone: P100/25/2.

3. The letter from Stephen Dudley Bridger is within the Bridger specimen volume for 1845. The late Leonard Robert Allen Grove was curator of Maidstone Museum between 1948 and 1975.

4. Giles Guthrie of Maidstone Museum very kindly searched its accession registers for the years 1967-68 but was unable to locate the entry for the Bridger specimen books. Mr. Guthrie remarks that 'Mr. Grove was known for his relaxed approach' [to the administration of the Museum.] After this article was written another Bridger specimen book, that for 1847, was in May this year recovered by Maidstone Museum from Bath, where it had been left by Mr Guthrie's predecessor for a bookbinding quotation several years ago. I have not yet seen this volume.

5. On Ferdinand Martin Briggs, *see*: CKS: Hadlow baptism registers and the 1851 Hadlow census; Samuel Bagshaw, *History, Gazetteer, and Directory of the County of Kent* (Sheffield, 1847); Post Office directories for Kent, 1851 and 1855; and Office for National Statistics (henceforth ONS): marriage and death certificates. Ferdinand Martin Briggs, draper, of Princes St., St. George Hanover Square, London, married on 6 December 1845; and died on 20 June 1887 at Brookwood Asylum, Woking, Surrey, his residence being in Brixton, London.

6. CKS: Hadlow baptism registers and the 1861 Hadlow census; and Post Office directories for Kent, 1859-71. Josiah Oliver was by 1872 in West Malling in partnership with Frederick Bailey as chemists, booksellers and stationers, as stated in *The Handy Directory and Guide for Maidstone* (Maidstone: W. S. Vivish, 1872).

7. CKS: Hadlow baptism registers and the 1871-81 Hadlow censuses; and Post Office directories for Kent, 1874-78. The *Sussex Agricultural Express* for 1887 lists Edwin Shrivell, chemist and stationer, as one of its agents.

8. CKS: Edenbridge baptism and marriage registers, and the 1851 Edenbridge census.

9. *Post Office Directory for Kent,* 1866.

10. For Henry James Humphreys, *see*: ONS: marriage certificate; CKS: Edenbridge baptism and burial registers. He married Agnes Stapley on 3 October 1861. For Agnes Humphreys, *see*: Post Office directories for Kent, 1871-74; CKS: 1871 Edenbridge census; and ONS: marriage certificate, which states that Agnes Humphreys, widow in Edenbridge, of no trade, married Robert Barling, grocer in Maidstone, at the Week Street Congregational Church, Maidstone, on 28 August 1879. The 1881 Maidstone census has Robert and Agnes Barling residing in Buckland Road in Maidstone.

11. The Norman family is variously noted in: Post Office and Kelly's directories for Kent, 1859-92; and CKS: 1871-91 Edenbridge censuses.

12. James Moran, *Henry George* (Westerham Press, 1972). Other sources consulted include the Westerham churchwardens' accounts in the CKS: P389/5/2, and *Perry's Bankrupt and Insolvent Gazette* for 1844, which names the two London book trade assignees as Richard Marshall, bookseller, and Richard Mason Wood, typefounder.

13. On Thomas Clare: Post Office directories for Kent, 1851-66; and CKS: Westerham churchwardens' accounts: P389/5/2, the 1851-61 Westerham censuses and Westerham baptism registers.

14. CKS: Westerham churchwardens' accounts: P389/5/2.

15. CKS: Westerham baptism registers.

16. *Post Office Directory for Kent*, 1855.

17. *The Post Office Directory for Kent*, 1859, describes Charles Hooker as a stationer. The first Post Office directory to describe him as a printer is the 1866 directory: bookseller, stationer, printer and bookbinder.

Charles Elliot's Book Adventure in Philadelphia, and the Trouble with Thomas Dobson[1]

WARREN McDOUGALL

THIS IS AN ACCOUNT, based on his business papers, of a critical episode in the life of Charles Elliot, bookseller in Edinburgh in the late 18th century, involving the Scottish book trade to America and Thomas Dobson of Philadelphia. Dobson found fame from 1790 as printer of the first American *Encyclopaedia*, but little is known of where he came from or how he got his start. The papers shed light on this, and do more, for they offer a narrative whose themes might be considered as generosity and trust, and enterprise and betrayal.[2]

Dobson in Edinburgh

Robert Arner, Dobson's biographer, notes his death age seventy-two on 9 March 1823, and places his birth near Edinburgh in 1751.[3] A case can also be made for his being born on 6 May 1750 in Galashiels Parish, Selkirk County, fourth child of William Dobson and Alice Walker.[4] The area was near the Oakwood Miln birthplace of Elliot (1748-1790), and indeed was the same parish as Elliot's cousin, the bookseller James Sibbald (1747-1803). A Borders friendship might help to explain the loyalty Elliot showed Dobson.

Dobson earned a working-man's wage to support his family in Edinburgh. At the age of twenty-six he became a clerk in Elliot's bookshop in Parliament Square. His first quarterly wage of £5 was paid in July 1777, which indicates a starting date of April. In 1782 this was raised to the next wage level at the shop, £6.5s. a quarter, (£26 annually), and remained that way until he left for America in 1784. James Sutherland, the senior clerk, was earning £7.10s. a quarter in 1783-84 (£30 a year).[5] With a secure job, Dobson married Jean Paton, a farmer's daughter, in October 1777 in Edinburgh and their first child, Margaret, was born 15 February 1779. At the baptisms of two further daughters in 1780 and 1782, one of the witnesses was Samuel Campbell senior, a bookbinder, whose word carried weight with Dobson.[6] It would appear that the younger girls did not long survive, as Elliot refers only to the eldest, 'Peggy', when discussing Mrs Dobson and the family in 1784-85.[7]

There is a glimpse of Dobson at work in Elliot's shop in 1780, in what must have been typical of his duties, he wrote to the bookseller John Blair, of Wigton:
Edinr 27 Sepr 1780 Mr John Blair Dr To Sundries £2.16.9
Sir
The above are this day put up for you and will be sent pr first carrier for your place.

You mistake the maths as to the prices from the Catalogue. The generality of Books are marked in Sale Catalogues considerably lower than the current shop prices, the design of sale Catalogues being to bring in Ready money. You also mention Books in Sheets, which are not extant but only in old libraries, and it is from the purchase of these that they come to be in Mr Elliots sale Catalogue.
Rapins Histy 15 Vols Mr Elliot can give you 10 pr Ct below the Catalogue price of 31/6. That is more than is commonly done and indeed there is never anything allowed, especially on old Books, from the Catalogue price.
Rollin he cannot give you in sheets as the Edition is out – can let you have one bound fine paper at 21/ & the Glasgow poets at 9d pr Vol in sheets—have made enquiry about throwing off your plates but cant get them done under 8d pr 100. Shall I Return the paper? You say you could send 8 or 1000 Quills at 8d pr 100 weighing 6 ounces. Are they Dressed? . If so send 100 by way of Trial and if they please Mr E will perhaps take a large Quantity. for C E T D[8]

Two weeks later he wrote again to Blair, filling another order, and politely explaining that the country bookseller could not get multiple copies in sheets of a 100 year-old book in the Elliot catalogue.[9] It is a picture of the bookseller's clerk expertly going about his trade.

During the seven years that Dobson worked in his shop, Elliot built up an extensive trade at home and abroad, and by 1784 was spending large sums buying medical copyrights. He published William Cullen, Benjamin Bell, Andrew Duncan, Alexander Hamilton, Alexander Monro I and II and other Edinburgh physicians and surgeons.[10] Money was flowing through the shop and the stock was huge. One of the booksellling schemes buzzing from Elliot related to the 10-volume *Encyclopaedia Britannica*, 2nd edition, being published by Macfarqhar, Bell and Hutton 1778-84. Elliot long saw its potential and a few months after Dobson left bought up all the remaining copies, turning the book into an international success. Clearly, Dobson, the £26-a-year clerk, was working for a man of wealth and reputation in the trade.

Elliot was impressed by Dobson and viewed him as a friend, and decided to serve both their interests by sending him to Philadelphia to sell his books. Together they chose the titles they thought would suit the Americans. There was no contract; the arrangement depended on Dobson's proven dependability, and on Elliot's trust in him. Neither were the financial rewards for Dobson explicitly defined. 'I am not able to fix any return for your Labours,' Elliot told him. 'I only will assure you that you shall not be a loser. I hope the return of this transaction will enable you together wt. your other consignments, to act somewhat independent for yourself in future.' [11] Elliot advanced £4 for Dobson's passage and arranged for him to receive £32 in cash and a letter of credit of £20 to £30 from Glasgow connections of the firm; Dobson would get more cash for his early needs in Philadelphia by collecting for book shipments sent others in America.[12] An account was opened in his ledgers in the expectation that Dobson would remit regular payments home.[13]

Elliot's Letters to Dobson 1784-87

In late October 1784 Thomas Dobson was at Greenock on the Clyde and had put on board the *Ann* forty-two trunks of books and some other goods worth £1964. His wait for a favourable wind enabled Elliot to write to him there; it was the first of forty-five letters, the salutation was 'Dear Thomas' and there was personal news along with business: 'Your Wife & Family are well... Little Peggy dined with us today.'[14] The letter also addressed a concern about the Customs charges. The invoice of books was for the retail prices, on which there would be a 2 ½ per cent *ad valorem* duty at Philadelphia. Elliot told him to make a second invoice for entry showing as the prime cost; the price of production in Edinburgh. '...and upon wc. you may freely Clear Your Conscience if necessary'. Future shipments would also be 'double invoiced', with the version for entry tax showing half the value of the other.[15] There would be a bigger tax to worry about: in 1785 Pennsylvania put an additional 15 per cent duty, making 17 ½ per cent on the value, of certain kinds of popular books. [16]

One of the letters of introduction Dobson carried with him was to the New York bookseller James Rivington. Rivington was buying and selling-on Elliot books (Dobson was to give him an invoice for £172), and was not told the whole truth about Elliot's part in the enterprise:

> Mr. Dobson... is a very deserving young man, who has been upwards of 7 years in my service. He intends settling if he finds it answer in some part of your Continent. I have given him a small Venture of Books as some others have done. If sobriety and attention be means of success he is sure of it. I will be obliged to you to give him your best advice. He can inform you of any thing new going forward here.[17]

While Dobson was still at Greenock, Elliot received letters from Philadelphia from Major William Jackson, who was starting as a bookseller, and from Dr Benjamin Rush, who recommended Jackson as Elliot's correspondent. Jackson had served with distinction in the American War of Independence, and was very well-connected, both socially and politically. He had recently acquired books in London and had just bought two cases of William Cullen's *First Lines of the Practice of Physic* that Elliot had sent to Rush on speculation. Elliot thanked Rush for passing on the Cullen and promised to do him or a friend any service he could.[18] Elliot told Jackson he hoped they would have many transactions together and, as with Rivington, played down his involvement with Dobson:

> Mr. Dobson has Carried a good number of Books from Different people in this place. From my knowledge of his fidelity, I made no hesitation of giving him what he asked of me that was my own printing. I am uncertain if he means to settle or not, with you, or sell off in wholesale, but I make no doubt you will give him your best advice.[19]

It was in the context of the Rush and Jackson letters, that Elliot gave a possibly fateful instruction: not wanting to disoblige, he told Dobson keep a wary eye on Jackson and to pretend to own the books.

> I wish you for your own Reputation to appear as if entirely upon your own bottom. If you are understood to be fitted out by me, it will hurt us both with the people that may worthy dealing with in the book way. You know a jealousy is a passion not to be accounted for... Look carefully about you with all men. This Gentleman may have been a very Good Soldier, but you'll be better after trial to judge of him as a Bookseller.[20]

Dobson took on the ownership so convincingly that it was not known in Philadelphia that Elliot was behind him, although there was a rumour of a Scottish connexion.[21] Jackson, the perceived threat, soon dropped out of bookselling, trained as a lawyer and became secretary of the Constitutional Convention in 1787. [22]

In April 1785 Elliot organised Mrs Dobson's passage for Philadelphia aboard the *Alexander*, telling Dobson 'Your Wife goes Passenger in the Cabin with many very respectful Personages, Viz. Dr. Nisbet of Montrose, & your Wife & Peggy are well, and shall want for Nothing. Your Mother is to continue with Sam. Campbell. Young Samuel goes out passenger in the Steerage and a maid Servant.' [23] The maid servant was for the Dobsons. Samuel Campbell junior, not yet twenty, would quickly succeed as a bookseller in New York. He had been apprentice to the Edinburgh bookseller John Bell, who like Elliot with Dobson, was funding his start in America, but with a much smaller supply of books. Dobson's mother was with Campbell senior until her death at an advanced age in 1789.[24]

'I wish [Mrs Dobson] may get safe & make you (from her Situation) better than you expected,' Elliot said. This appears to be a reference to the fine clothing with which he had fitted her out. 'On Mrs. Dobson's leaving this, I thought it was proper to Equip her a little better than she used to be, and more than your friend Samuel [Campbell senior] approved or knows of.' Elliot said he knew of the gaiety of the Americans, and it was important to give a good first impression. 'The Expence is not great & it is better the Philadelphians should say Mrs Dobson brought so & so wt. her than that she made it wt them.' [25] The expense for her passage and clothing was, in fact, £32, far more than Dobson had earned in a year at Edinburgh; Elliot paid it and added it to the account.[26] Mrs Dobson would arrive in Philadelphia dressed fashionably and with a servant; the wife of a merchant, not a clerk.

In the letter Mrs Dobson conveyed to her husband, Elliot talked of the financial arrangement, presumably in response to queries in the first letters back (Dobson had written to him on 3 and 27 December 1784 and on 11 January 1785). 'I have never fixed any Plan to Charge the Books, or how to settle with you. You'l be best judge from the prospect to name this.' [27] Dobson evidently kept coming back to the

unwritten terms of his recompense and Elliot's responses are a theme in the letters. As late as 1788, Elliot had to reply:
> There certainly was no settled bargain betwixt us at your setting out, but intention & Expectation was, (as I believe we both made the Selection to the best of our judgement) that I would allow you 25 p.cent upon the retail prices, only striking a proportion for binding upon which no discount could be given.[28]

Altogether in 1785 Dobson ordered five book shipments worth £1,400. A request mainly for London books caused Elliot to write to Robert Baldwin in Paternoster Row and Charles Dilly of the Poultry offering to exchange his own books for those on Dobson's lists. In the event, Elliot bought them from Dilly, George Robinson and Thomas Cadell on short credit, an expensive business.[29] He wrote that if Dobson had a greater demand for London books, 'I will make a trip to the City & try to lay in the different Articles of Books, Maps, Atlas, paper &c on the best advantage, being sensible that to push off my own books a very general assortment of every other is very necessary.'[30] Elliot intended to give him enough to sell to country stores and at great distances from Philadelphia. This, Dobson achieved: one of his customers was the Edinburgh bookseller William Wood sojourning in Charleston. (see below page 207.)

With well over £3000 worth of books now exported to Philadelphia, Elliot was worried about the lack of money coming back from Dobson, only £200 was received in 1785. He did not blame his friend: 'I make no doubt of your Anxiety and activity to remit and am certain also of the Difficulties,' Elliot wrote.[31] Dobson, without forewarning, did send some goods in kind—141 barrels of tar, 51 of pitch and 29 of turpentine—but Elliot could sell the tar only, for £11.[32] 'My Dear sir, to tell you honestly I begin too cool very much in my Expectations from My American Adventures, not in any the least blame on your account but from the impossibility of sending me remittances.'[33] Elliot pointed out that Sam Campbell had sent back a second shipment of gold and silver from New York to Sam Campbell senior and the bookseller John Bell.[34]

In 1786 Dobson made little payment on the books. 'I wish I had sent you to London or anywhere when America came across me, but this is not your fault,' Elliot said.[35] Elliot told his nephew William in March that it was not in Dobson's power to remit either bills, cash or produce.[36] By mid 1786 the account with Dobson stood at £4189.13s.10d, of which he had paid only £393.10s. The situation was beginning to damage Elliot: he had bought a new house in Edinburgh in 1786 and had depended on money from Dobson to pay for it [37] 'I am, Dr Thomas, in hope times will soon mend. If you do not think so, sell off directly, come home and I will do something for you at home.'[38]

In 1787 Elliot challenged a promise made by Dobson. 'You have repeatedly mentioned your sending Flour & Grain to the West Indies, but have never yet mentioned in what Bottom, quantity, or in short any thing like a plan when I may expect a tolerable remittance.'[39] He said Dobson should at least pay the interest on the debt. 'It surprises me very much Sam Campbell at New York transmits his father five pounds since he first set out, for your one, and he never had a sixth part of the credit.'[40] Elliot had opened a shop in London, and was very short of money. When no remittance at all arrived for eighteen months, he told Dobson,

> I have often wrote you my Dr Sir of the hard situations my adventures have brot. me into, & never more did I feel it than at this hour. In short, I am distress'd for a few hund[re]d Pounds, when you and some others amongst them have some Thousands of my property in your hands, and I cannot command one shilling. It has these 18 mos. surprised <u>me indeed</u> that I have realy in a manner got nothing from you when I know you must be laying out your ready Cash at a very high price for goods imported, & it leaves me without a Shilling to wait your Time & convenience, but this my friend will do no longer. I do think upon honor you have & must have taken unwarrantable Liberties with my property.[41]

Elliot, however, was incapable of staying angry or of suspecting Dobson's motives for too long. At the end of 1787 he sent him the current balance of £3583—saying he had paid nearly the same sum again in interest on it—and vowed not to send a single sheet unless he got a handsome remittance. He wrote that every one said how well Dobson was doing in Philadelphia, better than any of his neighbours, although he had been given no reason to think so, and that it was 'very odd to be employing my cash printing Books in America.' Elliot then enclosed a list of his new publications.[42] He often expressed contradicting views. In a letter composed between May and August 1788, as he was upbraiding Dobson for not remitting, and for buying a house in Philadelphia, two payments worth £86 arrived, and he changed directions:

> Every thing considered I must confess I cannot blame you so much as I perhaps insinuated. I have been made sensible of the impossibility of drawing much money from America for some years after the War. I hope however times are on the mending hand.[43]

The small payments were very encouraging to Elliot. He agreed to Dobson's request for a chemical furnace designed by Dr Joseph Black, and described what he was publishing. He wondered whether the American market would take an octavo edition of William Cullen's revised *Materia Medica*, which he would print in quarto in 1789. (Dobson never replied to this, much to Elliot's disappointment.)[44] Dobson would certainly have been interested when Elliot told him of the prospectus for the third edition of the *Encyclopaedia Britannica*: 'We are going on briskly with a new

Edit. of Encyclopaedia to be 15 vols at 21/ in boards or 300 1/ numbers. I will inclose you proposals.' These were in the box of books Elliot sent two weeks later.[45] Dobson reprinted the *Encyclopaedia Britannica* proposals on his own behalf, on 31 March 1789, and went on to produce the first number of his American *Encyclopaedia* 2 January 1790. His *Encyclopaedia*, an 18-volume reprint of the Edinburgh edition, with American alterations, and American engravings, was published 1790-98 and had a three-volume supplement 1800-1803. [46]

After failing continually to pay the debt, Dobson presented a new threat in 1788. He said he had a considerable quantity of the first shipment of books still unsold and proposed to send them back. He had never given an account to Elliot of the books sold or unsold or of his profits and losses on them. To have had books returned, at great expense, and in an unknown condition, would have been a great blow, but that was not all. Dobson was once again asking, surprisingly – since it had been more than four years – about the terms for taking the books out. Elliot told, or reminded, him that setting him up

> was a kind of mutual adventure, so far [as] all the advance & risque was on my part. The choice was made at both our sights to the best of our Judgements—but as there was no specific bargain an equal profit loss must fall on each (and at the worst you have had the advantage of a large Credit respect[ing] outfitting). Therefore if you say there are so many books unsold and will perhaps never sell let us make the most of them for our mutual advantage & we must do so; but you must come forward and Acct. for your profits on the goods that have sold . . .' [47]

Dobson had been clearly told that he could not evade responsibility for books that were unsold, and he did not send any back. But neither does he appear to have given an account of the Elliot books he had sold or exchanged. And it was these that had made his fortune in America.

Dobson in Philadelphia 1784-89

Dobson arrived in Philadelphia in December 1784 carrying both an introduction to Rush and a letter to Rush from William Cullen, thus starting a connection with the Philadelphia physician that served him well as both a bookseller and publisher. There he was, working independently in a vibrant city, an expert in his trade, with a great variety of new books valued at more than a clerk could earn in a lifetime, and with instructions to act as though the books were his. He was not long in opening the New Book Store on Front Street, and on 15 January 1785 placed two advertisements in the *Pennsylvania Packet*. One gave an indication of what was in the forty-two trunks of Elliot goods:

> T. Dobson has just imported a very large and valuable Collection of Books, in Various branches of literature, consisting of many thousand volumes, in general good editions, and the most elegant bindings: amongst which are: the Works of Shakespeare, Swift,

Pope, Sterne, Thompson, Hume, Robertson, Raynal, Smollet, &c &c. With a large collection of books in the different branches of medicine, Bibles of various Sizes, school-books. Books for entertainment [of] children, &c. Writing paper, quills, ink-powder, pencils, sealing-wax, wafers, music, &c. Also, a few dozen of fine old porter in bottles, an assortment of boots, men and womens shoes of the first quality. Catalogues of the books to be had gratis, of T. Dobson, at the store.

The other advertisement introduced Dobson's technique of advertising in themes. It was for a priced selection of his literature: *Evelina, Cecilia, the Theatre of Education by the Countess de Genlis,* and *A Select Collection of the most esteemed farces.*

The thematic advertisements that Dobson ran in the *Pennsylvania Packet* through 1785 (the reference dates are in the following text) show his professionalism, the titles available to Philadelphians that were despatched from Edinburgh, and the sheer volume of books that Elliot was supplying. The theme on 9 February was language – school books, self-help books and dictionaries – a list starting with William Scott's *An Introduction to Reading*, and *Lessons in Elocution* ('recommended,' wrote Dobson, 'by the celebrated Dr. Blair.') On 26 February the theme was French literature and language. On 21 May, it was medicine, with Bell's *System of Surgery*, Fourcroy's *Elementary Lectures*, Dickenson's *Enquiry into Fevers*, Irving's *Experiments on Bark*, Dr Cullen's *First Lines of the Practice of Physic,* and *The Chururgical Works of Percival Pott.* On 7 June the theme was divinity; 30 July: literature and novels; 31 August: popular religious work; 19 October: sermons by Scots ministers including Robert Walker, George Carr and John Smith. His advertisement on 7 November included more of the latest Elliot medical books, by Alexander Monro I and II, Alexander Hamilton, William Smellie and Andrew Duncan, and the promise that 'from the correspondence he has established in Europe, he hopes he will be able to supply the Public with every publication of merit on medical subjects.'

By May 1785, Dobson had moved to a new book store on Second Street and started to advertise how well he was doing. He hoped 'for a continuance of that favour of the generous public which he has already experienced'. [49] His business quickly spread beyond the Elliot titles when he began buying books from the printer Robert Aitken, apparently paying in cash.[50] In other transactions the Elliot books would have enabled him to extend his stock by exchanges with other booksellers. His first imprint appeared later in the year. This was an octavo: *Original Tales, Histories, Essays, and Translations by different hands*, Edinburgh: printed for Charles Elliot; and Thomas Dobson, Philadelphia, 1785. This collection existed in a previous edition in Scotland, and, thinking it would sell in America, Elliot bought the 150 remaining copies, put in a cancel title-page with their joint imprint, and shipped the books over.[51]

CHARLES ELLIOT'S BOOK ADVENTURE IN PHILADELPHIA

Robert Arner, in *Dobson's Encylcopaedia*, describes Dobson's rise as a bookseller and publisher from the time of his arrival: he presents a picture of energy and success where the Scots emigrant rapidly became a prospering American. He printed many books, and as a bookseller advertised reprints of British and Continental works under the heading of 'Books, American Editions'. The symbol of his success was the 'large, elegant store in the New-Stone House, in Second-street', which he built for himself and which he moved into in January 1788. The 'stone house' became famous in hundreds of imprints and was a resort for literary people in Philadelphia.[52] It took a while for Elliot to realise his money was paying for it. Its scale can be judged by its value: Dobson took out a first mortgage of £877.10s sterling in favour of a Mr Hockley in September 1788, and provided a second mortgage of £1000 as security for Elliot in June 1789; lawyers who inspected for Elliot's Trustees said, in 1794, that a sale of the premises would bring more than these sums.[53] (Dobson's stone house was more than twice the value of the four-storey house Elliot built for his family in Edinburgh New Town in 1786.) Contemporaries remarked on Dobson's progress. Benjamin Rush, writing to William Creech at Edinburgh in 1787 about the Philadelphia book trade, said: 'Mr Dobson, and a Mr [William] Young– from Glasgow – have succeeded, & will probably make a fortune in the course of a long life.'[54] In 1788 Francis Hopkinson told Thomas Jefferson that Dobson was carrying on publishing and bookselling in a large way and he seemed to have substantial capital and a large stock.[55] Dobson was doing very well in Philadelphia, and Elliot became aware of it.

Elliot's Letters 1789

In March 1789 Elliot began taking firmer steps to get his money, telling Dobson he should account for his profit and loss

> I dont mean to go very closely to work but there is a large sum my family cannot want conveniently and I wish in the first instance you will step forward and say what you propose or how you purpose to settle. I consider over and above the Balance there is a large sum of Interest besides due me. I wish this adjusted. Give me first what security you can and next give me your bond & Acknowledgement of the debt for the Balance.[56]

Elliot was ill in the spring but wrote that he had recovered. His next idea may have been genuine, or a way of getting Dobson to do something. 'I have often wished for a sail and very likely may visit the Continent of America.'[57] Dobson now acknowledged the size of his debt; in June, in front of a lawyer representing Elliot, he signed the £1000 second mortgage on the stone house for Elliot's security, and in July agreed to pay interest on the debt, and send money to Edinburgh, which he had not done for some time.[58] An anxious Elliot waited for months, but no money arrived.

Elliot was struggling in 1789. He was short of Dobson's money and paying interest on it and laying out money for copyrights and his shop in London was also a great expense. It is probably no coincidence that his final letters, written on 19 September 1789, were about Dobson. In one, to the Philadelphia lawyer Ralph Bowie, Elliot asked about the real value of the stone house, and said he was displeased with Dobson for asking for more books 'without a single penny of remittance'.[59] The other, to Dobson, began with sympathy for a loss in the family, then went through his grievances, including the grandeur of the stone house:

> I only knew lately that your superb tenement was the first & still the only stone tenement in the street. This was certainly most strange to sport my property in such a manner, when God knows I am at this moment going to sell my property for what it will fetch; to make good deficiencies, which I for some years depended on you to relieve. I hope you will send me all assistance you can directly, & send some bonds for the balance adding interest according to conscience. I have no doubt (& hope I shall not in future) of your integrity, altho' you have presumed by far too much on my property... Depending at least on the one half of the sum you owe me, has put me to dreadfull inconvenience... I am Dr Thos. wishing better times, for I never have been so much pinched these last 10 months. [60]

Soon afterwards Elliot suffered a stroke which left him paralysed, and unable to read and write.

The change in tone towards Dobson is startling. Elliot's book-keeper, John Greig, wrote to say Elliot was indisposed, bluffing that Elliot might go to America. He had witnessed the effect of the adventure on Elliot and the business and scathingly questioned Dobson's honour and honesty:

> From... Mr Elliot's Letters to you of late you will see the embarrassing effect produced on his affairs (which you well know were in a very flourishing state when you went out) by your retaining the Property he so generously entrusted you with, wholly upon the faith of your Integrity. Your conduct has at last forced him, tho' with great reluctance, to the fixed Resolution of either going out to Philadelphia himself or sending out some person sufficiently empowered to obtain that Justice he is so well intitled to from you above every person in the world, in case your own Conscience do not operate upon you so as to prevent it by making such Remittance now as will in some measure be adequate to the Sum you owe...
> In yours of 13th July last, you own receipt of two Copies of State of Accots. betwixt Mr. E. & you, <u>which you admit to be Right</u>, and Say, <u>That he is undoubtedly intitled to Interest for it</u>, But need not tell you that such Acknowledgements signify nothing of themselves, unless followed by actions corresponding to the import of them. Mr. E. has just now received an Order from Mr. Thos. Allan of New York, & a Remittance of £20 to purchase it with — Mr. Campbells sons send him money to make up their Orders. Compare Mr Dobsons conduct to Mr Elliot with this honourable & respectable manner of doing business, and then let Justice & Gratitude pass sentence upon it! But

it is impertinent in me to suppose I can influence you to do what you are bound to, by any arguments I can suggest after what Mr. E. himself has said to you.

I hope before this time you have taken the proper steps to vindicate your Honour & Honesty and make Reparation for the Loss & Damage Mr E. has sustained by the generous confidence he placed in your Care and Fidelity.[61]

In December, Greig wrote that Elliot still had sound understanding and every day he waited on the money from Dobson. 'But in this, like all other promises of the same kind, he has been disappointed.' [62] A payment of £150 did arrive on Christmas Day. At the time of Elliot's death, on 12 January 1790, Dobson still owed him £3691.[63]

Dobson at the Court of Session 1790-94

Sibbald v Dobson. In late December 1789, as Dobson was printing the first number of the American *Encyclopaedia* and Elliot was dying at his house in Queen Street, a summons was prepared against Dobson at the Court of Session in Edinburgh. It was taken out by James Sibbald who, unlike cousin Elliot, was never reluctant to sue. Sibbald sent books out to Dobson up to October 1787 but two years later still had not been paid the £42 owing. On 19 January 1790 a messenger-at-arms accompanied by two witnesses went through the procedure for accused who were 'furth of Scotland'. He marched up to the Cross on the High Street, which was the central gathering place, a few yards from Elliot's shop, gave several 'Oyez', yelled 'Thomas Dobson, bookseller in America!' read the summons and posted up a copy; the trio paraded down to the Pier and Shore of Leith and did the same thing at the water's edge. In June the court gave a decree against Dobson in his absence. Whether Sibbald actually recovered the money, awarded with interest and court costs, is unknown.[64]

Dobson v Wood. Dobson himself was not averse to suing for debts. The bookseller William Wood of Edinburgh owed him £68 for books and stationery bought between June and September 1786 while he was at Charleston, South Carolina. Dobson wrote out more than sixty Edinburgh, London and American titles he had given Wood and sent it, with a power of attorney gained from Philadelphia in 1791, to the lawyer Cornelius Elliot, Charles Elliot's cousin. In 1792, a summons was left at Wood's house in the Luckenbooths, and subsequently the court ruled in Dobson's favour. [65]

Cornelius Elliot v Dobson. Dobson not having paid his fee of £2.4s.10½d for this court-work, Cornelius issued a summons against him in 1793, and lumped him in with seven other petty debtors at a Court of Session hearing in February 1794; the judge ruled against the absent Dobson.[66]

Dobson and the Elliot family 1790-1807

It took some time for Dobson to pay his debt. The Trustees looking after the estate for Elliot's family – his widow, Christian (1761-1832), and two young children who survived, Anne (1782-1845) and William (1786-fl1846) – gave power of attorney to the Philadelphia lawyers Ellison and John Perrot to recover the money. In 1790 Dobson proposed to pay in instalments of £400 sterling a year, but nearly ten years later had paid only £1800. The Trustees had word that Dobson was 'in very good circumstances' and had informed an acquaintance in 1799 that the debt was paid. With compound interest of five per cent it still stood at £3938. The Trustees told the Philadelphia lawyers to recover the £1000 mortgage and sue for the balance. This moved Dobson to make ten large payments between 1801 and 1805 to clear the debt; in all he paid £6457. (Elliot's estate came to be worth £33 000.) [67] The repayment was twenty years from the time Dobson started up in Philadelphia with Elliot's books, and fifteen years after Elliot's death.

In 1807, Anne Elliot married the London bookseller John Murray II. Elliot's son, William, twenty years old, and training as a merchant, took advantage of the Murray relationship (it was to be his life-long habit) to write to Dobson. William asked him about bookselling prospects in Philadelphia, ostensibly on behalf of Murray, but more than likely seeking some kind of benefit for himself. If so, Dobson was having none of it. He did give William his perspective on the transatlantic book trade of the day and talked about their two families.

[Mr. William Elliot
care of Mr. John Murray.
Bookseller,
No. 32 Fleet Street, London]
Philadelphia Augt. 6th 1807

Sir

I was duly favoured with your letter of May 18th a few days ago, intimating Mr Murrays wish to know what prospects this country may offer for the extension of his business. My answer at present is not very flattering.

The duties on importing Books into the United States, besides freight, is nearly 20 pCent on the Invoice, and the demand for English printed Books, from the very high prices at which they now are, must be very limited. These high prices have induced many persons to reprint in this country the most saleable English publications, and sell them at lower rates; the number of these editions is much greater than a stranger could well suppose, and is still increasing. And the present state of intercourse between Great Britain and the United States holds out no flattering prospect. The number of Booksellers in this and the neighbouring states is very considerable; the greater part of these, however, are young men of more enterprise than capital, and who strain to the utmost all the credit they can get; of these some may be successful, but the number is small, and the spirit of speculation so great that the risk of an adventure is more than prudence would direct, as Books sent out on to sell on commission would yield returns very slowly indeed, and would generally turn out a losing concern.

The only safe way of doing business with this country would be as you have suggested, to have some respectable person on your side the Atlantic to guarantee the payment of the goods ordered, or to have a good Bill of Exchange sent with the orders. The few Booksellers in this city who may most be depended on, have their correspondence fixed and might not readily change, and their business is generally on a small scale, and would not be much of an object to Mr Murray.—-Messrs. Longman, Hurst, Rees, Orme, have an agent in this country, but I doubt if they reap much advantage from their trade to this country, taking it altogether. As to myself, I am still in business, but am not solicitous to extend it much, though I have no view of retiring from business while able to attend it. I should be glad to have a Catalogue of Mr Murrays Books, with the lowest prices for Cash, it might be of mutual service, a considerable part of my business is the sale of Medical Books, and Mr Murrays father was largely in that way.

My family now consists only of my Wife, one Daughter (Peggy) born in Edinburgh, who was some years since happily married to Dr Gallaher, a very respectable Physician in this city, and one son (Judah) about 15 years of age, who is attending to his Education, and at intervals attending the shop as a Bookseller, for which I intend him. All with myself in good health. From your mentioning your sister, I am induced to suppose you have but one. I am glad to hear of your Mother, please remember my Wifes Love & mine to her. We often think of your family.

I am with great respect, Sir your obt. servt
Thomas Dobson [68]

There was no advantage here for William. Three years old when his father died, he had, perhaps, no reason to see the irony of asking Dobson for help starting out in America, nor to reflect on the Dobsons' frequent thoughts of the Elliot family. The name had more resonance for sister Anne's descendants. A century after Elliot's death, his grandson John Murray III (1808-92), seeing Elliot referred to in a book by Samuel Smiles, wrote as marginalia that in 1789 'C.E. was in great straights from advances on copyrights in London also from having consigned property to on[e] Dobson of Philadelphia'. [69]

NOTES

1. This essay is from work in progress on a book-trade biography of Charles Elliot, which will include an index to entries in his papers. I thank Virginia Murray, archivist at John Murray, London, for her support in this project.

2. Elliot's papers, at the Archives of John Murray, consist of eight books of outgoing letters (1774-1790), four account ledgers (1771-1790), a Trustees Book, and financial records of his estate. I regularise the punctuation and, sometimes, the spelling, when quoting Elliot's letters. The copies were made by various hands, carelessly at times, and often without full stops; they do not reflect the standard of correctness of original Elliot letters. I have numbered the letter books by item, the ledgers by volume and page.

3. Robert D Arner, *Dobson's Encyclopaedia: the publisher, text, and publication of America's first Britannica, 1789-1803* (1991), 1.

4. General Register House, OPR 775/1, Selkirk County, Galashiels Parish, births (1714-1819) item 2. Siblings of this child were Andrew (1743), Isobel (1745) and Robert (1747).

5. Elliot Ledgers, L1/447 (1777) and L3/17-18A (1782-84), profit & loss accounts.

6. Arner, *Dobson's Encyclopaedia*, 1. See below for Dobson accepting Campbell's opinion in 1788.

7. Elliot letters 3120, to Thomas Dobson, [Greenock] 23 Oct 1784, and 3286, to Dobson, Philadelphia, 2 April 1785.

8. Elliot letter 1777, Dobson to John Blair, bookseller, Wigton, 27 Sept 1780. Copied by another clerk; I have supplied punctuation and initial capitals. See Dobson's 1807 letter below for his writing style.

9. Elliot letter 1793, Dobson to John Blair, Wigton, 14 Oct 1780.

10. See my paper, 'Charles Elliot's Medical Publishing and the International Book Trade', in C Withers and P Wood [ed] *Science and Medicine in the Scottish Enlightenment* (Tuckwell Press, 2002).

11. Elliot letter 3128, to Dobson, c/o William Poyntell, bookseller, Philadelphia, 30 October 1784.

12. Elliot letters 3112, to Gordon and Millar, shipping agents, Greenock, 16 Oct 1784; 3113, to Thomas Allan, 16 Oct 1784; 3114, to J & W Shaw, booksellers, Glasgow, 18 Oct 1784.

13. Elliot ledgers, L3/404 for Dobson accounts 1784-86, and L4/292 for 1787-1805.

14. Elliot letter 3120, to Dobson, 23 Oct 1784.

15. Elliot gave 11 trunks of books worth £406.3s.9d an entry invoice of £229.2s.6d., 19 trunks worth £615.17s.3d. an entry of £396.18s.10d. Elliot letters, 3381 and *3359, to Dobson, 2 July and 2 Aug 1785 respectively. 'Say how this answers,' Elliot said in the second letter, 'I am afraid in case such may lead you into Scrapes'.

16. On 'Testaments, Psalters, Spelling-Books and Primers, in the English or German languages; upon all Romances, Novels and Plays'. Stationery such as paper and blank books had a 10 per cent *ad valorem* imposed, making the tax 12 ½ per cent. *Laws enacted in the third sitting of the ninth General Assembly of the Commonwealth of Pennsylvania [23 Aug-23 Sept 1785]*, Philadelphia [1785], 671-72. Evans 19161; Charles Evans, *American Bibliography*, 6, 1779-1785 (1910), number 19161. I am grateful to James N Green for this information.

17. Elliot letter 3109, to John [ie James] Rivington, bookseller, New York.

18. Elliot letters 3123, to Benjamin Rush, Philadelphia, 25 Oct 1784, and 3128, to Dobson, 30 Oct 1784.

19. Elliot letter 3122, to Major William Jackson, Philadelphia, 25 Oct 1784.

20. Elliot letter 3128, to Dobson, 30 Oct 1784.
21. Arner, *Dobson's Encyclopaedia*, 3, quotes Francis Hopkinson telling Thomas Jefferson in 1788 that he believed Dobson was connected with some House in Scotland.
22. For Jackson's life see *American National Biography* (1999), 6: 778-79. His bookselling firm was Jackson and Dunn.
23. Elliot letter 3286, to Dobson, 2 April 1785.
24. Elliot letter 4402, to Dobson, 27 April 1789.
25. Elliot letter 3291, to Dobson, 6 April 1785.
26. Elliot ledger, L3/404.
27. Elliot letter 3291, to Dobson, 6 April 1785.
28. Elliot letter 4288, to Dobson, begun 25 May, finished in August 1788.
29. Elliot letters 3307, to Dobson, 20 April 1785; 3329, to R Baldwin, bookseller, London, 14 May 1785, with list of books for Dobson; 3330, C Dilly, bookseller, London, 15 May, 1785, with list for Dobson; *3359, to Dobson, 22 Aug 1785, mentioning Robinson and Cadell.
30. Elliot letter 3307, to Dobson, 20 April 1785.
31. Elliot letter *3359, to Dobson, 22 Aug 1785.
32. Elliot letter 3416, to Dobson, 30 Sept 1785.
33. Elliot letter 3488, to Dobson, 3 Dec 1785.
34. Elliot letter 3523, to Dobson, 31 Dec 1785.
35. Elliot letter 3565, to Dobson, 28 Jan 1786.
36. Elliot letter 3628, to William Elliot, bookseller, Fredericksburg, Virginia, 22 March 1786.
37. Elliot letter 3699, to Dobson, 30 May 1786.
38. Elliot letter 3745, to Dobson, 1 July 1786.
39. Elliot letter 4070, to Dobson, 27 Oct 1787.
40. Elliot letter 4070.
41. Elliot letter 4085, to Dobson, 13 Nov 1787.
42. Elliot letter 4121 (memorandum), to Dobson, 29 Dec 1787.
43. Elliot letter 4288, to Dobson, 24 May-August 1788.
44. Elliot letter 4402, to Dobson, 27 April 1789.
45. Elliot letter 4288, to Dobson, 24 May-August 1788.
46 Arner, *Dobson's Encyclopaedia,* 30-32, 45.
47. Elliot letters 4381, to Dobson, 18 March 1789; 4288, to Dobson 24 May-August 1788.
48. Elliot letter 4295, Sam Campbell sr to Elliot, copied to Dobson, 5 June 1788.
49. *Pennsylvania Packet*, 21 May 1785.
50. Historical Society of Pennsylvania, 'Robert Aitken Ms. Account Book 1771-1802', 412-41.
51. Elliot letter *3359, to Dobson, 22 Aug 1785.
52. Arner, *Dobson's Encyclopaedia*, 2-12.
53. Elliot Trustees Book, minute of 6 Nov 1799.

54. National Archives of Scotland, [*hereafter* NAS] Dalguise Muniments, RH24/26A reel 2, Benjamin Rush to William Creech, 30 March 1787. I thank Messrs J & F Anderson, WS, Edinburgh, for permission to quote this source.
55. Arner, *Dobson's Encyclopaedia*, 3.
56. Elliot letter 4381, to Dobson, 18 March 1789.
57. Elliot letter 4402, to Dobson, 27 April 1789.
58. Elliot Trustees Book, minutes 30 Jan 1790 and 6 November 1799. Elliot letter 4433, to Dobson, 19 Sept 1789.
59. Elliot letter 4434, to Ralph Bowie, Philadelphia, 19 Sept 1789.
60. Elliot letter 4433, to Dobson, 19 Sept 1789.
61. Elliot letter 4438, John Greig to Dobson, 3 Oct 1789.
62. Elliot letter 4461, Greig to Dobson, 14 Dec 1789.
63. Elliot Trustees Book, minute 6 Nov 1799.
64. NAS, CS226/8695, 'Summons James Sibbald bookseller in Edinburgh… against Thos. Dobson Bookseller in America' etc. (1790).
65. NAS, CS228/D6/22, 'Thomas Dobson & Attorney v [William] Wood (1792); includes Dobson's book list.
66. NAS, CS21/26, [Cornelius] Elliot v [Thomas] Dobson &c' (1794).
67. Elliot Trustees Book, minutes 30 Jan 1790, 1 March 1790, 6 Nov 1799, 19 June 1801, 23 April 1805. Elliot ledger L4/292. Accounts of Adam Bruce, factor for Elliot Estate, in letter to William Elliot, London, 8 March 1807.
68. John Murray Archives, ms letter, Thomas Dobson to William Elliot, 6 Aug 1807.
69. John Murray Archives, John Murray III's ms note in Samuel Smiles, *A Publisher and his Friends: memoir and correspondence of the late John Murray* (London: 1891), I: chapter 1.

P C G Isaac - Publications

Fine Printers

'William Bulmer, 1757-1830: an introductory essay', *The Library*, 5 ser, 13 (1958), 37-50.

Review of *William Bulmer and the Shakspeare* [sic]*Press: a biography of William Bulmer from A Dictionary of Printers and Printing by C H Timperley* (London, 1839), with an Introductory Note on the Bulmer-Martin Types by Laurance B Siegfried, *The Library*, 5 ser, 14 (1959), 75.

'William Bulmer, 1757-1830', *The Manchester Review*, 9 (Winter 1962-63), 333-343.

With John Dreyfus, 'William Bulmer's will', in *Studies in the Book Trade in Honour of Graham Pollard* (Oxford: Oxford Bibliographical Society, 1975), 341-349.

'Bulmer's influential supporters: an enquiry still in progress', in *Aspects of Printing from 1600*, edited by Robin Myers & Michael Harris (Oxford: Oxford Polytechnic Press, 1987), 49-68.

'William Bulmer (1757-1830) fine printer', *Archaeologia Aeliana*, 5 ser, 16 (1988), 223-237.

'Collecting William Bulmer fine printer', *The Book Collector*, 37 (1988), 225-233.

'William Bulmer (1757-1830): fine printer and Honorary Member', in Charles Parish, *The History of the Literary and Philosophical Society of Newcastle upon Tyne*, 2 (1990), 137-163.

William Bulmer: the Fine Printer in Context, 1757-1830 (London: Bain & Williams, 1993), 198. This book was expanded from the Sandars Lectures given at Cambridge University in 1984. Checklists of Bulmer's printing output were issued in 1961, 1973, 1986 & as an appendix to this work.

Checklists of the printing output, with short lives, of Thomas Bensley and John M'Creery were issued in 1989 and 1991 (revised 1999) respectively.

The Northern Book Trade

Review of Phyllis M Benedikz, *Durham Topographical Prints up to 1800: an annotated bibliography*, *The Library*, 5 ser, 24 (1969), 356.

Some Alnwick Caricatures: a Note and a Checklist (Wylam: Allenholme Press, 1965), 12 + plate.

History of Printing in the North: Some Highlights, (History of the Book Trade in the North Working Paper PH14, 1967), 10.

'The history of the book trade in the North: a preliminary report on a group research project', *The Library*, 5 ser, 23 (1968), 248-252.

With W M Watson, 'The history of the book trade in the North: a review of a research project', *Journal of the Printing Historical Society*, 4 (1968), 87-98.

William Davison of Alnwick, Pharmacist and Printer, 1781-1858 (Oxford: Clarendon Press, 1968), ix, 40.

Review of Michael Twyman, *John Soulby, Printer, Ulverston, with an Account of Ulverston by William Rollinson*, *The Library*, 5 ser, 23 (1968), 363-365.

'William Davison of Alnwick, pharmacist and printer', *The Library*, 5 ser, 24 (1969), 1-32.

Review of *Bewick to Dovaston, Letters 1824-1828*, edited by Gordon Williams; introduced by Montague Weekley, *The Library*, 5 ser, 24 (1969), 171-172.

Introduction to *Halfpenny Chapbooks of William Davison of Alnwick* (Newcastle upon Tyne: Frank Graham, 1971), 5-14.

Review of Frances Thompson, *Newcastle Chapbooks in the Newcastle upon Tyne University Library*, *The Library*, 5 ser, 25 (1970), 83-84.

Review of Derek Nuttall, *A History of Printing in Chester from 1688 to 1965*, *The Library*, 5 ser, 25 (1970), 366.

The Burman Alnwick Collection (Newcastle upon Tyne: University Library Publication 6, 1973), pp 88.

With C J Hunt, 'The regulation of the booktrade in Newcastle upon Tyne at the beginning of the nineteenth century', *Archaeologia Aeliana*, 5 ser, 5 (1977), 163-178.

'Fourstones paper mill: the documents speak', in G T Mandl, *Three Hundred Years in Paper* (Wooburn Green: Thomas & Green, 1985), 53-74; and *Yearbook of Paper History*, 6 (1986), 111-222.

An Inventory of Books Sold by a Seventeenth-Century Penrith Grocer (History of the Book Trade in the North, Working Paper PH53, 1989), pp 23; and Supplement (Working Paper PH53A, 1996), 4.

'A case of economic warfare in the late 18th century: 2. Sir John Swinburne and the forged assignats from Haughton mill', *Archaeologia Aeliana*, 5 ser, 18 (1990), 158-163.

Introduction to *William Davison's New Specimen of Cast-Metal Ornaments and Wood Types* (London: Printing Historical Society, 1990), 7-37.

[Edited] *Bewick and After: Wood-Engraving in the Northeast* (History of the Book Trade in the North, 1990), xii, 144.

William Lubbock & other Newcastle Bookbinders (History of the Book Trade in the North, Working Paper PH 76, 1997), 24.

[Edited] *Newspapers in the Northeast: the 'Fourth Estate' at work in Northumberland & Durham* (Newcastle, 1999), vi, 162. (History of the Book Trade in the North, Working Paper PH 78, 1999).
[Edited] *'A Very Good Public Library': Early Years of the Leeds Library* (Newcastle, 2001), iv, 171. (History of the Book Trade in the North, Working Paper PH 82)
Review of Nigel Tattersfield, *John Bewick, Engraver on Wood, 1760-1796*, *Papers of the Bibliographical Society of America*, 96.3 (2002).
Edited and published the Working Papers of the Book Trade in the North (PH 1-82, 1965-date).

Book Trade History

'Some early book-jackets', *The Library*, 5 ser, 30 (1975), 51-52 + 3 plates.
The Provincial Book Trade from the End of the Printing Act to 1800 (History of the Book Trade in the North, Working Paper PH46, 1987), 17, and *Provincial Printing in the Eighteenth Century: a Note* (Working Paper PH48, 1987), 5.
[Edited] *Yearbook of Paper History*, 7 (1988) (Marburg: International Association of Paper Historians), vii, 323.
Development of Written Language and Early Writing Materials (Newcastle upon Tyne: University Library, 1989), 23 + 2 plates.
A Penny Plain and Twopence Coloured: the juvenile drama (Newcastle upon Tyne: University Library, 1990), 30 + 4 plates; with Supplement (1990), 4.
[Edited] *Six Centuries of the Provincial Book Trade in Britain* (Winchester: St Paul's Bibliographies, 1990), xii, 212.
With Michael Perkin, 'The British provincial book trade', in *The Book Encompassed: Studies in Twentieth-Century Bibliography*, edited by Peter Davison (Cambridge: University Press, 1992), 176-181.
'The British Book Trade Index', *The Local Historian*, 24 (1994), 102-111.
'British Book Trade Index: development and progress', *Library Review*, 44 (1995), 17-23.
'William Davison of Alnwick and provincial publishing in his time', *Publishing History*, 40 (1996), 5-32.
[Edited with Barry McKay] *Images & Texts: Their Production and Distribution in the 18th and 19th Centuries* (Winchester: St Paul's Bibliographies, 1997), xiv, 188.
[Edited with Barry McKay] *The Reach of Print: Making, Selling and Using Books* (Winchester: St Paul's Bibliographies, 1998), x, 228.
'Charles Elliot and Spilsbury's Antiscorbutic Drops' in *The Reach of Print*, 157-174.
'Pills and print', in *Medicine, Mortality and the Book Trade*, edited by Robin Myers & Michael Harris (Winchester: St Paul's Bibliographies, 1998), 25-47.

[Edited with Barry McKay] *The Human Face of the Book Trade: Print Culture and its Creators* (Winchester: St Paul's Bibliographies, 1999), x, 228.

'Charles Elliot and the English provincial book trade', in *The Human Face of the Book Trade*, 97-116.

With Iain Beavan, 'Lamert, The Origin of Quack Doctors (1829) and its background', *Pharmaceutical Historian*, 30 (2000), 30-33.

[Edited with Barry McKay] *The Mighty Engine: The Printing Press and its Impact* (Winchester: St Paul's Bibliographies; New Castle, DE: Oak Knoll Press, 2000), xi, 205.

[Edited with Barry McKay] *The Moving Market: Continuity and Change in the Book Trade* (New Castle, DE: Oak Knoll Press, 2001), xiv, 201.

Editorial: *Ave atque vale* or 'meat and potatoes', in *The Moving Market*, ix-xiv.

'*Splendide mendax*: publishing *Landscape Illustrations of the Bible*', in *The Moving Market*, 145-160.

'The English provincial book trade to 1800', *Transactions of the Lancashire & Cheshire Antiquarian Society*, 97 (2001), 7-27.

'The English provincial book trade: a Northern mosaic', *The Papers of the Bibliographical Society of America*, 95 (2001), 410-41. Annual Lecture to the Bibliographical Society of America, January 2001.

Edited and published *Quadrat*, an occasional periodical of research in progress on the British book trade (1-16, 1995-2002).

John Murray II

'Byron's publisher and his 'spy': constancy and change among John Murray II's printers, 1812-1831', *The Library*, 6 ser, 19 (March 1997), 1-24. Presidential Address to the Bibliographical Society, 16 April 1996.

'Maria Eliza Rundell and her publisher', *Publishing History*, 43 (1998), 17-32.

'Byron's publisher and his printers', *Newsletter of the Newstead Abbey Byron Society* (July 2000), 86-96.

New Dictionary of National Biography

Articles for the *New DNB* on Thomas & John Bell, William Bulmer, Thomas Bensley, John McCreery, John Murray II, Thomas Slack, Anne Fisher, and Solomon & Sarah Hodgson.

Index

Aberdeen, book trade in, 148
Ablett, Joseph, 184
Adelaide, book trade in, 137
Advertisements, newspaper, 47,49,55,56,82, 85,86,87,88,89,90,132,141,177,203-4
Aitken, Robert, (printer), 204
Alcock, E, (printer), 133
Allman, Thomas, (publisher), 124
Alnwick, book trade in, 82
Archer, Caroline, 119-29
Arner, Robert, 197,205
Ashbourne, book trade in, 87,88
Ashburner, Thomas, (printer and bookseller), 54,57
Association for Promoting Christian Knowledge, (APCK), 79
Auckland, NZ, book trade in, 137
Auctions, book, 37,44,45,55,66,98,130,131, 132,134,135,165,168,173
Audubon, J, (artist), 143
Ayr, book trade in, 146
Ayres, William, (printer), 30

Bacon, Thomas, (bookseller), 55
Baker, William, (printer and circulating library), 131-40
Baldwin, Richard, (publisher), 66
Baldwin, Robert, (publisher), 203
Baldwyn, C M, (publisher), 113
Barber, John, (printer), 32
Barker, Christopher, (printer), 77
Barker, Robert, (King's Printer), 75
Baskett, John, (printer), 74,75
Bath, book trade in, 30,31
Baynes, William, (bookseller and publisher), 170,173
Beaufort, Lady Margaret, 18
Beavan, Iain, 141-52
Bell & Daldy, (publisher), 121

Bell, John, (bookseller), 200,201
Bell, William & John, (publisher), 121
Bendigo, book trade in, 133
Benson, Charles, 133
Bent, Andrew, (printer), 132
Berwick-on-Tweed, book trade in, 121
Bibles, printed, 75,76,77,80
Bill, John, (King's Printer), 75
Birkett, Mr, (newsagent), 56
Birmingham, book trade in, 122
Black, Professor Jeremy, 154
Blackie & Son, (publisher), 121
Blair, John, (bookseller), 197-8,204
Blake, John, (printer), 189
Boddeley, Thomas, (printer), 31
Bohn, Henry, (bookseller), 171,173
Book clubs (or societies), 95,98
Book of Common Prayer, bibliographical history of, 73-84
Book trade
- biographical directories, 2,3,5,6
- provincial, 1-12,27-36
- wholesalers, 7
Boston, Ray, 153
Bourne, Fox, 153
Boyd, George, (publisher), 142,143,144,145,146,148,149
Bridger, Frederick Marston, (printer), 189
Bridger, Frederick Thomas, (printer), 189, 191,193,194
Bridger, Harry Stephen, (printer), 189
Bridger, Stephen Dudley, (printer), 189
Bridger, William, (printer), 189,194
Bridger specimen books, 189-96
Briggs, Ferdinand Martin, (printer), 194
Bristol, book trade in, 30
British and Foreign Bible Society, 165
British Book Trade Index (BBTI), 2,6,9
Bruce, John, (printer), 80

Burges, Francis and Elizabeth, (printers), 30-1
Burton, K G, 154

Cadell, Robert, (publisher), 141
Cadell, Thomas, (bookseller), 203
Caernarvon, book trade in, 121
Cambridge, book trade in, 32
Cambridge University Press, 74-6, 79, 83
Campbell, Samuel, (bookbinder), 197, 200, 201, 206
Campbell, Samuel, (bookseller), 200, 201, 202
Canova, Antonio, (sculptor), 110, 113
Carey & Hart, (US booksellers), 149
Carlisle, book trade in, 51, 52, 55, 86, 97
Carnan, Thomas, (printer), 60, 67
Carnan, William, (printer), 30
Caslon, type founders, 176
Catalogues, library, 95-106
Cave, Edward, (printer), 32, 33
Caxton, William, 13, 17, 18, 19, 20, 22, 23
Census returns, official, 5, 109, 114
Chambers, W & R, (publisher), 121
Charles, Thomas, (publisher), 175
Charleston, book trade in, 207
Charnley, Emerson, (publisher), 120, 121, 123
Charnley, William, (bookseller), 57
Chase, William, (printer), 28
Chester, book trade in, 30, 155, 175, 176
Chetham Society, Manchester, 38
Chiswick Press, 74
Clare, Thomas, (printer), 193
Clarke, Adam, (collector), 165-74
Clarke, John Wesley, 169
Clarke, Samuel, 81
Clarke, T S, (printer), 165
Collier, John Payne, 110, 111-3
Collins, Benjamin, (publisher), 66
Collins, Freeman, (printer), 27, 28, 29, 30, 31, 32, 33, 34
Collins, Hannah, (printer), 33
Collins, John, (printer), 33
Collins, Susannah, (printer), 28, 30, 31, 32, 33

Collins, William, (Queen's Printer), 80
Cooke, John, (publisher), 61
Cooper, Margaret, 107-17
Copeland, John, (stationer), 57
Copeland, William, (printer), 57
Copland, Robert, (printer), 22
Copyright Act (1710), 34
Copyright Act (1842), 156
Copyright issues, 7
Cotterell, James, (printer), 28-9
Cotton, Thomas, (printer), 54-6
Coventry, book trade in, 65, 67
Cranfield, Geoffrey, 154
Crawfurd, John, 144, 145
Creech, William, 207
Cresswell, Samuel, (printer), 86
Crichton, Andrew, 146, 147
Cruikshank, George, (artist), 110, 112-3, 115
Cullen, William, 205
Cundall & Addey, (publisher), 121

Darker, Samuel, (printer), 30
Darton, (publisher), 67, 121
Davies, Owen, 176, 179
Davies, Robert, (author), 182, 184
Davies, W W, (printer), 132
Davison, William, (printer), 82, 155
Dawson & Payne (printing press manufacturer), 121-2
Dean, R & W, (printer), 173
Dean & Son, (bookseller), 122
Denbigh, book trade in, 175-88
Denbigh Cymreigyddion, 180
Denbigh Eisteddfod, 180
Derby, book trade in, 87
Deakin, Joseph, (newspaper editor), 156
Dicey, Cluer, (publisher), 67
Dick, John, (bookseller), 146
Dickinson, John, (papermaker), 148-50
Dilly, Charles, (publisher), 201
Dixon, Diana, 153-63
Dixon, Robert, (chapman), 54

INDEX

Dixson, Sir William, (collector), 132
Dixwell, James, (printer), 192
Dobson, Thomas, (printer), 197-212
Dublin, book trade in, 79
Dunn, John, (stationer), 57

East India Company, 145
Edenbridge, printing at, 190,191.193,194
Edinburgh, book trade in, 121,141-52, 197-212
Edinburgh Cabinet Library, (book series), 141-152
Elliot, Anne, 208
Elliot, Charles,(bookseller), 197-212
Elliot, Cornelius, 209,210
Elliot, William, 208
Elliott, R, (publisher), 121,123
Encyclopaedia Britannica, (2nd/3rd editions), 198,202,203
Ephemera, printed, 3
Episcopal Church (USA), printing for, 76,81,82
Evans, James, (printer), 177
Evans, John, (publisher), 67
Evans, auctioneer, 171,172
Everett, James, (bookseller), 165-74
Exeter, book trade in, 28,29,30
Eyre, Charles, (King's Printer), 74
Eyre, George, (King's Printer), 74
Eyre and Spottiswoode, (Queen's Printers), 75

Falkner, (publisher), 135
Farley, Felix, (printer), 31
Farley, Samuel, (printer), 29-30
Feather, Professor John, 1-12,27,34
Fell, John, (bookseller), 57
Fiennes, Celia, (traveller), 39,52
Foster, Allason, (printer), 57
Fraser, James Baillie, (author), 143,144, 146,147
Frost, Forbes, (bookseller), 148

Gale, John, 54
Gaskell, Nathaniel, (book auction of), 45
Gavin, John, 95-106
Gee, Edward Williams, (publisher), 180
Gee, Robert, (publisher), 180,186
Gee, Thomas, junior, (publisher), 180,185,186
Gee, Thomas, senior, (publisher), 175-88
Gent, Thomas, (printer), 33
George, Henry, (printer), 192-3
Gilpin, William, 51,52,53
Glasgow, book trade in, 121
Gloucester, book trade in, 28
Gordon, Peter, 144
Goulden, R J, 189-96
Grant, James, 153
Gregory, John, (publisher), 85-94
Greig, John, (bookseller), 206,207
Grierson, (printers), 79
Griffiths, David N, 73-84
Gwyneddigion Society, 178

Hadlow, printing at, 190,119,193,194
Hanley, Professor Howard, 107
Harland, John, 37,38
Harris, John, (publisher), 67,69
Harrold, Edmund, 37-49
Harrold, Thomas, 38,39
Hasbart, Samuel, (newspaper proprietor), 31
Haskoll, Joseph, 66
Haskoll, Lydia, 61-72
Haskoll, Margaret Holmes, 63,65,67,69
Haskoll, Mary Lydia, 65
Haskoll, Thomas James, 61,62-3
Haskoll, Thomas James Forbes, 66
Haskoll, William, 66
Heaton, Jenny, 62
Heaton, Martin, 62
Hereford, book trade in, 28,121,123
Heywood, John, (publisher), 121
Higden, Ranulph, 19
Hinks, John, 85-94

Hobart, book trade in, 132,136,137
Hodgson, W, (bookseller), 56
Hodson, Francis, (printer), 91
Holmes, Margaret, 62
Holywell Cymreigyddion Society, 183
Hooker, Charles, (printer), 193
Hooker, Sir William, 143
Hopyl, Wolfgang, (printer), 19
Hounslow, David, 61-72
Humphreys, Agnes, (printer), 191,193,195
Humphreys, Henry James, (printer), 192,194
Humphreys, John, (publisher), 175-6
Hunter Blair, Sir David, (printer), 80

Incunabula
- in general, 13-26
- sammelbande (collected incunables), 14-21
Isaac, Professor Peter, 9,81,155,213-6

Jackson, John, (engraver), 149
Jackson, Major William, (bookseller), 199-200
Jamieson, Robert, 143-4,149
Jenkin, David, (bookseller), 178
Johnson, Richard, (sixteenth-cent. reader), 22
Johnson, Dr Samuel, 32,74
Johnstone, Christian, 144
Johnstone, John, (printer), 144
Jones, Aled, 155
Jones, Robert, (printer), 178,182
Jones, Thomas, (publisher), 175,176,177,179,180,181
Jones, William Collister, (printer), 175, 176,177
Journals *see* Newspapers

Kaufman, Paul, 95,101,103,105
Kay, J R, 171
Kelly, Thomas, 105
Kemp and Fairfax, (printer), 132
Kendal, book trade in, 54,57,102
King's Printer, 74,75,79,80,81
Kinnier, David, (printer), 30

Kirsop, Professor Wallace, 131-140

Launceston, book trade in, 134,136,137
Lee, Alan, 154
Leeds, book trade in, 5,121,122
Legg, William and Martha, 62
Leicester, book trade in, 85-94
Leslie, Professor Sir John, 143
L'Estrange, Hamon, 82
Lewis, Lucy, 13-26
Libraries
- Barrow-in-Furness Free Public Library, 104
- Bethnal Green Museum (Renier Coll.), 120
- Birmingham, City Reference Library (Parker Coll.), 120
- Bodleian Library (Oxford), 66,67,157
- Bridwell Library (Texas), 17
- Bristol library, 101-2,103
- British Library, 55,68,107,120,156,157
- Bromfield library, 101,102
- Cambridge University Library, 21,22,157
- Carlisle Cathedral library, 97
- Carlisle library (Thurnam's), 102
- Chetham's (Manchester), 38
- circulating, 5,8,9,59,95,99-100,131-40 180,190
- Cotsen collection, 66
- Huntington Library,157
- John Rylands University Library (Manchester), 165,171,174
- Kendal library, 102
- Lake Counties (Cumbria), library catalogues, 95-106
- National Library of Scotland, 81,157
- National Library of Wales, 157
- Newcastle Central Library, 157
- Nottingham City Library, 87
- Penrith library, 103
- Pepys Library (Cambridge), 14,15,16,17
- Pierpont Morgan Library (New York), 17
- Sidney Sussex College (Cambridge), 16-7
- State Library of New South Wales, 132

INDEX

- Trinity College (Cambridge), 18
- Whitehaven Subscription Library, 98
- Yale University Library, 157
Licensing Act (lapsed 1695), 27,34
Lincoln, printing at, 155
Linton, David, 153
London
- book trade in, 1,2,3,6,7,8-9,27,28,29,32, 33,66,67,81,87,88,107-17,121,130,135, 148,170,173,177,201,206,208
- London Cymmrodorion Society, 183
- London Literary and Publishing Society, 113-4
Longman's, Green & Co, (publishers), 121, 141,173
Lowther, Sir James, 54,55
Lowther, Sir John, (book collector), 51,52, 53,54
Luckman, Mary, (bookseller), 67
Ludlow, book trade in, 28
Lumley, Edward, (bookseller), 137
Lyon, Benjamin, (printer), 31,32,

McDougall, Warren, 135,197-212
McKay, Barry, 51-9
Macfarqhar, Bell and Hutton, (publisher), 198
MacGillivray, William, 143-4
Machlinia, William de, (printer), 20
Macmillan & Co, (publisher), 121
Madden, Lionel, 153
Maitland, NSW, book trade in, 134
Manchester, book trade in, 5,37-49,121,167,173,174
Manchester Lit. and Phil. Soc., 167
Marriott, Thomas, 171,172,173
Marshall, John, (publisher), 67,69,185
Marshall, Richard, (publisher), 66,67
Martin, John, (painter), 107,110,111,114
Masheder, William, (bookseller), 56-7
Melbourne, book trade in, 134,135,137
Melrose, Thomas, (publisher), 121
Memes, Dr John, 145-6

Methodist Archives, 165,171,174
Methodist Publishing House, 167
Michael, Ian, 119-120
Milligan, Peter, (bookseller), 66
Millington, Jesse, (publisher), 122
Milne, Maurice, 154
Milton, John, 110,111,113,114
Mirk, John (fourteenth-cent. author), 17-8,19
Monmouth, Geoffrey of, 19
Moon, Marjorie, 66
Moran, James, 192
Morrison, Ian, 134
Moses, Henry, (artist), 110,115
Moxon, Joseph, 53
Mudie's, (libraries), 8
Mullen, Samuel, (bookseller), 134,135
Murray, Hugh, 142,144,145
Murray, John, (publisher), 141,143,144,145, 146,148,208-9

National Register of Archives, 160
Needham, Paul, 16,20
Nelson & Co, (publishers), 150
Net Book Agreement, 8,9
Newbery, Elizabeth, (publisher), 67
Newbery, John, (publisher), 60,64,66,69,72
Newcastle-upon-Tyne, book trade in, 3,56,57, 120,121,123
Newcombe, Thomas, (printer), 28
Newport, (IOW), book trade in, 66
Newspapers
- Alnwick Mercury, 155
- Baner ac Amserau Cymru, 175
- Bath Journal, 31
- Bendigo Advertiser, 133-4
- Bookseller, The, 7
- Cambridge Chronicle, 86,91
- Cambridge Journal, 86
- Christian Advocate, 170
- Courier de l'Europe, 87
- Coventry Mercury, 86
- Cumberland Pacquet, 56,58

- Daily Advertiser, 87
- Eastern Evening News, 155
- Family Magazine, The, 61,65,72
- Farley's Exeter Journal, 30
- Farley's Salisbury Post-man, 30
- Gateshead Observer, 157
- Gentleman's Magazine, 33
- George's Westerham Journal, 194
- Heads for the People, 132
- Horncastle News, 155
- in London, 8
- in Sydney, 129
- Kendal Courant, 54
- Leicester Chronicle, 156
- Leicester Herald, 156
- Leicester Journal, 85-94
- Leicester Journal and Midland Counties Advertiser, 91
- Leicester and Nottingham Journal, 86,87
- Literary Gazette, 107,111,113
- Liverpool Courant, 158
- London Evening Post, 55
- Loughborough Echo, 154,156,157
- Loughborough Monitor, 157
- Maidstone Chronicle, 191
- Manchester Guardian, 38,69,168
- Manchester Journal, 167
- Manchester Times, 167
- Middlesborough Evening Gazette, 160
- Morning Chronicle, 112,171
- New English Theatre, 89
- Newcastle Journal, 56
- Newcastle Weekly Chronicle, 108
- Northampton Mercury, 86,155
- Norwich Courant, 31,33
- Norwich Post, 30,31,32
- Nottingham Evening Post, 155
- Oxford Journal, 86
- Payne's Leicester Advertiser, 160
- Pennsylvania Packet, 203,204
- provincial, 3,4,5,153-63
- Reading Mercury, 30
- Salisbury Journal, 66
- Sam. Farley's Bristol Post-man, 30
- Sam. Farley's Exeter Mercury, 30
- Sam. Farley's Exeter Post-man, 30
- Slough, Eton and Windsor Observer, 155
- Tait's Magazine, 144
- Theatrical Magazine, 89
- Times, The, 167
- Westminster Gazette, 87
- Wharfedale and Airedale Standard, 122
- Whitehaven News, 155
- Whitehaven Weekly Courant, 55
- York Journal, 33
NEWSPLAN project, 6,157-8
New York, book trade in, 199,200,201,202
Nicholas, John, 91
Nicholson, Thomas, (librarian), 98
Nicol, James, 144,147
Nicolson, Bishop William, 97
Nineteenth Century Short Title Catalogue (NSTC), 6
Norman, John, (printer), 191,192,193,194
Norman, William Edward, (stationer), 192
Northampton, book trade in, 28
Norwich, book trade in, 27-28,30,31,32, 33,34
Notary, Julian, (printer), 18
Nottingham, printing in, 86

Oliver, Josiah, (stationer), 191
Oliver, Thomas, (publisher), 149
Oliver & Boyd, (publisher), 121,141,142, 143-50
Opie, Peter, 66
Otley, book trade in, 119-28
Oxford Movement, 78,82
Oxford University Press, 73-7,79,83

Parks, William, (printer), 28,30
Pattinson, Henry, (bookseller), 51,52
Payne, James, (printer), 195
Pele, John, (newsman), 54

INDEX

Pellin (or Pelin), Andrew, (bookseller), 53-4
Perkins, Maureen, 134
Philadelphia, book trade in, 197-212
Pickering, William, (publisher), 82
Piercey, (publisher), 65,67
Pite, Edward, (publisher), 121,123
Pontypool, book trade in, 30
Powell, Michael, 37-50
Powell, Sue, 17
Price, John, (publisher), 91
Printing, in fifteenth century, 13-26
Prowett, Edward, 112
Prowett, Robert, (dentist and publisher), 108, 109,111,113,115
Prowett, Septimus, (publisher), 107-17
Puddefoot, George, (printer), 190,193
Pughe, William Owen, 180,181,183,184
Pynson, Richard, (printer), 14,18,22,24

Queen's Printer, 74,75,79,80

Raffald, Elizabeth, (publisher and author), 38
Raikes, Robert, (printer), 28,31
Railton, George, (bookseller), 55
Read, Hugh Gilzean, (newspaper prop.), 160
Reading, book trade in, 28,30
Reeves, John, (King's Printer), 74,75
Reynolds, Linda, 119-128
Rhuthun, book trade in, 176,177
Ricci, Seymour De, 16
Rivington, James, (bookseller), 199
Roberts, H, (publisher), 66
Roberts, John, (printer), 32
Robertson and Mullen, (bookseller), 136
Robinson, George, (publisher), 201
Roden, Thomas, (bookseller), 178
Ross, James, (printer), 132
Rush, Dr Benjamin, 199-200,203,205
Russell, Revd Michael, 145,147

St Ives, book trade in, 28

Saunderson, Robert, (printer), 176,180
Schoolbooks, 141
Scotland, book trade in, 80-81,141-52
Scott, Sir Walter, 141
Scragg, Brenda J, 165-74
Sevenoaks, printing at, 193
Shepherd, William, (printer), 57
Short Title Catalogue, (STC), 73,74
Shrewsbury, book trade in, 81
Sibbald, James, (bookseller), 197,207
Simpkin, Marshall (publishers and wholesalers), 7,124,148
Smart, Christopher, (author), 64,68
Smart, William, (bookseller), 107
Smart & Allen, (publisher), 124
Smith, W H, 8
Society for Diffusion of Useful Knowledge, (SDUK), 141,146
Society for Promoting Christian Knowledge, (SPCK), 141
Sotheby's, auctioneers, 168
Spencer, Robard, (leatherseller), 14-5
Spottiswoode, Robert, (printer), 75
Sprange, Jasper, (printer), 189
Stamp Act, (1855), 154
Stanhope printing press, 76
Stationers' Company, 6,7,28,29,34,76
Stephens and Stokes, (printer), 132
Stephenson Blake, type founders, 126
Stevens Shanks, type founders, 125
Stoker, David, 27-36
Strahan, Andrew, (printer), 74,75
Strahan, William, (printer), 74
Stretch, J, (bookseller), 56
Sturch, John, (bookseller), 66
Sutherland, James, (bookseller), 197
Sydney, book trade in, 131-40
Syon Abbey, 16,17,18,19

Taylor, Samuel, (printer), 122
Tegg, James, (bookseller), 132,135,136
Tegg, Samuel, (bookseller),136,137,138,

Tegg, Thomas, (bookseller), 135
Thompson, James, (publisher), 85,86
Thorp, (bookseller), 173
Throsby, John, (author), 88
Tilt, Charles, (publisher), 114
Tomlinson, L, (publisher), 66
Tonbridge, printing at, 189-96
Tonson, Jacob, I,II,III (printers), 110
Trimmer, Sarah, (publisher), 61,65,70,72
Turpin, Homan, (publisher), 65,67
Type specimen books, in Kent, 189-97
Typography
- of children's readers, 119-28
- of prayer books, 77
Tytler, Patrick Fraser, 143

Uffelman, Larry, 153

Vaughan, Thomas, (printer), 178
Vizetelly, Branston & Co, (engravers), 149

Walch, Major J W H, (bookseller), 137,138, 139
Walcott, William, (bookseller), 107-8
Walford, Cornelius, 153
Walker, Professor Sue, 119-28
Walker, William, (publisher), 121,122,124
Walters, John, (author), 182-3,184
Warde, Beatrice, 119

Ware, John, (printer), 56,58,99
Watts, Isaac, 181
Waverley Novels, 141,142
Webb, William, (publisher), 122
Webb, Millington & Co, (publisher), 121, 122,124
Welsh-language publishing, 175-88
Wesley, John, 165,171,172
Wesley, Samuel, 171,172
Westerham, printing at.190,193,193,194,195
Wharfedale printing press, 121-122
Whitehaven, book trade in, 51-9
Whitworth, John, (bookseller), 42-3,44,45,47
Wickenden, John, (printer), 190,191
Wigton, book trade at, 197-8
Wiles, Roy, 154
Wilkie, J, (publisher), 66
Williams, Robert, (author), 182
Wilson, James, 143
Winchester, book trade in, 30
Wood, William, (bookseller), 201,207
Woodbridge, book trade in, 121,123
Worcester, book trade in, 4,107-8,111,115
Worde, Wynkyn de, (printer), 14,16,17,18, 20,21,22,24

York, book trade in, 30
Yorkshire Joint Stock Publishing & Stationery Company, 119-28